ASSASSINORUM KINGMAKER

ASSASSINORUM KINGMAKER

ROBERT RATH

BLACK LIBRARY

A BLACK LIBRARY PUBLICATION

First published in 2022.
This edition published in Great Britain in 2023 by
Black Library, Games Workshop Ltd., Willow Road,
Nottingham, NG7 2WS, UK.

Represented by: Games Workshop Limited – Irish branch,
Unit 3, Lower Liffey Street, Dublin 1,
D01 K199, Ireland.

10 9 8 7 6 5 4 3 2 1

Produced by Games Workshop in Nottingham.
Cover illustration by Darren Tan.

A CIP record for this book is available from the British Library.

ISBN 13: 978 1 80026 270 6

See Black Library on the internet at

blacklibrary.com

Find out more about Games Workshop
and the worlds of Warhammer at

games-workshop.com

Printed and bound by CPI Group (UK) Ltd, Croydon, CR0 4YY

*For Mom, who let me rent every spy movie on the shelf –
over, and over, and over again.*

For more than a hundred centuries the Emperor has sat
immobile on the Golden Throne of Earth. He is the
Master of Mankind. By the might of His inexhaustible
armies a million worlds stand against the dark.

Yet, He is a rotting carcass, the Carrion Lord of the
Imperium held in life by marvels from the Dark Age of
Technology and the thousand souls sacrificed each day so
that His may continue to burn.

To be a man in such times is to be one amongst untold
billions. It is to live in the cruellest and most bloody
regime imaginable. It is to suffer an eternity of carnage
and slaughter. It is to have cries of anguish and sorrow
drowned by the thirsting laughter of dark gods.

This is a dark and terrible era where you will find little
comfort or hope. Forget the power of technology and
science. Forget the promise of progress and advancement.
Forget any notion of common humanity or compassion.

There is no peace amongst the stars, for in the grim
darkness of the far future,
there is only war.

DRAMATIS PERSONAE

THE ASSASSINORUM

Sycorax	Callidus Temple	[REDACTED]
Absolom Raithe	Vindicare Temple	[REDACTED]
Avaaris Koln	Vanus Temple	[REDACTED]
The Liaison	[NO RECORD]	[NO RECORD]
Master of Operations	[NO RECORD]	[NO RECORD]
Tessenna Starne	Embedded Agent	Dominion Station

THE FREEBLADES

Sir Linoleus Rakkan	Knight of Stryder-Rau	*Jester*	Warglaive
Gwynne	Sacristan		

THE COURT

Lucien Yavarius-Khau (Stryder-Rau)	High Monarch	*Crown of Dominion*	Castellan
Baroness Sylva Achara (Rau)	Herald	*Voice of Authority*	Paladin
Baron Titus Yuma (Rau)	Kingsward	*Throneshield*	Warden
Baroness Symphonia Dask (Stryder)	Gatekeeper	*Basilisk's Gaze*	Errant
Baron Rallan Fontaine (Stryder)	Master of Judgement	*Axefall*	Gallant
Dorthiya Tessell	Arch-Maintenancer		

HOUSE STRYDER

Baroness Hawthorn Astair-Rakkan	Mother of Rakkan	*Greyhound*	Crusader
Sir Ishmayl Galvan	Squire to Astair-Rakkan	*Skystrike*	Warglaive
Sir Luca Sangraine	Knight	*Fencer*	Helverin

Sir Hortius Sabban	Squire to Dask	*Mauler*	Warglaive
Sir Viss Andricus	Knight	*Soaring Blade*	Helverin

HOUSE RAU

Baron Tiberius Kraine	Head of Rau	*Firedrake*	Errant
Dame Lidya Vossa	Daughter of Kraine	*Stormrider*	Helverin
Sir Selkar Fang	Father of Rakkan	*Jester*	Warglaive
Sir Sev Firscal	Knight of Rau	*Sprinter*	Warglaive

THE LISTS

Lord Bazile Daggar-Kraine	Son of Kraine	*Holdfast*	Crusader
Lady Lisille Lycan-Bast	Cousin of Rakkan	*Blood Oath*	Paladin
Sir Mauvec Kawe	Knight	*Typhoon's Teeth*	Gallant
Renauldus Tarn-Kegga	Lord	*Horned Hunter*	Warden
Lady Vagara Sakas-Varn	Lord	*Song of Renown*	Paladin
Lord Juul Lambek-Firscal	Lord	*Galeforce*	Crusader
Lady Baldonna Katline-Denshain	Lord	*Hand of Fury*	Gallant
Lord Sammel Tavona-Akava	Lord	*Chivalric Path*	Errant

>>*INDEX Alpha-13+*
>>File No. 5782-Gamma-KMKR+

Imperial Knight Classifications and Armaments

Primary Armaments in **bold**, alternate and/or optional armaments in *italics*.

DOMINUS-PATTERN KNIGHT

CASTELLAN:
ARM MOUNTS: **Volcano Lance / Plasma Decimator**
CARAPACE MOUNTS: **Siegebreaker Cannon / Shieldbreaker Missile**
CHEST MOUNTS: **Twin Meltaguns**

QUESTORIS-PATTERN KNIGHT

CRUSADER:
ARM MOUNTS: **Rapid-Fire Battle Cannon / Avenger Gatling Cannon** *[OR] Thermal Cannon*
CARAPACE MOUNTS: *Ironstorm Missile Pod [OR] Icarus Autocannons [OR] Stormspear Rocket Pod*
CHEST MOUNT: **Heavy Stubber** *[OR] Meltagun*

ERRANT:
ARM MOUNTS: **Thermal Cannon / Reaper Chainsword** *[OR]*
Thunderstrike Gauntlet
CARAPACE MOUNTS: *Ironstorm Missile Pod [OR] Icarus Autocannons [OR] Stormspear Rocket Pod*
CHEST MOUNT: **Heavy Stubber** *[OR] Meltagun*

PALADIN:
ARM MOUNTS: **Rapid-Fire Battle Cannon / Reaper Chainsword** *[OR] Thunderstrike Gauntlet*
CARAPACE MOUNTS: *Ironstorm Missile Pod [OR] Icarus Autocannons [OR] Stormspear Rocket Pod*
CHEST MOUNT: **Heavy Stubber** *[OR] Meltagun*

GALLANT:
ARM MOUNTS: **Reaper Chainsword / Thunderstrike Gauntlet**
CARAPACE MOUNTS: *Ironstorm Missile Pod [OR] Icarus Autocannons [OR] Stormspear Rocket Pod*
CHEST MOUNT: **Heavy Stubber** *[OR] Meltagun*

WARDEN:

ARM MOUNTS: **Avenger Gatling Cannon / Thunderstrike Gauntlet** *[OR] Reaper Chainsword*

CARAPACE MOUNTS: *Ironstorm Missile Pod [OR] Icarus Autocannons [OR] Stormspear Rocket Pod*

CHEST MOUNT: **Heavy Stubber** *[OR] Meltagun*

ARMIGER-PATTERN KNIGHT

WARGLAIVE:

ARM MOUNTS: **Thermal Spear / Chain-Cleaver**

CARAPACE MOUNT: **Heavy Stubber** *[OR] Meltagun*

HELVERIN:

ARM MOUNTS: **Twin Helverin Autocannons**

CARAPACE MOUNT: **Heavy Stubber** *[OR] Meltagun*

PROLOGUE

'A Knight who breaks their oath, must themselves be broken in atonement.'

– Lucien Yavarius-Khau, High Monarch of Dominion,
from his *Meditations on the Code Chivalric*

QUESTOR IMPERIALIS WORLD OF DOMINION

It was hot in the forgeshrine.

Hot like the steam vents near Rau Manor, in the volcanic highlands. Hot like sweaty sheets. Hot like *Jester's* cockpit had been during the summer tournament.

It had got even hotter when Rakkan had torn into Sir Mauvec Kawe's Knight, *Typhoon's Teeth*, during the challenge match, taking the big Knight down, *Jester's* chain-cleaver burrowing into the ablative tournament armour welded on for the occasion.

Arranging it had not been easy. After all, an Armiger Warglaive was a third the size of a Knight Gallant like *Typhoon's Teeth*. For one to emerge victorious in single combat was a prospect so remote, so entirely bizarre, that it had not been attempted in centuries. When last it had, the challenger – Sir Tusaveta Rawlin – had died in the attempt, chest crushed by a sweep of a reaper chainsword.

It had not been intentional. According to the songs, Rawlin's killer had mourned the young woman's death. But the simple truth was that while the tournament rules stated that any Knight could challenge another, the assumption had always been that the little fifty-ton Armigers would never choose to go plate-to-plate with a machine more than thrice their weight.

There was no way to do it safely.

With weapons at half-strength, chainblades slowed down, and ablative armour doubling their protection, two Questoris Knights could do nearly anything they wanted to each other with the pilots in relative safety.

There were still injuries of course. Broken limbs, ribs, internal bleeding – that should be expected in a tournament – but an Armiger was simply no match for the heavier builds, even with safety taken into account.

But there was a reason to try.

By the customs of Dominion's Code Chivalric, a victorious challenger could opt to take the defeated opponent's Knight suit. Indeed, the bested pilot would need to offer it freely.

Generally it was a courtesy. Knight pilots liked their suits. Grew attached to them, and knew best how to carry them into battle. No pilot truly wanted to undergo the Becoming ritual a second time, their consciousness merged with ancestors who had piloted the Knight in the past. Indeed, some of these venerated ancestors might even reject the usurper, angered by the sudden change of pilot.

And it carried a social stigma – it just was not done. The offer was a formal courtesy, never accepted.

Sir Linoleus Rakkan, though, had intended to accept. He'd challenged Kawe specifically because he wanted to steal *Typhoon's Teeth*. To finally be rid of the little Knight Armiger that had been his father's, and that of the Fang line for millennia. Forever squires and skirmishers, never piloting the towering Questoris Knights.

Linoleus Rakkan had sworn to rise from his blood.

And, he thought, as he turned a corner in the forgeshrine and saw his suit, he had almost succeeded.

It stood in the forgeshrine cradle, its left pauldron removed and laying at its feet.

Jester. The little Armiger's split colours indicated that Rakkan was in the Lists, a man with no house, no loyalty. The removed pauldron had a motley pattern of cross-hatched diamonds that, legend had it, gave the Knight suit its name. It hung in chains, lifted off the marble and wire-mesh floor by hoists secured beneath its massive arms. The left leg was gone below the knee servo, where *Typhoon's* thunderstrike gauntlet had torn it off as though it were the drumstick on a game bird.

Jester. Rakkan's blessing. Rakkan's curse. A perfect name for a Knight suit so notoriously troubled. Once Rakkan had been so promising. Flown through trials of wits when he reached his majority, gritted his way through the trials of strength and combat, relying on his head rather than raw power. Even with his questionable bloodline, he might've been accepted if he'd taken *Typhoon's Teeth* for his own.

But they'd not wanted it. Low-born Rakkan, with his foreign grandfather, always striving for more. Put him in a Questoris Knight, he might rise high enough in the Lists to be eligible for succession.

House Stryder always preached achievement, and Rau droned about honouring the ancestors, but the truth was that neither liked the idea of this boy with his debased bloodline and insolent smile being a serious candidate for the throne.

It had still been worth it, though, to see the expressions on their faces.

'Gwynne,' he called. 'Did *Typhoon* do us a permanent injury?'

Rakkan saw the sacristan's shadow before he saw her. She

leaned out from a motorised ladder, her red robes lit by the sparking of a pinpoint welding torch in her right hand.

Black protective shielding retracted from the lenses of her metal eyes.

'By the blessed protection of the Omnissiah, it is reparable. Given time you will fight again.'

'*Jester* will fight again, you intend.'

'It is the same,' Tannah Gwynne said. She descended the ladder in a slide, augmetic hands scraping on plasteel uprights.

Rakkan winced, but appreciated the sprightliness.

Most sacristans, most tech-priests for that matter, were dull. Slow. Missing whatever quantum of humanity gave living people a spark, their decade of Cult Mechanicus training seeming to snuff out their personality. Even the young ones seemed impossibly old.

Gwynne was not like that. She was full of energy and enthusiasm. Not warm, precisely, but full of excitement. Her family had been vassals looking after the limited motor pool in the House Stryder garages – enginebikes and auto-carriages, with the occasional Taurox armoured transport. To service an Imperial Knight, even an Armiger, was an elevation of status beyond imagining. The very act of ministering to the machine made her bubble over with enthusiasm and joy.

'But sir,' she said when she hit the ground. 'It was close. Thunderstrike gauntlets are nothing to tangle with. Had the fracture occurred two feet higher, we would need to replace the entire leg.'

'If it had, then we would.'

'Leg assemblies are in short supply, my lord. I'm merely warning you that the challenge was fraught with risk. Honourable Machine Lord *Jester* could have been crippled, cursed with a limp for the rest of its service life. Would that have been worth the small chance of success?'

'Small chance?' he sniffed. 'If they hadn't stopped the bout, you and I might be working on *Typhoon's Teeth* right now.'

'Yes,' Gwynne nodded. She had been with him. Watched as he leaned on the edge of the box seat, elbows to the wood, his untouched vin goblet swirling in his left hand. Knew what he had seen – the slight servo malfunction in the hip traversal gears of Honourable Machine Lord *Typhoon's Teeth*. Heard him mutter that, with *Jester* having ranged armaments and the *Typhoon* having none, he could bait the bigger Knight suit into the soft, sloping ground of the lower field. Run around it so it twisted towards him and activated the malfunction, pausing in its traversal in an unbalanced moment.

And if his Armiger slammed into the big Knight Gallant during that two-second window, he could topple it and render the big machine temporarily defenceless. Face down, its broad back ready for his Armiger Warglaive to leap upon it like a wolf on the back of a wounded grox, pinning the bigger animal and chewing for arteries.

But just like they would not let Rakkan place high in the Lists, they would not let him take a Knight suit from a more 'deserving' candidate.

'The problem,' Gwynne said, 'is one of readiness, my lord. While it is true you would have defeated Lord Kawe, the result would have been two damaged...'

'Nonsense,' he snapped. 'If we worried about damage, we would not conduct tournaments. They simply didn't want one of my blood–'

'Lord!' Gwynne seized him by the arms.

For an instant, he was shocked. Sacristans did not touch nobles. Not even if they served together. Different classes. Different codes of...

But then the violence of her enhanced strength threw him to

the side and he realised she'd tackled him, the awkward tangle of them staggering towards the mechanical ladder.

The force twisted him around, and he saw the hooded figure emerging from the shadows, a matt-black laspistol extended in one hand.

He swore he saw the bone-white finger slam down on the trigger.

Crack. Crack. Crack.

The gunfire brought footmen, voices shouting, boots scuffing the floor. The hooded figure had already disappeared.

'Gwynne,' said Rakkan. 'I… the pain. I can't.'

But then he felt the hole in Gwynne's back, a hole leaking oil and coolant. And his knees buckled.

Noble and sacristan fell in a tangle at the feet of the deactivated Knight suit, blood and oil spreading across the floor.

Their bodies reflected in the dark glass of *Jester*'s single cyclopic eye.

PART ONE

ASSASSINS

ONE

Tessenna Starne figured she had about twenty minutes to live. Thirty, if she'd lost them on the moor.

The headlumen on her dirtcycle, hooded with a cap and its lens red to avoid detection at range, cast a thin crescent of light ahead.

. Curved and crimson, like a slashed throat.

She leaned forward over the handlebars to counterbalance the bucking hydraulics as her cycle clawed up the dirt road, cresting the last rise before her target.

Road. What a jest. It was nothing better than a shepherd's track, a weaving line of pounded earth that climbed into the fog-bound moorland hills, used by none except the sure-footed curlhorns that picked their way up the foothills.

Once they'd been livestock, overseen for generations by the region's herd-serfs. Then the reorganisation came and the displacement shortly thereafter. House footmen had moved in with lasguns to escort the herdsmen to their new home, two duchies over.

She'd been just a girl, then, but she remembered. Remembered how the footman who'd come into her home had looked apologetic as he did it. Uncomfortable. Said he was a servant, just like them. Empathised, even as he forced them from their home at gunpoint. Nothing lived here but the proud curlhorns now. It's why Starne had picked it.

She stopped at the crest of the hill, raised her visor and spared a glance behind, picking out the weaving line of lanterns emerging from the trees at the bottom of the hill. Canine barks echoed up from the valley floor.

Then she slapped the visor down and gunned her dirtcycle's engine, took the plunge down the other side of the slope – curlhorn track forgotten, feeling her machine buck beneath her as she jarred and wheeled over the humps, briefly catching air halfway down as she leapt a rise.

She'd done this once every season for the last seven years. Stealing out of her quarters at Gathering Palace with forged errand-orders that bought her a full day. Making it to the shed where she'd stashed the bike, heading into the hills. Always on the new moon. Transmitting her check-in codes and short reports. *Dominion Station / Status Rep. Alpha, Rift+742dys / NTR.*

NTR – Nothing to Report.

Tonight's message would be significantly longer. She could feel the codebook heavy in the pocket of her leather jerkin.

A las-bolt streaked above her, stabbing blind in the deep shadows of the valley, briefly splashing her with an arc of passing colour as it sizzled overhead. Lighting the fog that gathered like poison gas in the bowl of the valley floor.

Starne jagged the handlebars, slewing the bike right, spewing gravel, to change her position and angle.

Two more spears of red lashed behind her, close to her old position, searing away the night vision in her left eye and leaving purple streaks she blinked away as she hit the valley floor, fully enveloped in the fog. Doused her light.

She could see the crumbling village emerging from the fog ahead. Thick rock walls and moss-colonised roofs. What doors and window shutters remained hung by single hinges, precarious.

Though she could no longer see the lanterns, she knew they were close. Shouts carried down from the hill behind.

Revise the timeline. Ten minutes to live. Make them good minutes.

It was right, somehow, that it would end here.

Starne left the bike at a fence in front of the first dwelling, hoping it might misdirect her pursuers. Give her another sixty seconds as they searched the wrong house. She snapped down the kickstand to activate the trigger and gingerly leaned it upright, then slipped into the tangle of houses.

Perhaps her sense of poetic justice had betrayed her. Her home village, after all, was a matter of house records. Any Gatekeeper or Kingsward would ken the pattern immediately. Displaced herder girl, promoted through house magnanimity to an important communications role, privately nurses her grief and resentment until it curdles and she turns traitor to her oaths.

A simple story, easy to understand – and true enough.

The Imperial spymaster had come to her during the Tallaxian Campaign, when the house Knights were crushing a subterranean tyranid infestation, and asked her if she wanted to do a service for the Emperor.

With compensation, of course.

Dominion had no currency, or at least none serfs could use. But life-saving pharms – blister packs that could be easily hidden in belongings and protect both her and what remained of her family from the plagues that regularly swept through the labouring classes – those were welcome.

Starne weaved through the buildings, found the tumbledown shack with the tree sprouting from one corner, roots worming through the foundation and big trunk forcing its way through the roof like a chimney.

A perfect frame for the long wire aerial that she'd coiled around it.

Starne could hear dogs barking in the fog-shrouded streets. Stablights glowing on the weed-choked common. Shouts of discovery.

Despite the tension, she smiled.

A *whump* of detonation on the far side of the village. Orange-lit fog boiling into the sky, rolling away in a visible shockwave.

They'd found the dirtcycle, moved it enough to trigger the plas-tek charge she'd planted behind the promethium tank.

The stablights in the common swung towards the explosion, bounced as the footmen began to run.

She reached the door to the hovel and gingerly stepped over the tripwire stretched taut across the threshold, its trigger keyed to the frag mine that sat above the door, pointing down from behind a false stone. She slipped in, closed the door and barred it.

In the night of mist, darkness and red lights, the blinking green and amber of the vox-caster comforted her.

She put her dirtcycle helmet on the table, pulled the autopistol from the back of her waistband and checked it. Set it down by the transmission unit so it would be within easy reach.

She dropped her codebook next to it and opened it to the message she'd just finished composing when that meddling arsehole Calthius – head serf-master of Gathering Palace, mes-senger wing – had walked into her chamber.

He'd taken an interest in her the month before. Made advances. Invited her to private training. She had said no, but Calthius was obsessed. He kept trying.

Starne didn't know what Calthius intended when he'd slipped his master key in her room's lock and walked inside. Perhaps he'd wanted to search it, find something that would give him leverage over her. Or to get her alone.

He'd definitely not expected to find her leaning over her personal trunk – the secret compartment in the lid dropped open to display a row of gold coins, message wafers, a codebook and a well-oiled autopistol all nestled in purpose-fit foam.

Starne killed the leering bastard, of course. But he was a big man and didn't go quiet. The footmen came. Swordsmen, naturally. Nothing the autopistol couldn't handle.

And now she had only minutes.

Dominion Station / Status Rep. Alpha, Rift +1088 dys

She typed with the trained speed of a lifelong messenger-serf. Accurate and decisive. Tuning out the growing volume of barking and iron-shod boots on turf. Of rotted windows and doors getting beaten down.

Just like when she was a girl.

A thump on the door, someone trying to force it.

Bad idea.

Ch-chink. BLAM.

The frag mine above the door frame. Starne could hear the little ball bearings shredding the footman's flesh, cracking bones and rattling off the entrance flagstone to pepper the men behind.

She hit TRANSMIT.

She closed the codebook and strained, bending it in half, cracking the incendiary flare hidden in the spine. She dropped the smouldering hardback into the mould-eaten stone fireplace as the fizzling chemical flames started to lick up from its pages.

Las-bolts tore through the door behind her, stinging her left bicep, leaving an orange glow on the uneven piled-slate walls. Nearly hit the vox.

Starne grabbed up her autopistol and jammed it directly into the smoking hole in the door, squeezed off two bursts to keep them off her. Looked back at the vox.

SENDING... SENDING...

More las-fire lanced through the window to her left, blowing a brick out of one corner of the chimney, throwing it into the wall. The shutter broke inward and hung at a crazy angle.

SENDING... SENDING...

Starne slid to the window and opened up in the footman's face point-blank. Bullets threw sparks from his stamped-metal helm as they drilled into his cranium and scoured her knuckles with slivers of metal shrapnel. He dropped.

She looked back.

SENDING... SENDI–

TRANSMISSION COMPLETE

Starne leapt across the room. Made the corner with its tangle of invading roots. More blind las-fire stormed into the windows, chipping the stones and boring black burn-holes in the vox-set.

She grabbed the roots and pulled herself upward, alarmed at how weak her left arm felt. She realised halfway up that the stinging las-shot had gone clean through her bicep. Above her, she could see the gap where the tree had forced its way through the roof, stars shining above.

The door gave in, boots behind her. Shouting.

She grabbed up through the hole, found the handle she'd embedded in the moss-slick roof just in case. Pulled herself through just as the first las-bolts drummed into the tree.

Rolled. Dropped, broke her fall poorly enough to bruise, but well enough not to cause injury. Roofs in her village, poor as it had been, were only about seven feet high.

Starne flipped the switch in the back of the hut, pulled her aching body up and ran.

The tube-charges under the vox went in a line like flame-crackers. One-two-three. Tore up the vox to destroy any trace of the final transmission. Lifted the roof right off the house.

Starne threw herself into the dry streambed just as the rain of stones arrived, thumping into the soft turf. Her exfiltration plan was, at least, going well. The fog was working to her advantage.

She ran crouched through the streambed, hearing the shouts and wails of wounded men in the mist. She passed under the stone bridge that was her waypoint, turned two points north-west and ran across the moor, her torn jerkin flapping.

The field was excellent concealment tonight. The fog made land navigation difficult for anyone who didn't know the terrain. Starne hit the split-rail fence pen and slithered under, keeping the ghostly shade of a rock wall to her right.

She'd hidden a second bike in the forest up ahead, wrapped in a waterproof tarpaulin and wheeled into a thick bush. Escape would've been impossible but for the fog. Yet she might make it. Even still be alive when the Imperial intervention arrived.

Then she stopped.

Before her was a hillock she did not recognise.

But was that possible? These were her fields, where she'd played and worked as a child. She knew every row and pen – had the fog-disorientation and blood loss confused her? Was this a rotting haystack she'd never noticed, or an outshed that had passed into the shadows of her own memory?

She took a step forward, peering, then another. Reached through the thick fog to touch the hill.

Felt cold metal.

The hill began to move. Rise. Big servos whining. Pistons hissing. Three eyes the size of Starne's hand lit the fog with an electric green glow.

The Knight Armiger rose above her, straightening from its

hunched position. Fog condensate rolled off as the armour plates warmed from the nuclear furnaces within.

Starne could only stand, transfixed, as the terrible machine straightened and took a step, planting its feet in a wide stance to block her path. Allowing her to take in its massive stature as it shook the fog off.

Nearly three times her height. The span of its autocannon arms wide as a Valkyrie.

It had been waiting for her. A huntsman allowing its dogs to flush the prey into the open.

Starne yelled defiance. Pointed her autopistol upward and fired into the glowing eyes. Bullets flattened against the crystal of the ocular systems.

The Armiger hunched over her, her small form dwarfed by its bulk, unhurriedly pointing both autocannon barrels at the girl from the ruined village.

And the world ended in noise.

TWO

As autocannon rounds tore Tessenna Starne apart, her message was already in the wind.

She had known little about the technical specifications of the vox-set she'd been given. She had not needed to know. Indeed, even the nameless spymasters who had given her the instructions did not fully understand its workings.

Which was fitting. Because while the purpose of the organisation was to gather information, its operatives understood that natural curiosity was to be directed outward, at the enemy. One did not ask questions. Knowledge about sources and methods was something superiors granted if they deemed it necessary, not a thing one should seek out.

But despite its unremarkable drab green casing, the vox-set Starne operated for seven years was no ordinary unit.

Known as a subliminal astropathic-caster, or sub-caster, the unit had beamed its encoded message over the heads of the milling footmen – still trying to break down the door, at that point – past the shadows lumbering in the fog, over the forest, and to the chivalric fortress-halls of Gathering Palace.

There, it flashed over Heaven Defence West, one of the two fire-control stations that coordinated the planet's air defences in case of enemy attack.

It beamed over the tournament ground – empty this time of year, its banner poles struck and stowed, the opposing box seats painted in the heraldry of House Stryder and House Rau empty. Come tilting season, the empty fields would fill with the Knights of the rival houses, their engines pulsing and weapons loaded. And clad in ancient and irreplaceable armour, they would tear at each other with great chainblades and massive cannons, egged on by the wild cheers of their kinsmen. These martial exploits would then be broadcast back to their home manors via its giant aerial vox-tower.

That tower was the message's destination, and it used the reliable point to renew signal strength and change direction, redirecting its beam to the Chancel Fortress of the Adeptus Astra Telepathica that sat on the mountains overlooking Gathering Palace.

There, it met a young astropath named Drusus Mak. Or rather, it met a small coin-sized implant in his forebrain, inserted shortly after his successful soul-binding. Mak was unaware of the implant's nature or function. He knew only that, on occasion, an encrypted message would float up from his subconscious and repeat, like an obnoxious hymn lyric, until he channelled it into the message harmony of the larger astropathic choir and sent it on its way through the warp.

Mak had no idea that this act, done without thought twice a year, was the entire reason why he'd been assigned to the backwater Knight world of Dominion.

Within the warp, the message piggybacked upon other astropathic traffic, the theory being that the best way to hide deeply secret data was amidst a stream of similar data. Yet when the stream hit the first relay station of Shautin, another implanted astropath separated the message from the stream of traffic, re-encrypted it, sanctified it, and sent it through the warp to astro station Pacificus Deep. There the process repeated before the final delivery into the sanctified atmosphere of Holy Terra.

At last, deep underneath the Obsidian Keep of the Adeptus Astra Telepathica, it reached its final destination.

A reception choir of three astropaths received the communique, picking apart its layers of psychic encryption until only the original coded message remained. Never allowed to leave the keep, and living in dwellings that adjoined the reception room, they spent their lives off-shift in study and chant, and on-shift parsing messages that they could not read. Which was in fact a mercy, given that if by some impossible chance they *did* divine the contents of the message, they would be immediately executed.

It was a silent world of scratching quills and murmuring, as the astropaths sketched each communique via automatic writing, sealed it in a secure tube, and inserted it into the chest of a delivery servitor. At any one time, a dozen servitors idled in ranks, some with armour painted red for the Mechanicus fortress, green for the Militarum, blue for the Navy or purple for the Navis Nobilite.

The Dominion communique, on the other hand, received unusual care.

The chief of the astropath triarchy loaded it, with caution, into the chest-port of a matt-black, up-armoured servitor. She took such care because she knew that the cylinder port sat between two melta charges designed to trigger if they detected tampering.

Then the astropath spoke the code word that sent the tracked, vat-born monstrosity trundling down the tunnel marked with a skull and cross, its cranium bisected with a dagger.

To the Officio Assassinorum.

* * *

Despite the Officio Assassinorum's dark reputation, it is well named. Much of it is indeed an *office*, and were some Administratum official to find themselves in one of its control centres, they would not think themselves out of place until they made the fatal mistake of looking carefully at the paperwork being processed.

Because for every operative firing a killing shot or wielding an alien phase blade, there are a thousand clerks, analysts and logisters determining where the operatives should go, who they should kill, and how their equipment will arrive.

Managing the vast amount of incoming signals traffic falls under the purview of the Office of Missions, and that was where the Dominion Communique first landed on the desk of Eadwinne Foe.

An overworked man in his middle fifties, balding and with a clerk's perpetual stoop, he was no one's idea of an assassin. Indeed, his wife and friends thought he had a rather dull job in the Administratum, processing and approving requests for agri-chemical shipments.

Yet it was his job to intake each communique from field agents, send them through decryption, then route the decrypted messages through the analysts for vetting and verification.

Normally, should the message be considered genuine and of sufficient importance, Foe would elevate it to the next level of bureaucracy where the process would repeat, but with those of a higher security clearance. Should it fall short, he might route it, anonymously, to the Militarum or Office of Planetary Governance.

But the Dominion communique stopped him cold.

The reaction was delayed – with so many requests for intervention coming through, focusing on one thing could be difficult – and he paused halfway to handing the decrypt to his assistant when he snatched it back and read it again.

'Throne of Terra.' He ran a hand through what remained of his hair. 'Get the casket with my seals.'

'Yes, sir.'

'Quickly, boy! Quickly! You're not a damned Ecclesiarchy messenger any more.'

The boy – who was actually twenty-three, but who Foe would ever see as a boy – brought the silver-chased casket and held it steady as his superior fitted his signet ring into a cavity.

Internals whirred. The chest sprang open to reveal a row of seal-stamps in escalating order of priority.

He took the heavy one on the far right, stamped the back of the decrypt SPECIAL ESCALATION: M of O, rolled it, and stuffed it in a pneumatic tube of impact-proof crystal so the red ink could be seen through the glass. Then he smeared the hinged door with his desk candle, pressed his signet ring into the wax and held it out.

'To the dispatch hub, immediately. Run.'

Minutes later, the communique shot upward through the network of delivery tubes, carried via air current past floors and floors of analysts – literally bypassing levels of bureaucracy as it flew up the hidden headquarters of the Office of Assassins.

It arrived with a hollow *thunk*.

White-gloved hands removed it, inserted it into a nano-sniffer that would detect any explosives, chemicals, biological materials or nerve agents. The machine showed a green light and ejected the tube, and the white gloves broke open the hinged door, confident that the message would have been incinerated at the slightest hint of an anomalous substance.

The man with the white gloves read the message, swore, and then ran. Through two blast-proof doors that opened upon his biometric signature. Into a comfortable but windowless office stacked high with paper, its walls covered in galactic charts.

'Master,' the white-gloved man said, holding out the communique. 'It's Dominion. Special Elevation. Just came through.'

This Master of Operations – the description of whom is so sensitive that it should not be recorded here – turned in their high-backed chair and read the message.

'Contact the Grandmaster,' said Operations. 'Tell him I am coming for an appointment. In person, not by vox. Tell him Operations politely requests that he convene a meeting of the lords.'

'There is one scheduled for tomorrow evening,' said the white-gloved deputy.

'Let us hope,' Operations said, interweaving their fingers, 'that's soon enough.'

THREE

'Look at these schematics carefully. These are the weapons
you will wield. Both rifle and pistol are called Exitus. Those of
you who are scholam pupils may know that translates to end,
outcome, or death. They are the means you will use to bring
ends to others. And you will almost certainly meet your own
end with them in your hands.'

— Initiate's Primer, Vindicare Temple, title and author withheld

Sea foam and roaring water.

Absolom Raithe could feel the wave's power as it sucked the
water out from under him, its jewel-blue face streaked with
bubbles. A mountain forming above his head, the rolling bulk
of its front flattening as it hit the reef and broke.

He slashed through the foaming surf towards the thirty-foot
breaker, ignoring the burn in his shoulder as he built up speed
before hitting the base and diving under.

In the lenses of his spy mask, he saw the wave break over
him. Noted the boiling impact of the crashing water. Cavita-
tion bubbles swirling in spirals. Felt the shockwave as it went
through him with a great thump, his body whipped up and
down like a carpet being shaken out.

Raithe liked that feeling. Liked the force of it hammering him,
punishing him. Reminding him of his mistake – pounding the
lesson into his body.

For it was not his brain that had erred, it had been his *instinct*.

Turava Beta, Lotus Chain. Four Terran months back. A straightforward mission with a tricky infil-exfil problem.

Target had been Archmagos Tabulatum Vrain, an archeotech researcher who, Raithe assumed, had looked a bit too deeply where he shouldn't. Started experimenting with the conqueror_ wyrm code-virus, and expanding on the work of its heretek creator, Programmator Quivarian.

Raithe didn't need to know the details. Didn't want to know the details. They hadn't been pertinent to the central challenge.

Which was how to put a turbo-penetrator round through Vrain's augmeticised brain.

Above him, the boiling water swept by and the wave rolled past, its sucking pressure gone.

He surfaced, took a breath from the recycled oxygen of his spy mask. The next breaker rushed towards him – again, thirty feet of overhead, about to break.

He shoved his thumb between the bottom of his spy mask and his neck, breaking the seal. He paddled forward at the approaching monster and went under just as the water began rising around him.

As he descended, water flooded his mask. His lips tasted salt a moment before the bottom of his face went numb.

Vrain's fortress, the Monastery of the Cliffs, had too many sensor nets and air defences for a direct insertion and recovery by Valkyrie. Even a grav-chute would have been risky.

So he'd gone in by sea, disassembled Exitus rifle slung in a dry bag across his back. Pistol sprayed with sealant to proof it against the seawater. Rode the grav-chute down into the chop and ditched it before the weight pulled him under. Swam a mile to shore.

Inserting had been the easy part. Exfiltration had not gone quite so smoothly.

He hadn't expected the waves to be so high on his way out. Swimming a mile into shore with thirty-foot overhead surf and a high-calibre rifle was one thing – swimming out against the waves was another, even with his synskin suit partially inflated.

His muscle memory had failed him a quarter-mile out. A momentary lapse of control, a second of swimming past the point he'd needed to dive.

The big wave had rolled him. Thrashed him around like he were a phial of evidence in a centrifuge. Dragged his body face first across the dead reef below, cracked one eye-lens on his spy mask.

That's how the mask flood had happened. Salty water pouring into his eyes, blinding him, creeping behind the mouth seal so his next breath gagged on a teaspoon of cruel ocean.

Then his right arm had snagged in a reef hole – the lair of some local eel. It stopped the drag, but left him underwater and helpless, caught in the wash, each big wave blowing him back and forth like a strand of seaweed. The ligaments in his shoulder straining and tearing, the long nerve that connected his neck and fingers stretched over and over like a rubberine cord. Each *zing* of pain causing him to suck in an ever-increasing flood of water.

Training took over, as training should. He reverted to his contingency plan. Sealed the broken eye-lens with a palm and triggered an emergency valve blow that blasted air into his mask, purging the water.

At the cost of nearly all its oxygen reserve.

Vision restored, he'd activated the mask's blast cover on the left side, blocking the broken lens apart from a weeping trickle of water. He'd drawn his Exitus pistol and fired into the bone-dead coral trapping his hand. Each bullet, driven by compressed air, made an odd *fwump-fwump-fwump* sound in the cold water. He'd freed himself. Got back topside and removed the mask. Swam out to the Valkyrie rendezvous without it.

His superiors had applauded him. In truth, Raithe had got lucky.

And he hated that. Luck was the refuge of a bad operator. Luck meant you'd screwed up, but hadn't been punished for it. It was an ephemeral ghost, coming and going, a construct of the weak-minded who wanted to feel comfort about their vulnerability. Who interpreted their random survival as a virtue, not a simple quirk of probability.

Raithe did not need luck. He had tradecraft.

It was the Vindicare way. True, Raithe's amplification surgeries had made him faster, stronger, more observant than the ordinary human. But the Vindicare were not uncanny shape-shifters like the Callidus, tech-freaks like the Vanus, or created monsters like the Eversor and Culexus.

Instead the Vindicare had craftsmanship.

They overcame via rigorous preparation. Fanatical training regimens to stay at peak performance. Obsessive operational planning. Contingencies upon contingencies upon contingencies. A dedication to understanding and maximising technology.

And hammering every lesson home.

Raithe's mask flooded. He still made the dive correctly, eyes full of water and mouth tasting sea brine. Continued swimming as he initiated the mask purge procedure. Felt the force of the wave bang through him, driving in the message.

Mess it up again, and you'll die. Had that happened nine more times, you would've died in all nine. You are the one in ten. You don't beat the odds, the odds beat you.

His shoulder felt like it was on fire. Like the blood in it was congealing. The punishing swim out had wound it tight as a sailor's knot.

He was coming up, mid-self-flagellation, when he noticed the next wave wasn't the proper height. Only fifteen feet, and rolling not breaking.

Raithe trod water, rising and falling over it.

Someone had turned off the generator of the Natatorium wave pool. Dropped the bottom so the waves wouldn't break. He looked back towards the shore of the big generator pool, six hundred feet behind.

He saw two figures standing on the edge of the simulated ocean, their high-collared bodygloves and robes looking incongruous against the pink tile of the Natatorium walls. Their forms breaking the mosaic of the Imperial eagle that soared behind them.

'Absolom Raithe,' said a voice through the speaker system. *'Report for orders.'*

FOUR

'You're sure he's the right man?' asked the Liaison. He nursed a lho-stick held in a long stem. His narrow eyes watched Raithe pull his way towards the artificial shore, cutting through the diminishing waves.

'Oh yes,' said Tallica Vare. 'You've seen his file.'

'That I have.' The Liaison tapped his ash on the tile floor, a man used to others cleaning up his messes. 'Impressive.'

'Forty-nine missions is a record for our sector temple,' Vare added. 'The average lifespan for a journeyman operative here is about eleven missions. Thirty-three for a master operative.'

'We don't want average, not even *your* average, Vare.' He sucked at the lho-stick, the orange ember lighting up his hooded eyes. 'I mean no disrespect in that, but the matter is a tricky one. Now, you're sure?'

Raithe reached the shore break and rode a wave in, head down like a torpedo, letting the surf streak him towards the officers.

'Absolutely sure,' Vare said. 'I only hate to do it because…'

The Liaison looked at Vare, one eyebrow raised.

'Well,' said Vare, 'it would be his fiftieth elimination, wouldn't it? That means nomination for Sicarius Primus. He'd get to pick his targets, right of first refusal on any sector-area mission, even poach assignments from other temples.'

'Plus the possibility of advancement to Terra,' said the Liaison, dryly.

'It would mean a great deal to us,' Vare said. 'Vindicare Pacificus hasn't produced one since the War of the Beast.'

'He could succeed, you know.'

'Even if he does,' said Vare, 'there's not much chance of him getting back to have the jade laurel affixed to his mask, is there?'

Raithe emerged from the surf, cold seawater dripping from the angles of his spy mask, flowing from the ridges of his hardened muscle. He wore only the mask and a pair of aquatic trunks. Rivulets traced the scars that crossed his brown body. The scars were not the same. Some, arrow-straight and faded, were surgical, remnants of the enhancement regimen that had made him what he was. Others were battlefield scars – marks engraved on his flesh by xenos claws or hot shrapnel. Asteroid craters of old gunshot wounds.

The Liaison looked him up and down with an appraiser's eye. He guessed that the lack of bodysuit was part of the Vindicare's notoriously gruelling training regimen. Even standing feet back from the lapping water, he could feel its chill.

One tank over, to their left, a dozen teenage initiates gasped and dived through a lake-sized tank of seawater slicked with burning promethium. Each time one surfaced, a gun-servitor swung towards them and peppered the water with live rounds.

Raithe didn't even look towards the sound of gunfire as he approached them.

'Operative Master-Grade Raithe,' said Vare, dropping into an at-ease stance. 'Present yourself.'

Raithe strode forward and came to attention before them, back rifle-barrel straight yet somehow still exuding comfort. He tilted forward in a bow. 'Sector master,' he said, the words coming out flat through the spy mask.

'Unmask and at ease,' said Sector Master Vare. 'I have someone I would like you to meet.'

Raithe paused, removed his mask.

Five decades in the Assassinorum bureaucracy had taught the Liaison that, beneath their masks, assassins rarely looked like you expected them to. But given Raithe's reputation he'd thought that, this time, things might be different. A vicious scar down one cheek, for instance. Blued-steel eyes or a blade-like face.

But Absolom Raithe did not come from the propaganda-picts. And killers rarely looked like killers – that was, after all, the point.

The Liaison saw a man of almost indeterminate origin. His skin was brown, like nutwood. It was difficult to determine if the colour was genetic, or tanning due to solar exposure. Raithe's face was handsome, in a way, but not striking or characterful. His black hair was cut in a tight style that was identifiably civilian, but close-cropped enough to pass as Militarum regulation.

The eyes were, the Liaison was disappointed to find, copper brown.

He was plain, forgettable. The Liaison wondered if his face had always been that way, or a chirurgeon had purposely sculpted his inconspicuous features.

'Before anything,' said Vare, 'how is the shoulder, Absolom? Fully rehabbed and fit for duty?'

'Yes, master,' said Raithe. 'Fit and ready for action.'

'None of the pain discussed in your medicae screening a few months back? I see it's riding a bit high.'

'No, no pain, sir,' said Raithe, dropping the shoulder a fraction.

'It bunches in extreme cold. I'm training it out of the habit with the daily swims.'

'Good, good,' said Vare, turning towards the Liaison. 'Are you satisfied?'

'Indeed.' The Liaison sucked his lho-stick and gave a slight bow. 'Honoured to meet you, operative. Your reputation is… extraordinary. Known even on Terra. I'd be quite curious to hear details about a few missions, if we have time to exchange anecdotes.'

'You've come from Terra, sir?' Raithe glanced sidelong at his master. 'Inspection isn't for another seven years standard, correct?'

'Not an inspection,' the Liaison chuckled. 'A mission.'

'And you are?' Raithe asked.

The Liaison smiled. 'Let's save that for somewhere quiet, shall we?'

'We're clear,' said Vare, as he keyed the sonic dampener. An extra measure, in case the room's foot-thick adamantine door proved insufficient. He gestured to three chairs surrounding a large ebony table, the Vindicare symbol inlaid in gold. 'Make yourselves comfortable. It's just us.'

A miniature elevator, connected directly to the secure archive, chimed. Vare slid open the hatch and extracted a stack of parchment folios.

The Liaison slumped into one of the high-backed chairs and lit another lho-stick. 'You asked who I am, Absolom. Well, I'm not going to tell you that. Not pertinent. But I can tell you my function.'

He slid the heavy ident-ring across the table. Raithe trapped it and inspected the device.

An Assassinorum symbol, a skull impaled with an operative's dagger.

On the forehead was an O.

Raithe twisted the bezel on the ring and activated the holo-lith, reading the credentials and clearances.

'I see,' he nodded, voice betraying a hint of interest. 'You're from the Master of Operations?'

'As far as you're concerned, I *am* Operations.' The Liaison gave a wry smile. 'I'm their operational legate. I have full powers to act on behalf of M of O.'

'Exciting,' said Raithe, matching the Liaison's smile. 'We usually get an encoded beam-message or dead drop. Must be something big.'

The Liaison chuckled.

'Perhaps too apt a choice of words, Absolom,' said Vare, suppressing a smile.

'Are you familiar with the world of Dominion?' asked the Liaison.

'Knight world, isn't it? Has a noble house there.'

'Correct, after a fashion. There are *two* knightly houses there. House Stryder and House Rau. Each rules a hemisphere.'

'Sounds complicated,' said Raithe.

'Very much so,' said the Liaison. 'Especially since they detest each other. Bad blood. Dates back to – well, who knows when. Back to the Great Crusade, probably. The last time there was a succession crisis they nearly descended into civil war.'

'Succession crisis in which house?'

'That's the interesting part,' said Vare. 'A single High Monarch rules Dominion. Has absolute power over both houses.'

'Sounds like an inherently unstable system,' Raithe said. His brow furrowed. 'Each faction wants their chosen successor, only one can win.'

'As you said.' The Liaison paused to puff his lho-stick. 'It's complicated. Owing to the power-sharing agreement on Dominion, only a candidate with the right bloodline can ascend to the throne. Namely, they must be the offspring of political marriages between the houses. Those in the succession line are considered part of neither house, unless they declare allegiance to one. In fact, to ensure that no house can overly influence them, they alternate houses each year until they come of age. One year with the mother's house, one year with the father's.'

'Is there a succession crisis on the horizon?' asked Raithe.

'Yes,' the Liaison smiled. 'Because you're going to start one.'

FIVE

Absolom Raithe had long ago learned that, when surprised, the best tactical choice was to say nothing.

The Liaison pulled a heavy piece of parchment out of a case and rolled it open on the table, holding it just out of Raithe's reach as if it were a piece of priceless art.

'Absolom Raithe,' said the Liaison. 'Vindicare master operative, service number fifty-nine-theta-stroke-three-seven-three. By order of the Senatorum Imperialis, I hereby task you with the execution of Lucien Yavarius-Khau, High Monarch of Dominion, Commander of the Noble Questor Imperialis Houses Stryder and Rau.'

The execution order was inscribed on thick vellum, the calligraphic ink that made up the words a shining royal blue of lapis lazuli. Heavy wax seals – twelve in number – crowded the document's right side. Raithe made out the triple eye of the Navis Nobilite, the scales of the Arbites, and the impaled skull of the Assassinorum among the grouping before the Liaison gingerly rolled it up and stowed it back in his document case.

'I've never seen one in person before,' said Raithe. 'Usually we receive a data-facsimile.'

'This is an unusual case, Absolom,' said Vare. 'Special, really. It's been quite a while since we removed the head of a knightly house. Long enough that we've lost any operational data about how it was accomplished.'

Raithe leaned forward, sheer interest cracking his stoicism. 'I suppose you have parameters?'

'We do,' said the Liaison. 'It will be a challenging operation. A delicate operation. One where the hand of the Assassinorum must not be detected.'

'So I suppose an inferno round to the cranium isn't what we're looking for,' said Raithe. 'Understood. But in that case, why come to us? Why not the Vanus Temple, or the Venenum? Perhaps even the Callidus. Those methodologies seem more suited to that purpose.'

'Don't talk yourself out of this assignment, Absolom,' said Vare with a smile. 'The Master of Operations did not pick our temple due to its tactical capabilities, but because of its operational planning. Is that not correct, my lord?'

The Liaison balanced his lho-stick holder on a crystal ashtray, folded his hands and looked Raithe in the eyes. 'The M of O proposes an execution force. You, operative, will be given command as well as the remit to form your team however you like. Carte blanche. Anything the sector temples can provide, you may have. Your team will insert onto Dominion, remove the High Monarch, and steer a suitable successor to the throne.'

'Just to clarify,' Raithe interjected. 'We are to both kill the High Monarch and stage-manage the ensuing succession crisis. That's... unusual.'

'Indeed.' The Liaison picked the lho-holder back up and took another drag.

'And difficult,' Raithe continued.

'I have no doubt,' the Liaison said. 'To level with you, it's more than difficult. When united, the forces of Stryder-Rau are nearly unstoppable. They were a lynchpin of the Lotus Subsector's defences even before the Heresy. Rode to battle alongside Macharius himself. Most recently, they were instrumental in suppressing the tyranid incursions on Pharaxes.'

'But they're not united, at least going by what you were saying.'

'Correct. Of course a certain amount of disunity is to be expected given their unique form of government – but things have taken a disturbing turn.'

'Around two years ago standard,' said Vare, 'just after the beginning of the Indomitus Crusade, Terra invoked its treaty with Stryder-Rau, calling them to fulfil their obligation to muster for war and join Fleet Tertius. With the current troubles in Pacificus, the fleet requires every available asset.'

Raithe nodded. 'Dominion's response?'

'None,' said the Liaison. 'That's the trouble. With the Rift, and its associated communication difficulties, no one even knew if Dominion received the message. So it was re-sent. Twice. Then we received an alarming report from an embedded agent suggesting that an anti-Imperial camp has arisen and is talking secession. Our analysis people put two and two together. They say that Yavarius-Khau's power is such – and Dominion's culture of oaths so rigid – that if he ordered a muster for war, it would have happened already. A treaty violation of that magnitude is de facto secessionism. He needs to be removed.'

'Why not let them fight it out?' asked Raithe. 'Break off a few frigates and throw military aid towards one side. Make Dominion an example. With a political rift like Stryder-Rau's, it would be easy to exploit divisions and solidify a pro and anti-Imperial camp. Why use the Assassinorum?'

'Because a civil war is what we're trying to avoid,' the Liaison replied. 'Attrition takes its toll. Their Knight suits are ancient and irreplaceable. Even if none are destroyed, if too many suffer damage, their combat effectiveness will not be sufficient for what is required of them. Stryder-Rau's reserve of suits is running low.' He pulled the stub of the lho-stick out of his holder and flicked it in the ashtray. 'If such precious machines must be damaged or destroyed, it should happen while fighting the Emperor's enemies, don't you think? Rather than some petty dynastic struggle.'

'And a succession conflict would be spectacularly ill-timed,' said Raithe. 'Given the conqueror_wyrm outbreak in the sub-sector's north. From what I hear, the heretek data-contagion is spreading. Two forge worlds lost to the infection this year, and the Vypaan Salient barely holding. If the feral machine-cultists break through, Dominion will be crucial for blunting the assault.'

'I told you he was sharp,' said Vare, his pride evident.

'That's an accurate assessment,' said the Liaison. 'If reductive. The heretek broadcast virus conqueror_wyrm and its hard-wire precursor heart_wyrm are proving decisive. The difficulty is that the defences in this sector are reliant on Mechanicus forces – and we can no longer count on the skitarii. We throw units at the Cult of the Transmuted, and within days they get infected via enemy broadcasts and defect. Titans and Imperial Knights, though – whether due to the extreme age of their technology or their differing vox-pickups, no one's sure – appear immune.'

'So the Imperium needs Stryder-Rau,' Raithe nodded. 'You have briefing documents?'

'Here's a dossier outlining what we know,' said the Liaison. He extracted a parchment bundle from his document case and held it out to Raithe. It ran to several hundred pages, and strained the black ribbon that bound it. 'It includes the original report from the intelligence operative we embedded on Dominion to keep an eye on things. And more besides. Give it a read and then we can discuss what you require.'

The Liaison sat back and lit another smoke. He did not realise that he would nearly exhaust his jewelled lho-case before Raithe was finished.

Most operatives, in the Liaison's experience, would read quickly in the presence of authority. Rush through, feeling social pressure not to waste time.

Raithe did not rush. He went slowly, methodically. Page by page. He did not even glance up at the other two men, and did not speak, apart from asking absently for water, a stylus and a writing pad.

It took three hours, and when he was done, he flipped back to the beginning and started taking the bundle apart, undoing bend-studs and clamps that held the pages together. Re-ordering them in a grid of stacks before him so he could easily reference them by topic. Took notes.

For a further three hours.

It was then that the Liaison saw the assassin in him. Deep focus and dogged purpose. An augmented mind turning over possibilities and analysing vulnerabilities. He drew family charts on his writing pad. Scribbled marginalia onto schematic drawings of Knight suits. He drank the water in one long draught, without looking up from the papers, as if the rehydration was nothing but preventative maintenance to keep his body running.

The Liaison would rather have left, but that was not possible. His remit would not allow him to be separate from these sensitive documents, or leave them even with trusted operatives. Data-slates were not allowed in the secure briefing chamber, and apart from eating the two meals that came up via the elevator – cold after being carried through to the archive – he smoked and mentally reviewed his schedule.

'My masters,' said Raithe. 'Thank you for your patience. I have a tentative plan.'

'Yes?' It was Vare.

'It will be a small team,' said Raithe. His copper eyes snapped up to the Liaison. 'Otherwise there will be no possibility of remaining undetected. Three members, including myself. Here's a list of the temples I would like to request, as well as a preliminary approach to the kill.'

Raithe slid a sheet of paper across the table. It had two names, followed by a single page of blocky handwriting.

'Not what I expected.' The Liaison pursed his lips, nodded. 'But direct and quiet.'

'Direct and quiet,' said Raithe, 'is the Vindicare way.'

'Very well.' The Liaison rose, bones creaking after the six-hour wait. 'I will contact the temples and request dossiers on their best. You will have your choice, along with any logistical support required.'

'Who will bring them in?' asked Vare.

The Liaison raised his eyebrows. 'Why, I will.'

SIX

LOCATION: PANOPTIC, LOTUS SUBSECTOR
OPERATION: ADJUDICATOR
MISSION DESIGNATION: SINKHOLE

'Haderaxes was a good enginseer. Been with us since the Ferrodine Gap. Saved my crew once, when our Exterminator threw a track and got stranded between the lines. What I mean to say is, he was trustworthy. But when that broadcast came through our vox, he became someone else. Eye-lenses went purple. Every drill and saw coming off him started to whine. He went at us like an animal, on all fours. Killed three crew before I stopped him, and that was only because I happened to be in the top hatch, and managed to swing the pintle-mount around before he climbed the tank. Even then, chopped up by a storm bolter, it was like the mechanical parts of him were trying to crawl free of his body... We ran over what was left – twice, just to be certain.'

– Lieutenant Yaal Kaskar, Cadian 34th Armoured Shock, from an after-action report regarding a new Archenemy weapon encountered on Graydon.

'Signal them again. Come on, do it!' Governor-Warden Salvarius Dio made a shooing gesture with his hands as he spoke, as if encouraging speed. When he dropped his meaty palms back to the command throne, his heavy rings clanked against the armrests. 'We have nine suppression teams deployed, *one* should be able to hear us.'

'Attention, attention. All suppressors report,' said Andocius Drawl, pressing down the SEND button of his hand-vox. As Chief of Discipline, the militarised aspects of governing Panoptic fell to him – usually without oversight. When the governor-warden bothered to get involved, well, it never meant anything good.

And a servitor rebellion certainly wasn't good.

He let go of the button. Heard the fuzz of static. Switched channels and sent again. Tried it over the address system – nothing.

'Lines still dead, governor,' he said. 'Chief? How are our visuals coming?'

Twenty feet away, Morala Zon, Chief of Processing, stood at a bank of monitors. Her mechadendrites struck and wove, adjusting dials and plugging into inputs one after the other. The light of the security monitors – stacked in a grid ten feet square, screens rolling and flashing – bathed her crimson robe in a blue light.

'I… I do not understand it,' the tech-priest howled, distraught. 'All visuals from Number Eleven Deep Shaft are cut off. I can't connect to the combat zone, and I… I… I…'

'Chief of Processing?' asked the governor-warden, brow furrowed.

Chief of Processing Morala Zon turned, her wheeled under-chassis rotating to face them. The flesh around her right ocular implant twitched in some kind of spasm. The other side of her face had gone slack.

'Is she having some kind of stroke?' asked the governor-warden, recoiling. He'd always found the tech-priest and her function repulsive – her greyish skin, the way she lobotomised and augmented the inmates into mining servitors – but now the thought occurred to him that the plague might have found her as well.

'*Governor-Warden Salvarius Dio.*'

The voice boomed from the laud-hailers overhead, shaking the decking beneath the command centre, as it echoed throughout the command cell block.

But that scared Dio less than the fact that each booming pronouncement was preceded by a whisper from the lips of Chief of Processing Morala Zon.

'Do not concern–' the tech-priest started.

'Do not concern yourself with the uprising,' the voice boomed, cutting her off. *'All is in hand. I am managing the clearance operation remotely. Your suppression teams have improved lethality by one hundred and twenty-two per cent, and recaptured the mag-lifts in Number Eleven Deep Shaft.'*

'She's possessed!' wailed the governor-warden. 'Plagued! It's got to her!'

Chief of Discipline Drawl did not wait for an order. He drew his laspistol and pressed it against the tech-priest's head.

The crack of the shot echoed through the command centre three times before Morala Zon's body hit the floor, mechadendrites writhing and knotting in the confusion of neural death. Something inside her cranium burned, filling the chamber with the stench of fried logic boards and cooked meat.

Drawl shot her twice more.

'It's not necessary to do my work for me, Discipline Chief Drawl,' said the voice. *'But no harm done…'*

Avaaris Koln held the code-casket up to the light, turning it to see the lights dancing red and green along the length of the dark brick sealed inside its sanctified sample tube. 'I already have everything I need from *her*.'

One of the cogitators pinged an alert from suppression team two. The amber light of the data-burst illuminated the copper hair of the machine's operator, who lay face down on the input board. Koln lifted the corpse up by the hair long enough to type a hatch-opening command, her augmetic fingers scraping unnaturally on the metal keys.

'Poor Morala Zon,' said Koln. 'She didn't know she was infected with the code-virus. She wasn't a cultist, just an asymptomatic carrier.'

Koln pushed the dead systems controller away on his wheeled chair, the body lolling backwards and rotating slightly as it drifted into the gloom of the access control centre.

There were nine other bodies slumped on workstations or sprawled on the floor. All of them armed, not that it had helped them.

Koln's eidetic memory archive flashed back to the fight.

Open door. Down three with digital laspistol embedded in her right index finger.

See guard approaching with taser-goad.

Dodge backwards to let the weapon pass, then grab the arm and break it, slam the elbow the wrong way until it comes apart like a wing on a roast bird. Chop to the larynx with her metal hand.

Two guards, shotguns. Activate ion buckler from left palm to absorb fire. Down one with digital laspistol. Trigger kinetic impulsor in right knuckles and send the other sailing sixteen feet across the room. His neck snaps as he hits the ceiling.

See cogitator operator go for hardwire alarm. Use dataveil to find path of the power supply cables. Rip them out of the wall. Shoot cogitator operator as he pulls dead alarm…

She blinked away the intrusive thought. Shook it off, continued.

'Morala Zon was at an early stage. The heart_wyrm infection hadn't mutated into the conqueror_wyrm variant. You were lucky. If it had, it would have been broadcast, and every prisoner-servitor in the mines would be trying to kill you, not just those from Eleven Deep Shaft. See, in the beginning, the virus needs a direct neural link for infection. But if allowed to circulate in the population for a year or more, it starts to adapt and…'

She looked at her vid-feed of the command centre, black and white, slightly distorted by the low-light conditions taxing the picter of her micro-drone skull as it nested in the ceiling. Saw the governor-warden's team of personal suppressors hammering at the door to the outer corridor. Chief of Discipline Drawl, shooting out every monitor one by one, in a vain attempt to stop whatever had taken them over.

The governor-warden himself standing behind a wall of officers with riot shields, blubbering.

'…but,' sighed Koln. 'I can see you're not really listening.'

'*Governor-warden, you should know all this from the sector-wide threat alerts on the epidemic,*' the voice boomed. '*Which from a cursory search of your data-slate, I can see you haven't read.*'

'It's not fair,' moaned Governor-Warden Dio. He spoke to the ceiling, tears streaming down his jowls as if he talked to the Emperor Himself. 'She did it. Zon. I didn't know. I didn't know.'

'*No,*' the voice boomed. '*You didn't know, at first. But when Discipline Chief Drawl first discovered the infection, well. He thought he could handle it…*'

'No! That's not…' Dio looked across the command floor at Drawl, saw his subordinate's face greasy with sweat. The bank of cogitators destroyed.

Drawl's eyes. Guilty.

'*But everyone knows that the warden punishes subordinates who bring him bad news – so they don't. Drawl kept it quiet, until it got so big you* had *to be informed. And at that point, well, you had an outbreak bad enough that raising an alarm would've meant calling in sector authorities and the Inquisition. And who wants to give them* bad news?'

'Please!' Dio yelled up at the ceiling. 'I-I have erred. Remove me. Strip me of my position. Banish me to a posting on the furthest penal labour moon and...'

'You would've got away with it, if you hadn't listed Eleven Deep Shaft as still actively producing on your tithe forms. The lithicarium your prisoners mine goes straight into the lasgun cells of the Indomitus Crusade. Did you think no one would notice you were debasing the minerals in order to make your quota?'

'Get off your knees, you coward,' snarled Drawl. He slapped the warden a stinging blow across the face. 'Collect yourself. It's talk. Just talk. He's trying to scare us into surrendering. We have a full suppression cohort in here. Riot shields. Shotguns. Electro-staves. Let him try to storm us.'

'If you were smart,' the voice continued, *'you'd have informed them of the outbreak and positioned Drawl to take the bullet. It might have exposed your incompetence, but you would've lived. But instead...'*

The bank of monitors blazed bright red. Half of them, their cathode tubes damaged by Drawl's laspistol, burst outward with the surge of energy as they activated simultaneously. Sparks fountained into the room.

A few, undamaged, showed a black symbol against the alert-red background: an X device, emblazoned with a knife impaling a skull.

'...instead, you got me.'

Jets of gas erupted from above, washing the room in a fog of white cloud that chilled skin and frosted metal. Governor-Warden Dio clawed at Drawl. He tried to beg his lieutenant for help, but his hyperventilating lungs could get nothing from the thick smoke.

His panic was already feeling distant, unimportant, when he was shoved to the floor and panicking boots stomped over him in their rush to escape.

* * *

Koln watched as the fire suppression system washed over the struggling men. Gouts of retardant foam and concentrated carbon dioxide filled the command centre from bottom to top, like a glass filling with kaj-milk.

Drawl clearly had Militarum experience. Probably a gas attack survivor. He managed to get up on a console, holding his head high above the fog bank as the room filled.

It bought him a few more seconds of life.

Koln leaned back in her chair. 'Dictation on, data stream to satellite. Memo to self. Operation Adjudicator, Mission Designation Sinkhole is transitioned to closed matter. Ensure all data on heart_wyrm outbreak is forwarded to Inquisitorial sector office for follow up after removing privileged sources and methods. And...'

It had been days since she'd connected her augmetic brain to the micro-satellite that she offloaded mission data to, in case of failure or death. Things had been moving fast over the last few days, and Eleven Deep Shaft was far enough underground that connection wasn't possible.

So she hadn't received the message alert until now.

It floated in the upper right corner of her dataveil, blinking red.

>>URGENT: EXTRACT FOR REASSIGNMENT<<

SEVEN

LOCATION: GENEXES, LOTUS SUBSECTOR

OPERATION: COUNTERCOUP

MISSION DESIGNATION: FISHHOOK

The darkness, like all else in the manse, felt comfortable. Hidden audio-ambiance units filled the air with calming vibration. Perfume wafted, light and fresh, from the circulatory ducts. A small stream wound through the room, burbling over smooth river stones and cascading in waterfalls down the steps where it wandered into the garden terrace outside.

A key scraped on the door lock. Muffled giggles drifted through the thick, iron-banded door. More laughter.

'*Intrusion detected,*' the voice of a security system bleated. '*Full alarm in ten, nine, eight, seven–*'

A male voice spoke what sounded like a name.

'*Apologies, lord. Alarm deactivated.*'

The key finally bit the lock pins and turned. And when the door came open two figures stumbled inside, laughing.

'Can you imagine?' said the woman. She staggered slightly, the neck of a vinfindel bottle in one hand. 'If it had called the enforcers? And they found us here?'

She laughed. It was an attractive laugh, and she was an attractive woman. Not the most high-born accent, true. And the clothes, while well cut and worn, were clearly bought from the rack rather than tailor-made.

But wasn't that exactly what a young industry noble liked after a long week of tithe inspections? Something easy. A girl with big eyes who was enthusiastic and easy to impress. One who wouldn't make you work too hard.

'Oh, no,' Lord Hectur Silanus slurred. He closed the door, turned the bolt so they would not be disturbed. A mop of his hair, so fashionably tangled, lay over one eye. 'We have an arrangement with the enforcers.' He played a finger across the lumen-controls, bringing the room to a soft, sunset glow. 'They don't come without ringing up first.'

'Is that so?' She smiled, taking a few coquettish steps back into the room. 'Gallant of them, eh? Ringing you up. And tomorrow are you going to ring me up, my lord industrial?'

She drew out the title, as if savouring its novelty.

He went to her, the smell of good quality obscura suffusing his clothing, and put his hands on her hips.

Which was when they both noticed the man in the chair.

'Sycorax,' nodded the Liaison.

'Who the devil are you?' said Lord Silanus, his face going white. His eyes darted left, towards the servants' quarters, before remembering he'd given them the night off for religious observances. 'What are you doing in my home?'

The girl whimpered and took a step back, sliding behind him for protection.

'I'm afraid you've been reassigned.' The Liaison flicked a gram of his lho-stick ash on the mosaic floor. 'Top priority. You'll have to end it quickly.'

A knife flashed jade in the dull light.

The girl moved with inhuman swiftness, grabbing the noble

around the waist from behind and pressing him to her, one arm hooking around to plunge the alien blade into the man's throat.

Silanus caught the girl's wrist and held it, the blade tip immobile an inch from his skin.

Then he forced the curved dagger up above his head, turned under the girl's raised arm like a dancer doing a ballroom spin, and slammed the knife down into her chest, embedding it in the soft spot just above the ribcage.

The girl's mouth opened in shock, blood spilling over her plump lower lip and down her chin.

Purple blood. Sycorax released the target, stepping back as the girl slid down the wall and slumped to one side, death-spasms rattling her frame.

The Liaison took a pull from his lho-stick and stood, ambling over to look at the stricken creature.

'Well done, assassin. For a moment I didn't know which was which.'

'Isn't that the point,' Sycorax said, not phrasing it like a question. Her features were flowing, shifting.

Even used to assassins as he was, the Liaison did not like to watch this part. He kept his eyes on the twitching woman, seeing the hate that burned in her eyes. Noticing that, sometime during the reverse-grapple, Sycorax had also plunged an envenomed blade into the target's stomach. The muscle spasms were decelerating now, their regular *tick-tick* pattern growing slower like a dying wrist-chrono.

'The Sanctus Cabal of Genexes,' he said, pursing his lips. 'My congratulations. Quite a catch.'

'Not finished. This is only the second of three.'

'I have requested another operative to take over the file.'

When the Liaison looked up, he saw that Sycorax's features had settled into those of a woman. Plain and severe with straight, light-brown hair, her only notable feature a mouth that sat slightly upturned on one side, giving her an air of playful malice.

He wondered if this was her natural face, or one she chose.

'Who?'

'Tatania Leite.'

She snorted. 'Tatania. Suppose she'll do fine. Targets are easy enough.'

'Easy?' repeated the Liaison. 'They've killed eleven industry nobles, brought the planet's steel output close to collapse.'

'They're good at what they do,' admitted Sycorax. She opened a chest on the shelf and extracted a heavy pistol, its bulbous forward housing cradling a crystal phial that was clouded with neon-green gas. 'But they only have one trick. Go to the spirit-clubs, attract nobles with an easy conquest, kill them with poison. If they'd changed their modus operandi, finding them might've been a challenge. Still, I suppose the plan was effective enough, provided the targets were sufficiently careless and stupid.'

'And how is Lord Silanus?'

Sycorax keyed the neural shredder live, saw a miniature lightning strike crackle through the ionised gas of the bulb. 'Shacked up in a chalet with all the obscura he wants. Probably quite happy.'

'Well, if you're looking for a challenge,' said the Liaison, 'we have one.'

'Sounds fun,' she said, the lopsided mouth twisting upward. 'Now if you'll stand aside, sir, you can never be too sure about these things.'

She pointed the neural shredder down at the drooped head.

The sanctus sprang upward, xenos mutations flooding it with one last burst of alien adrenaline when it was clear it could not play dead. Needle fangs slashed from hidden pockets in the pink gums. A psionic shriek howled from its lips.

Sycorax pulled the trigger. Lightning cracked in the gas chamber.

From outside, the dark windows of the manse flashed green once, twice.

Then all was still.

EIGHT

Targets remaining: 34

Range to targets: negligible

Air temperature: +40 degrees from Freeze Point

Wind speed: 0 mph

Conditions within acceptable equipment tolerances

The cool green data-chain of the spy mask, resting peripherally in his enhanced vision.

Targets remaining: 33

Raithe ran the kill maze with his Exitus pistol.

Door kick. Sweep for target. Fire. Sweep. Fire.

Targets remaining: 31

Roll to avoid a spatter of low-power las-fire, line up a head shot while rising.

Execute.

Targets remaining: 30

The Exitus rounds were dummies, but they struck the training servitors with such kinetic force that it threw them backwards into the stone walls of the maze.

Grab a falling servitor as a body shield, down two more. Roll into cover. Reload.

It was the rhythm of his weapons. Fire and reload. Evade and attack. Climb to the higher levels for a vantage point and switch to his rifle, downing targets one by one.

Shot. Shot. Shot.

Pain. Pain. Pain.

Targets remaining: 25

His shoulder. Tired. Aching. Bunching no matter how many muscle relaxants he shot into it.

Normally this was calming. The regular pattern of his gunshots. His firing bolt sliding to and fro like the precision machine it was. A drumbeat of efficiency, as soothing to him as a monastic chant or repeated prayer. Keeping him cool and sharp. The meditation of action and muscle memory.

Instead, there was frustration and agony.

His shots were drifting. Not with the pistol – there the recoil was manageable – but every shot with his longrifle jammed into his injured muscles and twisted his nerve taut as a violin string. He'd turned off the kill maze's accuracy recorder.

Raithe's shot groupings were off. Not badly enough to affect close-range fire, within a few hundred yards, but at his normal engagement range of one mile plus, he'd barely be able to hit an ogryn.

This was supposed to centre him. Prepare him. Calm him for the trial ahead.

He knew the briefing was going to be a difficult start. An execution force was no easy thing to direct – and to do it, he would have to become something that he was not.

A leader.

And the kill maze wasn't building his calm.

He felt only torture.

Shot. Shot. Draw utility knife. Bury it in a throat.

Targets remaining: 22

Raithe walked into the briefing room smelling of fyceline, Exitus pistol still holstered on his thigh.

'I see everyone's here,' he said, placing his briefing packet on the table and sitting in the empty chair, next to the boxy slide-caster controls.

Three chairs around the circular, symbol-inlaid table. Two of them filled with women who Raithe, even if he had not known them, would pick out as assassins. Both toned and muscular, in peak physical condition. Eyes that scanned their surroundings, missing nothing. Each had a briefing packet in front of them.

The taller, straight-backed one – Koln, he guessed – had already dissected hers, laying it out in front of her in stacks. The amber shine of a dataveil glossed her brown eyes. Across from Koln, the Callidus, Sycorax, lounged backwards, her briefing packet unopened, tracing the table's inlaid Vindicare symbol with a finger.

'First of all, thank you both for arriving with such speed.' Raithe turned a knob, dimming the lights. 'Once you are read in, I think you'll agree the haste was warranted.'

'Pardon the interjection,' said Koln. 'I don't doubt that this operation may take precedence, but did we need to be dragged out so…'

'Clumsily,' said Sycorax, her voice flat as the polished table in front of her.

'*Abruptly,*' corrected Koln. 'My last mission had heretical elements. In general, I would brief Inquisitorial representatives before handing the matter over. Especially when a drop in the world's production capacity could impact the crusade. Were there no other operatives that fit this brief?'

'A fair question.' Raithe took a breath before continuing, calling on a marksman's patience. 'Operations recommended you based on unique criteria. You, Mistress Koln, are an intrigue specialist, with a track record operating in closed societies with heavy Mechanicus presence.' He paused. 'I read your monograph on the unspoken power structures among the sacristans of House Griffith. It was insightful.'

'I'm working on a follow-up,' she said. 'On strategies to alter, forge or sabotage their documentation system. It's unique and–'

'But to answer your question,' Raithe cut her off. 'No, there was no one else. Lord Commander Guilliman's order to deploy the entire strength of the Assassinorum has left us short-handed. Not enough supplies, not enough logistical support and especially not enough operatives. To reassign, we have to pull from the field and...'

Sycorax raised a languid hand, as if she were in the scholam, then spoke before Raithe acknowledged her. 'Why is a Vindicare in charge of this operation?'

'My temple,' Raithe said, planting his fists on the table, 'was given leadership of this execution force because of our operational planning and command-and-control capabilities.'

'Templum Vanus has planning and analysis skills well matched with Vindicare,' said Koln. 'And superior intelligence-gathering capabilities. This is not a challenge, I merely want to understand the command structure and reasoning behind it. Why not Vanus?'

'Or Callidus,' interjected Sycorax. 'After all, if I'm here it's an infiltration job, isn't it? That's our specialty. And we have the flexibility to adapt to changing conditions when Vindicare is, well... your tradecraft is mostly about getting a line-of-sight and pulling the trigger. All...' She traced a zigzag in the air with her finger. 'Straight lines.'

In a flash, Raithe saw how he'd kill them.

Draw Exitus. Sweep left to right with two trigger pulls. Koln in the head, Sycorax centre mass. The Vanus was the greater threat. The Callidus probably had nothing but a poisoned blade, but Koln's file listed six digital weapons in her augmetic hands.

There was no malice in it. He was trained to see firing solutions when threatened.

Raithe opened his mouth to reassert power, but a voice cut him off.

'Vindicare is in charge of this execution force,' said the Liaison from his chair in the corner. 'The Master of Operations picked Absolom Raithe, out of all other operatives in this segmentum, to lead it. If either of you wish to dispute that decision, give your complaint to me in writing and I will personally take it to Terra and convey your message to the M of O.'

Silence followed.

Assassins feared very few things. Not death, for it was the inevitable end point of an operative's career. Pain was expected and prepared for. And of course, the inhuman monsters of the Eversor and Culexus Temples likely feared nothing at all.

But among the sane, none relished the idea of coming to the notice of authority. In a bureaucracy of murderers, the nail that stood out got hammered back in – usually with a bolt shell.

Raithe took a breath.

'I understand your frustration,' he said. 'We are, all of us, independent operators. We aren't used to having eyes looking over our shoulders. But I assure you, the target is big enough that none of us could take him down alone. And frankly, I'm glad you're angry about getting dragged out of your assignments. It shows you take pride in your work.'

Koln tapped the table with a finger. Sycorax pulled a dental pick from her bodyglove and planted it in her mouth like a lho-stick, toying with it as she stared at Raithe, expression unreadable.

'We don't have matching skills,' continued Raithe. 'We don't think alike. That's good. It's what I wanted.' Raithe pointed to the door. 'I could've asked for a team of ten Vindicare who would've shut up and done everything I told them without question. But if I did that, the operation would fail. This isn't a target we can stake out and murder with a hellfire round from two miles away. I need operatives with skill sets I do not possess, who can help formulate and execute a plan. Can you do that?'

'Apologies,' Koln nodded. 'I was out of line.'

Sycorax shrugged. 'What are we killing?'

Raithe pressed a button on the tabletop controls. The caster mounted to the ceiling clicked and clanked, its wheel of pict-glass slides rotating like the drum of a grenade launcher. A dim, hand-illustrated image of a planet splashed on the wall.

'The famed technology of the Vindicare,' Sycorax murmured.

Raithe continued, refusing to be needled. 'Dominion is not a world that has attracted many resources lately. Many of our archive holdings on it are, shall we say, venerable. You'll see from the briefing packet the distinct crimson tint of its seas, due to the contamination from an off-world algae.'

'Perhaps we can skip what was in the briefing packet,' said Koln, glancing at Sycorax for confirmation. 'We had two weeks to study it in transit. We're well aware of Dominion, Stryder-Rau, the potential for a succession crisis. All that is laid out…'

'We don't have a target, security estimate, obstacles, operational constraints,' added Sycorax. 'Let's start there.'

'Fair enough.' Raithe passed them two sealed envelopes. 'Read them and hand them back for destruction.'

Tearing envelopes. Paper rasped on paper.

Koln swore and flipped the page.

Sycorax chuckled. 'He did say it was big.'

NINE

>>OFFICIAL ORDERS: OPERATION *KINGMAKER*
>>Issuer: Master of Operations
>>Method of conveyance: By hand only
>>Date: REDACTED
>>Location: REDACTED
>>Clearance Level: Vermilion Plus
>>DO NOT TRANSMIT<<
>>DO NOT DUPLICATE<<
>>DESTROY AFTER READING<<
SANCTIONED TARGET:

Lucien YAVARIUS-KHAU, approximate age 187.

High Monarch of Dominion, Knight-Commander of House Stryder, Chieftain of House Rau, [for full titles, see MAGENTA-level clearance briefing materials, separate packet]. He has ruled Dominion for 104 Terran standard years.

The first century of YAVARIUS-KHAU's reign passed smoothly, with him serving as a competent and popular ruler – leading the forces of Stryder-Rau to victories against aberrant Chaos cults and the fallen Knights of House Morvayne – on the border of Segmentum Solar. However, in the past decade his behaviour has become increasingly erratic and partisan, seeming to intentionally pit one house against the other.

At times, he and members of his court have intimated the possibility of a temporary or permanent severing of relations with the wider Imperium. A recent call for military aid from Terra has been ignored, violating treaty obligations – perhaps a sign YAVARIUS-KHAU either intends to, or already has, seceded from Imperial allegiance.

With the fine balance of political power and patronage upset, Dominion is in danger of falling into civil war upon YAVARIUS-KHAU's likely imminent demise. Should this happen, even if pro-Imperial factions emerge victorious the combat effectiveness of Stryder-Rau may be permanently degraded or damaged.

SECURITY THREAT LEVEL:
EXTREMELY HIGH

The high court of Stryder-Rau is made up of highly combat-proficient Imperial Knights of varying classes. Particularly notable are BARON TITUS YUMA, Kingsward [royal guard], and pilot of the Knight Warden THRONESHIELD, and BARONESS SYMPHONIA DASK, gatekeeper [security chief] and pilot of Knight Errant BASILISK'S GAZE.

However, the most dangerous and difficult obstacle will be YAVARIUS-KHAU himself. As High Monarch, he pilots the ancient Knight Castellan CROWN OF DOMINION. Due to war wounds, YAVARIUS-KHAU has settled permanently into the ancient machine and conducts all royal business through it. A party of sacristans fulfil his corporeal needs, and few see him in person.

* * *

PROVENANCE:

Initiating report came via embedded agent TESSENNA STARNE. Her crash alert, received via subliminal astropathic caster, follows:

Dominion Station / Status Rep. Alpha, Rift +1088 dys

CRISIS ALERT: Call to crusade spurred talk of Imperial secession in House Stryder-Rau. [STOP] Factions coalescing, outbreaks of violence. [STOP] Both sides awaiting death of YAVARIUS-KHAU, who will die within year. [STOP] Despite insanity, YAVARIUS-KHAU sole unifying figure. [STOP] Houses are primed for conflict, plots to kill YAVARIUS-KHAU in progress. [STOP] Factions poss axtempting [sic] to assassinate monarch to kickstart conflict. [STOP] Cover blown. Enemies closing. Will destroy vox. Emp. Protecs.

MESSAGE ENDS

While the typing style of the message does suggest it was written by the agent in question, the typing error as well as short-hand suggests a message transmitted quickly and under stress. Consider it genuine.

The vox transmitted a death-pulse confirming itself inoperable, and therefore it is the opinion of this office that TESSENNA STARNE is dead due to hostile action.

MISSION OBJECTIVES AND PARAMETERS:
OBJECTIVE PRIMUS:

Operatives of the execution force are cleared by the Senatorum Imperialis to use *any and all methods* to eliminate YAVARIUS-KHAU.

OBJECTIVE SECUNDUS:

Operatives are cleared to use *any and all methods* to mitigate the damage of any succession crisis that follows, and are given remit to guide a stable candidate to the throne.

* * *

PARAMETER ALPHA:

As the point of the operation is to minimise damage to the strength of House Stryder-Rau, operatives are to avoid any unnecessary damage to Knight suits. Pilots are expendable, Knight suits are not.

This in particular applies to the Knight Castellan CROWN OF DOMINION, which must not suffer irreparable damage due to operatives' action. The cultural and political significance of CROWN OF DOMINION to Stryder-Rau is important for stable continuity of government.

EXITUS ACTA PROBAT: THE OUTCOME JUSTIFIES THE DEED>>ORDERS END, DESTROY IMMEDIATELY<<

TEN

'Questions?' Raithe asked. He held his hands out for the orders.

'It's difficult,' said Koln. She handed back the envelope. 'To eliminate him without overly damaging the suit… we'll have to get close. And this is a closed society, very difficult to penetrate. Infiltration would have to be in the guise of a noble, and that means mimicking unique social behaviour, suit interface – there are a lot of levels.'

'I've infiltrated worse,' said Sycorax. She slid her envelope across the table. Raithe had to snatch it up before it fell on the floor. He dismissed the insubordinate gesture, pleased at the note of eagerness in the flat voice. 'Replacing a pilot is nothing. Two years ago I had to infiltrate a Dark Mechanicum research station. For that, I had to…' Then she stopped, laughed. 'That's why I was chosen, wasn't it?'

'It is,' said Raithe. 'You have the hardware.'

Sycorax swept her braided hair up so Koln could see the augmetic port at the base of her skull. She tapped it with a finger. 'Pre-frontal cranial cortex, same as the pilots use to control their suits. All the research subjects in the station had one, so I needed to get it installed.'

'I'm not saying it's impossible,' said Koln. 'It's probably our best course of action. I just want you both to appreciate the intricacy of this society. Knight worlds are only nominally Imperial – it's a veneer on top of something much older. They date back to the early exploration fleets. Not so much under the Imperium as allied with it – they each have individual social rules, protocols and cultural references. And it's a place where all the people of consequence have known each other since childhood. You might be able to remove and replace one subject, but slip up on one form of address or stumble on an old memory or nickname and you'll blow the operation.'

Raithe stepped on the foot pedal of the crematorium bin beside the table, dropping the envelopes and their contents inside the open hatch. When the flap cover closed, the dark seam between cover and barrel flared orange. He ignored the wisps of smoke that crept out from the join.

'Tight-knit social groups are hard,' admitted Sycorax. 'But there are ways to mitigate that. Personal problems usually work. Trouble at home. As soon as I remove and replace a subject I have a public row with their spouse, maybe hit the bottle too hard – hells, once I staged a head injury. Everyone chalks the differences up to a personality change or mental distress. Best part is, rumours spread that explanation so you don't have to, and everyone is too uncomfortable to ask about it.'

'That might help,' said Koln. 'But you'll be exposed. The world of court is one where every gesture is observed and dissected. And you will need to bond with the Knight suit, which has its own dangers. It could realise you're a plant and reject you. If we had the option... do you think you could replace a sacristan?

Get into the group that cares for Yavarius-Khau's physical state and sabotage his life support?'

'Infiltrating the Mechanicus isn't much of a problem,' said Sycorax. 'But replacing a specific priest long-term is very, very difficult. You generally need to kill them and harvest their augmetics, since those are hard to replicate convincingly. Then you have to surgically implant them, which might not be reversible – even speeding up the healing process with polymorphine would push the timeline...'

'How long?' asked Raithe.

'Rough estimate?' asked Sycorax. 'Six to ten months.'

'What about light augmetics?' asked Koln. 'Say, oculars and some data-ports. Just what can be seen?'

'Three months.'

'That's out,' said Koln. 'He'll be dead and the planet in civil war.'

'I could,' mused Sycorax, 'come in as a replacement from Ryza with forged orders, but they definitely won't let me work on the monarch's life support when I'm fresh off the boarding ramp.'

Raithe cleared his throat. He'd been learning a great deal about them from their conversation, and had not wanted to intervene.

'For all those reasons,' he said, 'I've determined we should impersonate a pilot. One who has been away from Dominion for a long period.'

Raithe clicked the button and the drum-fed slide-caster once again rotated with a mechanical clack. The dim star map slid upward like a fortress portcullis and a fresh image slammed down in its place.

Despite the indistinct nature of the pict-capture – it had been taken from some distance with a long-lens – the ghostly image of the man on the wall was striking. Oiled hair parted in the centre, falling down in waves nearly to his collar. Golden-brown skin and a nose so straight it spoke of good breeding and a childhood free of fist fights. He wore some kind of technical suit, and an odd scalloped helmet in his hand.

'Sir Linoleus Rakkan. He's currently acting as a Freeblade, an unattached Knight-in-exile serving on the Vypaan Salient. That will mean extracting him from a warzone, which will prove tricky and extend our timeline, but…'

He stopped, seeing the smile on Koln's face, and her hand in the air.

'Yes, operative?'

'I can save us some time here,' she said, then turned to the Liaison. 'Did you get my package?'

'As it happens,' said the Liaison, 'it arrived an hour ago.'

'Colleagues,' said Koln, 'meet Linoleus Rakkan. Formerly of House Stryder-Rau and pilot of the noble Armiger Warglaive *Jester*.'

The man on the other side of the one-way glass slumped across the spare metal table of his onboard stateroom, face buried in the crook of his arm. An empty amasec bottle lay upended in front of him.

'Charmed,' said Sycorax. 'So the whole time you were poking holes in our planning, he was already here?'

'I said the infiltration would be difficult,' said Koln. 'Not impossible. I just wanted you both to understand the risks. I also picked up his sacristan, Gwynne, though she is being held elsewhere. Theoretically either one could be your cover, but Rakkan does seem simplest.'

Raithe stepped up to the glass. Koln could see his brow furrowing in the reflection. 'You did this without authorisation?'

'Strictly speaking, yes,' she said. 'But this was your plan, wasn't it? You were about to announce an intention to take Rakkan from his warzone posting of Kumalia Secundus, and have

Sycorax impersonate him. It's as good a plan as we could get. Provides us access to court, and he's been away for four years.'

'Long enough to explain any difference in personality as growth,' said Sycorax. Her nose wrinkled. 'Pity he's a drinker, my last cover was too. I'm going to need a detox if I survive this. Does he slouch?'

'What?' asked Koln.

'Is he a sloucher?' Sycorax gestured towards the bent back. 'I can't stand slouchers. I once played a scribe who spent his whole life bent over a desk. My spine didn't feel right for a month afterward.'

'No,' said Koln. 'I think due to his breeding his posture is quite good.'

'That's something,' said Sycorax.

'I did not authorise this action,' said Raithe, staring through the glass.

'I did,' said the Liaison, hovering in the background. He flicked his finger across a data-slate. 'En route to contact Operative Sycorax, Operative Koln suggested that arranging Rakkan's transport here would shave three weeks off our timeline. I agreed.'

Raithe took a long breath, turned towards Koln. And in his eyes, Koln knew the Vindicare was subliminally ranging her for a shot. 'How did you know my intentions? That wasn't in the preliminary materials.'

Koln nodded at the Liaison. 'He had a draft of your operational plan scanned into his data-slate.'

'But it's a secure data-slate,' said Raithe.

'With all respect, sir,' Koln answered, 'there's no such thing as a secure data-slate.'

'You requested a master-grade Vanus operative,' said the Liaison, breaking from his reading to glance up at Raithe. 'This is what they do.'

Raithe's jaw tightened. Koln calculated a need to salvage the situation fast.

'I apologise for surprising you,' she said. 'If we had met before the briefing, I would have apprised you of the situation. I know your temple prizes methodical procedure, but mine looks for efficiencies. Why do step alpha, beta, etcetera, when you can do steps alpha and delta simultaneously? By executing your orders before you issued them, it's saved us weeks. As you Vindicare say: *Exitus Acta Probat.*'

'The outcome justifies the deed,' Raithe repeated, by rote.

In her peripheral vision, Koln saw Sycorax hide a lopsided snicker.

Koln watched Raithe's eyes search her. Noticed his body tensing, his right shoulder rising slightly above the left. She wondered what that was about. An intentional overtraining of right-side muscles to deal with recoil? Her dataveil mapped his face, storing the micro-expressions to help read future moods.

Her data-collection suite picked up a hum, a tremble in the ambient subaudible buzz of cranial augmetics – a calming catechism, she realised, running through the Vindicare's mind.

Raithe's shoulders relaxed. 'How was it done?'

'And how much does he know?' added Sycorax.

'About us? Nothing.' Koln banished the facial-mapping algorithm and stepped up to the glass. Rakkan was starting to stir. 'I forged an order from the Fleet Tertius command section, politely requesting a redeployment. His recent combat actions have been against the Transmuted. He believes this is part of a standard three-week quarantine to ensure he's not infected with conqueror_wyrm.'

'Probably smart anyway,' said Sycorax. 'All three of us have neural augmetics, and we don't want to risk infection. Is he Stryder or Rau?'

'He's shared heritage between the two,' said Raithe. He jumped in fast, trying to take back control, and Koln let him. 'A Stryder mother and a Rau father – technically in line for the throne, though too far down the list to matter. Four years ago, something happened back on Dominion and he went into self-imposed exile. Sycorax, I want you to study him. Convince him to co-operate. Learn his habits. Koln can interrogate him and extract cultural details en route to Dominion. Then, we kill him and dump him out the airlock.'

Silence.

'Thanks to Koln's… initiative,' he continued, 'we can leave for Dominion immediately.'

'Hold on,' said Sycorax. 'Do we have time for post-operational rehabilitation and rearmament?'

Raithe nodded. 'Do you have requirements?'

'Polymorphine,' said the Callidus. 'Normally I would get my post-mission dose after extraction but… I've been without for two weeks now.'

Raithe narrowed his eyes.

Koln's focus snapped to Sycorax, mentally cataloguing the signs she'd missed. Irritability. Languidness. Lack of care with social boundaries.

'Are you informing me,' said Raithe, 'that you're chemically dependent?'

'Of course I'm chemically dependent,' snapped Sycorax. 'No Callidus can go three weeks without a polymorphine hit, not if they've been in service for ten years. I've been patient about it until now. A few more days, and I could wake up with my muscles sliding off my bones.'

'Understood,' said Raithe. 'Callidus Pacificus station sent a chest for you. I'm sure it has everything you require.'

Koln read Sycorax's body language, gauging her. Filed a micro-memo to herself recommending that she review the audio she'd collected and analyse the Callidus' speech patterns for signs of impairment.

'Are you satisfied, Koln?' Raithe asked.

'Oh, I have everything I need.' She laced her augmetic hands together, feeling the familiar weight of the devices embedded in each finger. 'We can lift anytime.'

'Good,' the Liaison said. 'This ship is the *Stiletto*. I've allocated it as your headquarters for this operation. It's not comfortable, but it's warp-capable and has all the standard functions for an Assassinorum vessel. Fuelling is already in process.'

'You heard the Liaison,' said Raithe. 'Pick your berths and get your gear aboard. Thanks to our… accelerated timeline… we'll seal hatches in three hours and lift in four. Dismissed.'

Raithe saluted, turned on his heel, and walked out of the room. The Liaison followed, data-slate in hand.

Leaving Koln alone with the Callidus.

'How thick,' asked Sycorax, pressing a hand up against the glass, 'is the adamantine plating on a Knight Castellan?'

'Hard to generalise,' answered Koln. 'If you're talking about the sheer amount of metal between the exterior air and the pilot's body… four feet thick at the chest. Perhaps three feet on the top carapace? That's not counting the ion shield, of course.'

'He's going to get us killed,' Sycorax laughed. 'You know that, right?'

ELEVEN

> 'There are two kinds of chaos. One comes from outside, a thing
> of the empyrean, which the Emperor's fleets keep blockaded
> within the Eye. The other is an internal chaos. It is the selfish,
> bestial, covetous animal lying within the human heart. And
> that beast of chaos, no fleet can contain – only oaths can
> bind it. Oaths are not about gaining honour, they are about
> keeping order.'
>
> – Lucien Yavarius-Khau, High Monarch of Dominion,
> from his *Meditations on the Code Chivalric*

Twenty minutes after launch, as soon as the small ship cleared
the atmosphere, Sycorax went to her cabin to take her dose.

Her armaments had been delivered in a knee-high casket,
pressurised and sealed with sensors bio-encoded to her genetic
signature. Latches sprang open at her touch, and she opened
the casket and felt along the inside lid for the catch to the secret
compartment.

With a click, the false top of the lid dropped down slowly on
its hydraulic pistons. Wisps of super-chilled air spilled out as if
it were the drawbridge of some wraith-haunted castle.

Polymorphine phials lay in neat ranks like bodies after a mass
killing, organised by dosage from the maintenance syrettes as
small as a lho-stick's butt, to transformation injectors big as her
thumb. The latter paired with the subdermal injector hidden in

the flesh of her left thigh, but the former had capped needles ready for surface injection.

Her secret. *The* secret of the Callidus Temple. So sensitive, that all Callidus operatives were instructed to destroy them rather than let them fall into outside hands – even those of other Assassinorum operatives.

She took the first out of its shell foam housing and closed the chamber so the precious pharms would not warm. Before long the void would chill their vessel to an uncomfortable degree, but this soon after slipping atmosphere the cabin was so sti-fling and humid that the sheets of the narrow bunk were moist when she lay down on them.

Sycorax uncapped the syrette, found the vein on her thigh and knit the needle into it. Squeezed the cartridge until the seal popped.

Polymorphine flooded her system. Chilled it like coolant through an engine.

'I destroy the enemy by becoming them,' she said, relaxing her jaw and using the mantra to regulate her breath in a way that dulled the pain. Stared at a bolt on the ceiling, as if resting the pain there, outside her body.

'I wield the weapons of the xenos against them. I will mimic the corrupt body, yet my mind shall be focused on human purpose.'

Her heart, fortified against the assault of the pharm, pushed it through her body. For a suffocating moment, it felt like her blood had congealed, moving syrupy through her veins. She couldn't breathe.

Then the throttling chemicals released, and she sucked a desperate breath.

For another thirty seconds she looked at the bolt in the ceiling, then sat up and felt her face.

The fever she'd suffered for a week had broken.

'Damn that blue bast…' She stopped herself, swallowed the sentence. Reasserted her indoctrination-programming. 'The lord commander only did what he needed to.'

Every Callidus was a subversion agent. It was, Sycorax knew, the way she was built. An instinct rather than a choice. But she had to be cautious what she turned that instinct against. Especially in a temple ship that probably had recorders everywhere.

'Damn this galaxy,' she said instead, finding it safer to condemn the whole cosmos than one man.

Guilliman's total deployment of the Assassinorum had stretched the logistics chain thin. As Raithe had said, none of them had recovery time any more. This was Sycorax's fourth mission straight, a total of two years in the field.

Before the sanctus it had been a t'au earth caste scientist. Before that it had been Programmator Quivarian.

And she'd missed her resupply between missions three and four. During the hunt for the sanctus of Genexes, she'd rationed polymorphine to dangerous levels. Used her last maintenance dose on the way to the Vindicare Temple – been so moody due to the withdrawals, in fact, that she'd locked herself in this very cabin en route and not even met the Vanus until she'd arrived.

The Vanus. Sycorax wasn't sure she liked her, but then again, Sycorax had not been trained to like people – she'd been trained to use them. And Avaaris Koln appeared very useful indeed, if she were even half as knowledgeable as she claimed.

But the Vindicare, Raithe, was another thing entirely.

He seemed capable enough as an operator. Indeed, even in Callidus circles Absolom Raithe had developed a certain notoriety. There was that story about the jackal Alphus, when he was just an apprentice assassin. The Dark Apostle on Zaccharine. Rumours that he was the one Operations called when the

Assassinorum had to remove one of its own. That's how he got the call sign *Headsman*.

He would, Sycorax knew, try to control every aspect of this mission. She'd seen how tense he'd got when Koln had carried out orders, his own orders, out of sequence. It had got under his skin. For all his talk of wanting them to augment his skill set, he'd hated Koln taking initiative.

Step by step, deliberate, planned, that was the Vindicare way.

The Callidus way, by contrast, was to take advantage of turmoil. Improvise each step in turn, using the vagaries of fate and social manipulation to approach the target. Adapt quickly to changing conditions, not even pretend that your plans could be fluid enough to match the shifting circumstances.

It was said that no stratagem survives contact with the enemy – and Callidus operatives had more contact with the enemy than anyone else. To try and plan an operation tip to tail was building a house upon the sand.

Still.

She picked up the data-slate she'd tossed on her bed. Each of them had one, their data streams entangled so notes or changes made on one would show up for the others. That was the Vanus' doing, and not a bad idea, at least as far as bad ideas went.

Sycorax clicked through each page of the shared dossier one by one. An intercepted letter in Rakkan's handwriting. A star map of Dominion's place in the Lotus Chain, the bow-shaped arc of worlds that straddled the border between Segmentum Pacificus and Segmentum Tempestus.

And finally, the Knight Armiger. *Jester*.

She tapped a nail against her teeth, then got up on shaky legs. Ensured no one was in the corridor before slipping out, past the gleaming refectory galley and into the dark of the cargo bay.

Grasped in the dark until she found the cable and its switch.

She threw it, igniting the tripod flood-lumens that cast a womb of light in the cavernous space.

Jester stood in the centre, towering and broad-shouldered as a sanctuary statue. Heraldry glowed under the harsh light. Heartblood crimson of Rau on one side, sky-blue of Stryder on the other. A battle-honour pennant, removed in combat, hung between its legs like a tabard. It bore Rakkan's personal device of a sword emerging from Dominion's blood-coloured sea. Above it flew the hooded falcon of Stryder, its wings spread over the storm cloud of Rau. The falcon's claws grasped two red lightning bolts that lanced from the cloud – though whether it was catching them, or being burned, was up to interpretation.

Sycorax gave a slight bow before the great machine, and approached. White ribbons were wrapped in spirals around *Jester*'s weapon-capped arms, and when she took one between her fingers, she saw it was inscribed with the names of former pilots who now lived, ghostlike, in its Helm Mechanicum.

As was Stryder-Rau custom, a great leather hood covered the Knight's face when it was inactivated – mirroring the falcon on the Stryder-Rau crest. After a moment of hesitation, Sycorax reached up on her toes and touched the adamantine armour plating of the machine's leg, right where it capped the knee.

It was warm. It felt alive.

'I've done many things,' she said to the machine, 'but I've never driven a Knight before.'

In the executive sleeping compartment, Absolom Raithe sat in front of his wide bunk.

He had taken the stateroom – the largest on the vessel – as his personal quarters and nerve centre. Raithe considered this both appropriate and practical. He was both leader and senior operative, his longrifle required the most space to store, the room

had the best security suite, and the attached officers' mess provided an ideal meeting space for operational planning.

And the second bed was an ideal place to service his weapons.

He sat in front of the bed on a high-backed chair of Cata-
chan glosswood, looking at the disassembled rifle parts laid out
in front of him.

Selecting a barrel, one of four he'd brought for this mission,
he gingerly inserted a las-micrometer into it and measured the
internal spiral – assuring himself there were no flaws, and that
the test rounds he'd fired through it before embarking had not
fouled the intricate channels meant to grip the bullet and spin it.

This was a medium-range barrel, a fact he knew by feel alone.
Ideal for targets that closed on you fast, like genestealers or the
drukhari – both of which he'd ended in his time.

A good tool, he reflected, holding it to the light and looking
through it like a scope. Hardy and precise. Effective.

And like all good tools, it did what it was supposed to.

Two compartments away, Avaaris Koln stood in the centre of
her cabin, adding the dossier to the collage of research materials
already papering the walls.

The Liaison had taken her for a tour of the half-dozen cabins
available – and expressed no little surprise that Koln chose this
one. It was technically a belowdecks crew berth, designed for six
souls hotbunking on twelve-hour shifts. Three roll-out sleeping
pods were set in one wall, like drawers in a medicae mortis
facility.

Indeed, she had noticed that their temperature controls went
unbelievably low, sufficient to store a corpse in the rare instances
when orders dictated that a target's body be recovered.

She did not sleep in the drawer-beds, instead using them as
storage for her gear and file boxes.

The room had no other furniture apart from a separate neces-sarium so narrow she could barely slither inside between the steel, prison-style toilet and sink. A semi-functioning water nozzle in the ceiling and drain in the floor took care of her hygiene needs.

Apart from an inset galley shelf on one wall, containing nothing but a caffeine brewer, the four walls were completely bare – all the better to fill with research notes. Koln slept in a net hammock that she slung from the ceiling, and could stow away for the bouts of extended pacing she was so prone to.

She sat in it now, partially reclined, one leg trailing a bare toe onto the floor as she looked at the evidence grid on one wall, the documents sheathed in plastek and secured with friction tape.

It was not the grid she'd built to examine the culture of Dominion; that was to her right. Nor did it lay out Stryder-Rau succession laws; that nightmare was to her left. Behind her was the barest wall, with only a few documents, labelled LINO-LEUS RAKKAN.

The one in front of her, by contrast, contained two pict-captures surrounded by a cloud of documents, labelled INTERNAL CONCERNS.

The two picts were front and profile views of Absolom Raithe and Sycorax, captured during the briefing by the picter implanted in her augmetic eyes.

She looked at the data grid with soft focus, letting the dataveil in her vision conjure the network of connecting lines, associ-ated documents and personal notes she'd mentally inscribed over them.

'Fire up audio dampeners. Start dictation,' she said. Techni-cally unnecessary, but like the pacing, the physicality of talking often helped her work through data. 'Classify Eyes Only Avaaris Koln. Destroy upon unauthorised access.'

She paused her light swinging to collect her thoughts, then resumed it, taking comfort in the metronomic creak of the hammock cords rubbing the overhead piping.

When her skin felt the hum of the dampeners reaching full strength, she began. 'Initial impression of Execution Force Kingmaker: mild to moderate pessimism. Current leadership style presents mid-level concerns. May upgrade that level as operation continues.'

She paused, speed-reading the briefing transcript in her dataveil, focusing on exchanges between Sycorax and Raithe.

'Raithe is a phenomenal operative with good intentions, but a poor leader. While he believes we need to work together for a positive outcome, and understands that our skills are necessary, he is unused to the varying styles of Templum Vanus and Callidus. By training and personal inclination, he looks at problems as if through a scope, a direct and narrow-minded approach that risks sidelining the force's Vanus and Callidus skill sets. It did not surprise me when I learned that his previous multi-operative missions have all involved other Vindicare. If he continues in his current leadership style, he risks alienating Sycorax.'

Koln shifted her vision to the Callidus' pict, searching the brown shoulder-length hair and wickedly tilted mouth. She sighed.

'Sycorax is another difficulty. After analysing her vocal patterns for indications of impairment, and testing sweat collected from an exercise bodyglove, I believe his scepticism of her chemical dependency is misplaced. Not only is it an occupational hazard of the Callidus Temple, but the service record I harvested from Raithe's data-slate shows an excellent success rate – so clearly her dependency is managed and does not affect her tradecraft. While she lacks the experience of Raithe and myself – I suspect she is right in saying that she was chosen primarily for her cranial port – she is a veteran operative. Their conflict appears to primarily rest in a clash of personal styles and differing outlook. Callidus operatives by nature are improvisational and fluid, an approach Raithe no doubt considers cavalier and sloppy.'

Koln swung her trailing foot into the hammock, looking at the data-mandala she'd projected on the ceiling, letting its repeating patterns and intricate depths calm her and trigger packaging subroutines that cleared her mind of loose ends and stray evidence points.

'Note for follow-up – she referenced her prefrontal cortex cranial port as having been installed to facilitate infiltration of a corrupted research station, but that particular action appears to have been removed from her service record. Ultra-sensitive.' She removed the data-casket from her pocket, and held it up to the light. Watched the red and green lights blink. 'Programmator Quivarian, creator of heart_wyrm and conqueror_wyrm, disappeared around that time. Rumour was a Callidus got the assignment. Was controversial among the Vanus, since as he was a heretek code-sorcerer we considered him to be in our wheelhouse. Will probe further.'

She placed the sample back in the velvet-padded lockbox resting beside her and sealed it. Put her eyes back on the data-mandala.

'As for myself, I currently see my function as twofold. My stated role is to fulfil my mission parameters as a cultural advisor and manage the court intrigue and human interactions. However, this function is actually secondary. For now, my personal objective must be to keep this execution force operating efficiently and build bonds between the three of us.'

She sank into the data-mandala. Felt her nocturnal rest subroutines kicking in so she could process data while she slept.

'Because if I fail to do that,' she said as sleep came, 'Sycorax is correct. We'll all be dead before we get within rifle shot of Yavarius-Khau. Even a successful mission is unlikely to allow us to walk away.'

Just as her eyelids dropped, a thought occurred to her.

Maybe that was the point.

Sir Linoleus Rakkan woke when the amasec bottle rolled off his table and smashed on the floor. Had he knocked it? Pushed it away in his disturbed dreams? No.

The hanging chain-light above him was tilted. The unsteady rocking motion he'd first taken for the world rolling from drink was actually happening.

The ship was moving again.

He wiped his face with his palms and tried to stand. Failed.

'Oh, hells,' he swore, before reaching down to turn on his augmetic braces.

He got up, the steel leg armatures straightening their knee pivots to hold him upright.

That was one advantage of his injury: no matter how drunk he got, he never had trouble standing. That had saved him on the line a few times, when he'd been in his cups and the Transmuted opened up a frontal attack. When he'd suddenly had to mount *Jester* at the sound of a raid siren and cover the ground in heretek blood. Facing wave upon wave of corrupted tech-priests and thralls, purple eyes burning with the conqueror_wyrm. Electro-flail arms and implanted saws...

A bone-white finger, pulling a laspistol trigger.

'No,' he told himself. 'Keep those in dreams, please.'

He skirted round the shattered glass and pounded a fist on the door.

'Hail!' he said. 'Out there! I have broken glass. Bring a broom and pan, please.'

No answer. Never an answer. The food appeared. Clean blankets appeared. Diagnostic tests he was supposed to plug into his neural port once per week. When he was sick, pharms in little paper cups.

A week in, he suspected that he was being observed through the big mirror. Two weeks in, and he didn't care any more.

Because bottles also appeared, and he appreciated that. After his stock had run dry, they kept bringing them from his personal reserve. Though fewer and fewer lately.

'Maybe they're drying you out,' he said to himself. 'Ready for combat. Fit for duty. Back with *Jester* and Gwynne. Another warzone.'

The last one he'd served alongside the Cadians. Tough people, but quite mad. It almost seemed as if they enjoyed it. Perversely revelling in the opportunity to demonstrate how hard they were. He remembered one officer, a violet-eyed lieutenant from the 24th who he'd briefly courted when they were both in reserve rotation, saying facial scars were considered attractive among Cadians. Particularly vain soldiers were known to mess with their medicae stitches to ensure healed wounds would show.

She'd had a wavering white line slicing from brow to jaw. It creased when she laughed.

Rakkan stepped back over the glass, and washed his face in the basin. Looked up and saw himself.

Red eyes. Puffy cheeks. Not quite the lean, hungry Knight he'd been four years ago, when he'd taken two las-bolts in the spine and left Dominion.

He stretched the skin, as if his own face were a mask. Trying to find that younger version of himself, before he was a Freeblade, drifting from battle to battle. No plan but to fight until he and *Jester* were too broken to be of use.

'That's your problem, Linoleus,' he told himself. 'You're a questing Knight without a quest.'

Ka-chunk.

His neck twisted at the noise, the familiar sound of the rotator hatch.

Inside the alcove stood a small hand-brush, a pan, and a half-size bottle of amasec.

'Thank you,' he said, to whoever was listening. 'And let me the hell out of here.'

PART TWO

REGICIDES

The Storm and the Falcon,

The Falcon and the Storm.

Over moorland, over seas,

Battle Falcon and the Storm.

The Falcon tries to catch the Storm,

The Storm to drown the Falcon.

Which will remain, at break of day,

The Falcon or the Storm?

The Storm or the Falcon?

— Traditional lullaby, Dominion

TWELVE

'I'm not going to do it,' Sycorax said.

Koln recited a psalm to herself in order to keep herself calm, stop her body from tensing and adding to the sense of threat in the room.

'Why not?' said Raithe. He didn't look up as he said it, just slid his carving knife through the square of braised grox-meat on his plate. The cut was clean, precise, and done with such force it sent a small shriek up from the porcelain underneath.

When he raised the piece of meat to his mouth, Koln saw that it was bloody.

'It's what your temple is known for, isn't it?' he said, before taking the piece in a single bite.

'That's a bit reductive,' Koln said. She'd hoped that her support would stop Sycorax from exploding, make it a three-way debate rather than a two-way argument.

Sycorax slumped over her plate, elbows on the table. If Raithe was a combat knife, all sharp edges and straight lines, she was a whip. Languid and flexible, lifeless until the moment it snapped into the air to strike.

The officers' wardroom was small. A C-shaped booth around an oval table. If things came to violence, it would be like two big felines locked in the same cage.

To manage her own tension, Koln catalogued the meal on Sycorax's plate. Mostly vegetables. Aerated water instead of the tall glass of scarlet vin Koln had poured for herself, and the half-glass Raithe hadn't touched.

'Seduce him.' Sycorax's eyes regarded Raithe with a micro-expression that Koln's algorithm identified as bored contempt. 'That's your plan. I seduce Rakkan into helping us.'

'Yes.' Raithe swallowed. 'What is your objection? You find it distasteful?'

'I find it impractical,' Sycorax answered. 'It doesn't make sense in the current environment.'

'We need him to help us.' Raithe's knife swept through the grox-steak again, blood welling from the cut. 'He needs to be motivated. Incentivised to cooperate.'

Koln interjected. 'What if–'

'No, no,' said Sycorax, raising a hand. 'I want to play this idea out. So you, Master Raithe, have been locked three weeks in quarantine and you don't know why. You're fresh from a battlefront and have spent most of that three weeks soaked in amasec and have barely washed yourself. Then suddenly a... what? Comely medicae comes in and sympathises with you and you fall hard?'

'Something like that,' said Raithe.

Sycorax snorted.

'What's the problem?' he said, getting those range-finding eyes.

'The problem is, you don't know how humans work. Socially, I mean. I'm sure you've studied enough anatomy to plunge that knife into any number of arteries, but manipulation isn't in your training.' Sycorax lifted her glass and took a drink.

'I asked for you to critique the plan,' said Raithe. 'Not me.'

'All right.' Sycorax put her glass down hard. 'First of all, it's too fast. Seduction only works if given time, and it's better if the target comes to *you*, not you to it. Speed raises suspicion. Don't get it twisted – if you want me to play a medicae with a weakness for the bottle who hears Rakkan has a private stash and wants some, I can do that. But he'll smell something wrong the second I try to question him.'

'So he falls for you,' said Raithe. 'And we tell him our purpose afterward.'

'Bad idea,' said Sycorax.

'I concur,' Koln broke in. 'He'll feel betrayed. It'll likely produce the exact opposite of our desired effect.'

'We also know little to nothing of his psychology,' said Sycorax. 'We don't know his preferences. His romantic history. For all we know, even if we were successful it'd put him into a self-destructive spiral of loathing. If I'm to study him, I need him acting as normally as possible – including with his sacristan. She's the one most likely to find us out when I replace him.'

'Unless we tell her,' said Koln.

Both assassins turned towards her.

'What?' said Sycorax.

'We tell her,' she repeated. 'And him. We tell them both.'

'No,' said Raithe.

'We played out your idea,' said Sycorax. 'Let's do it for this one. Why? That seems a risk.'

'Not really.' Koln opened her data-slate, the micro-projector she'd grafted onto it casting flickering blue document-holos in the air. 'It's eminently practical. If we try to dupe them, we might succeed. But we have the problem of there being two of them. Replace Rakkan and kill Gwynne, and once we get to Dominion they'll assign a new sacristan we have no leverage over. Conversely, it will be difficult to successfully pass Sycorax off as Rakkan in Gwynne's presence – she knows him well, and has been with him during the last four years.'

'I had worried about that,' admitted Sycorax. 'So you want to recruit them as assets?'

'We get the best of all possibilities,' Koln said. 'Open knowledge sharing, available immediately. Deep familiarity with Dominion and its systems. Real-time advice delivered by micro-bead.'

'Dangerous,' said Raithe. 'They'll give us up the moment we land.'

'I don't think they will.' Koln slid a finger across her data-slate, changing the holo to a schematic of a skeleton, its legs braced with metal clamps. 'My scans of Rakkan brought up an interesting feature. He has augmetic leg braces, the kind used to provide mobility after a spinal injury. At first I thought it was due to a war wound, but when I scanned the state of the augmetics' micro-plasma reactors, I found out the half-life of their coils suggest they were first activated around four years ago.'

'When he left Dominion,' said Raithe. 'And went into exile as a Freeblade.'

'Correct,' nodded Koln. 'But there's more. Before he was brought aboard, I rigged his stateroom with a full pict-audio suite. It has proved illuminating.'

Sycorax laughed.

'What's amusing?' Raithe said.

'People in quarantine for three weeks with a case of amasec,' said Sycorax, 'tend to talk to themselves.'

Koln triggered the audio file.

'*Damn them all,*' said the voice of Linoleus Rakkan. It appeared as waveform floating above the data-slate. '*Stryder, Rau. A pox on both their bloodlines. And damn the mad tyrant Yavarius-Khau.*'

'He goes on like that,' Koln said, shutting the file down. 'For weeks. When he's intelligible.'

'So,' said Raithe. 'You're suggesting Sycorax talk to him, give him an option.'

'Not at all,' Koln said. 'I'm suggesting that I do it.'

>>Interrogation Transcript 1
>>Operation: Kingmaker
>>File No. 5782-Gamma-KMKR
>>Mission Day: 8
>>Recording Device: Ear canal augmetics [stereo]
>>Recorder: Avaaris Koln
>>Cleared for Reading: Koln, Avaaris; Raithe, Absolom; Sycorax
>>Clearance Level: Vermilion Special Privileged
>>DO NOT TRANSMIT<<
>>DO NOT DUPLICATE<<
>>PURGE DATA ON MISSION COMMENCEMENT<<
KOLN: Good morning.
RAKKAN: Who...
KOLN: A friend. You are safe.
[Pause: 2 seconds]
RAKKAN: You've... kidnapped me. Given me a deployment order... locked me in here as a prisoner... told me nothing...
KOLN: Yes, I apologise. The quarantine was necessary due to the threat of the wyrm. We have recruited you for an endeavour. To serve the Emperor.
RAKKAN: Emp... ror...
KOLN: Linoleus, I'm going to need you to stay awake and

sober. This is very important. I have given you a stimulant to help, but I need you to focus. Here.

[AUDIO: Tin cup and porcelain on metal.]

KOLN: I have brought you some caffeine and breakfast. Please have some. I put a little extra kick in the caffeine to help you out.

[124 seconds removed; sounds of drinking and utensils on plate]

RAKKAN: My regards. The scrambled embriyolks were quite good.

[Pause: 1 second]

RAKKAN: This chair… There are straps on the arms of it. Are you going to bind me?

KOLN: I doubt they'll be necessary.

RAKKAN: Aren't you worried I'll overpower you?

KOLN: In a word, no.

RAKKAN: That's fair, I suppose. You've kept me locked here for weeks. Probably more people on this ship than just you. Even with my armatures, I doubt I'd make much headway.

KOLN: Let's put that aside for now, shall we? I apologise for detaining you and keeping you in the dark, but we had your best interests at heart.

RAKKAN: [laughs] You sound like my mother.

KOLN: [laughs] You're funny. That wasn't in my profile of you. That will make this go easier.

RAKKAN: Where is my sacristan?

KOLN: She is aboard, and we are seeking her cooperation as well. You can see her if you like, though I don't need to tell you that any conversation will be monitored.

RAKKAN: So I *am* a prisoner?

KOLN: Of course not, your cooperation is voluntary. You can leave whenever you like.

RAKKAN: Would you return me to the front, or drop us off on a planet or…

[AUDIO: Metal object on table.]

[Pause: 3 seconds]

RAKKAN: And we were having such a nice conversation.

KOLN: It's a short-pattern stubber, cross-drilled bullet for maximum damage when it breaks up after entering your cranium – and so any fragments from the exit wound won't puncture the hull.

[Pause: 2 seconds]

KOLN: Personally, I'd recommend putting it just here, at your hairline. Or I can do it, if you prefer. I also have pills. Whatever you want, you're a free man.

RAKKAN: For a minute I thought you really were giving me a choice. Should've known better, at this point.

[Pause: 2 seconds]

RAKKAN: I suppose that's why there's a drain in the floor.

KOLN: Those are your choices. There is no going back. Either you join your sacristan in cooperating, or you don't. I'd prefer you did – this is not a bad place. It has quite an impressive liquor cabinet and better quarters than these. We are serving the Emperor in a great task, much greater than fighting waves of Transmuted on a losing battlefront.

RAKKAN: What do you want from me?

KOLN: I want you to tell me about your life. About the culture of Stryder-Rau in both generalities and particulars. About the succession system. And most of all about High Monarch Yavarius-Khau.

RAKKAN: Why?

KOLN: Because we're going to kill him.

RAKKAN: Kill the High Monarch? [laughs] Who hired you? Kameela Rau? Jaskan Synk-Stryder? Whose side are you on?

KOLN: The Emperor's.

RAKKAN: So your price for my life is to help you murder my great-uncle?

KOLN: Yes.

RAKKAN: Mamzel, if you'd woken me up with that, you wouldn't have needed the gun.

Tap. Tap. Tap.

Sycorax came up from her bed in an instant, rolling from the mattress to a combat crouch on the floor. Yanked the vox-bead from her right ear, the sound of the interrogation audio still droning between her fingers.

Tap. Tap. Tap.

Knuckles on her cabin door. She slid up beside it.

'What?' she asked.

'It's Koln. I found something I want to share with you.'

Sycorax swore. Last thing she needed was a new ream of data to read. She did not like reading – the audio interviews were different. Her brain had been augmented to handle conversation, to read intonation, emotion. To find hidden layers of meaning and mimic accents, but that had come at a loss to her visual processing.

Words would not stick if she read them, and the thought of looking through another inch-thick stack of cultural essays and family trees scraped her nerves – already raw from the polymorphine comedown.

Sycorax cycled the wheel lock and opened the door a crack.

'What is it?' she droned.

Then she saw Koln's grinning face – and the amasec bottle in her hand.

Sycorax cocked her head, then opened the door and let the Vanus in.

'You can take the wall chair if you like.' Sycorax nodded to the far wall. 'There's a folding table stowed next to it. I'll take the bed.'

'Quite a planning session,' said Koln, dropping the table from the wall and sitting in the take-off jumpseat. She leaned forward so the shoulder buckles didn't dig into her back. 'Thought Raithe might hit you.'

'Wish he had,' said Sycorax. 'Instead of being so damned... controlled. Controlled and controlling. Not for me, thanks.'

Koln paused, the amasec bottle hovering over the second glass. 'Sorry, from what you said when we met, I thought you did.'

'I do a little. I like a nip of amasec and a half-lho-stick after a kill. But I'm going from playing one drunk aristocrat straight into playing another. I need a break. Besides, my vocation puts enough poison in my body – no sense doing it for relaxation.'

'Interesting, and understandable.' Koln reached inside her coat. 'Personally, I like to experiment a little. Given how many chemicals we pump into our bodies to enhance our physical selves, I find that mind and emotional expansion is occasionally useful. For example.' She raised the amasec glass, looked at the amber liquid rolling around the bottom. Thick and syrupy, leaving a slight golden film on the glass that drained as she tipped the tumbler around. 'Amasec. Always found it instils a certain nostalgia, a golden lens on the past. A nice drink with friends. Or...' She pulled a small stoppered bottle from her coat, placing it on the table. 'Purple wine. A fine soporific. Fuzzy and floating, a sense of well-being. Still not tempted?'

'At another time.'

Koln raised a finger, dug in another pocket. 'I foresaw this.' She drew a cylinder thermos, small as a frag grenade, and tossed it to Sycorax. 'Klaava.'

Sycorax popped the catch and sniffed for poisons. 'Alcohol?'

'None at all. It's a weak narcotic. Think of it like caffeine, but it takes you down instead of up. I know this is a time of heightened emotion, but emotions are just neurological chemicals so...' Koln raised her glass. 'You change the chemicals.'

Sycorax took a tentative sip. Then a larger one. 'Thanks, it's good. Now what do you want? Or are you here because you don't like to drink alone?'

This felt calculated, suspicious. She didn't like it.

Koln turned the crystal tumbler in her hand, staring into the amasec. 'What did you think of that approach plan, confidentially?'

Sycorax felt the prickle of sound-dampeners on her skin.

'Don't worry,' said Koln. 'He won't hear us.'

Sycorax set the thermos down on the shelf next to the bunk. Stayed silent, looking at Koln. What was the Vanus' game, here? Get her to bad-mouth Raithe then run to him with the audio? Feign friendship and then use what she revealed as leverage?

'I'll go first. I think Raithe is out of his depth,' said Koln. 'His approach plan for Rakkan was wrong, and it was patronising.'

'It was a groxshit plan, and I said so. Telling us what we should do, instead of asking what we *can* do.'

'Exactly.'

'And you backed me up on that.' Sycorax leaned forward in a toast, and crystal tumbler met thermos in an ugly scrape. She waited until Koln took a drink before adding: 'But you're no better.'

Koln brought the tumbler down, swallowed. In her enhanced vision, Sycorax saw a faint movement behind her pupils. Amber rings, rotating.

'Sorry?' asked Koln.

'Apology accepted.'

'No, sorry, I was unclear–'

'Apology accepted.'

'I–' Koln stopped. 'You're manipulating me. To prove a point.'

'Yes. Because it's what I do. As a Callidus. Social manip-ulation. It's the specialty the temple designed me for with their indoctrinations, and scalpels, and training. The reason I was selected for this mission, other than this.' She tapped the skull-port. 'By all rights, it should've been me making the approach to Rakkan. You poached it, just like you initiated Raithe's plan and snatched Rakkan before getting an order to.'

'It increased–'

'Efficiency, I know. But deep down, I also think you believe Templum Vanus should be running this operation. Maybe you're even right. But working how you are is pissing me off, and Raithe too. You collect an entire structure of evidence supporting your own plan of action, and tell us at the last minute. That's not collaboration, it's a power grab. To be honest, I can't blame you for it. Intrigue and data collection is your specialty.'

'But you didn't object.' The rings in Koln's eyes were rotating again, adjusting. A tell. Sycorax had unbalanced her. Good.

'There were reasons to let you do the approach,' admitted Sycorax. 'I need a good rapport with Rakkan. And if it fell to threats, he might not have forgiven me. Besides, your technocratic undermining act is annoying, but if it's effective enough to handle a Vindicare, you could handle a Knight pilot.'

'And now,' Koln laughed, 'I'm the one being handled.'

'Don't take it personally. I'm just offering you a fair warning. You're good at what you do, but just remember that I am too. It's Raithe I'm worried about. This mission doesn't match his standard modus operandi.'

'You said he's going to get us killed.'

'Because he is.'

Koln took a drink, eyes staring into the bulkhead. Not a social affectation, Sycorax decided, but a focusing technique. Accessing the thoughts of her augmented conscious.

'Have you considered that might be the point?' Koln asked. 'That we're not meant to come back?'

'Plenty of missions are one-way.'

'No...' Koln's eyes darted back and forth, as if she were reading a document only she could see. 'This is different. It's *specific*. I've been reviewing our operational histories. After-action reports. There are commonalities.'

'Like?'

'Both Raithe and I are fresh off missions involving the conqueror_wyrm. Raithe killed a heretek researcher who was trying to further mutate Quivarian's infection algorithm. I identified a penal world outbreak, and you...'

'I?'

'You killed Programmator Quivarian.'

Sycorax kept breathing. Didn't blink. Just snorted like it was ridiculous.

'Don't deny it. I got a hold of your unredacted service record. Not many details there, but I was able to piece enough together. That research station you mentioned. It was Quivarian's, where he developed heart_wrym into a broadcast virus. To get in, you got infected.'

'No.' Sycorax tossed the thermos back to Koln. The Vanus caught it without looking. 'No, I wasn't. When they uploaded heart_wyrm to my skull jack, it got funnelled into a segregated neural implant that the Mechanicus later removed and destroyed. Six months of screenings turned up no taint.'

'But they still suspect you. Treat you like tainted goods. Reason enough to send you on a one-way mission.'

'Raithe's about to be Sicarius Primus. They wouldn't throw him away.'

Koln raised her eyebrows, looked back at Sycorax. 'Oh, Templum Pacificus would mourn him. But not the command structure. Every Sicarius Primus in history has moved into leadership if they survive, most to Operations. You think M of O wants to deal with a potential rival? If Raithe succeeds in killing Yavarius-Khau but dies, everyone gets what they want. M of O eliminates a threat. The Assassinorum rids itself of potentially infected operatives, and Vindicare Pacificus gets their Sicarius Primus hero, but only posthumously.'

Sycorax thought on that a moment. It was true that the bureaucracy of the Assassinorum was a deadly place. Most senior leadership roles only turned over when the office holder expired, and almost never of natural causes. Generally, one advanced by removing superiors.

And the suspicions about infection... that scanned. Quivarian's wyrms could only infect those with neural bionics. Artificial or synthetic cranial augmentations that interacted directly with the thought-centres of the brain. So while organic humans were immune – it would not affect an augmetic eye or limb – the priests and thralls of Mars were uniquely vulnerable.

And every assassin had some degree of neural augmentation, from Koln's cogitation-centres to Raithe's neurally linked spy mask, to her own synthetic memory storage with its expanded recall of names, faces, conversations and relationships.

'I remotely accessed the Templum Vanus archives,' said Koln. 'I have a copy, though it's six months out of date – and pulled some data from the Vindicare ones as well. In ninety-seven per cent of cases, operatives deployed against the Transmuted subsequently received an assignment with a threat level rated "very high". Eighty per cent did not return from those missions.'

Sycorax leaned back on her hands, looked up at the glow-globe in the ceiling, sitting in its wire cage. 'You're saying we're being culled.'

'Yes,' Koln said. 'And I don't know about you, but I intend to survive.'

'And how do we achieve that?'

'First,' Koln said, 'we need the best, up-to-the-minute intelligence on Dominion. Meaning we need to keep Rakkan alive.'

'Raithe is dead-set against that, and to be honest, I'm not convinced. It's never preferable to have two of the same person dashing around. Both Callidus doctrine and common sense.'

'Do you really think you can learn everything there is to know about being Rakkan within two weeks, even with his help?'

Sycorax thought. 'No.'

'So we need to keep him alive, and since Raithe has already entrenched in his own position, we can't convince him by debate or argument. He needs to feel like he's in charge.' Koln held out the thermos again. 'Some more?'

Sycorax took the klaava. 'You want to trick him.'

'No, I want him to trick himself.'

'Difficult.'

'Not really, it's just about presenting the data in the correct way.' Koln tapped a few commands into a wrist-cogitator. A small network of dots and lines hovered in the air. 'What's this?'

'Don't play scholam instructor,' said Sycorax. 'It's the constellation Ursid Majoris, from the holy sky over Terra. I *have* seen the dome frescoes of a cathedral before, Avaaris.'

'And it's called Ursid Majoris because…?'

'Because it looks like a bear.'

'Does it?' Koln tapped a key and the lines connecting the dots disappeared. She rotated the constellation, the dots turning as if on an axis. 'What about now, do you see a bear?'

Sycorax leaned forward, said nothing. But she liked Koln's expression of mischief, so she reciprocated with a tilted half-smile. 'No.'

'At some point, when you were very young, someone told you it was a bear – so you see a bear. Yet these random points of data only look like a bear when viewed from a specific perspective, and with the right prompting. Your conclusion comes not from the data, but how it's presented.'

'So what are you proposing?'

'Simple. Raithe distrusts your instincts – so I want you to start agreeing with him.'

THIRTEEN

'A squire serves a knight, a knight serves a lord, a lord serves a baron, and a baron serves a monarch. So, who does the monarch serve? He serves every subject, from the rudest serf to the members of the court. Chivalric fealty, when ideally practised, is not a pyramid but a circle.'

– Lucien Yavarius-Khau, High Monarch of Dominion,
from his *Meditations on the Code Chivalric*

The drukhari wych came right at him, leaping a cargo crate and springing off the wall as it made for Raithe, splinter pistol extended in one hand. She was all lithe, deadly grace, her ritualistic gladiatorial armour cut out in sections on her right side. Flame hair done up in a topknot, a sickle blade raised above her head.

His Exitus pistol round hit her directly in her scar-crossed face.

An alert in his spy mask.

He dropped and spun, landing on one knee and firing through the abdomen of another wych, right as her segmented razor-flail sliced above his head. She burst into stardust, the round over-penetrating and clipping another leather-bound aeldari behind her.

Alert.

Above him, on the catwalk they used to service the Knight Armiger. Three targets dashing left to right. Trying to flank him.

His mask marked them in red, ballistics equations measuring range and speed spooling above their heads.

Three trigger pulls. Three more depraved xenos snuffed out.

He dived to his right, taking cover behind a cargo crate as he reloaded the pistol. Ghostly splinter rounds flashed past above him.

Splinter hit on left leg, the mask informed him. *Targets remaining: 4.*

He cursed.

Well, he'd wanted difficult. It wasn't satisfying otherwise.

The Cult of the Ragged Edge. Six years dead. He'd been tasked to kill their succubus after she'd attacked the hives of Castus IV one by one, spilling so much blood it coagulated in the streets and made them impassable.

Killing her had not been as difficult as escaping her blood-bride coven – the fastest enemy he'd ever faced. That was why he'd used the recorded mission data from his spy mask to construct an internal training simulation.

Raithe slapped another magazine home and charged the first round. Reached down and unsheathed the long utility blade in his right hand. Saw the incoming target tags around him in the peripheral vision of his mask.

Developed a plan.

Executed.

He ran crouching to the wall, wedged himself into the space between the tarp-draped cargo pallets and slid around the other side. Came at the drukhari trio from behind as he closed on where they *thought* he was.

His blade slid through the first, punching in the side of the throat and ripping outward. Before the throat-cut aeldari had even dissolved into pixelated nothingness the other two were already felled by his pistol, their blue-tinged forms exploding into cubes like shattered safety glass.

'Not bad,' said Sycorax. 'For fighting ghosts.'

Raithe drew a deep breath, the meditative calm of his exercises bleeding away just as he'd reached the state of pure, unconscious action he'd been chasing.

He tapped his mask, disabling the simulation, and removed it.

Sycorax leaned against a wooden cargo crate, sheathed in a black synskin bodysuit, vambrace on her wrist and neural shredder mag-locked to her thigh. Her mask hung like a hood at the nape of her neck.

'Knowing my tools has kept me alive for a long time,' Raithe said. He manually ejected the last round from his pistol, caught it as it arced spinning through the air, and slipped it into a loop on his webbing. 'We turned this cargo bay into a training arena, and yet I'm the only one who's used it.'

'I've been studying my schematics,' she said, thrusting her chin out at the Knight Armiger standing at the end of the rear hatch, tied down with guy-wires like it might float away. 'At the end of this voyage, I have to know how to drive that. Koln says she's made progress with Rakkan, might be ready to bring him out and let us start lessons.'

'Good news.' Raithe walked to a sheet lying on top of a crate and began disassembling his Exitus pistol with sure, quick movements. As each component came away, he wiped it with an oil rag, pausing to scrub the barrel with a pipe brush. 'You will need to learn everything you can in the next week. Then we'll kill Rakkan, liquefy the body and present you to the sacristan as him. A good test run to see if she considers anything amiss.'

He said it without taking his eyes off the gun parts.

'Agreed,' she said. 'Koln might say she can keep Rakkan safe on the ship once we hit orbit, but do we want to risk that? Not sure I trust her.'

'I trust her,' said Raithe. 'It's a risk but I'm sure it's calculated.'

'Still, don't want him to be found. Though who knows, I might kill him before the week is up, just get it over with.'

Raithe had picked up his pistol barrel and began scouring its insides with a brush, cleaning away any powder fouling. The brush stopped halfway.

'What?' he said.

'I've watched him with Koln.' The Callidus was looking at his pistol parts, speaking with a casual disinterest. She reached down and plucked up his utility knife, testing its weight. Snorted in disapproval. 'So unbalanced! And this serrated edge...'

'Do not touch that.' Raithe took it out of her hand, and in a flash, he saw how if he reversed the motion he could plunge it between her collarbone and ribcage. 'It's classified. Part of the sacred armament of Templum Vindicare.'

'It's a knife,' she said. 'Sharpened metal. Not exactly a secret weapon – we should spar sometime, you can see me use the phase blade.' She raised the vambrace fixed around her right forearm. Even with the alien blade stowed, Raithe could sense a slight, almost eager vibration.

'It's not a weapon,' he corrected, annoyed at the edge creeping into his voice. 'It's a tool. A utility knife. There are functions beyond killing. It can cut climbing rope. Dig handholds. The serrated edge can saw through foliage to build shooting hides. And yes, it cuts a throat just fine.'

'Multipurpose. Does more than one thing.'

'Yes,' he said, slapping the Exitus together, before she could get a closer look.

'Much like me.'

He looked at her, trying to find an expression of mirth in the tilted mouth. 'Excuse me?'

'You tried to herd me into the approach you wanted. For Rakkan.' She stepped towards him, within an arm's reach. 'I gave you my expert opinion that it wouldn't work, but you pushed. Then you took away the approach and gave to it Koln. There were any number of ways that I could've–'

'Koln knows how the chain of command works,' he said, stepping back. Giving himself enough space to fire the Exitus pistol if she came for him. 'She gives me options and analysis, and I choose which to execute. There is a clear process.'

'And in Templum Callidus,' she said, stepping to the side, circling, 'we improvise. Go by instinct. Seize opportunities. I know my optimal methods, and won't be micromanaged. Because when we get to Dominion, and I become Rakkan, I can't act like some automaton you can order around or we'll get found out.'

Her flat grey eyes seemed to look right into him. Raithe's father had been a planetary vice-governor on Balmoran. When the old man had died, the diocese confessor had placed silver coins on his closed eyelids. One of Raithe's first memories. And it was those cold silver discs that he thought of when she looked at him.

'Trust me,' she said.

'You're carrying this whole operation,' he sneered. 'I chose you to perform the most crucial part. Isn't that enough trust?'

'Then act like you believe I can handle it.' Her features began to melt and distort, muscles and bone sliding beneath the surface until Rakkan's face emerged. 'Because I can.'

Raithe took a breath, steadied himself. 'Sycorax, you can transform into anyone, isn't that right?'

'Yes.'

'Then for the duration of this mission,' he said, enunciating each word, 'please transform into a person who respects authority.'

'No,' she said, voice alien in Rakkan's mouth.

'What do you mean, *no*?'

'Master assassin, I can become anyone you want me to be for the mission. I will live other people's lives. I'll lie in their beds and eat their food. I'll make friends and nurture lovers, then turn around and kill them if it's required. I'll blaspheme against the Emperor and lick the wounds of alien masters – but when we talk, I'm me. No one else.'

She brought her hands up to her face, cupping it, and when they parted she was herself again. In his stomach, Raithe felt an unusual squirm of discomfort at how easily she flowed into and out of identities. He had so long trained for one role, that the possibility of playing all roles felt like staring into a bottomless abyss.

'I could kill Rakkan tomorrow,' she said, 'and still be convincing.'

'I absolutely forbid that,' said Raithe. 'We will keep him alive at least a week.'

Sycorax shrugged. 'You said we were going to kill him, sooner or later. My gut tells me sooner would–'

'I have not made a final determination on when to terminate Rakkan.'

'Very well,' said Sycorax, voice dripping in vinegar. 'Commander.'

Raithe watched her walk away, hands already disassembling the Exitus to clean any areas he'd missed.

He didn't see Sycorax smile at the security picter in the corner.

In her cabin, Koln couldn't help but laugh.

FOURTEEN

>>Interrogation Transcript 6

>>Operation: Kingmaker

>>File No. 5782-Gamma-KMKR

>>Mission Day: 11

>>Recording Device: Ear canal augmetics [stereo]

>>Recorder: Avaaris Koln

>>Cleared for Reading: Koln, Avaaris; Raithe, Absolom; Sycorax [LIST ENDS]

>>Clearance Level: Vermilion Special Privileged

>>DO NOT TRANSMIT<<

>>DO NOT DUPLICATE<<

>>PURGE DATA ON MISSION COMMENCEMENT<<

[Transcript begins at 1:12:35 of recording]

KOLN: So let's take two steps back.

RAKKAN: Very well.

KOLN: For completeness, I'm going to review the Dominion succession process.

RAKKAN: We've been through it in detail for days…

KOLN: Humour me. I want to create a brief record for my associates.

RAKKAN: If you wish.

KOLN: To succeed to the planetary throne, and pilot the Knight Castellan *Crown of Dominion*, a candidate must be of a specific parentage. Namely, they must be born to one parent from House Stryder, and one parent from House Rau.

RAKKAN: That's correct. It is impossible to succeed to the throne without direct parentage from both houses. It was originally a measure to prevent civil war – not that it has.

KOLN: These children then form a line of succession depending on the status of their ancestry, their genealogies going back to the original settlement ships.

RAKKAN: Yes, we call it the Lists. Though not all marriages are within the two houses or between the two. Members of Stryder or Rau will on occasion marry outside. It degrades the succession placement of any descendants in that line for a generation or two, of course, but it also enriches the genetic pool by introducing new blood – all the lines have married outside, strategically, at one time or another. A few internal marriages usually recover some status, as the outside marriage passes into history.

KOLN: And where were you in the succession line?

RAKKAN: It's hard to say, really. Far down. All successors have a worth – a points score, to put it crudely. Your starting worth and placement in the Lists is based on your genealogy, which affects what kind of Knight you inherit. My initial worth was fifty, since my grandfather was an outside marriage and even before then, the Fang line was never worth much. We've ridden *Jester* for Emperor knows how long. Ten millennia, if you believe the chronicles. Most start out with one hundred, or a hundred and fifty – those families have Questoris-pattern Knights. The best bloodlines might have an initial worth of two hundred...

though by that time, a line is generally so inbred as to be unable to pilot a Knight.

KOLN: And whoever has the highest worth ascends the throne?

RAKKAN: No, no. [laughs] That would be too easy. Worth is really only there to demonstrate suitability. When the High Monarch dies, the court convenes in a conclave to elect the new monarch – each casting a single vote. There's... bargaining. Land swaps. Undermining. Often the candidate with the highest worth doesn't get chosen – but only once in history has a candidate not in the top seven places in the Lists been chosen.

KOLN: So you could ascend the throne.

RAKKAN: That would assume the system is fair. It isn't. Yes, worth can be accumulated, my score could go up. But it's via tournament victories, or success in war – an Armiger will never do as well as a Knight Paladin, for instance, in either field. Really, my numbers can only go down.

KOLN: How?

RAKKAN: If you marry or sire a child as a candidate, you lose all worth and are out of the line. If I married, I'd join my partner's house.

KOLN: Explain that, please.

RAKKAN: The whole point is that the candidates have no formal allegiance. They're between houses from birth. Growing up, we spend a year in our father's house, then a year in our mother's, alternating until we reach our majority. Usually as we do that, each house tries to sway us one way or another in our sympathies. Each house hopes that should one of us reach the throne, that candidate will secretly favour them. You have to understand – apart from my parents' wedding day, they had no contact.

KOLN: So how were you...

RAKKAN: An artificial womb, implanted with my mother and father's genetic material. They started that three centuries ago.

There were too many… emotional attachments forming in political marriages. The houses didn't like it. Things got messy. It divided loyalties. Spouses caring more about each other than the good of the house. There were a few double-suicides when they tried to break couples up. So now the marriages are only contractual, for the purposes of producing a single child.

KOLN: Sounds a difficult way to grow up.

RAKKAN: I've come to realise it was… unusual.

KOLN: And the Armiger? It seems *unusual*, as you put it, to mount a possible future monarch in a vehicle for a bondsman.

[Pause: 2 seconds]

RAKKAN: When I became of age to become a pilot, my worth was not large enough to rate one of the more sacred machines. Outside marriage in my father's line. And *Jester* was his Knight. The court thought that was proper.

KOLN: So if you were so low in the succession order… your great-uncle, Yavarius-Khau. Why would he try to have you killed?

RAKKAN: I don't know. Perhaps because I'd bested one of his favourites in the summer tournament. Or he worried my mother's line was getting too powerful. Who knows? The man is senile and insane.

Hot in the forgeshrine. Hot like the steam vents near Rau Manor. Hot like sweaty sheets.

Gwynne, jumping for him. The impact. A bone-white hand holding the laspistol.

Crack. Crack. Crack.

Rakkan sat up, shouting. Scrambled to rise and could not.

Hot. So hot. The sheets pressing down on him, damp and warm like the air of the forgeshrine. He threw off the blankets, gaining mastery over himself. Fought the panic that he couldn't take his feet.

He put his face in his hands. Controlled his breath.

It had been a long time since the dream.

Knock. Knock. Knock.

Not the splitting crack of a laspistol. A fist on his door.

Not unable to rise, just injured, the nerves of his spine severed by the assassin's second shot.

He reached down and activated his leg armature, swung his feet over the bunk and stood. The lock on the door cycled – he did not have control over that – but they preserved his dignity by letting him open the door himself.

Outside stood Avaaris Koln, her tall, broad-shouldered frame swathed in a blue Navy coat. And behind her was a small woman with fine features, offset by a cruel mouth. She wore a deep cloak and hood.

'Good morrow, ladies.'

'Good morrow, Sir Rakkan,' said Koln. 'I wanted to introduce you to the person who will be impersonating you upon our return to Dominion – you remember we discussed that.'

'Yes,' he said. 'Yes, of course. Please take me to him.'

No one moved. The woman gave a rasping laugh.

'This is her,' said Koln.

'But… she…' said Rakkan. His brow knit. He seemed to be searching for the correct response. Trying to discern whether this was a joke at his expense. 'But she looks nothing like me.'

'Everyone always thinks they're one of a kind, so unique and irreplaceable, but…' said the cruel-mouthed woman, her voice shifting as she lowered her head into the cowl. 'The truth is that everyone can be replaced, sir Knight. Everyone.'

Rakkan had to grip the door to keep from falling – because the voice coming from the woman's lips had become light but masculine.

And when the cowled head rose, he saw the face looking back at him was his own.

FIFTEEN

>>Interrogation Transcript 8

>>Operation: Kingmaker

>>File No. 5782-Gamma-KMKR

>>Mission Day: 12

>>Recording Device: Ear canal augmetics [stereo]

>>Recorder: Avaaris Koln

>>Cleared for Reading: Koln, Avaaris; Raithe, Absolom; Sycorax [LIST ENDS]

>>Clearance Level: Vermilion Special Privileged

>>DO NOT TRANSMIT<<

>>DO NOT DUPLICATE<<

>>PURGE DATA ON MISSION COMMENCEMENT<<

[Transcript begins at 1:01, interview preparations excised]

KOLN: Do you mind if we conduct this interview in Low Gothic rather than binharic?

GWYNNE: You know binharic?

KOLN: Yes, though with a pronounced Ryzan accent.

GWYNNE: You've been to Ryza?

KOLN: I have not been, no, but I was trained by a Ryzan of the Sacred Archive.

GWYNNE: Marvellous. You have my envy, freely given. Also for the sensor suite installed in the ceiling. I presume you're scanning my chain of thought?

KOLN: You presume correctly.

GWYNNE: Most intriguing. This is an excellent ship. It doesn't look like much at a glance, but scan beneath the internal hull panels and there's all sorts of...

KOLN: You're quite a curious little thing, aren't you?

GWYNNE: Yes, everyone says so. I'm sorry. [subaudible buzzing]

KOLN: What is that?

GWYNNE: The Catechism of Admonishment. My masters taught it to me as a self-correction measure whenever I... well. It feels like whenever I do anything, but particularly when I start asking questions. We're not supposed to do that.

KOLN: Ask questions?

GWYNNE: Yes. Or wonder about things. A sacristan is not a tech-priest, you see, not really. We are not delvers and researchers. Our path is to maintain. Maintain the noble Knights we serve, repair their damage, ensure their human component is kept safe.

KOLN: Human component, you mean the pilot?

GWYNNE: The pilot, yes.

KOLN: So you know everything about how *Jester* works.

GWYNNE: [laughs] You are funny. We're not meant to know how the Knights work, it is a consecrated mystery not for mortals like us. I can repair the sacred Knight *Jester*, ensure it runs smoothly, but I am not to investigate its workings. To do so would be a most terrible insult to the ancient creators, and a violation of the ancestors contained within.

KOLN: So you're not curious.

GWYNNE: However could I not be curious? A divine machine like *Jester*, made by the Omnissiah and maintained by thousands of the Machine God's servants... But temptation to delve is not the same as delving. Yet that mere inquisitiveness was enough to receive reprimands from Arch-Maintenancer Tessell. I do not remember much before the damage to my mem-banks, but I do remember her saying that I was always sticking my diagnostic sensor where it didn't belong. In addition, my comportment is lacking, my tone far too light, and altogether...

KOLN: Too much of everything.

GWYNNE: My masters thought so. But *Jester* seemed to like me.

KOLN: That is lucky. Because right now I'd rather have a bad sacristan than a good one.

GWYNNE: Whatever for? Against all training, I'm intrigued.

KOLN: Tell me about the sacristan order on Dominion.

GWYNNE: There is not much to tell. We serve the Knights.

KOLN: The machines, or the human component?

GWYNNE: The blessed machines, of course. Human components wear out or break and get replaced, their spirits subsumed into the throne or helm, but the Knights are eternal. *Jester* itself has existed since settlement, and was activated and took its first steps ten thousand years ago.

KOLN: Are you allied to a specific house?

GWYNNE: The houses are nothing to us. We serve the machines. Should a machine's human component go on to their afterlife within the soul chamber, and a human component from a new house take over, we travel with them. It is not the so-called pilot we are loyal to, it is the Knight. Indeed, my order are the only impartial force on Dominion. It is often the Arch-Maintenancer's swing vote that decides the next monarch. And we have prevented civil war on numerous occasions.

KOLN: Is that so?

GWYNNE: Yes, we don't want the Knights to get hurt. Not over human pride. We are their custodians. Should one die, it should die fighting the Archenemy. A worthy death for a great machine.

KOLN: So if my goal was to prevent such a civil war, you would work with me?

GWYNNE: Of course. It would be my duty.

KOLN: Even if it meant killing High Monarch Yavarius-Khau.

GWYNNE: Don't be morbid. You can't kill Yavarius-Khau. His soul will simply live eternally with his ancestors within the *Crown of Dominion*. But you shouldn't anyway.

KOLN: Why not?

GWYNNE: Because it isn't how things are done. We will wait until he dies and use due process to choose the human component to replace him.

KOLN: From what I have learned, the High Monarch is senile and mad. Mentally damaged. And if you have a damaged component, isn't it better to replace it early before it causes a total breakdown? It's the same as you'd do for a capacitor or join servo.

[Pause: 2 seconds]

GWYNNE: Yes, that is logical.

KOLN: Would you have any qualms?

GWYNNE: You're monitoring my thought-chain traffic. Do you see any?

KOLN: No, I think we understand each other.

GWYNNE: I think we do.

'This is what confuses me,' said Sycorax.

She tapped her finger on the manual's schematics, open to a

hand-drawn layout of the Armiger's controls that matched the instrument console in front of her. It folded out of the larger manuscript like a map. Unfurled, it was half of life-size, covering her entire lap and flowing onto the arms of the command chair.

She had no idea where Koln had obtained the manual. But by the spidery calligraphic writing, she suspected the Vanus had written it herself by hand.

'Well, that,' Rakkan said, 'that's the most important part.'

'That explains everything, then.' To Sycorax's left and right, the walls – padded with leather to protect her skull in case a solid hit rattled her cranium against the bulkhead – pressed in on her, claustrophobic. Above, Rakkan hung over her like a gargoyle, his torso leaning into the top of the open hatch. She could smell his cologne, a salt tang she assumed was a specialty of his home world.

They had spent a week together, now. Discussing the structures of Stryder-Rau. His family. Cousins' names, and what they liked to eat. Endless questions like: *When a conversation has become tense at a party, what do you say to dispel it? What are the sensitivities around money? If you bump or jostle a person of lower rank, do you apologise to them, or them to you?*

Sycorax knew the way she looked at him made him uncomfortable. And she tried to accommodate that – but study was study.

'Apologies, lady, that was obtuse. You are only seeing half the mechanisms. This panel' – he leaned in far over her shoulder to trace the bottom panel – 'constitutes the physical instruments, which are manual controls. Among them are our dials and switches. The throttle lever for your right hand, fire-control stick for your left. Chain-cleaver stick just ahead and to the right of the throttle. If you're ever rendered thought-dead – if your connection to the Helm Mechanicum is cut – you can rely on these. You will be slow and stilted. More like a Militarum walker than a fusion of human consciousness and archeotech, but it might be enough to keep you alive.'

Rakkan's words grew less stilted as he spoke, not quite natural but faster.

'This part.' Rakkan indicated the top of the sheet. 'These are your cerebro-spinal impulsion instruments. Not so much literal controls but thought-patterns.'

'I thought that once I was plugged into the Helm Mechanicum, the Knight would do what I do.' She looked up over her shoulder, and she saw Rakkan's eyes flick away from hers.

'Not exactly. With practice, it feels like that.' Rakkan fixed his eyes on the curve of the Armiger's hull. He began rubbing it as if to buff out a scratch. 'But in the beginning it's unnatural. Like controlling a new augmetic. An Armiger doesn't move like a human body does. Not only do you have to separate your thought-stream to compel the Armiger's movements and actions, while still commanding your own body to work physical controls when needed, you also have to merge your consciousness with the machine to an extent. Mingle it with the previous pilots. Become both someone, and something, else.'

'I've never had trouble becoming someone else.'

'There is no hiding from them. They may sense the difference in your blood and reject you. It would be entirely impossible with a larger Knight – the Becoming ritual cannot be replicated with a stand-in. Even now, I worry it is not possible. Even with you... changed...'

She folded the control schematic and closed the manuscript. 'All right, Rakkan. Out with it.'

'Out with what?'

She reached up for the hoist handles and pulled herself upward, one toe pushing off the back of the chair to give her leverage. In a moment, she sat on the hump of the Armiger's back, her legs dangling into the cockpit. 'You're tense. Muscles tightened. Breathing accelerated. My guess is that you're grinding your teeth at night. Over the last two days, I can practically smell the anxiety coming off you. I'd hoped you would relax, and I've done everything I could to make this easier, but it's not helping.'

He stood back on his augmetic braces, mouth open.

'We only have a week left,' she said. 'And if at the end of it, I can't pass for you or pilot this Knight' – she rapped on the armour – 'we're all going to be dead. So what's your problem with me?'

'I… I suppose it's questions more than anything.'

'Ask away. If there's an answer, I'll give it.'

Rakkan chewed the inside of his cheek. Sycorax stared at the movement, studying it. He didn't so much knead the cheek between his teeth as most might. He bit down and held it, pinched, between his molars. 'I suppose it's… You're a strange one, but you're the most normal of them. That man Raithe feels like he's almost as much a machine as Gwynne. Avaaris seems personable enough until she opens her mouth, but it's not natural, the way she thinks. But with you, I can't pin it down. I keep thinking that the person I'm talking to might be as much of a construction, as much of a disguise, as when you assumed my shape.'

'I'm not hearing a question,' she said.

'Who are you? The Inquisition? High-level Militarum intelligence?'

'Classified.'

'Are you all… human? Or something else like the venerated Adeptus Astartes?'

'We are human, if augmented.'

'Augmented how?'

Sycorax thought about her girlhood on medicae stretchers, the wounds of the augmentation surgeries fresh. Her body looking like it had been sewn together from spare parts. Years of gene-therapies and injections to develop chemical tolerances.

'Classified,' she said.

'Are you going to kill me when this is over?'

'Not provided you remain useful.'

'How do you... change into other people? Is it masks and cosmetics? Maybe combined with juvenats or–'

'I can't tell you.' Then, her crooked mouth lifted. 'But if you want, I can show you.'

'Please.'

'Are you sure? People tend not to like it.'

'Show me.'

'Give me your glove.' She wore Militarum-issue black pants, and a sleeveless undershirt. Light and breathable in the stuffy Knight cockpit.

His brow furrowed. 'Do you need to scan it?'

'Just give it to me. I'm going to have to wear your compression suit eventually.'

He handed it to her – his right-hand one, heartblood-red in the colour of House Rau. The gloves were an intrinsic part of his combat rig, wire-inlaid for better interface with the machine.

Sycorax pulled the glove on, held it out to him, palm down.

'Well, Sir Rakkan,' she said. Her flat affect failed to hide the tone of mischief. 'Doesn't Dominion teach you to take a lady's hand when it's offered?'

He stood frozen an instant, puzzlement and reticence splashed across his features. His hand moved to take hers, then retracted at the last moment, as if the hand in the oversized glove might bite him.

'I won't hurt you. We're allies, remember?' She turned the

hand so that instead of a demure lady's gesture, it was a hand-shake of companions.

Trembling, he laid his hand in hers. Limp, unembracing. Touching her as little as possible.

When Rakkan's hand closed over the glove, he found it slack in his grip, the fingers so slim, long and delicate that the leather of it flopped around them. Her fingers closed on his hand.

One year, while staying with his mother at the Stryder court, he'd become separated from her on a hunt and found a secluded glade. In the centre lay a desiccated cervus, its antlers tangled in bramble. It had become trapped there and starved, the heat baking it until it was naught but skin around the bones.

He'd touched it, curiosity warring with revulsion. A feeling so specific he'd never experienced it again, until now.

The hand slithered under his grip, like a serpent in a bag. Bones shortening. Fingers plumping like they were swollen by venom. He tried to tear his hand backwards, but she held him fast with incredible strength.

He ripped his gaze away and looked in horror at her. The woman Sycorax was concentrating, her yellow-brown eyes looking at him. Through him.

Brown eyes – hadn't they been silver before?

The rest of her changed not at all, even as the hand gripping him grew sinewy, its fingers thick. Knuckles popping out into definition beneath the leather with a soft *tuk-tuk-tuk* sound.

Her other hand seized his wrist and the transforming hand released him.

'Don't look away now,' she said, tugging the glove off with her sharp teeth. 'This is the best part.'

She raised the naked hand – its thickness obscene on her thin wrist, curls of black hair sprouting from the back, familiar freckles and scars all where they should be – and brought the fingers close to his face.

In the harsh light of the cargo bay, he could see the fingertips of her hand, his hand, swimming and worming into a new shape.

Then she released him, and he rocketed backwards into the rail of the maintenance ladder. Grabbed purchase, leaned over, and retched.

Partially digested grox-steak and starch-lumps spattered the decking twenty feet below. He kept vomiting, face red, feeling the acid in his sinuses.

Sycorax reversed the transformation. Waited for him to be done. Cast a keen eye at his body language.

'Are you all right?' she said. 'I told you people didn't like it.'

He put his forehead to the cool steel of the railing. Breathed deep.

'It's not human. You're not human.'

She shrugged. 'People make bigger physical transformations during puberty than I do from one role to another. A child becomes an adult, who becomes an aged elder. A huge amount of difference compared to a face or a hand.'

'How do you even know who you are?'

She paused. 'I'm a servant of the Emperor,' she answered, and raised the manual. 'And right now, we're neglecting our duties. Come on, tell me about the uplink ritual. I don't want any surprises when I plug into the Helm Mechanicum.'

Rakkan wiped his mouth with the back of his hand. 'I don't know if I can do more today. That was...'

'Rakkan,' she said. 'People die for the Emperor every day, you're just being asked to talk to someone who makes you uncomfortable.'

He nodded, and approached the cockpit. Keeping well clear of the mimic within.

SIXTEEN

>>Memo to Absolom Raithe: Internal Progress Report
>>Operation: Kingmaker
>>File No. 5782-Gamma-KMKR
>>Mission Day: 19
>>Recording Device: Ear canal augmetics [stereo]
>>Recorder: Avaaris Koln
>>Cleared for Reading: Koln, Avaaris; Raithe, Absolom [LIST ENDS]
>>Clearance Level: Vermilion Special Privileged
>>DATA WILL PURGE IF INTRUSION DETECTED<<

The following brief updates summarise and memorialise pre-operational planning for KINGMAKER and related operations.

SUMMARY:

We are three Terran standard days out from arrival on Dominion, and while preparation progresses, the short time-frame continues to worry me. Particularly given our current plan to terminate Rakkan after Sycorax bonds with *Jester*.

INSERTION PREPARATION:

Our preparations to insert Sycorax in place of Rakkan continue, though with a few adjustments. I have been spending a great deal of time preparing the documentation necessary to support our cover for Sycorax/Rakkan and bring her to the most advantageous position with greater access than a standard return from war. Rakkan's assistance and insight into the complex court and family politics of his home world continues to be invaluable.

SYCORAX, TACTICAL PREPARATION:

Having never worked with the Callidus Temple previously, I am more than impressed with Sycorax and her tradecraft. Rakkan is compliant. Scared of her, as he should be.

Yet since she has fully transformed into the Rakkan double, incorporating his eccentricities, that fear has become increasingly mixed with fascination. In my estimation, it is born of egotism – he seems to enjoy the constant attention Sycorax's study necessitates, and her mimicry of him occasionally has become so excellent it has unnerved even me.

As you know, the charade has reached a point where you requested Sycorax induce a tattoo – the Arms of Stryder-Rau on the back of her left hand – to differentiate the two lest we become confused and disclose confidential information to the real Rakkan.

Sycorax and Rakkan's test of this system – with them switching places at the common dinner four days ago – was clearly a gross security violation. And you were right to deride it. However, it did make the point that Sycorax has perfected the role enough to fool even us for a period. It also brought Rakkan and Sycorax closer, since he enjoyed the theatricality of the deception.

Though I have put a demerit on Sycorax's file as requested, I will admit her instinct seems to have been correct. Bringing him into a relatively harmless conspiracy seems to have made him feel included in Sycorax's deception, rather than a victim of it.

Tomorrow, Sycorax will attempt to pilot the Armiger using the Helm Mechanicum. Though she has become relatively proficient with the manual controls – as good, Rakkan says, as someone fresh out of training – it remains an open question whether she will be able to fool the shades in the machine as well as she fooled us.

RAKKAN, ELIMINATION OF:

As you know, current operational planning calls for Rakkan's elimination following the bonding ritual. I have prepared strike packages for both eliminating Rakkan and reformatting Gwynne in order to corrupt her memory of the last week, leaving Sycorax as the only Rakkan she can recall.

I know Sycorax is keen to put these into motion, but given that we have extended the deadline for Rakkan's execution twice – and the valuable intelligence we have gained in the process – I worry that we are eliminating our best window into Dominion. This is especially true given even Rakkan's intelligence is four years old, and the situation may have evolved. I currently deem both Rakkan and Gwynne to be compliant and at low risk of exposing us – particularly after the subliminal programmatic chants I have been bombarding Gwynne with during her inactive periods.

After studying the *Stiletto*'s schematics, I have noticed that the vessel includes an isolation chamber in the engine room. It is my determination that we can secure Rakkan there once on the surface if you decide to issue a stay of execution.

If necessary, we can eliminate him there anytime.

RETURNED WITH DIRECTIVE: Given current progress, rescind previous orders to eliminate Rakkan and sterilise Gwynne's mem-banks. We will do so at planetfall.

SEVENTEEN

> *'It is rare fortune that we can speak to our ancestors. Or rather, that they can speak to us. The wisdom of the deceased is open to us. Unfortunately, much like the living, the dead tend not to agree.'*
>
> – Lucien Yavarius-Khau, High Monarch of Dominion,
> from his *Meditations on the Code Chivalric*

Sycorax stood in front of the Knight Armiger *Jester*, Rakkan's compression suit tight around her, the weight of the helmet comfortable in the crook of her arm.

'Careful,' said Rakkan. '*Jester* is a rough ride. Renowned, really. Doesn't always do what you want her to. And her memory choir is notoriously querulous.'

'I like her already.' She put out a hand, and he helped her into the second glove, mating its metal cuff with the one on the compression suit's sleeve. When the metal rings twisted, they sealed the join with a click. 'Should I start the ritual, then?'

'As we practised.' He sniffed. 'Suppose I should go. *Jester* will see the deception if it awakens to find two of us here and–' His voice caught. Sycorax saw his throat bob. 'I don't know that I can see another pilot in there anyway.'

He patted her on the shoulder plate and ambled towards the exit on crutches, his armature temporarily clamped to Sycorax's frame. Koln was making her a copy, but it was not yet ready.

Sycorax looked back over her shoulder – Rakkan's shoulder, but the cover had settled in enough for her to consider it hers – at Raithe and Koln. The Vindicare leaned against the wall, fingers in his belt and trying not to look tense. Koln stood next to him, feet apart to hold herself steady and her arms crossed. Likely recording the event with an ocular implant, standing braced to minimise shake in the vid-clip.

Sycorax gave them a thumbs-up gesture, picked up the blocky cooling unit that fed cold air into her suit via a rubberine pipe, and began her walk towards the machine.

Jester stood oiled and gleaming, detached from its hanging chains and glossed to a sheen. Paint chips and scoring from its last deployment had been repaired. Banners and battle-honour pennants hung from its arms and between the tree-trunk legs, silk rippling in the wash of the hold's ventilation systems.

Banks of incense burned in front of it, so the cleansing smoke drifted up past the hooded head. Before it lay a slab of roasted porcine, given as an offering to the ancestors within. Usually it would be a whole animal, but the side of ribs was the largest cut in the ship's meat locker.

Sycorax stopped with a double-stomp of Rakkan's pilot boots. Bowed low.

Gwynne, standing on a maintenance ladder, removed the hood.

Jester's cyclops eye burned green in its chrome skull.

'Honourable war machine *Jester*, vehicle of the Emperor's wrath, chariot of victorious ancestors and mausoleum of their memories. A pilot requests your consent to approach and swear oaths.'

Sycorax stared at the deck. Heard nothing but the creak of the vessel's hull shifting around them. The warp had been kind – small ships attracted less attention – but the vessel still groaned with the strain of keeping hell out. Sycorax resisted the temptation to look up at the machine. Knew that Gwynne would be scanning it, attempting to divine the will of the Knight suit.

'Noble pilot,' the sacristan buzzed in her odd beelike voice. 'You are given leave to approach.'

Sycorax straightened, walked five more steps forward and bowed again.

'Venerated mount, I request the privilege of donning the Helm Mechanicum, and joining the choir of my ancestors.'

Rakkan had said the ceremony was important. The helm was not to be taken on lightly, and the machine-spirit of the suit would not cooperate if oaths were sworn without the proper rites. Though Sycorax had now spent over a week controlling the suit manually, walking up and down the cargo bay, running simulations, manual control was no better than rudimentary movement. A clumsy procedure, intended for positioning the suit in maintenance bays or moving it short distances – a function mostly there for the sacristans that cared for it.

To mingle consciousness with the machine would be another thing entirely.

Raithe had argued a full ritual was not necessary, that they would be better served with more control-hours in the machine, but Sycorax and Koln had convinced him. Koln argued that running roughshod over Dominion's cultural practices would risk breaking their alliance with Rakkan and Gwynne. For her part, Sycorax doubted there was much to the superstitions of the Dominionites. No doubt the programming memory of previous pilots remained, and after a few centuries the collected layers of mysticism had brought them a spiritual dimension. She'd seen societies that worshipped storm clouds and misconstrued the Adeptus Astartes as gods – it would not be the first time.

But it was still crucial to comprehending Rakkan. The rote

operation of the ritual, the mystical experience of it, would help her understand Dominion.

The odour of roast porcine filled her nostrils. Gwynne had glazed it with machine oil before the roaster, giving the sweet scent an undercurrent of burn.

'You may mount and assume the helm, noble Knight,' said Gwynne.

When Sycorax straightened the Knight suit was utterly still, joints locked. She walked a circle around it three times, reciting its battle honours and previous pilots. For a week she'd studied the litanies, her augmented brain absorbing the information so quickly Rakkan had gained a new respect for her. Memory was a prized asset in both houses, but particularly venerated among the Knights of Rau.

First circle. Forging.

'Made on Terra, during times of darkness ill-remembered. Her artisans were Sukhumvit Tallah, who forged her armour. Jemson Lye, Master of Locomotion. Wallum Jau, Armsmith…'

Second circle. Combat record.

'Was first through the breach at Clortau. Stood against the hrud in the Crusade. Marched beside the holy Lord Solar at Saviam and killed six daemons in view of his shining eyes. Broke the line at Tavelion…'

Third circle. Pilots.

'Mount of the mighty Sangraal Destin. Carried Valarine Soo-Palvar to her glorious martyrdom at the Gate of Blades. Fought one hundred years under the command of Calibris Horth, and carried him home, wounded and unconscious, so he could die in the arms of his lady…'

She ascended the stairs, one at a time, reciting the last of the pilots with each step. At the top, she disconnected the mobile cooling unit's hose and handed the box to Gwynne.

'The last was Selkar Fang,' she said, dropping into the cockpit. 'My own father. Who saved the High Monarch's life at the Blazing Heaven. And now…' She closed and locked the hatch above her and took the helmet from under her arm. Connected the heavy interface cable with its curved skull-jack to the pivoting mechanism at the helmet's base, so the bundle of fibre-cables trailed away like a long hair braid. Rakkan said this bundle of wires fed into the Helm Mechanicum, the control centre that housed the data-revenants of previous pilots.

Sycorax raised the helmet above her head, feeling its weight.

'Now the honour comes to me,' she said, in Rakkan's voice.

She lowered the helmet onto her head, the eyes a few degrees off-centre until the helmet's rim slotted into the metal collar of her suit.

With a twist like breaking a man's neck, she snapped the seal closed and felt the suit engage, vacuuming to her body.

One breath later, the scorpion tail of its neural jack snapped forward into her skull-port.

Darkness. The visor of the helm was shut. Her breath washed back on her, the humidity of it prickling the skin around Rakkan's moustache.

Nothing happened.

Had she done it wrong? Misremembered a step?

No. Gwynne was responsible for all that. She needed to hit no buttons or run power; the suit was technically already active and ready.

'Gwy–' Sycorax started, then shut up.

There was a small icon on the bottom left of her vision. A Stryder-Rau coat of arms, blinking. Disappearing and reappearing. The text below it almost too small to read.

Invocation in progress…

Invocation in progress…

Invocation in prog–

It disappeared. Once again, the claustrophobia of silence.

Hail, Knight.

Sycorax jumped so hard her helmet hit the padded cockpit wall. She reached up to the helm, hoping to open the visor manually. 'Gwynne?'

A noise filled her ears. A sound like a broom across flagstone, or the soft hiss of blade-edge on a whetstone. A quiet sound, an alarming sound – more alarming when she realised she had not heard it with her ears.

Hisses and scratches formed into whispers. A hushed voice that was not from one throat, but many, spiralling together, each out of sequence but coalescing as it spoke.

You have come.

You have come.

You have come.

'Noble ancestors,' said Sycorax, inclining her head. 'It is Linoleus Rakkan, Knight of Stryder-Rau. Candidate for the *Crown of Dominion*.'

Why have you initiated this reconsecration protocol? You have piloted this war machine for nigh on a decade. Thisss is irregular.

The sound of a hundred hushed voices speaking in unison sent a chill down Sycorax's spine, settling in her belly. It was unnatural, strange. Flashed her back to Programmator Quivarian's research station, and the rising tide of whispers that had engulfed her when they'd uploaded her false consciousness with the heart_wyrm. *Upgrade yourself. Transmute your soul. Embrace the Power of Eight!*

She banished the thought, lest the data-ghosts perceive it.

If they detected she was an intruder, Rakkan had said, they could kill her. Drive her into madness. Surge her consciousness so full of traumatic memories from ten thousand years of war that they would permanently burn into her neural pathways, breaking her psychologically and reshaping her entire brainscape.

The whispering chorus fragmented, splitting into voices identical in affect, yet distinct.

He wishes to change his allegiance, hissed one. *And will support valiant Stryder.*

Fool, said another. *He has been injured in the brain. I detect neural anomalies…*

He has seen the light and will favour stalwart Rau.

Enough, said the majority voice, a chorus drowning out the dissenters. *Knight, state your purpose.*

'I, Linoleus Rakkan, wish to reconsecrate my questing vows.'

You will renounce the quest of the Freeblade? Has the war against the hated foe ended?

To renounce is no small thing.

But it may be done, should it lead to the greater glory of one's house.

'The foe is not defeated. But my destiny lies on Dominion. I have served the Emperor, but now it is time to serve my own.'

The highest calling a Knight may have, they whispered together. *To serve the house and the High Monarch. Are you prepared for the rituals?*

'I am.'

We–

What about the neural changes?

Changessss?

I sense cranial implants. Linoleus Rakkan has none, apart from the helm port.

'I was wounded, ancestors,' Sycorax lied. It was second nature. 'A shuttle crash in transit. In healing the trauma, I was also augmented.'

Sycorax had gone so far as to reshape her brain, matching the folds of her grey matter as much as possible to a cranial scan conducted on Rakkan. It had been difficult and painful, but now she was glad Koln had insisted on it.

Very well. Tell us who you are.

'Linoleus Rakkan, Knight of noble birth, the blood of Stryder and Rau united within me. My mother's people descend from the Astair line. My father's people are of the Fang line, of which I am the last. By blood and trial, I am a candidate in the Lists.'

Go on.

'My mother is Baroness Hawthorn Astair-Rakkan, pilot of *Greyhound*, who fought the Great Devourer at Magravor. Her father was Baron Selenus Rakkan and her mother Dame Salkerk Velkus Astair. Dame Astair's mother was Baroness Halvarina Astair, pride of the Astair line, who alone held the Tovernian Bridge against the fallen Knights of House Morvayne...'

Memorising the lines had taken more time, even, than learning the Knight's controls. Rakkan would know his genealogy all the way back to the Long March ships that carried their voyaging ancestors away from Holy Terra. It was a component of him as familiar as his facial features and unique as a fingerprint. A thousand generations passing their blood and legacies to form him.

And if she forgot one title, mispronounced a single syllable, the machine would know she was an impostor.

Sycorax sank deeper into the impersonation trance she'd developed in the days of study and reflection. Lived inside the constructed identity. Let it take over. Willed her body not to react to the data-jack pressing on the back of her brain. Channelled the mem-recording of Rakkan's recitation of his genealogy through her brain's speech centre. Hoped the tone of his voice, uncomfortable at speaking such a personal and ritualised chain of information, had not corrupted the recording.

When she finished, four hours had passed.

The voices lay quiet and cool on the coils of her brain, considering.

And who are your father's people?

'My father was Sir Selkar Fang, scion of the Fang line and loyal servant of House Rau, pilot of this very Knight Armiger, martyred defending High Monarch Lucien Yavarius-Khau from the fallen Knight *Dawn of Slaughter*. His father Malnus Selkar was an outsider of noble rank. His mother was Sevana Khal, matriarch of the Fang, and favoured servant of the Machine God. Her father was Milvian Hunyad, Kingsward, and her mother was Lariana Taan, diplomat who piloted no Knight, but steered the machine of state. Milvian Hunyad's father was–'

STOP.

She faltered. 'Yes, ancestors?'

The data-jack twisted into the back of her brain case like a screw. Sycorax felt pain shoot around her head like a crown. She saw fire, curtains of it, with two dozen hulking Knight suits sprinting through the flames, murdering the fleeing tides of humans before them with fire from their spiked guns.

Milvian Hunyad had no father.

'He–'

Traitor blood grants no legacy. Hunyad is not responsible for his parent's sin, but he may not claim the noble ancestors of that line – no true noble line produces a traitor. That line is forgotten and forbidden. Milvian Hunyad's father joined the traitors of Dread House Morvayne, and his line is damnatio memoriae.

The data-jack twisted like a burrowing worm, boring towards her hindbrain. Pain exploded through her temples and shot down her spinal column. Internal stimm-dosers flooded her system with pain suppressors and mental stimulants.

Disconnected images of torment. Around her, a circle of Morvayne Knights in their magenta armour, closing for the kill. Chainblades on her adamantine armour, smoking with the friction of teeth on metal. Green eyes igniting in underwater darkness. A Knight looking down to see that shrapnel had penetrated his cockpit and severed both legs. The sky, full of smoke, rising blood choking her as it flooded the helmet.

Voices broke up, arguing with each other, the chorus of the dead descending into riot.

What had she said wrong? Had Rakkan played them false? She ignored the pain, the horror. Focused on her expanded recall to fish out the detail she'd missed...

'Cascar Tyranno!' she shouted. 'Cascar Tyranno was his father. Under law. Adopted Hunyad to redeem him when his natural father turned heretic.'

The data-jack stopped twisting, her head pressed so far forward in the throne restraints that, seen from the outside, she must have looked as though she were bowing to the controls in front of her.

Under law... A pause.

There is no law but blood, half the voices intoned. *It is the way of House Rau.*

And yet, came the answer, *every soul makes its own legend. It is the way of Stryder.*

Cascar Tyranno believed the child's blood could be valuable to House Rau. He took the boy as his own, gave him his line.

It is legal, answered the Stryder voices.

It is tradition, intoned Rau.

Why did you forget this shame? Why say that Hunyad had a father, when Tyranno was only a father under law?

Sycorax took a ragged breath.

'I misspoke. I do not commemorate nor remember the obliterated line. Struck it out from my soul. To remember it would be to honour it, so I have forgotten. Milvian Hunyad has no father in law or spirit but Cascar Tyranno.'

A pause.

You honour us with this answer. You may continue.

Sycorax continued naming the Rau line for a further five hours. As she did so, her mind conjured pages of the great lineage tome Rakkan had given her to study – it had been heavy and thick. There was one volume for each house, each folio-sized, and as wide as her hand. On every page lay the story of an ancestor, hand-illuminated by a living scribe, for no soulless servitor could create work so exquisite. Most pages included a facing illustration, illuminated in gold and platinum leaf, depicting the ancestor and their mount.

Each noble on Dominion, she was told, had such a lineage tome. The pages added as the generations passed and the book was handed down to heirs. If Rakkan were ever to renounce his claim and have children, he would pass it to his primary heir and make copies for other children. The oldest pages were ancient and brittle, turned with a special repulsor rod that minimised tearing and the ravages of the mild acid on human fingertips. It had clearly been rebound several times, expanded, had things inserted.

And one section, she'd noted, had been removed and replaced with newer pages.

The line of Milvian Hunyad. The boy with the traitor father.

As the pages passed before her eyes, both sense-memory and filed in her expanded consciousness, she felt tears welling from her eyes. Wetting her cheeks, running through Rakkan's pointed beard.

It was no stratagem, the tears were her own. Because despite lacking any connection to these past Knights, the litany of self-lessness and heroism, victory and defeat, touched her. She'd known death and sacrifice, she told herself, and it had triggered something deep. She tried to activate a shot of emotional dampening solution but it had no effect. So deep in this role was she that Sycorax was *feeling* Rakkan's emotions. A dangerous and worrying thing.

Or else, the stories of consciousness mingling with the machine were no folk tale – but the thought of it was so disconcerting she pushed it aside as a distraction.

When she had named the last name, they interrogated her. Asking her to name the birth and death dates of certain ancestors. Recount stories of their heroism or where they placed in the lists of a tournament that had occurred four thousand years gone.

Then, there was silence.

We have found you true and worthy, Sir Linoleus Rakkan. Your reconsecration is complete. Does any have course to question this?

Silence. Then, a hissing voice. Small and alone:

He lies.

Noble cousin, why say you this?

He lies, he is different. I cannot know how. Perhaps he has been corrupted by the Ruinous Powers.

The longer the chorus spoke, the more Sycorax had come to recognise the parts of the whole. She could see it now, a crowd of shadows in the back of her brain. Like being surrounded in a dark room, sensing the presence of bodies rather than seeing them.

This hissing voice, the detractor, had a female cast to it. A long-ago bondswoman, the same who'd said she was different.

Present your evidence.

No evidence. A feeling only. He is wrong.

Do any others believe this?

I have thirteen others who support me. They sense a difference.

But you have no evidence?

No.

Your faction are suspicious of every pilot. It is not your first accusation thus. Vigilance against treason is a virtue, but this is paranoia. If you have no evidence, and have not the votes to reject a pairing, you are overruled. The consecration is complete.

We shall watch. And we shall see.

Noble Knight, have you raised the banners?

'I have,' she said, tasting sweat on her lips. The closed helm and active cockpit, stuffy from hours of the reactor running as the Knight stood still, sweltered. Below her, she could feel the damp seat of her pilot armour sticking to the leather throne. 'I have raised the four banners and am ready to pledge.'

Before her eyes, the helm's vision slit slid open.

Even Sycorax's ocular orbs, surgically enhanced for night vision and to resist sudden changes in light levels, were briefly dazzled by the first sight.

Before her was the cargo bay, its sodium lumens hard and bright as though the light was pouring into her skull.

Colours blazed full, the table in front of her with its crackling pig and crimson vine-alcohol showing almost neon. Rust speckling the far reaches of the ceiling vault overhead. Across the bay, Raithe and Koln turned from a discussion and looked at her. Koln curious, Raithe anxious, one arm across his chest and cradling the opposite elbow, the fist clenched in front of his mouth.

But most of all, she saw the four banners. On the left, a heartsblood-red one with the stormcloud of Rau. On the right, a sky-blue one with the falcon of Stryder. And in the centre, a plain-white chevron with the Imperial aquila, and the immortal banner of Stryder-Rau – quartered with the houses' colours, its badge an image of a hooded falcon gripping a stormcloud.

And she realised she was not looking at a screen.

This she saw through the eyes of *Jester*.

Four banners, said the chorus, echoing itself. *Four choices. Were you a mere squired bondsman, as most of your Armiger kin, you could only choose to serve your master or the path of the Freeblade.*

But you are in the Lists, of the succession line. You must choose a path of glory, power or service.

You may kneel to Rau or Stryder, abandoning your claim forever in order to pledge to a house. You shall spend your remaining days winning glory for your kin.

You may choose to kneel to the High Monarch's banner and win power for yourself, for the path of court is also the path to the Crown of Dominion. *But we caution you, Linoleus Rakkan, no one of your humble bloodline has ever achieved the crown, nor has any Armiger pilot. Yet still, the life in service of court is still a life of power.*

Or as you did in your last vow, you may choose to serve the Emperor – a Freeblade with no pursuit of the crown or house glories, a soldier in the wars of the Terran God.

Glory, power or service. Arise and choose!

Sycorax looked down at the clawed feet beneath her, feeling their pistons stir, waves of disorientation crashing upon her as she moved legs that were not hers, swung down a limb topped with a thermal spear to help her up.

She rose, pistons sliding, steam venting from her back. Pendulous arms followed. Her head felt too low, as if she were once again mimicking a hunched genestealer cultist. Everything appeared too bright, too vibrant. She saw Raithe and Koln move, startled and excited, and blink-dismissed targeting indicators as the Knight painted them as possible threats.

Sycorax hesitated, tottering on the backwards-facing legs, and took a step.

It was like nothing she'd ever experienced. The foot – clumsy like a newborn grox – came down on the table of offerings and fractured it. Splintered wood and metal rods ground under her foot like dry leaves.

She wobbled on her feet, took another step, feeling the vibration run through the walls from the footfall.

Within the clumsiness, the drunken confusion of it, she felt power. Power like she'd never imagined. In her career, Sycorax had killed many men – many things that were not men, for that matter – cutting down eight and ten at a time without thinking.

But this was entirely different. She could bash aside daemons with a flick of her wrist. Hole a Land Raider in a single shot. Kick straight through the bulkhead of this ship and into space.

Her steps became steadier. One. Two. One. Two. She had to think about each one. Plan how the foot fell, make up for the unfamiliar balance. To keep steady, she swept the arms out wide and saw the vicious teeth of the chain-cleaver.

He stumbles, hissed a voice.

He was head-injured, responded another. *His brain is not the same as it was.*

And then, she stood before the banner of Stryder-Rau. Looked at its divided colours and badge of the falcon and the storm.

Carefully, heavily, she knelt before it, beweaponed hands finding the floor to keep her from tipping. Her cycloptic lens nearly touched the deck in reverence.

You choose power, you choose the crown, said the voices. *May the Terran God and your venerated ancestors have mercy on your soul.*

EIGHTEEN

>>Operational Planning Transcript 4

>>Operation: Kingmaker

>>File No. 5782-Gamma-KMKR

>>Mission Day: 21

>>Recording Device: Ear canal augmetics [stereo]

>>Recorder: Avaaris Koln

>>Location: Officers' mess, transport craft

>>Cleared for Reading: Koln, Avaaris; Raithe, Absolom; Sycorax [LIST ENDS]

>>Clearance Level: Vermilion Special Privileged

>>DO NOT TRANSMIT<<

>>DO NOT DUPLICATE<<

>>PURGE DATA ON MISSION COMMENCEMENT<<

[Transcript begins at 3:22]

KOLN: –given that, I anticipate no problems with access to–

[AUDIO: Door opens, shuts.]

RAITHE: Good of you to join us, Sycorax. Three minutes late.

SYCORAX: Apologies. Rakkan was running me through engagement simulations. They take–

RAITHE: I am aware of your daily schedule. Armiger familiarisation checkouts from 0900 to 1300 hours, shipboard time. My question is if *you* are aware of it. This preoperational strategy meeting was marked, and none of us have time to waste.

SYCORAX: It's difficult–

RAITHE: If it's so difficult, why were both Koln and I here on time?

[Pause: 1 second]

RAITHE: What?

SYCORAX: Nothing.

KOLN: If we are concerned about time, perhaps we could just leave this issue and move on. No sense squandering more by arguing.

RAITHE: What were you going to say?

SYCORAX: Because, sir, with respect, you and Koln are not living as three different people.

[Pause: 1 second]

RAITHE: Explain.

SYCORAX: I am expected to be Sycorax. But I'm also expected to be Rakkan and Rakkan's mind is comingled with *Jester*. Ordinarily when I take a legend, I have to suppress my own consciousness to become them convincingly. Fade into the background. Hide my real self away as the constructed role takes over. How deep I go depends on how much I need to become someone – convincing a squad mate is one thing, but convincing a spouse? A child? For that I have to temporarily forget who I am. And this Armiger.

[AUDIO: Chair being pulled out.]

SYCORAX: *Jester* isn't a machine like a Sentinel or even a

Dreadnought. There's no machine-spirit in the way we usually think about it. There's a life to it that–

KOLN: Careful.

RAITHE: Machines are not alive. Abominable intelligence is banned. Rakkan's superstition is getting to you.

SYCORAX: Let me finish. I don't mean it's alive. It has imprints of previous pilots. Whatever data-cogitation chains run through it get altered by the neural patterns of those that it has been connected to. Their personality programs are ingrained in it, but they can't learn or grow like living things. It's like... like when a data-slate is put into a cogitator. Even after the slate is removed you have programs that have transferred over to the cogitator's main drive.

KOLN: Not exactly how data-slates work.

SYCORAX: It's an analogy, Avaaris. Not all of us are info-cytes. The point is they're data-ghosts projected by the machine, functions of its security algorithm or central stratagem drive masquerading as intelligences. They're cunning. Whatever security protocols are inbuilt make themselves known through them, and if I let my mask slip even once they'll root me out and drive a data-spike through my brain. And they... show you things. Visions. From the past, I think.

[Pause: 2 seconds]

RAITHE: Are hallucinations a side effect of your polymorphine regimen?

SYCORAX: No.

KOLN: I'm interested in these visions. Please give me a detailed debrief if any occur.

SYCORAX: Anyway, that's why I'm late. I was deep enough into cover that I was thinking about Rakkan's life, not mine. An occupational hazard.

RAITHE: The Callidus Temple seems to have quite a few of those.

SYCORAX: If it makes it any better, I consider that an indication that the cover has taken hold and is doing well. I can walk in the Armiger without any difficulty, do most of the movements required for a ceremony or parade well enough to go undetected. Even learned a few basic court dances.

KOLN: What about combat?

SYCORAX: That's trickier. I'm still… clumsy. Unnatural. It doesn't move like a human. Think of it like learning to use a new augmetic, but instead of an eye or arm, it's every part of your body. And I can feel the machine fighting me.

KOLN: But you can pass if you're just doing courtly movements?

SYCORAX: Yes.

RAITHE: So it's unlikely we can use the Armiger to cut a path to Yavarius-Khau?

SYCORAX: That's accurate.

RAITHE: That removes an entire slate of options.

KOLN: But we have others. Direct assault with *Jester* always presented some difficulties.

SYCORAX: Not least because it would be suicidal for me.

RAITHE: The Vindicare teach that it is our function to die for the Emperor. It is an honour.

SYCORAX: The Callidus teach that it's our function to make *others* die for the Emperor, and the more we can do it, the better. Dead operatives eliminate no more targets.

KOLN: In any case, it's out of the question. That still leaves us fourteen strike packages.

SYCORAX: You two have been hard at work, I see.

RAITHE: Koln has suggested that we keep our options open currently, and focus on insertion. I agree. Would you like to show Sycorax what you've devised?

KOLN: Gladly. Our largest problem is not just to get the court to accept you as Rakkan, but to admit Rakkan to the inner circle. When he left, he was a divisive figure. An outsider.

SYCORAX: To hear him tell it, they hated him. Yavarius-Khau tried to have him killed.

KOLN: Right. So why would they let him anywhere near the High Monarch? They wouldn't, not unless we play on a value both houses crave – glory. The Stryder amass glory and achievement for themselves. The Rau do great feats in order to honour their ancestors. And I've gotten my hands on something that provides both. Here... see for yourself.

[AUDIO: Clasps opening, object sliding on tabletop, hinge opening.]

SYCORAX: Where did you get this?

KOLN: I made it.

SYCORAX: You're joking.

KOLN: You have your talents, I have mine.

SYCORAX: Forget the inner circle, they'll make him part of the royal guard.

KOLN: Our thought precisely.

[END RECORDING]

NINETEEN

'When the ancestors speak, listen. Many a Knight has been saved by wisdom from a dead man's tongue, or seen victory through other eyes. Pray that is all you see...'

– Lucien Yavarius-Khau, High Monarch of Dominion, from his *Meditations on the Code Chivalric*

Smoke. The entire skyline was smoke – rising from burning vehicles, belched from the muzzles of the big guns that lit the horizon like heat lightning, billowing in acrid blossoms from the flaming promethium wells.

Sycorax urged the Armiger forward, ploughing through the haze, *Jester*'s sensor array marking vehicle wreckage at the Knight's feet lest the great machine trip.

Engines revved to her dexter side, and she twisted on the run to see a pair of Hellhound tanks emerge from behind a blown-out hab-block. Blasphemous equations marked their soot-blackened chassis, human organs nailed in parabolas and cosines, formulae painted in human gore.

Dangerous things, if they got close, Hellhounds. The inferno cannons could wash over an Armiger, burning away its exposed cabling and overheating the power plant.

But she was a pilot of House Rau, born of a proud line, and piloted a war machine that had borne the battle even when the God of Terra had walked among men.

And they were too late. Their turrets swivelled towards her, stilted and mechanical, as she slung her thermal spear to one side and fired from the hip as she ran.

Yellow-white columns of superheated air lanced from the over-under muzzles, splashing over the glacis of the lead tank, turning its armour a glowing red for a nanosecond before its payload of promethium gelatine went up, splitting it in two and blasting a rolling inferno skyward. But already she'd raked the melta-beam across the second tank, which was trying to reverse back behind the building, using its destroyed squadron-mate as cover.

She swept over its right track, liquefying the treads and fusing them to the body. She turned the stricken vehicle's backwards escape into a rotation that swung its inferno cannon and heavy bolter away from her. Crew began bailing out, knowing what would come next. Crude stitching held their gas masks to their faces. Most wore hardly any clothing, better to display the needled spines that grew from their skins.

She cut short the melta-blast to preserve her ammunition, then sent a directed shot straight into the helpless vehicle's spine.

The roiling explosion overtook the heretics, bestowing on them the fiery end they deserved.

Peripheral augurs pinged a warning, and Sycorax wheeled, pivoting at the hip. Contact signals chimed and she realised that during her evasive run, *Jester* had charged through a pack of traitor Guardsmen, mashing one beneath its quad-toed foot and booting another into a wall fifteen feet away. She stooped and swept through them with her chain-cleaver, wincing at the ghost-touch of their polluted blood on her skin as they came apart and spattered *Jester*'s chassis.

The last two broke and ran into the war-fog, their lasrifles abandoned in the shell hole they'd tried to shelter in.

Blood singing with the battle-joy, giddy with how the clean kills honoured her ancestors, she plunged into the choking clouds.

'Dame Yattaya,' she voxed, dodging by a holed loyalist Demolisher. 'Yattaya, declare your position.'

Vox-clicks answered, signals fouled by the number of metal wrecks on the field. By the time Stryder-Rau had dropped from orbit and planted their banners here, the Mordian armoured divisions had been fighting on this ground for three months.

'Sir Fang,' Yattaya's broken signal returned. 'I am ahead, in the fog-break. No-man's-land. We are to clear a path. Skirmish formation, I–' A signal break. 'Foes! Foes! I am in melee!'

I am not Sir Fang, Sycorax thought. It was an idle observation, one that dissolved the moment it passed through her consciousness, like a handful of sand dropped in a river. Swept away, only visible in shape for a brief moment. Because she *was* Sir Fang of House Rau. Oath-sworn pilot of the noble Knight Armiger *Jester*. Charging into smoke to aid her fellow lancer.

Plunging head first, running low to avoid the shells streaking overhead, she broke from the fog bank and into no-man's-land. Into the clear.

Into hell.

Low forms stalked forward through the clearing on canine legs that bent backward. Their heads slung low on their humped backs, arms simian. Sycorax felt her gorge rise. War Dogs. Corrupted Armigers like her proud mount, twisted and defiled. Stretched, tattooed skins covered their pauldrons. Chains woven with skulls dangled from their arms. Beneath the charnel trophies, she could see the iridescent magenta of the thrice-cursed house.

A hunched War Dog with a viper's mask sighted her and turned its twin autocannons, unleashing a stream of golden tracer rounds that lashed overhead and spanged off her upper chassis. Even the clipping blow rattled her hard enough that her consciousness briefly disconnected from the interface, and she felt the hot claustrophobia of the cockpit and sweat-beaded leather of the throne.

She dived back in, throwing the great machine into a forward roll that ended with her kneeling behind the inert form of a destroyed Baneblade super-heavy.

'Yattaya,' she voxed, as autocannon rounds hammered the far side of the wrecked tank. 'Identify position, I have met the foe. It is Hou–'

Her vox crackled, squealed. *'WE ARE HOUSE MORVAYNE. WE CARRY THE BROKEN MANACLE, FOR WE ARE FREE. THROW AWAY THINE SHACKLES AND JOIN THE DANCE OF LIBERTY. CHANGE THYSELVES TO–'*

She switched frequencies, blocking the raving madness.

'Yattay–'

'Fang! Aid! Aid!'

A transmitted location-ping flared on the ghost map in her sinister quadrant peripheral. She searched the land ahead and saw it.

Yattaya's Warglaive, *Ranger*, was giving ground as two War Dogs of the Warglaive type boxed it into the shell of a ruined cathedral. The walls were naught but rubble, the fire-gutted buttresses merely a cage for the duelling machines. Ion shields crackled and flashed, their field-on-field contact lighting up the ribs of the hollow sanctum. As she watched, *Ranger* dodged backward, avoiding the sweep of one foe's chain-cleaver and catching the other's blow on its own weapon, the two great chainblades juddering and throwing orange sparks, smoke leaking from their overtaxed drive plants.

'Hold fast!' she screamed. 'Stand and show your blood!'

She ran, casting her ion shield right to catch the autocannon fire, smashing aside the shells of dead civilian groundcars and vaulting the fallen statue of a saint as she negotiated what had once been a great traffic plaza. Hard rounds slammed her ion shield, bubbling the dexter side of her vision to the milky white of ball lightning.

Before her the snap-pop of field discharges lit the cathedral columns, her lenses only able to catch the rising and falling of chain-cleavers and bright fountains of teeth meeting adamantine.

'*Yattaya!*' A scream – anguished, afraid.

She burst through the cathedral's main portal, feet crunching the charcoal remnants of wooden pews and the blackened skeletons of parishioners who had died in them.

It must've been a major airburst that burned the cathedral, because the congregation was still there – bones fused to the disintegrating benches, a silent audience watching the duelling giants in the cathedral's heart.

One traitor Knight lay dead, punched through by *Ranger*'s thermal spear, and burning internally. Tongues of blue fire licked out of its shattered eye-lenses and vox-emitter, the joins between its adamantine armour plates glowing orange-hot.

And above it, using the body as a stumbling block, was *Ranger*. Heartblood-red armour lit by spot-fires, face mask cracked and falling away from a chainblade blow. Shield guttering, eyes dull from the power output of valiantly fighting twice its number. One leg greave torn away, and a delta of cracks across the cuirass. As she watched, Yattaya caught an overhead strike with *Ranger*'s thermal spear, the revving teeth fracturing the fuel tanks of the weapon and spraying a geyser of pearlescent gas into the air. With her chain-cleaver, Yattaya wrestled aside the foe's questing thermal spear so the two machines locked together and knocked shells in the shove of the challenge.

A valiant stand, one worthy of Rau blood, the sort of expert duelling that had vanquished dozens of opponents on the tournament field.

But Sycorax saw the death before it happened, and knew she was too late to stop it, even as she tore through the dead congregants towards the melee.

The War Dog's pintle-mounted meltagun dipped as the two Knights drove close, its vented tip nearly kissing the top of *Ranger*'s pilot hatch.

'I will speak your deeds!' she screamed into the vox. 'I will hang your mask in the basilica!'

She wanted that promise to be the last thing Yattaya heard.

A spear of white light flashed from the meltagun, drilling through *Ranger*'s top hatch and flaring through the spiderweb cracks of its damaged adamantine. Her hero, her mentor, incinerated in an instant. The noble Knight *Ranger* naught but cooling slag.

She smashed into the traitor from behind as it bent, trying to disentangle its chainblade from *Ranger*'s burning corpse. Came upon it with a springing avian leap so her quad-toed feet bashed the cylindrical plasma reactor in its back and knocked it sprawling face first to the marble floor.

It tried to rise, its weapons pushing it upward, but she was on it, armoured greaves digging into its back, thermal spear smashing down like a club to fracture the meltagun as it tried to swing around and spear her as it had noble Yattaya.

The War Dog wriggled and thrashed under her, perversely alive. Its squeals, sickeningly organic, set her teeth on edge. Her great metal body ground down on it, shredding its flayed-skin trophies, popping skulls into powder. Sycorax's skin crawled with the sensation of them.

And she carefully, slowly, placed the tip of her chain-cleaver on the vent grille just above the plasma reactor. She cycled the teeth once, twice, digging in a guide cut as though she were using a power drill. Ensuring the blade would go where she wanted it to, and not rupture the reactor and end both of them in starfire.

The traitor shrieked, writhed. She could feel its mind reaching out to beat against hers. Bonded Knight talking to bonded Knight.

'Your name ends here,' she snarled, and ignited the chaincleaver.

It dug its way downward, tip first, scything through servos and pipes, throwing purple coolant-bile and festering semi-organic oil into the air in a gushing fountain. Below the weight of her armour, the wriggling turned into a panicked thrashing. The War Dog bucked beneath her so violently that if it had been organic it would've torn its own muscles from its bones.

She forced the chainblade deeper, pressing it through layers of adamantine and steel, her own arm straining as she unconsciously put it into the same movement. Then, the teeth hit the empty space of the cockpit and suddenly drove forward, ripping through the fallen pilot inside.

The War Dog went limp under her, and she gasped in a breath.

It was quiet in her cockpit module, sheltered from the battle. No screaming chain-cleavers. No rush of thermal spears. Just the sound of her own ragged breath.

She back-revved her cleaver to extract it and stood, shaky after the intensity of the killing. And that's what it was: a killing. No tournament-field duel, no valorous clash, but the culling of an animal that had succumbed to madness. A livestock slaughter.

She could feel the hollow eyes of the remaining congregation upon her adamantine shell. Empty sockets staring from the pews, from the bleached skulls scattered among the pulverised bone fragments scattered by the clash. From the ranks of silent singers looking down from the choir loft.

And then she heard the noise.

It was a howling, braying sound. Like a bull pachyderm about to charge. And with the noise came a putrid pink-red glow in the sky, a light the colour of infected flesh that pulsed to a metronome beat. Illumination resolved into the shape of three eyes and a mouth that gaped like an open furnace.

Sycorax walked unsteadily towards the side of the cathedral as if bewitched, leaning her thermal spear against one pillar to keep her feet. As she watched, even the War Dog skirmishers to her dexter side turned, raising their weapons in a salute.

Dawn of Slaughter charged from the war-fog. Three-eyed. Mouth afire. Swinging a barbed reaper chainsword the size of a battle tank, the talons on its thunderstrike gauntlet long and curved like a raptor's claws. Chains thick as a man dangled from its breastplate, links warped and snapped where the forces of the Archenemy had tried to restrain it. One thick cable still stood taut, and as the hell engine exited the war-fog, Sycorax saw that it was dragging a capsized servo-hauler, its twisted crane arm still extended in a vain attempt to arrest its charge. To keep it leashed with chain until the right moment.

Dawn of Slaughter howled like a possessed locomotorvator and ignited the reaper chainsword, smashing it downward onto the piece of equipment. The weapon's teeth threw armour plates and struts a hundred yards before it turned the keening blade on a War Dog that was too close, bisecting it at the midsection ball pivot.

It howled its steam-boiler howl.

And to her sinister side, Sycorax heard an answer, like the song of the great cetaceans that played off the cape at Gathering Palace.

She traversed her head to see an answering blue glow light the cloud bank. A calming, noble illumination. The light of angels.

A plasma column lanced out of the fog, spearing across

no-man's-land to burst in a solar flare on the traitor Knight, its ion shield lighting up like a cataract on a milky eye.

The traitor staggered, the readjustment of its ion shield not fast enough to take the whole hit. But Sycorax's eyes had already turned away.

She was looking at the blue-lanced fog bank, and what she knew was about to emerge.

A plasma decimator pierced the dirty smoke, the heavenly glow resolving into the bright light of a power coil. A great volcano lance was held level like an equestrian at the charge. There were gold-chased eyes and a crusader faceplate, half heartsblood-red, half sky-blue, cream pauldrons set with Imperial aquilas and the campaign badges of ten thousand years. Heraldry caught the light even on that dank battlefield.

It came out of the smoke like a breaching cetacean. Like the *Leviathan* of legend, who arose from the sea to kill Baron Morvayne during the Heresy. Trails of putrid air caught on its angles and streamed off behind it. Wisps caught in the golden crown that surmounted its head.

The *Crown of Dominion*.

'Yavarius-Khau!' she screamed in pride. 'Yavarius-Khau!'

All along the line, she heard the shrieking whir of chain-blades, the keening of plasma reactors and thermal cannons. From the smashed Imperial line, she saw skirmishing Armigers emerge from the twisted detritus of the battlefield. Armoured Wardens stalked out of the fog and added their weapon clamour and vox-enhanced voices, humming the *Song of Deeds*. Weapons hammering their tilting shields in time.

Mmm-mmmm-mm. Clang-clang. Mmm-mmmm-mm. Clang-clang.

The song, she realised, was coming from inside the Helm Mechanicum. Voices of the living and the dead joined the same chorus, beating the dirge.

Preparing to witness the challenge.

Sycorax raised her chain-cleaver and let it rev along with them. 'Khau!' she yelled. 'Yavarius-Khau!' There was moisture on her helm lenses, and she realised they were tears.

Dawn of Slaughter tore across the wasteland, smashing aside battle tanks and shouldering through a factorum wall in a mad rush towards the High Monarch.

And High Monarch Yavarius-Khau met the beast's challenge. He set the *Crown of Dominion* into a run, coming straight at the traitor – volcano lance raised, the red beam of its discharge rocking Sycorax's insides but breaking apart on the traitor's ion shield.

Then they met directly in front of Sycorax, the traitor cutting the great lance aside so the two Knights came together in a crack of thunder.

Even through *Jester's* armour plating, she felt the shockwave.

Adamant on adamant. Masks hammering each other like two anvils colliding again and again. Wrestling, weapons locked, the *Crown's* arm-mounts firing into the sky. Yavarius-Khau's twin meltaguns boiled the air with point-blank shots, hazing her view of the combat.

Dawn of Slaughter's gauntlet gripped the long barrel of the king's volcano lance, pushing it upward, sending bolts of lightning dancing along the weapon.

The High Monarch hunched down, trying to protect his cockpit with his thick upper carapace, and get low enough to fire his shoulder-mounted battle cannon turrets. One discharged, shattering *Slaughter's* left pauldron.

But the cheer died on her lips as she once again saw how it would end.

Slaughter let go of the volcano lance, swung down and under. The clenched fist reached through the monarch's guard and under the carapace – a direct line to the cockpit.

It was too short, unable to land a blow.

But it didn't have to.

Sycorax saw the spikes embedded in the gauntlet's knuckles spring outward with a discharge of dirty smoke. Not spikes at all: harpoons.

The three spears drove deep into the *Crown*'s breastplate, impaling the cockpit housing. The chant along the Stryder-Rau line failed as the cables leading from gauntlet to embedded spikes lit with corposant flame.

Crown of Dominion shuddered, buckled. Fell to one knee.

Dawn of Slaughter raised its reaper chainsword.

'No!' yelled Sycorax.

The sword dropped, cycling teeth gouging deep into the *Crown*'s upper carapace. Sparks arced fifty feet high.

'Khau!' Sycorax yelled. 'Yavarius-Khau!'

She was running before conscious will told her to do so, sprinting through the wrecks and smoke. Dashing past a War Dog, who, braying in victory, did not even pursue her until she was well past.

NO! the ancestors wailed. *A challenge is a challenge! Do not interrupt a contest. The code forbids...*

But she would not let her monarch die to keep an oath. She would sacrifice her honour if it meant saving her king. Did her oaths not say that she must protect her monarch?

'*Dawn of Slaughter!*' she howled, and let off a blast from her thermal spear. It flashed harmlessly off *Slaughter*'s bruise-coloured shield, but it made the monster turn to look at her, its next blow faltering.

She could see other Stryder-Rau Knights moving now. Knight Wardens and Crusaders. Knight Paladins and Errants. In the Stryder blue and Rau crimson, or the quartered livery of the court.

She wished they were closer. Wished she were in a Questoris-pattern that could match *Slaughter* in size. Wished, in absurd vanity, that the venerated *Leviathan* would rise up like in the old stories and deliver the Knights of Dominion from their enemies.

But no. Fate had not constructed that destiny.

Only the little Knight Armiger *Jester*, standing beneath a giant twice its size.

'I challenge you!' she yelled, blasting a melta-stream that burst the monster's ion shield. 'I challenge you, beast!'

Slaughter regarded her, shaking. It emitted a meaty, wet laugh that boiled through her vox-speakers. It still held the *Crown*, the Knight's systems limp and arms hanging, upright with its gauntlet. Ghost-light danced over the harpoon cables.

With contempt, *Dawn of Slaughter* turned away from her to make its kill.

'For Dominion!' she called, as she charged full tilt at the monster's flank, spitting melta-beams from her thermal spear and her pintle-mount.

'For the ancestors!' she said, as she ducked below the backhand swipe of the massive chainsword, its whirring teeth showering *Jester* with the oil-blood of her stricken monarch.

'With the strength of *Leviathan*!' she declared, as she brought her melta-beams together on the Achilles piston at the rear of *Slaughter*'s back foot. Heating the metal orange.

'I strike!'

Her chain-cleaver bit deep into the monster's piston, severing it clean. Unbalancing the beast so it tumbled forward and to the side, unable to stand upright. She leapt atop it, cleaver biting adamantine, slashing away grotesque ivory horns that pushed through the armour, meltaguns boiling away eyes that squinted at her in mute fury as she carved at the beast's reactor.

When the thunderstrike gauntlet hit her, she didn't even feel it.

Just knew that she was on her back, looking at the smoke-twisted vault of heaven.

'My son...' she tried to say, but gagged, choking.

Blood filled her mouth and throat, and pooled in her sealed helmet, so when she coughed it only sent bubbles into the red, sticky fluid that was now creeping up to the bottom of her eyes.

She tried to remove her helmet, but her arms would not respond. She sent a mind-impulse to *Jester* to initiate an emergency helmet flush, but received nothing but damage reports.

She raised her head, feeling broken vertebrae grind, coughed to clear her throat.

'My son,' she choked, as more blood welled up. 'Tell Rakkan... to rise from his blood.'

Then she was nothing but a panicking mind, in a broken body, entombed in a shattered suit without even breath to comfort her.

Drowning in her own blood.

Sycorax sat up in her bunk, blankets soaked with sweat, hands shaking in the palsy of combat adrenaline.

There were tears on her face, and her ears rang from the impact of the great warriors.

Rakkan opened the door on her second attempt to knock. He was up, a crutch under one arm. Red eyes and puffy skin showed that he'd been drinking.

'I–' she stared. 'A dream.'

'You had it too then?' he said. 'I thought you might. The Battle of the Blazing Heaven. It's the anniversary. Forgive me, I did not think to warn you. You probably have questions.'

'That was... Sir Selkar Fang, wasn't it? So that...'

'Yes,' he said. 'That was how my father died. And now, in my dreams, I get to see it – and you do too, apparently.'

When she said nothing, he opened his door wide and gestured to an open bottle of amasec. 'I think you'd better come in.'

>>Daily Briefing // Historical Background // File No. 5782-Gamma-KMKR

>>Mission Day: 21

>>PURGE DATA AFTER READING<<

Good morning, colleagues. Emperor keep you.

Given the extensive amounts of briefing material I have provided, and the general complexity of this mission, multiple force members have requested scaled-down, more easily digestible versions of pertinent information.

In the spirit of teamwork and clear communication, I will be sending daily digests of information that I consider pertinent to this phase in the operation. Today, we will be exploring the origins of the rift between House Stryder and House Rau.

As you are aware from your briefing materials [see Preamble 4: Section 6] the origins of Knight worlds date back to the Dark Age of Technology, when fleets of Long March settlement ships struck out into the dark of space. They carried with them instructions for how to found human settlements in hostile environments, along with instructions concerning how to repurpose their ships into combined construction-defence platforms we now know as the Imperial Knights.

According to oral tradition, in late M23 an autonomous survey probe landed on Dominion and marked it as suitable for settlement. The soil was good for terraforming, and the native wildlife non-sentient. Sometime in M24, House Stryder was granted exclusive colonisation rights to the world and set off to claim their prize.

However, the would-be colonists were caught in a warp current and lost in the eddies of the empyrean. When fifty years passed with no contact, they were assumed lost. House Rau took over their settlement charter and staked a claim – successfully establishing a settlement in the northern hemisphere.

It was quite a shock for the colonists, then, when the Stryder settlement fleet arrived three standard centuries after the first Rau colonists set foot on the world.

A more perfect impasse could not have been created. Both factions had paperwork declaring Dominion to be their sole and exclusive homestead. And both sets of documents were technically still in force.

Whatever legal edge Stryder held by possessing the older settlement charter could be rebutted by Rau, who had claimed rights under the Statute of First Arrival that had remained uncontested for three centuries.

The result was the First Settlement War, a nine-decade conflict wherein Stryder made planetfall and entrenched themselves in the lightly occupied southern hemisphere. Rau, however, held onto their possession in the northern hemisphere.

With both factions fighting to exhaustion, they agreed to appeal to Terra for mitigation. But their timing could not have been worse.

The warp storms of the Age of Strife descended, cutting all communication and travel back to Terra.

And so, to avoid mutual destruction and fight back the darkness, one of the most curious power-sharing agreements in human space came into being...

Absolom Raithe pushed the briefing away, dropping it on a pile of Koln's other background material.

Closed his eyes to rest them, preventing strain that might affect his accuracy. Counted one hundred and twenty seconds.

Then opened them, and picked up the dossier marked FIGURES OF INTEREST.

The first page was Yavarius-Khau. High Monarch. War leader. Dead man. An approximate facial reconstruction and vital details. Raithe flipped past it.

He pored over the subsidiary files again and again. Court figures. Close associates. Relatives. Looking for a crack in the armour. Any exploitable weakness. An angle of attack.

A clear firing line.

He reached for the glass of amasec. Light from the overhead desk lumen hit the gold surface of the liquor and set it glowing – little splinters of soft light refracting out of the cut crystal, spilling in starlight shards across the slide of his Exitus pistol.

He took a sip. Small, tentative. Lips closed tight so most of the amasec broke across them then spilled back like surf on a shore. This way, the drink could last three or four hours, which was exactly his intention.

Raithe allowed himself a drink every other night. Exactly two ounces, offset by an extra forty minutes of cardiovascular conditioning. Even his pleasures, when he took them, were regimented and mitigated.

He placed the glass down and settled his hand on the desk, laying it within a reassuring two-inch distance from the pistol grip.

His left index finger tapped the sketched picture in front of him, a reconstructed likeness based on Rakkan's description. A thick face and wide forehead, regal and statue-like – nearly worthy of a Space Marine. An arc of geometric tattoos decorated the right side of his shaven skull, like a mathematical rainbow.

Baron Titus Yuma. Kingsward. House Rau, but sworn first and foremost to the protection of his High Monarch. Pilot of the Knight Warden *Throneshield*.

The briefing materials tagged him as threat-level Alpha. And according to Koln's debriefs with Rakkan, Yuma would be their most formidable physical obstacle. As royal bodyguard, he would always be there. Even dismounted, he was known as a fierce opponent at close range.

Sixteen years ago, a group of Knights from House Rau had attempted a coup. After years of Stryder-friendly candidates dominating the Lists, a Rau candidate had made an incredible showing at the Sanguinalia Tournaments and edged to the top. Knowing Stryder would likely retake their spot in the next tournament, a cabal of Rau Knights drew powerblades and tried to run Yavarius-Khau through as he knelt at prayer in his private chapel.

All were dead by the time Khau got to his feet – helms and breastplates caved in by the Kingsward's power mace.

Four dead Knights. All from his own house. That was how loyal Yuma was.

Raithe moved his finger to another sketch portrait – this one a woman, thin-faced and angular, black hair held in a bun with a decorative jewelled comb and suspicion pooling in the one eye not replaced with a spidery augmetic. She looked no older than her early forties, but too-youthful skin contrasting with wrinkled eyelids hinted at regular courses of juvenats.

Symphonia Dask. Gatekeeper. House Stryder, but outwardly sworn to the throne. Pilot of the Knight Errant *Basilisk's Gaze*.

Dask was just as dangerous as the bruiser Yuma, if not more so. In most houses, Koln had said, the Gatekeeper served a security function – countering any threats to the capital or palace. In short, they neutralised any danger before it reached the person of the monarch. The inner sphere was the purview of the Kingsward, the outer sphere that of the Gatekeeper.

Stryder-Rau, however, was not a traditional knightly house. Except when the house was mustered for war, the monarchs of Stryder-Rau had no fear of a traditional strike at their power centre. No xenos armies or megafauna would be smashing against the walls of Gathering Palace, and peasant uprisings, while fairly regular, were not a credible threat.

Internal security, however, was another matter.

So for thirty-six years, Symphonia Dask had served as Stryder-Rau's counter-intelligence head and spymaster, her network of informants penetrating every servants' quarters, alehouse and private nobles-only revel within the walls of Gathering Palace – and some said even in both houses. Her operations were not as splashy or bloody as Yuma's. No foes vanquished with a mace for her. Rather, her targets often ended face down in a lake.

Yuma and Dask. Inner circle and outer circle. Raithe wasn't sure who he was more concerned about, the mace or the–

His hand was on the pistol before his brain even registered the sound.

He whirled, ducked low into a shooting stance. Twisted in his chair to bring the weapon to bear on whoever had entered the room.

Over the sights of his pistol, he saw Sycorax sitting on the edge of the bed.

Flash, he saw it. Shot to centre mass. Ride the recoil up to place a second shot in the cranium.

'I was wondering when you'd notice,' she said.

He dropped his aim, not away from her, but not a kill shot. 'How did you get in here?'

'You left the door open.'

'I did not.'

'You might as well have done.' She cocked an eyebrow. 'All those door sensors, and not one on the overhead steam vent in the necessarium.'

'That vent,' he said, gaze flitting briefly to the necessarium door, 'is ten inches across and barred.'

'You wanted the best,' she said. 'Or the best with a pre-frontal cranial mind-impulse unit, at least.'

'Why are you here?'

'We get to Dominion in the morning,' she said. 'And our current orders are to kill Rakkan.'

'They are.'

'I want to do it,' she said, sitting forward, those dead-coin eyes flashing. 'I've been working with him. I know him.'

'Koln thinks he can be useful. She's asked me to retain him after we make planetfall.'

'He's a risk,' she said. 'Let me pull the trigger.'

'Very well,' said Raithe. 'You have my permission. I'll inform Koln.'

He set the pistol on the desk and turned back to his files. Read a paragraph.

She was still there.

'Is that all?' he asked.

'How long have you known?' she asked.

'That you and Koln were trying to handle me? I'm not stupid.' He took a small taste of his amasec. 'You are specialists in intrigue and social sabotage. Controlling others is what you do. It's how you're built. You are operating, to be honest, within expected parameters. Doing what you were made to do.'

In his expanded peripheral vision, he saw Sycorax stiffen. Her easy languidness seizing up. An act, he wondered, or real? He could never be sure. It's what made her so interesting. Indeed, she had been much more convincing and subtle than Koln – he would've been convinced, had he not known what she was. Studying her methods up close had given him a greater appreciation of her powers.

'Rakkan,' Sycorax said. 'We can't kill him.'

'Why not? He's a discovery risk, you said so.'

'Our greatest risk is not knowing the inner workings of the

court. There are so many knowledge gaps we could fall into. Not recognising family members by sight. Each day I... see things. Things that I need him to explain.'

'Agreed,' he said, cutting her off before her voice rose further. 'Koln has made a very convincing case. Rakkan can stay alive, for now.'

He turned towards her fully, zeroed her with his eyes. 'But if that risk calculus changes, he and the sacristan die. Immediately. Understood?'

Sycorax rose. 'Understood.'

'Good. We hit atmosphere at oh nine forty-five. I want everyone prepped by oh five hundred so we have a few hours to sand off any rough edges before we let Yavarius-Khau know that his wayward great-nephew has come home. You're dismissed. Leave now.' Then he added, 'By the door.'

'If I must.' She unlocked the door, paused before opening it. 'Raithe?'

'Yes?'

'Get some sleep.'

'I don't need to. Biologically. Part of the modifications.'

As she left, he listened for the click of the lock engaging.

And asked himself why he had lied to her.

Because while it was true Absolom Raithe did not strictly need to sleep, the dictates of the Templum Vindicare suggested that during non-mission periods he do so for at least four hours each day cycle.

Except he couldn't. Not any more. At times he lay for hours in the dark, muscles chemically relaxed, eyes shut against the world.

Hearing each creak of a transport vessel. Night insects in their mating reveries. The chanting of initiates at the Vindicare Temple. Or the squawk of vox-units as armed enemies passed beneath his shooting hide.

There was a difference between not needing to sleep, and not being able to.

Raithe hadn't slept in three years.

TWENTY

Ten years as an Assassinorum operative had brought Sycorax many places, and shown her many cathedrals. For seven months, she'd even been a Sister of the Orders Famulous, sent to inspect various holy edifices as she hunted for the heretic architect Slatnev Borane.

But even then, she had never seen anything like the Basilica of Dominion.

It was roofless, its columns and buttresses open to the slate-grey sky – which was likely necessary, since it was of far too vast a scale for a traditional dome or roof. Above, the heavens flickered slightly, distorted by a squall of rain spattering the arc-field that kept the interior dry.

The Armiger's environmental sensors scrolled, unable even in their vast computational powers to estimate the size of the space. Equine skulls buzzed through the vaults above, blowing humid air out of their bone nostrils and trailing banners beneath them a hundred yards long.

The banners were deep scarlet on the left, sky-blue on the right.

She walked slowly into the gloom, so the long back-jointed legs of the Armiger wouldn't outpace the followers walking alongside: Gwynne, in her crimson sacristan robes, and Koln, in a high-collared jacket with a double row of brass buttons, her waist tied with the yellow sash of the Verser trade consortium.

And then there was Raithe, clad in an armoured black body-glove – his head buzzed into a Militarum-issue fade. Regimental tattoos of the 14th Varansi Grenadiers decorated his wrists and neck.

When Sycorax had first seen him that morning, she'd laughed. It was the perfect legend for him, a tight-arse soldier with no sense of humour.

'No acting involved,' she'd said. 'You'll fool everyone.'

Now that jest didn't seem so sharp. The magnificent scale of the place hammered home the danger of their mission – that for all their skills, they were a group of very small people amongst the lords of war.

She felt her pulse spike as they passed through the vaults. It was not a place built for men, but giants. Flagstones large as super-heavy tanks made up the floor, and each vault was big enough for a Warhound Titan to pass beneath.

On her right, a stained-glass window the size of a Baneblade depicted the salvation of Yavarius-Khau at Blazing Heaven. In the foreground, Arch-Maintenancer Dorthiya Tessell and a Tech-marine of the Iron Hands Chapter gingerly lifted the shattered monarch from the *Crown of Dominion*'s top hatch, their faces solemn. Angels levitated above the scene, one holding a shield, the other an arc-welder.

It was soon blocked by one of the pillars that lined the central vault, each as large around as a tower keep, and studded with the face masks of ancient Knight suits, some verdigris-green or furred with rust.

'Death masks,' whispered Koln into her throat-mic. It came through as a whisper in Sycorax's auditory implant, effectively subaudible. 'When a pilot is killed, their knight's face mask is removed and converted into an urn for their ashes.'

Above them, banner after banner passed overhead, the standards carried or won by the Knights of Stryder-Rau. Some were bright and brazen, their colours still fresh. Others had faded, their reds run to pink, the blues to charcoal, what was once pure white now a dirty beige. Among them were standards so ancient they'd decayed to threads, looking like nothing so much as spiderwebs hanging from poles.

All of them had been won through Stryder-Rau blood, granted in thanks by warmasters and warlords stretching all the way back to the Great Crusade. Bought with deep sacrifice and unimaginable violence.

It was four hundred yards to reach the basilica's chancel, long enough that they had time to examine the members of the court standing before the altar.

They were so tall and immobile that in the dim light they appeared to almost be part of the cyclopean architecture. Two wings of them, arrayed in a V, their sloped carapaces catching the fractal kaleidoscope colours of the stained-glass rose window behind them. The eyes of their low-slung heads glowed bale-green behind their masks.

And in the centre, a monstrous king, spot-lumens lighting it from above, so its heraldry shone. Burnished gold trim flashed with such radiance that the whole image blurred in the Armiger's visual sensors.

Unlike the Knights that stood beside it, the *Crown of Dominion* did not have peace ribbons tying its weapons.

'Throne, look at the size of it,' said Koln. 'It must be fifty feet tall, thirty wide.'

'You read the schematics,' said Raithe.

'In the flesh is different,' retorted Koln.

'We're being scanned,' said Sycorax. Sensor barrages pinged on objects to both sides, painting hard contacts on the tactical map and manifesting in her consciousness as a crawling sense of being watched.

She rotated the Armiger's head right, and saw heat plumes in the shadows of the cathedral. A left rotation betrayed the same.

'We're flanked, either side,' she said. 'Looks like both house-holds have turned out to welcome us.'

'Vox silence,' said Raithe. 'Who knows their capabilities.'

It was another five minutes before they reached the stairs to the chancel. The attendants fell to their knees at the foot of the stairs, and Sycorax took two steps forward and knelt, chain-cleaver planted on the floor, thermal spear across her armoured body as if it were resting on a knee.

'Most excellent and honoured High Monarch Yavarius-Khau,' she broadcast through the laud-hailers. 'Now kneels before the dais your servant Sir Linoleus Rakkan, scion of House Stryder-Rau and pilot of the Armiger Warglaive *Jester*. Candidate in the Lists and most obedient nephew. Returned from a Freeblade quest to take arms with Warmaster Law.'

She held the kneel, lens-eyes on the bottom stair, waiting to be acknowledged.

This is the first test, Rakkan had said. *You shall not move. No matter how long it takes, stay on your knees. Not a single twitch, not a word until the herald acknowledges you.*

She did not have to wait.

'The *Crown* acknowledges you, Sir Linoleus Rakkan. Great-nephew and Freeblade.'

Not Yavarius-Khau – he did not speak directly to those out-side the court. He relayed his thoughts to his herald, Lady

Achara. It was the trumpet-like laud-hailers on her Knight, *Voice of Authority*, that rattled the instruments in *Jester*'s cockpit module. Sycorax could hear the voice reverberating in her teeth. Rakkan had warned her, when discussing the unusual intricacies of Dominion's High Gothic courtly language, that the High Monarch always referred to themselves as the *Crown*. A constant reminder, Rakkan said, that the reigning monarch did not speak merely for themselves, but the spirits of all monarchs who haunted the Throne Mechanicum.

As she spoke, the lights in her mask turned red to show she spoke for the king, not herself.

'Five years past, you fled this court in the blue of night,' continued Achara. 'With next dawn's light illuminating a wake of rumour and scandal. Wagging tongues repeated sharp-edged curses. It was said that you called this *Crown* "murderer" and "tyrant". That you renounced your ancient blood and took the Freeblade's quest to be rid of us. What say you to this?'

The light in *Voice of Authority*'s visor slit went from red to green.

It was the signal to begin speaking. To interrupt a High Monarch was treason – a sentence it would be easy to execute, given the amount of firepower in the room – and the system was designed to ensure the *Crown* was entirely finished speaking before a subject responded. Better, and safer, for everyone.

'My fair monarch,' she began, 'for you are the fairest man I have known. Perfectly balanced, as the *Crown* must be – and in this proclamation you have maintained equilibrium.'

Red light in the visor.

'How so?' blared the herald.

'You are balanced, for you have done me justice with one hand, and injustice with the other.' She raised the Armiger's head, though she did not look at the *Crown* directly. 'It is true that I flew from this place, and it is true that in my youthful foolishness, clouded by suffering, insensate with intoxicating medicines and mourning for my severed nerves, I did misattribute my attack and slander you. Indeed, it was for my own protection that my mother spirited me from Dominion before my fevered ravings made me lose my head. She put me on the path of the Freeblade out of love for her wounded child. In this, you have truth.'

'If that is truth, then what has the *Crown* said that is not?'

'Great kinsman, though in delirium I have transgressed, I never did renounce my blood and duty. Neither living kin nor dead ancestor have I disowned. My heraldry remains unblemished, never overpainted. For upon my healing I took the Freeblade not as a quest of exile but one of redemption. An oath not to return until I could bring an honour to the houses greater than the dishonour I had left.'

Red light, gleaming, ever-eager for increased glories.

'What deeds have you done, Knight?'

As Sycorax opened her mouth to respond, a low rumble went through the cockpit module. Not a rattle like the voice of the herald, but a tuning-fork ring punctuated with the sound of the anvil. *Clang-clang.*

Humming. Every Knight in the great cathedral was humming a low, rising march interrupted at intervals as chainblades and ordnance thumped the tilting shields that sat over the left breast of every Knight suit.

Mmm-mmmm-mm. Clang-clang. Mmm-mmmm-mm. Clang-clang.

'I have brought the war banner of Stryder-Rau to three worlds,' she said, ratcheting the vox-pickup higher and shouting to be heard above the rousing dirge. 'On Sysiphon, I slaughtered ungrateful separatists who had seized the southern hives. At Ama Hymal, I defended the great mountaintop stupas and monasteries from a tide of orks so thick, men in voidships above could not see the snowcap. And at Graydon, oh, at Graydon.'

The humming dirge rose higher, the nobles sensing a culmination of the tale.

Mmm-mmmm-mm. Clang-clang. Mmm-mmmm-mm. Clang-clang.

Sycorax let the drama stretch as she removed the Helm Mechanicum, and reached for the vox-set on the wall. She cued the broadcast clacker. 'On Graydon,' she said. 'In the Vypaan Salient, did I face the heretek forces of the so-called Transmuted. And when their faithless flesh and twisted machinery met my chainblade, they died with lamentation in their throats and the terror of our colours burning in their sickened minds. Through wastes I strode, through blood did I wade.'

Sycorax popped the top hatch, the coiled cord of the vox stretching to full extension as she clambered out onto the carapace for the final act. She didn't have to mimic Rakkan's unsteady gait – the borrowed augmetic leg braces enforced his stiff movement.

'My steed, *Jester*, was six times mentioned in dispatches, given letters of commendation from the commanders of four Militarum regiments and the warmaster herself.'

Raithe stepped forward, his head bowed and holding out a document tube encrusted in so many seals, its green marble surface could barely be seen. The documents were expert forgeries, a testament to Koln's skill. One was even – and Sycorax could not fathom how this was possible – on a true copy of Warmaster Law's letterhead, complete with a chip-embedded wax ident-seal.

But that was nothing compared to the final reveal.

'And a month ago, as Graydon City trembled and the faithful woke in nightmare, the heretek Magos Brabatina Markov drove her daemon engines and crackling machines at the cantonment earthworks – their electrical discharges lighting the sky with aurorae.'

Mmm-mmmm-mm. Clang-clang. Mmm-mmmm-mm. Clang-clang.

She stood full on the armoured shell now, right hand braced on the open hatch, within easy reach of the gold braid hanging down from the banner pole behind her. The pole was affixed to the Armiger's back, sprouting from a housing just fore of the reactors, a rolled piece of embroidered cloth on its crosspiece.

'And when Markov came, her machine-daughters scuttling through the war-fog, claws rending the flesh of reality itself, I rode to meet her amid the falling shells, the vassals of the Militarum all about my feet. And when she met me, she opened her great maw wide and unleashed a shriek that slew nine of those brave soldiers, their powercells exploding in their lasguns. Silver aquilas around their necks liquefying in molten streams. Organs cooking so their bellies burst.'

She let the image hang.

He lies, whispered one of the ghost-choir. *The heretek Markov died in an artillery barrage.* Jester *saw it from a mile distant.*

It is embellishment for glory and advancement, hissed another. *A story that brings renown to both Dominion and* Jester. *It is custom. It is permitted.*

'And as her warp-befouled breath washed over my adamantine,' said Sycorax, ignoring the whispers. 'I raised my thermal spear and fired it straight into the blasphemer's mouth.'

Clang-clang.

This time she joined the movement too, slamming a closed fist on her heart before finishing.

'For this deed, Warmaster Law sends her thanks – and her personal banner.'

Sycorax pulled the cord, and the thick roll of cloth at the top of the banner pole dropped, unfurling with a flash of brocade and bone.

It was a skeleton, woven in silver thread on the tapestry of the banner, holding a torch in one hand and a sword in the other.

But the skull, the skull was real. The rear of the cranium was cut away so it rose out of the banner, a jade laurel wreath on its head, and rubies glowing in the eye sockets. The skull of Law's own father, a strange martial tradition on her home world of Declis.

The dirge-song stopped dead. Silence in the great cathedral.

Sycorax could hear nothing but the background thrum of the Knights' reactors, a few grinding creaks as the giants repositioned to get a closer look.

Sycorax had no idea how Koln had managed to weave the banner in so short a time, not to mention doctoring the holes from lasgun fire and age. Indeed, the deception was so brazen she worried that the Knights might not buy it.

But she need not have been concerned.

For after the silence, came the noise. A banging, raucous cacophony of such force, Sycorax worried her eardrums might rupture.

Sir Linoleus Rakkan had been welcomed home.

TWENTY-ONE

The clamour stopped, its reverberation echoing through the megalithic hall.

All waited, unmoving, for the High Monarch's judgement.

'Take the banner down,' said the herald. 'The *Crown* wishes to see it.'

Sycorax nodded. With the Armiger kneeling prostrate, the banner pole dipped far enough forward that it was no difficulty to clamber up and deactivate the magnets that held it in place.

It was heavy, even in her augmented arms. She took a step down towards the floor then saw the red light in the herald's visor.

'Halt there!' the herald blared. 'The servitors will come fetch it.'

Sycorax heard the buzzing of anti-grav motors and held the banner up with both arms. Two winged servitors snatched it up with augmetic foot talons, jerking it out of her hands with surprising strength. Feathered wings of brass grafted in place of their arms beat hard trying to bear the weight aloft, and Sycorax noticed that cap hoods covered their faces, penetrated only by a beaklike ceramic protrusion.

Servitors fleshworked into hunting falcons.

In her enhanced vision Sycorax could see how ancient and finely wrought the augmetic components were, and how inflamed and jagged the sutures where they met the sallow flesh. The inorganic components were from another age, a better age, scavenged and fused to new vat-grown servitor bodies whenever the previous body became inoperable.

High technology, eternal and lasting, fused to flesh that decayed and fell away.

Much like the Knights themselves.

Sycorax felt an unusual flutter in her chest, and realised it was a shudder.

The servo-falcons flew the streaming banner up the dais, the tassels of the bottom edge grazing the stone steps, until they drew level with the *Crown of Dominion*'s facemask. Blue light shone through the back of the thick fibres – clearly some form of scanning beam.

The court waited, still as statues.

And finally, slowly, the *Crown*'s great head tilted upward and cast its gaze to the open sky above.

The servo-falcons bolted skyward, beating their brass wings as they took the banner to hang amid the others chained to the columns on the great procession of victories. One more honour among a parade of honours.

'The *Crown* is pleased,' said the herald. 'You may raise your eyes to it.'

Sycorax raised Rakkan's head – not all the way, still dipped into a slight bow – enough to look at the *Crown of Dominion* directly.

The great machine's head was tilted to one side, as if regarding this strange little Knight with more curiosity than before. Looking upon it fully, up close, it seemed impossible that a machine so massive could die – much less that she could kill it. Such a thing was nearly unthinkable, like trying to execute a mountain, or run a tidal wave through with a sword.

'Great honour deserves a great reward,' said the herald, the thunderous words pounding on Sycorax's unprotected eardrums. 'Name what you wish.'

Rakkan had warned them of this. It was, in truth, the most dangerous part of the insertion. Impressive as Rakkan's embellished war glories were, he was still a mere Armiger pilot. A nothing. So far down in the Lists, there was no reason to coddle or ingratiate oneself to him in case he ever rose high.

If she asked for too much, they would blow any goodwill they'd gained with the presentation – but to grovel was not Rakkan's way, and asking for too little would cause suspicion.

Green light. Sycorax raised the vox to her lips. 'This man, Sergeant Jethus Pyne,' she said, as Raithe stepped forward, head low, 'swore a death-oath to me on Ama Hymal. I came to the aid of the Varansi Grenadiers when greenskins swarmed their position – he was the lone survivor, and now serves as my lifeguard.'

Koln stepped forward.

'This woman,' Sycorax continued, 'is Engine-Master Axanda Dak, of the Verser trade consortium. She has granted me passage from warzone to warzone, on permanent assignment from her masters. I ask, good king, that both of them might take my livery as bonded men and be granted the freedom of Gathering Palace and all places where I go.'

Red light. The herald chuckled. It sounded both booming and hollow, because she was repeating a facsimile of the monarch's genuine reaction. 'The *Crown* is amused. Your liege lord offers you a horse, and you take only its shoes. He gives you a jewelled pendant, and you care only for the silver chain on which it hangs. Want you nothing else besides these vassals?'

'Yes,' said Sycorax. 'My liege, I have discharged my oath as

Freeblade, and reconsecrated my mount. I wish to pledge to the court as a bondsman, to re-enter the Lists, and to be the most loyal servant to my lord High Monarch Yavarius-Khau.'

A pause. Red light showing in the herald's visor, as if the High Monarch did not want to be disturbed whilst in the depths of thought.

'So you pursue power and influence,' said the herald, slowly. 'I should have thought no different. You have your mother's ambitious Stryder blood as well as your father's warlike spirit. That is admirable. But as to your request, I can no more force members of my council to take on a bondsman than I can pull stars from the firmament, but if one will have you, you may rejoin the court – and the Lists, for what good it will do you. And at the request of your uncle Baron Kraine, head of House Rau, we will give you this.'

Baron Kraine. Rakkan's uncle. A servitor walked forward with a battered helmet on a cushion, laying it in front of Sycorax.

'Your father's pilot helm. Worn when he saved the High Monarch's life at the Battle of the Blazing Heaven.'

Green light. Sycorax awkwardly knelt in the cockpit's open hatch, Rakkan's augmetic braces stiff and slow to respond. 'Undying thanks, my liege. You honour me with this gift.'

'We will now adjourn,' the herald said, her visor light amber to show it was her speaking rather than the monarch. 'To the Feast of Welcome.'

Sycorax closed the hatch just as the *clang-clang-clang* of weapons on shields announced the closing of court.

It was time to attend a party – and find their path to kill a king.

Though as she watched the hulking edifice of the *Crown* stomp backward, never turning its back on the court, she wondered if the better word would be monster.

* * *

On the *Stiletto*, in a cabin locked tight and accessed via a door set into a false coolant tank beaded with condensation, Rakkan watched the court lumber into the shadows of the basilica.

How often he'd dreamed of returning in glory. In vengeance. Of being hailed as the repentant child, come to claim the laurel of victory so long denied him.

And now he watched it through the pict-capture feeds, switching between the augmetic embedded in Koln's left eye and the wire-lens stealthily drilled and implanted into Sycorax's skull, shrouded by the right eyebrow. A procedure, he assumed, that was less traumatic given her shape-changing abilities.

This way he could watch, from her perspective, as she lived his life. He could even communicate, to a certain extent.

He pulled the cogitator's clackboard towards him and laboriously tapped out a simple message with two crooked fingers, eschewing all complicating punctuation, before hitting TRANSMIT.

congratulations, it read, *you got the homecoming i never had*

He reached for the glass of amasec next to the cogitator bank, drained it, toyed with stopping there, then poured another and returned to the clackboard.

someone always dies at these parties, he sent.

make sure it isn't you

He drained the second glass, feeling the warmth spread and chase away the cold of the artificially chilled bulkhead to his right, which masqueraded as the coolant tank. It was a clever device, and no one would ever find him.

On reflection, he thought, perhaps it was safer having his own party in here.

But if they died, what exactly would happen to him?

* * *

'Sir Rakkan, you should give your oath to Baroness Dask,' said Koln. 'Proximity, but also access to information.'

She spoke openly as they walked the Hall of Fields, the refractor-shielded bridge that connected Gathering Palace's stable, where they'd left *Jester* and Gwynne among the other Knight suits. To any capture-voxes, it would seem a normal conversation. The standard jockeying of court, a minor Knight and his vassals vying for power.

'Eh,' said Raithe.

'You disagree, sergeant?' said Koln, putting some vinegar into the last word, the same way a mid-deck engine-master might when being grunted at by a grubby infantryman.

'Speak your thoughts,' chided Sycorax.

'Achara the herald.' His copper eyes drifted everywhere in the slow, thorough manner of a good lifeguard. Except he wasn't scanning for threats, his vision angled too high. Raithe was eyeing sniper positions on Gathering Palace, assessing its battlements, firing slits, gargoyles, the narrow lance-like roofs of the round towers. 'Her, or Yuma. Swearing service to Yuma would give us greatest proximity to the *Crown*, but at the greatest danger. He is formidable. Achara not only gives us access but also insight into the High Monarch's thoughts.'

'Baroness Dask, by contrast, gives us information,' argued Koln. 'Getting close to Dask means access to information coming into her web of spies and informants. That would be... useful.'

They knew what she meant, merely by implication. Dask handled what passed for Dominion's counter-intelligence services and secret police, meaning a position close to her could be used to monitor any effort to find them.

'Excessively dangerous, too much vetting,' said Raithe. 'But it has to be one of the three, and I say the herald.'

'Four,' said Sycorax.

'I'm sorry?' Raithe responded.

'The Exalted Court of Dominion is always four officers. Two from Stryder, two from Rau,' Sycorax said. 'Today we were missing the Master of Judgment.'

'Rallan Fontaine,' said Koln. 'House Stryder, pilot of the Knight Gallant *Axefall*. The Exalted Court's executioner. He's in the hinterland, putting down a small uprising.'

'Not the best choice,' said Raithe.

'Lord,' said Sycorax.

'What?' asked Raithe.

'Not the best choice, *lord*,' Sycorax corrected. 'Know your place, sergeant.'

'I'll tell you my place, *lord*,' Raithe nodded upward. 'Right in that window up there. Above the palace gate. It's inside the refractor field. Clear line of fire all the way down the Hall of Fields. Control access to the Knight suits.'

'Such a beautiful walk,' Sycorax said, looking to her left. 'I used to come here as a child, you know. To play Hektur and Heretics with my cousins, dreaming of being pilots.'

Koln had too much self-mastery to let the smile show, but she turned her head to look at the view in order to conceal even the slight twitch at her lips.

It was, she thought, an incredible landscape.

Gathering Palace was built on an isthmus that connected the northern continent dominated by House Stryder, and the southern one ruled by Rau. Water, flashing dull crimson in the deepening winter, covered the horizon on either side. And behind the hulking grey keep of Gathering Palace – itself as large as a small city – her augmented eyes could see the heat plume and carbon emissions of the first city in Stryder territory, just as behind her, the last city of Rau territory reared its great walls.

Both were built like fortresses. And between them, Gathering

Palace stood as a small area of peace and interchange. The isthmus was bright green and loamy, though she knew that granite layers underlying the earth made it perfect for fortress construction.

That's all Gathering Palace was. A city-fortress, with a village at the base for the poorer vassals, a Knight stable primarily used by those in the Lists, and a tournament ground. Just to her right, on the plain of the isthmus, she could see the fortified bastion of Heaven Defence West – the hemispheric fire-control station bristling with weapons liberated from destroyed Knight suits and repurposed as defensive artillery.

They passed through the enormous gate, looking up at the spiked portcullis made of pure adamantine – a portal large enough for two Questoris Knights to march through abreast.

'So our favoured patron?' asked Sycorax. 'Herald, Kingsward or Gatekeeper?'

'Herald,' said Raithe.

'Gatekeeper,' said Koln.

'I say we go by feel. And we have forgotten our first and most formidable obstacle,' said Sycorax.

'What is that?' Raithe paused. 'Lord.'

'My mother.'

TWENTY-TWO

*'Noble Stryder and Stalwart Rau. Many long winter nights
have I lain awake trying to ken their future. Sometimes, I think
they are like hammer and anvil, that the force of their beating
together shapes the candidates that take the throne. At other
times, I imagine the falcon and the storm, like in the old poem.
But increasingly, I see them as two drunks, mutually supporting
each other as they stagger home. If one slips, the other may
laugh at his misfortune – but both will fall.'*

— Lucien Yavarius-Khau, High Monarch of Dominion,
from his *Meditations on the Code Chivalric*

'Linoleus, my boy, my child.' Baroness Hawthorn Astair-Rakkan
held her arms out to her son, tears in her eyes.

'Mother,' Rakkan said, and embraced her. The baroness was
tall and angular, her shoulders back like the diving falcon of the
Stryder heraldry. And when Rakkan – for Sycorax had slipped
into the legend deep enough that she thought herself to be
Rakkan now – took the woman in his arms, he felt how slight
she was underneath the layered ballgown.

Pulled close, Baroness Hawthorn whispered in her son's ear,
'You could have told me you were coming, you ungrateful little
coffin-worm.'

'And ruin the surprise, mother?' He leaned in to do the oblig-
atory cheek kisses, glad he'd been so thoroughly briefed on this
relationship.

Hawthorn's eyes burned, but she smiled for the benefit of anyone looking. 'If I'd known you would be such trouble,' she said, kissing Rakkan's left cheek, 'I would have ripped you out of me and thrown you to the hounds.' She kissed his right.

Baroness Hawthorn, he knew, was publicly a lady in every respect. Impeccably dressed in the latest fashion, a connoisseur of fine vintages and a hostess of parties. Well-regarded pilot of the Knight Crusader *Greyhound*, with a history of excellent tournament results, if mostly in the ranged events.

Privately, though, she was infamous for having the filthiest mouth in Dominion. The joke was that when Stryder needed to strip a Knight suit for repainting, they simply stood it in front of Hawthorn when she was in a foul mood, and within minutes not a shred of paint would remain.

Indeed, she was so formidable that court had abandoned her last names entirely, and simply dubbed her Hawthorn. As if there could be no other.

'A true Stryder homecoming,' he answered. 'In my defence, I did bring a gift.'

He gestured to Warmaster Law's banner, hung on one wall of the great hall, half in the Stryder side of the feasting hall, half in Rau.

The great hall of Gathering Palace was bisected, one side hung with the red banners and heraldry of Rau, the other in the blue of Stryder. But even without the decor, the guests' apparel was enough to show the delineation. The crowd was similarly divided by colour, and a ten-foot moat separated them to prevent an affray. Only the raised dais at the end of the hall, with the table laid for the High Monarch and his Exalted Court – currently empty – was not delineated by house. The only way to pass over the moat was a small raised bridge between the two sides.

No one had crossed since Rakkan entered.

'Political capital from your banner is impressive, Linoleus,' said Baroness Hawthorn. 'But you immediately wasted it on grubby vassals and a go-nowhere appointment.' She turned to Koln. 'Hasn't my son trained you? My glass is empty. Get me more vin-ferment. The gold not the red, twenty-year summer crop.'

'Yes, baroness,' said Koln, who – if she wanted to – could've caved in the woman's skull with a jab of her fist. 'Right away.'

'At least they're polite,' Hawthorn mused. Then she saw a woman in a fitted tunic striding towards them and her face lit up in a smile bright as a search-lumen. 'Careful, well-wishers incoming. Hello, Lisille! It's been so long.'

The woman smiled in greeting, crinkling the scar that ran across her otherwise flawless lips and chin, and bowed. 'Well met, baroness. A son returned, eh? My lady, you must be so proud, and relieved to have him home. And of course, Sir Rakkan, we are all grateful to you for representing us in the crusade.'

She turned to Rakkan and saluted by beating her fist twice to her heart. Her double-breasted dress tunic, quartered in the colours of both Stryder and Rau, was starched so stiff it crinkled under the blows. A ceremonial sword, its blade made from harmless plasteel so it could be worn into court, hung from a wide baldric that crossed her shoulder. 'A bondsman to the court, very interesting idea. Do you recall me?'

She stood back, fists on her hips. A great groomsman loomed behind her, and Rakkan suddenly realised she was young. Painfully so. No more than nineteen or twenty.

Rakkan searched his memories, those both implanted and learned until the name formed a connection. 'Lisille!' he said. 'Lisille Lycan-Bast. Cousin, you've grown so much. You're a pilot now?'

'The Errant *Blood Oath*. Mounted her two years ago. Tournaments and uprisings, nothing as exciting as slaying hereteks.'

'And this?' He wiggled his finger before the lip scar.

'Nothing much,' she smiled. 'Cockpit straps got rattled loose in the... summer tournament, two years back?' She turned to her footman, who nodded. 'Sir Tavlar mashed me with a thunderstrike gauntlet and my skull hit the control console.' She smiled and clicked her front teeth with a fingernail. 'Ceramite replacements, better than new. I daresay I'll see you in the melee at tomorrow's midwinter tournament?'

He raised his glass. 'See you in the Lists.'

She swept away, smiling, walking through the sky-blue crowd, up onto the bridge, and crossing into the half where red tabards dominated. A fish swimming in many streams.

Hawthorn waited until Liselle was out of earshot and said, 'She's rutting that footman of hers.'

'Mother.'

'Well, she is.'

He raised his eyebrows. 'And you aren't?'

'No. Well, once or twice each, but that's hardly the same thing. They've been carrying on for a year – it's unseemly. I could've told you by letter but you do realise it's been two years since you wrote, hmm? And that we only knew to expect you because of reports Dask picked up from some listening station she keeps in the out-system.'

So they'd gotten the manufactured signals traffic. Clever Koln.

'I was engaged,' Rakkan said.

'Hopefully not, unless you want me to finally have that aneurysm you've been trying to induce ever since you were knee-high. Now tell me, what daemon possessed you to trade that ratty banner for being bonded to the Exalted Court? When I heard you say it, I nearly called for the exorcist.'

'It is an honourable appointment.'

'And one that does nothing for Stryder,' she snapped. 'When you came back, if you ever came back, I had hoped you would join your true house. I could use you.'

'Yes, that's what I was worried about. I am not a Stryder, mother, I'm a Stryder-Rau.'

'Please,' said Hawthorn, a word she only used as a type of curse. She had been in the Lists herself – thus her dual name – but had left in order to head House Stryder. Yavarius-Khau, after all, did not seem to be going anywhere. 'Your father left you nothing but a diluted bloodline and a few hazy memories. You know Rau only offered the match with your father because they wanted to neutralise our line from sitting as the *Crown* for a few generations. Wouldn't offer anyone suitable. I was so furious that I put it in the contract that you would only have my name – your father didn't fight it. Didn't even care you'd be just Rakkan rather than Rakkan-Fang.'

'Yes,' Rakkan sipped his vin, and tilted his head. 'So you've told me. But you can't smear a chivalric war hero, can you?'

She snorted. 'Awful position your father put me in. Saves the High Monarch and dies doing it, and we can never speak ill of him again. Even though his outsider father was some upstart frigate commander, stinking of void reactors–'

'Post-captain,' corrected Rakkan. 'Grandfather was a post-captain. And he made vice-admiral.'

'Posthumously,' she spat. 'I don't see why I must respect a man merely for being killed by the aeldari. Neither his sacrifice, nor your father's, did anything for this house or this world – and now you've traded your leverage.'

'Is it that bad?'

She shot him a look, lips curling in – what? Disgust at his ignorance? Resentment that he'd missed so much? Beneath the constructed consciousness of Rakkan, Sycorax felt herself stepping into deep water.

'That bad?' she hissed. 'The High Monarch is... well... you can't say what he really is. He's capricious, let's say, or eccentric. Last year he was a devoted partisan of Rau. Favoured them in the tournaments. Gave them Telshen Hall...'

'Finally solved that, did he? It's been disputed since you were in frills.'

'Be serious, Linoleus. I never consented to wearing frills, even when I was a babe. He also had your poor cousin slapped from his assignment at court for nearly no reason at all. Some nonsense about not showing Rallan Fontaine enough deference in a meeting.'

'Which cousin?' Rakkan frowned.

'Mauvec, of course.'

'Ah,' said Rakkan, scanning the blue-clad crowd. 'I don't look forward to that meeting.'

'Well you *did* try to take *Typhoon's Teeth* from him. But it's been years, I doubt he'll break more than a few fingers. But the point is, last year the High Monarch was antagonising us – then he wheeled around and dropped his lance straight for Rau. They can't get a good ruling on anything this year. And when one of our squires killed one of theirs in a duel, well, the law states that it made our man a proper target in the blood feud. But he disallowed it, refused to let Rau fulfil the vendetta.'

'Strange.'

'He's also closed their machine sanctuaries.'

'What?'

'Disallowed the ancestral machine sanctums. Referred to them as absurd superstition. The sacristans are livid, but they never make waves – after all, they can continue bowing and scraping to the Omnissiah, it's just the Rau ancestral halls that are forbidden. He's declared them a subversive belief – said they should be listening to his orders, not the ancestors – and threatened to bring in the Inquisition.'

'That's insa–'

'Intemperate,' she corrected. 'No High Monarch is mad. And if one is, it is not said until after they've left their mortal shell and been absorbed to the Throne Mechanicum. You know the rules.'

'Still, good for your faction, eh?'

'One would think so,' she said, 'if one was a simpering moron. We're hostage to him, Linoleus. He could change his patronage at any second and drive as hard at us as he did at Rau. Anything he wants now, Stryder will give him. He's riding us to spit-froth like a horse. We'll collapse soon. And if we don't, Rau will rise up and kill us all. They think we're behind it, that we've bribed or coerced him somehow.'

'What do you think caused this change in his mind?'

The baroness turned and regarded him with sharp eyes. 'You're quite interested in house politics. Exactly whose son came back to me?'

'War changes a man,' Rakkan said. 'At least it did for me.'

A textual dispatch from Rakkan, the real Rakkan, flashed across Sycorax's vision.

ask about dogs

'The hounds are well, I assume?' Rakkan enquired.

'They are!' Hawthorn gestured to a footman, who weaved through the crowd with three lean stalkerhounds at his side. The man held the leashes taut in case the tall canines lost control and nipped at a plate of sluk mutton. They pushed ahead, snouts low, straining to get to their packmaster until they were able to lick Hawthorn's outstretched hand. 'Here, my lovelies. You remember Rakkan, don't you?'

They sniffed Rakkan, the lead one growling low.

'Yarrick,' scolded Hawthorn. 'You know Linoleus. Remember?'

'I've been gone a long time,' Rakkan said in excuse, glad the interviews concerning Hawthorn had been so extensive. He reached out to scratch the creature.

not behind the ears

Rakkan pulled his hand back, just as Yarrick opened his jaws.

'He's an old man now. And cranky. Now, that must be Macharius, but... who's this one? Where's Creed?'

Hawthorn sighed, then knelt and rubbed Yarrick's silvered face. 'Creed lived up to his name a bit too well. Squared up against an ursid on a hunt rather than running away. The new one is Ibram Gaunt. He's a good little bird dog, aren't you, Ibram? You lovely boy.'

'The next time we have a Militarum delegation,' Rakkan said, 'best not to mention the names. They wouldn't appreciate it.'

'Why not? It's a tribute. And it's proper. Isn't that what the Guard is for? Flushing the prey out of the bushes for us to shoot?'

'It's verging on heresy.'

'A heretic? Me? What a thing to say about your mother. Besides, this is our world, we can do what we want.'

'They leave us be as a courtesy, mother. We are part of the Imperium, whether you like it or not.'

Hawthorn wrinkled her nose. 'Only in a technical sense. We have an understanding with the Imperium, Linoleus, we are not *Imperial*. Dominion was a settled world with ancient chivalric traditions when Terra was just feuding warlords and techno-barbarians. Never forget that, my son. We are older than their empire. It suits us to be a part of them.'

'They might not see it that way, if it came down to it.'

'If it came down to it,' she said, lowering her head and looking at him hard, 'we have a stack of treaties thick as a hymnal.'

'Paper, I've found, provides very little armour when the lasguns start firing.'

'Good thing *Greyhound* is made of adamantine, then,' she said. 'The Freeblade life has made you morbid, my dear. It's quite boring. Where is that woman with my vin?'

When the cogitator screen snapped off, and the lock on his door disengaged, Rakkan assumed his duties for the night had concluded.

Was it alarming that the lights snapped briefly off, before red emergency light threw everything into crimson shadow?

Two drinks ago, it might have bothered him more. But the fourth drink always did him in. And how many had he had now? Six? Seven?

When he'd begun watching the ceremony in the basilica, the amasec bottle had been half full. Now it… wasn't.

But how could they have expected less, making him watch his own homecoming? His mother speaking to that Sycorax woman. You'd think she'd recognise her own son.

Though she hadn't, had she?

'Old Yarrick knew,' he mumbled to himself. 'He could tell the scent was off.'

The dog knew him better than his own kin. If that wasn't just a perfect encapsulation of his upbringing on Dominion, he didn't know what was. One year with his mother's people, changing custody at midwinter to spend the next year under his uncle and the shadow of expectation cast by his dead father.

A life split between hemispheres. Two families, two bedrooms, two different sets of cousins for friendship. Two lives.

And in each house, a constant berating of the other. Endless screeds about who had stolen the world from who. The failings of his mother's people, and his father's people.

That was their one thing in common: they all seemed to have a lot of failures.

In a way, he was glad to see this homecoming from a distance. Festival days and tournaments at Gathering Palace were always stomach-churning affairs, his two families uniting in a dance of revulsion and spite. No one able to talk behind anyone's back any more.

All of them bragging, fighting, manipulating for his approval. Hoping that he would either join their house or – if he should be successful at court – grant them favour.

Better to be here.

Except, no it wasn't. This deep in the bottle he could admit that.

Anyone could've told him that this would sting. Watching Sycorax be better at being him than *he* was. So clever. Deflecting, probing, keeping it light when he might have gone stormy and caused his mother to raise her ion shield. Being the person he once was. Getting the approbation, the attention.

She was a monster, of course. His mother certainly, but Sycorax even more so. They all were, these new companions-in-arms. Raithe with his steely coldness, looking at you with those copper eyes like you were equipment. Koln, who studied people like they were insects pinned to a board. Sycorax, with the brilliance to manipulate others' emotions without the empathy to understand the damage she did.

Did they even know how badly this would hurt? Was that simple humanity beyond them, or did they simply not care?

At least the dog knew him. You can't fool a dog. Good little vassals, them.

His eye fell on his father's helmet. Sycorax had little interest in it – she'd tried wearing it as a prop when they returned to dress for the party, but it was dead, a curiosity – so she'd forwarded it on to Rakkan on the *Stiletto*.

'Well, father.' Rakkan picked it up, looked into the frosted eye slit. 'Looks like we're both observers now, eh? I'm two steps from a spirit in the helm.'

Staring at it, he felt his back prickle. Felt a pull of morbid curiosity.

The helmet they'd pulled off his father's body when he'd piloted the Knight *Jester*. The great and martyred Sir Selkar Fang.

He could see that the padding around the chin was stained crimson. He lowered it onto his head, saw a cursor blinking in the left margin of his vision.

>*Hail, Sir Selkar Fang*
>*What is the duty of a wounded Knight?*

Taste of blood in his mouth. Choking. Smoke-twisted sky.

Rakkan tore the helm off his head. Looked inside, held it up to the light. For an eye-blink, he thought he saw the gleam of wet blood smeared around the mouth seal. But when he touched his face, all he felt was fear-sweat.

Dead. It was dead. Spitting nonsense. A venerated relic rumoured to have been used with *Jester* from the Settlement Era, irreparably damaged when his father died. But still and all, just an old helmet.

Throne, he was jumpy. He needed more amasec.

The first clue that he was too far gone was when he got up from his chair and had to catch himself on the table. What with the dark and the drink, he'd forgotten that Sycorax was wearing his leg braces – damn her for that too. He reached out for his crutches and slowly made his way towards the door, leaning heavily on one as he opened the heavy bulkhead and shuffled into the gangway.

Red emergency lights splashed this corridor too, deepening the shadows and enhancing the strangling claustrophobia of the ship. There seemed to be so much less space inside this ship than out. This was partially due to the locked cockpit with its hardwired flight crew. Likely there were smuggling compartments too.

Tricky people.

Rakkan clicked down the engine room corridor, rubberine caps on his crutches snagging slightly on the grated floor. When he boosted himself through the oval hatch to the mid-deck crew area, the going became easier.

'Throne-damn Koln,' he cursed. She'd promised him a facsimile pair of braces, but she hadn't delivered. Clearly it hadn't been high on whichever of her twenty priority lists took precedence that day.

No amasec in his cabin. Cadian Leolac, yes, but he'd learned his lesson overindulging on that during his last deployment. Besides, no good to mix. He was already going to be in for it tomorrow morning.

He swung to the galley. One advantage of the drink was that his pain dulled, making it easier to move around. Rakkan leaned one crutch against the galley sink and unlocked the liquor cabinet, rifling through the wire racks to a good amber.

There. A Culanaan. Thirty-one year. Probably a waste to drink it when this far gone, but what the hells, everyone else got a homecoming party, didn't they? Even Gwynne was off with the sacristan order, chanting and being solemn at machines.

He pulled the cork, tilted it towards a glass.

Bang.

He froze, neck of the bottle poised over the tumbler.

That was an exterior hatch. Not the big cargo hatch at the back, or the crew hatches on the side – this was towards the cockpit. One of the emergency escape hatches Koln had shown him in case the craft ever went down. No more than a chute with a handle above it, meant to slide down, not climb up.

His brow furrowed.

Bang, bang. A squeal of protesting metal then: *Crack.*

That was a seal being prised open.

'Gwynne?' he called. He wondered if she was doing some kind of maintenance. He immediately felt stupid; silence answered and an icy trickle went down his spine, even to the vertebrae he could not feel.

His free hand fell to his jerkin pocket. The crisis vox Koln had given him. He'd joked about it then. *Is this a call bell? Will you come and bring me another glass of drivet?* he'd asked. *Hot water for a shave, perhaps?*

His pocket was empty. A flash memory: the crisis vox in his safe room, next to the amasec bottle. In the safe room he'd left when the power went out.

No, when the power was *cut*.

He swung himself around the kitchen, praying that the hitch-click of the crutches was not as loud as it appeared in his ears.

'My apologies, baroness,' said Koln, sliding up with a stemmed glass of vin as if called telepathically. She bowed low as she presented it. 'I had to dispatch my colleague on an urgent errand.'

'How dare you,' Rakkan said with humour. 'What could be more pressing than a woman with an empty glass? Pardon me, mother.'

'Not at all, dear. I've monopolised you. A parent's right.'

Rakkan stepped to a quiet corner, Koln at his elbow and speaking low as she activated her vox-dampener. 'Anything serious?'

'An alert from the *Stiletto*. Power loss, followed by a hatch breach.'

'A welcoming party from Symphonia Dask?' said Rakkan.

'Possibly. Counterintelligence. Or some other faction trying to gauge us for inter-house reasons.'

'Could they find our guest, or anything else they should not?'

'Not with a cursory search. I have hidden the usual caches of false secrets. Private letters, an obscura pipe. A few pornographic data-slates. They might stop there. But this party will go late into the evening. The sergeant decided to take care of it.'

'Is our guest in danger?'

'Not if he stayed put, but the data-spike says his hatch door is unlocked and open. No bleat from the crisis vox, which means they might already have him.'

'Damn it,' Sycorax swore. And for the first time since they'd walked into Gathering Palace, it was Sycorax speaking rather than Rakkan. The accent slipped back into place. 'We're blown if they find him. No way to explain that. Unless we do a double-bluff, plant my kit on his body and claim he's an infiltrator.'

'Our man is on his way. Whatever else you think of him, he is capable of handling things. If we're blown there's not much to do but exfiltrate as cleanly as possible and re-approach, but in case that doesn't happen, I need to stay and assess the political situation. It's unlikely we'll ever get both houses in the same room again.'

'Suppose you're right.' Rakkan sucked air through his teeth. 'Let's just hope our man doesn't take matters into his own hands if there's been an exposure – he saved me with the dogs. More pertinently, dear mother's opinion on Imperial ties was… enlightening. Borderline secessionism.'

'The talk at this party is much less restrained than I'm used to.' Koln bowed, keeping the outward appearance of subservience for the benefit of onlookers. 'I've placed a few micro-voxes in the environment and the servants' halls. Later audio analysis will be needed to harden determination but the public belief seems to be that you're not fully independent, Sir Rakkan. That your move into court is part of a stratagem by Stryder.'

Rakkan grunted. 'Well, Baroness Hawthorn leads the house. It would be hard to see it differently. We'll have to balance that, won't we?'

'Access is our primary concern. Can't be cut off from half the court. If it's all right with you, I might suggest you talk to your uncle, Baron Kraine. With your mother, that would be the two heads of house contacted within a single evening.'

She nodded across the hall, across the moat and to a knot of red-tabarded courtiers gathered around a tall man with a black forked beard, a blue tattoo crossing his forehead like a circlet.

'Good plan,' said Rakkan. 'But stay close.'

'Why?'

Rakkan pointed towards a pair of nobles shouting insults across the moat. One, a smallish Rau woman with a short haircut, threw a vin goblet that splashed across the Stryder man's tunic. Shouts rose above the general buzz of conversation, causing the crowd to turn like hunting birds towards prey.

'Because I think someone's about to die.'

'Let us hope,' said Koln, 'that it's not us.'

TWENTY-THREE

As Rakkan turned to step through the hatch to his room, he saw the first stablight beam fan across the interior of the galley he had retreated from. The light beam traversed the space, dappling over the crew table and the cups of eating utensils set into it. When it hit them, it threw their shadows unnaturally long across the tabletop, the cup of forks sprouting a hedge of dark thorns like in the goblin stories. The knives stretching into dark swords.

Then it fell on the uncorked amasec bottle and abandoned glass.

Rakkan had not made it to the safe room. Instead, he shuffled into the humid dark of his own cabin, pushing the heavy door closed an inch at a time so it did not…

The hinges hit the sticking point and howled.

Running feet. Leather boots on metal decking.

Rakkan leaned into the door, put his shoulder into it to both keep him upright and slam it, one hand fiddling for the lock.

Instead, he found another hand. Leather-gloved, curling around the side.

He slammed himself into the door and heard a yowl as the hatch mashed the man's fingers. Rakkan put his back into it and shoved again, hearing the brittle snap of skeletal digits.

It gave him time. Time to fumble with the crook of his left crutch, the one the Imperial agents had never examined closely. He pressed the catch-stud and the saddle came free, the curve of its padded surface fitting his hand perfectly. He slid the long duelling barrel free, the folded trigger springing out and locking with a *click*.

The man on the other side of the door heaved, sending Rakkan sprawling backward.

He landed in the room's rotating chair, only staying upright because it was bolted to the floor.

A dark figure came at him, the red ammo runes of a pistol like a predator's eye in the darkness.

Rakkan's concealed laspistol was already levelled, two-handed. His fall into the chair had taken him below the assailant's firing line.

Rakkan's first shot lit the cabin red for a brief instant. He saw a footman in unmarked black livery, wearing a de-burnished breastplate and helmet common to the household guard. It holed his breastplate just below the sternum, boring a black hole through him.

Second flash, the shot hitting higher this time. Glanced off the top of his breastplate and ricocheted up and under his chin. The footman's head snapped back and he tumbled into the corridor, twitching.

He fell nearly into the arms of a second man, tangling up his primitive las-lock. Rakkan put two shots into him, the first burning a smear onto the bulkhead behind him, the second drilling his shoulder. The man screamed and writhed on the floor, the red-lit corridor smoky from the las-discharge.

The crutch-pistol's powercell was big. It took up the whole of the crutch saddle it was contained in. Rakkan could hold out a long time. He fired another shot towards the side of the door to make the point.

'Go!' he shouted. 'Take your damn men and go.'

Instead, a heavy metal object clattered into the room, nudging his numb feet.

Rakkan didn't realise it was a grenade until the room filled with noise.

'What started it?' asked Koln as she watched the two nobles inspect their rapiers.

They were standing back, outside the crowd so they could speak with some privacy and allow Sycorax's personality to re-emerge with minimal danger. The shouting had led to a blow, then challenges, and now the two stood on the bridge over the divided hall, the soles of their boots seeming to float a few inches above the heads of the boisterous crowd.

'I heard the one on the right, the Rau one,' Sycorax murmured, nodding at the black-haired woman who was looking down the tang of her blade. She was a serious type, hair cut short to her shoulders, perhaps in imitation of the Adepta Sororitas. It was both fetching and severe, complementing her angular frame and catlike eyes. 'She said that at the tournament she would put her feet on the other's Knight suit.'

Koln clicked her tongue. 'A great insult. One of the worst. My family tree is a bit outdated, but I do believe she's Lidya Vossa, pilot of *Stormrider*. Baron Kraine's daughter. Making her your first cousin.'

'Everyone's my cousin,' Sycorax scoffed. 'And the other, the boy?' She nodded at the young man on the other side of the bridge, who was seating his leather gloves and shaking out his shoulders.

'Sir Ishmayl Galvan,' Koln answered. 'Pilot of the Armiger Helverin *Skystrike*.'

'Dear mother's squire.'

Galvan was fair and pleasant to look at, hair parted off-centre and falling to one side like a breaking wave – his moustache, though, was not thick enough to be really convincing.

'Throne,' said Sycorax. 'They're barely of age. Must be sixteen, seventeen at most.'

'We weren't much older.'

She tilted Rakkan's head, pursed his lips. 'True.'

Baroness Hawthorn stepped up onto one side of the bridge, and Baron Kraine the other.

'State your reason for challenge,' said Kraine.

Galvan pointed at his opponent, slicing his rapier through the air. 'This loathsome villain–'

'Keep it brief,' interrupted Hawthorn. 'State your grievance.'

'She threatened to deface the honoured Knight suit *Skystrike*. To place her feet upon it, wipe her hands on its banners. Spit on its weapon mounts.'

'Can anyone swear oath that she spoke thus?' asked Hawthorn. A scatter of hands raised on the Stryder side. 'And you, young lady, what say you?'

Vossa grinned. 'He has stolen the words out of my mouth, baroness – just as his house stole the planet from beneath our feet. Now both will answer.'

Cheers from the Rau side, greeted by a wall of hisses.

Baron Kraine, Rakkan noticed, was not quite so cavalier. He dropped a hand on his daughter's shoulder, as if trying to restrain her.

Or, Sycorax thought, to have one last touch.

The baron raised his voice. 'Must we do this, Hawthorn? Is it not enough that their footmen skirmish in the palace? Do we need to mar this happy occasion with your nephew's death?'

'Ah,' said Hawthorn. 'We are playing to death then – I had

expected it to be blood, but if you want to send little Vossa to the ancestors I will not stop you. But either we must accept your apology, or you accept our challenge.'

Kraine whispered in his daughter's ear, but she shrugged his guiding hand off her shoulder.

'On behalf of house and ancestors,' she said, dropping into a guard stance and raising her weapon, 'I accept your challenge!'

Hawthorn and Kraine stepped away amid the roar.

'Kraine muttered something,' said Sycorax. 'As he stepped away. Did you get a read on his lips?'

'Stupid,' said Koln. 'He said don't be stupid.'

Then the fencers stepped forward and the blades met with a stinging clash.

The slap rocked Rakkan's head back. Brought him out of the muffled comfort of unconsciousness and back into the world of red light and blood.

Rakkan's vision blurred and drifted, doubling the man in front of him.

'Good morrow, Sir Rakkan,' the blur sneered. 'How strange to find you here.'

Rakkan responded by voiding his stomach on the man's shoes.

It wasn't intentional. Between the amasec, the stress response, and the smell of las-bolt-cooked flesh it was nearly inevitable – but his captor hit him anyway. Bright lights in his face, dazzling him. Not the compact stablights Guardsmen fixed to their lasguns or the headlamps of the granite mines of the northern hemisphere – these were chunky and barrel-shaped, their faces as big as a saucer.

If they hit him with one, Rakkan reflected, it would break his neck.

The questioner passed in front of the stablight, betraying his silhouette for a moment. Rakkan got the impression of broad shoulders and forearms thick with hair. The big man dragged a chair over and sat so close their toes touched. Rakkan smelled breath made rich and thick by spiced mutton and a coal-pipe habit.

'I have a quandary for you, Sir Rakkan.'

He paused, and Rakkan saw a glowing orange point in the light-washed darkness. A pipe. Rakkan could smell the sweet smoke, the coal plug soaked in barandictine liquor.

'You' – Rakkan felt a tap on his chest, and realised it was the pipe stem – 'are as of this very minute being banqueted in the great hall. And yet, here you are.'

Click of pipe on teeth. The orange glow again.

'Do you know Saint Cederic?'

Rakkan said nothing. Though he *did* know the old folk stories. They were pre-Imperial. A favourite among Dominionites, so much so that the Ministorum had successfully petitioned to make the local hero a minor saint – hoping that elevating a familiar figure would assist in conversion efforts.

'My old pater, he used to talk about how wily Cederic could be two places at once – fooling heretics into confessing up in the Stryder lands, while leading prayers in the domain of Rau. Know you that story?'

Rakkan said nothing.

'Are you a saint, Rakkan?'

Rakkan laughed, despite himself. Shook his head.

'So it's witchcraft then.' The questioner clicked his tongue. 'You know we burn witches here, *sir*. Have since time immemorial. That's why we survived the Age of Strife, when all those other worlds ignited with psyker eruptions. We torched the witches. Fire and blood, eh?'

The questioner stepped hard on one of Rakkan's shoes, then the other.

Rakkan felt a thump on his lap, saw the orange coal between his legs. Felt the searing pain of the lit plug burning through his trousers, the fabric under it blackening and curling away, with threads of orange around the expanding hole.

Instinct sent his hands flying to his lap, but the questioner grabbed and held them together. The smoker tried to force Rakkan's arms down, but after years on crutches and braces, the pilot's upper body strength was massive. The smoker grunted, and two footmen holding the lights put them on the deck and took his hands, each forcing an arm until the clenched fists rested knuckle to knuckle on the back of his neck.

Rakkan fought them, but it was hard to win a contest of strength when you could smell your own flesh cooking. Rakkan tried to jump his legs and throw the coal off, but without his braces, what leg muscles could respond were no match for the questioner's feet pinning them to the ground.

He fought the panic that clawed and convulsed in his gut. Breathed. Acknowledged the pain. Divorced his emotion and terror from the raw feeling. It was a familiar exercise – he'd had to do it before, when Gwynne built his augmetic braces and ran him through exercises as he learned to walk again.

Take the fear out of it, and Rakkan was well used to pain.

Instead, he focused on the smoker's face. He could see it now, between the ghostly after-images of the stablights that still floated in his vision.

He was a footman, Rakkan was sure of that. But one with a high rank. Possibly even a minor noble. The man was older, perhaps fifty, with a pitted face covered by a large mutton-chop beard that met above his thin lip. He smiled a bit, two teeth on the right worn halfway down where he seated his pipe.

Rakkan memorised the face. Thought about how he would draw it. He'd sketched as a child, still did on occasion. He met the man's eyes with hate.

'Tell us who you are,' the interrogator said. 'And how there are two of you, and this can end.'

Rakkan said nothing.

The smoker shrugged, and leaned down, using his pipe stem to nudge the coal an inch towards Rakkan's crotch. It was blackening, cooling. He pursed his lips and blew, flaring the little lump orange again.

Rakkan took another breath, growled as he let it out, settling into this new pain. Sweat slid down his brow and into his eyes. For the first time, he thanked the Throne that he'd drunk too much. Between that, the numbness of his injury, and his deep knowledge of managing pain, he could keep this up.

Not for long. But at least for a time.

'Come now, you know I don't like doing this,' said the smoker. 'Terrible, this kind of thing. Unpleasant for both of us. I'd just as soon get it over with. Because when that glowing little beauty reaches where it's going, you're going to squawk. And if you don't, you'll regret it.'

Rakkan knew it. And the pain was rising, along with the panic. The second one was the worst. He could feel it clawing up his throat from his belly, throttling him. Hitching his breath. Cutting off the supply of oxygen that was the lifeline keeping him calm.

'Who are you running this farce for, eh? Rau? Stryder? A member of court? The Inquisition?'

The smoker pushed the coal closer.

'You don't understand,' Rakkan said, tasting the tears that flowed freely down his face. 'These people. You don't know.'

'What people? Specifics, sir Knight. What don't I know?'

'They're terrifying.'

'I'm terrifying, goodsire.' He reached down to push the coal the last inch.

'Not like them,' said Rakkan. 'Not like them.'

Outside, a body clanged against the bulkhead.

TWENTY-FOUR

'When does a law come into being? When it is written? No. A law is merely ink on paper until it is used. It is the swing of a headsman's axe that conjures it into reality. A law comes into force when you apply exactly that – force. Fail to enforce the law, and it is broken.'

– Lucien Yavarius-Khau, High Monarch of Dominion,
from his *Meditations on the Code Chivalric*

Lidya Vossa scored the first hit, a savage lunge that brought her so far onto her front knee that the back of her calf and thigh touched, her long blade whickering in beneath the boy's guard and plunging into his chest.

The audience exploded, one side with cheers, and the other as if they'd been struck collectively in the stomach. The wind driven out of them.

Galvan hammered the pommel of his rapier down into Vossa's skull with a *crack* that reversed the noise – raising shouts from the Rau side and stunned cheers from Stryder.

The fighters parted, Galvan with a hand to the dark stain spreading on his jacket, Vossa with a wrist to her brow. When she removed it, a trickle of blood rolled down her pale face and collected in her eyebrow. They each retired to their sides of the bridge, as Hawthorn and Kraine assessed whether either injury was a mortal wound.

'Glancing hits, both of them,' mused Sycorax. Of all the assassins, she was the expert fencer. 'He twisted at the last minute, got pierced but managed to keep the blade outside of his ribcage. She twitched her head so the pommel strike didn't fall square.'

'They learned from the Balrissi-Cadmus manuals,' said Koln. 'Very good form.'

'That's the problem,' said Sycorax. 'Neither are very good. Good at drills and stances and technicals, sure. But they're playing regicide rather than fighting. Too ritualised. Doing everything like it was taught. Trying to outthink each other when they should be trying to out-feel each other.'

'I can think of a certain colleague who might like their regimented approach,' said Koln.

'Vossa has a little spontaneity – it was a good lunge.'

'You think so?' said a man, sliding up on Sycorax's right side. He wore bisected livery on his silver-chased doublet. An eyepatch, embroidered with a stylised lightning bolt, rested over one eye. 'It's been a long time, Linoleus.'

'Well met, Mauvec,' Sycorax said, fully submerging into the legend. Rakkan held out his hand and grasped the man's forearm, hoping Baroness Hawthorn hadn't been right when she'd said the man would break his fingers. 'Sir Mauvec Kawe, may I present Engine-Master Axanda Dak of the Verser trade consortium. Engine-master, this is my cousin Mauvec Kawe, my competitor in the Lists. If one could even call it a competition.'

Kawe snorted. 'I'm about as likely to end up in the *Crown* as you are, Linoleus. Two years back I stopped pretending neutrality and came out for Stryder. The Rau electors will veto me without question now.'

'So why stay in the Lists? Why not pledge Stryder, get married and serve the house?'

Kawe leaned in, his eyebrows high. 'Because of what you

just said, cuz. While I'm in the Lists I'm my own man. Court appointments and people interested in my support. Exit the Lists and vow to Stryder and I get to live under your mother's thumb for the rest of my life. She'll press me right into my grave with it. Besides, if I pledged Stryder I'd never be able to lay a wager on a Rau fighter at a tournament again. And I've made a good purse off Rau fighters on the field of honour recently.'

'Yes…' Rakkan faltered. 'I worried there might be a bit of poison between us, Mauvec. Because of the tournament, you know.'

Kawe shrugged, brought up his goblet. 'Embarrassing. But my own fault for not withdrawing and getting that hip rotation fixed. A mistake I'll never make again. Banish it with a tap.'

'With a tap,' Rakkan said, clicking his goblet to Kawe's.

'The important thing right now is…' Kawe turned and gestured with his glass towards the duellists, who had stopped assessing their injuries and were beginning to reapproach, testing each other with feints of their blades, trying to judge who would make the first true lunge. 'Are you going to lay out money on this, or are you going to be dull?'

Rakkan looked taken aback at the prospect, then swallowed a grin, like a man who should know better falling back into adolescence. 'I'll take Vossa. Shorter reach, but better speed.'

'True, but she's tiring out,' said Kawe. 'I'll venture a quarter purse.'

He held out his goblet, and the metal cups meeting joined the sound of clashing blades.

Through his magnoculars, Raithe could see two footmen outside the *Stiletto*'s cargo ramp.

Short-pattern autoguns. Black jerkins and bodygloves. Each with a dagger at the waist. An auto-carriage lurked nearby, the glow of a lho-stick ember in the driver's seat.

Raithe lay on a hilltop above the transport. It was a disused part of the landing fields, countryside that would otherwise have made good pastureland if embarking and disembarking starships hadn't burned circles in the grass.

Few void-worthy craft called at Dominion, but Raithe had specifically chosen a remote and inconvenient landing site to ensure they would not have visitors.

Yet they'd got them anyway.

Raithe took a comm-bead out of his pocket and nestled it in his ear canal. Twisted a winder to dial it in. Sounds of searching, hoarse orders in low voices.

He laid out a gun cloth as he listened, drew a Klavell stub -compact from the shoulder holster concealed under his jerkin. Raithe ejected the magazine and laid the body of the gun down as he inspected the magazine spring and ensured the bullets were not askew, risking a jam. Undid the slide and held the barrel up to the starlit sky before test-fitting the silencer, which was longer than the pistol itself.

In the event of a breach, Koln had rigged vox pickups in the *Stiletto* to broadcast in a local field, so any observers knowing the frequency could listen in and judge the threat from the outside.

Ideally, their response would be to let the unidentified hostiles search, as if the *Stiletto* had nothing to hide. It was why Koln hadn't rigged auto-weapons, explosive traps, or anything past a silent alarm and vid-recorder system. Better to look unremarkable and insecure. Let the enemy think they'd penetrated your defences, but keep your true secrets hidden a layer deeper.

But if they found Rakkan...

Voices in his earpiece, drifting in and out of audible range. Raithe froze and reached up to his ear bead to isolate the half-muffled voice between crackles, gingerly coaxing them to clarity as if he were dialling in range on a scope.

'*Are you a saint, Rakkan?*'

Laughter. Sardonic, tinged with pain.

'*Then it's witchcraft. You know we burn witches here, sir.*'

Raithe's hands flew. Barrel into slide. Slide onto gun body. Silencer threaded onto the barrel with deft twists of his hands. The magazine slid into the pistol's grip. He chambered the first round.

He came down the hill on the guards' flank, keeping the big auto-carriage between him and the sentries.

Even if he'd been spotted, his speed and the night would protect him. His dark blur racing down the slope could be dismissed as the shadow of a night bird passing overhead. Only seconds now, until the torturer did permanent damage. Raithe could hear Rakkan's breathing heavy through the vox-pickup.

'*Tell us who you are,*' said the voice in the comm-bead. '*And how there are two of you, and this can end.*'

Raithe opened the door of the auto-carriage.

The driver twisted, lho-stick glowing in his lips, brow furrowed.

Raithe grabbed him by the front of his jerkin and shot him point-blank. The long suppressor swallowed any flash or report from the Klavell, leaving only the *clack* of its slide. Not silent, not exactly, but a sound more like an industrial paper binder than a gunshot.

Raithe dragged the body free, let it fall to the ground.

The Klavell was no Exitus pistol, that was for sure. But even a tool as superb as the Exitus was not made for every job. The slab-like Exitus was difficult to conceal without disguising it as another object, impossible to carry into a party. And it was messy. An Exitus round would've blown the man open, spreading forensic evidence around the auto-carriage cab. They would have to ditch the vehicle later, and it was better to have no traces of violence.

The Klavell, by contrast, was easy to hide and supremely quiet. Its accuracy and range were nowhere near that of his beloved Exitus, but it sufficed for close work. Small, high-speed rounds made for minimal mess. No exit wounds. They entered the cranium and bounced around inside. Clean.

Raithe liked clean things.

And the recoil was gentle on his shoulder.

'Come now, you know I don't like doing this,' said the voice in Raithe's ear.

He leaned into the carriage's cab and turned its headlumens on the brightest setting. Put on the chaperon, the brimmed flat cap, that was sitting on the seat.

'Terrible, this kind of thing. Unpleasant for both of us.'

The two guards at the ship's rear-hatch ramp were coming towards the carriage, autoguns pointed down, hands up to shade their eyes.

He walked towards them, coming out of the light.

'Aye, Mikkal!' one said. 'What's with the lumen–'

Clack. Clack.

Both crumpled. Raithe walked between them without a glance.

'I'd just as soon get it over with. Because when that glowing little beauty reaches where it's going, you're going to squawk.'

Raithe walked into the cargo bay.

'And if you don't, you'll regret it.'

'Can you come help me with this?' said a footman prising at a hatch with an axe-tool. He barely looked over his shoulder.

Raithe pistol-whipped the man into unconsciousness. Better to leave one for interrogation. But the man's axe clattered as it hit the floor.

'Who are you running this farce for, eh? Rau? Stryder? A member of court? The Inquisition?'

'Clumsy ass!' came a voice, just around a stack of cargo caskets. 'The master said to do it fast and qui–'

Raithe grabbed the man as he came around the corner, wound the garrotte twice around his neck, then dragged him into the shadows. Raithe bent forward and rolled the man over his shoulder, back to back, as if he planned to throw him.

'*You don't understand.*' Rakkan this time, sounding pained.

When Raithe heard the man's spine snap he let the body down gently and released the garrotte, letting it zip-retract back into the bracelet fastened to his wrist. He drew the dagger holstered at the man's waist.

'*These people. You don't know.*'

Raithe moved fast now. He could hear Rakkan about to break, and if he could hear it, the interrogator could too.

'*What people? Specifics, sir Knight. What don't I know?*'

Raithe swept out of cover. Running now. Needing to clear a path to the asset.

A footman to his right spotted him, actually managed to swing his autogun up.

Raithe dropped him on the run. *Clack-clack.* First shot struck centre mass before the second tore out his voice box.

'*They're terrifying.*'

Raithe saw movement on the catwalk above, and threw himself sideways into the maze-like warren of containers.

'*I'm terrifying, goodsire.*'

Raithe took a flanking position, peered around to see a footman above with his autogun shouldered. Sweeping for movement.

'*Not like them...*'

It was a far shot for the Klavell. Out of its effective range for almost any marksman. Line of fire through hanging chains, railings and pipework. Hard cover. Only the top half of the target's body visible.

Less than ideal.

'Not like them.'

Raithe spun out of cover, wrists braced against one another, pistol and knife pointed in the same direction. The footman saw him and wheeled.

Clack. Clack. Clack.

Three shots, tight grouping. One spanged off the autogun casing and ricocheted into the footman's chest. Another drilled his shoulder. Third was a cranial.

But the target didn't drop, he flew – so surprised by the hits that he spasmed and jumped backward, his back hitting the railing so he went over.

And clanged hard on the inward-sloping curve of the cargo bay's bulkhead.

Silence in Raithe's vox-bead. Then…

'Someone's here,' the interrogator whispered. *'See what that was.'*

Raithe was out of ammunition. It didn't matter – no need to be quiet now.

He met the two footmen as they came through the darkened galley. Took the first one by grabbing his laslock barrel and yanking him forward, into the blade Raithe had taken from the dead footman.

Raithe rushed the other, using the dying man as a shield.

The second footman let off a panicked burst that drummed his comrade's back, the muzzle flash of the suppressed autogun lighting up the room, making the targeting easy as Raithe drew the laspistol holstered across the chest of his human shield and put two bolts into the shooter's chest, then as he hit the floor, another in the head.

Raithe's lip curled, disgusted, as he dodged into the officers' mess.

Lasweapons. Not proper firearms at all. No consistency from shot to shot. Power output always fluctuating. A miracle of engineering? Certainly. But no way to pack your own ammunition or hold a single round in your hand.

He dropped the laspistol on the table, pressed his hand to the false wood of the tabletop so the handprint scanner read his palm. Reached into the hidden vault when it slid open and felt the heavy, relieving weight of his Exitus.

Augmetic contact pads in his fingertips interfaced with the weapon, bringing it online.

'Listen, eh?' said a voice in the hall. The interrogator. 'I have Rakkan. We know your game. You withdraw right now or we burn his brains up with a las-bolt, understand?'

Raithe stepped into the corridor, and saw Rakkan on the floor of the hallway – dumped there, head resting against the opposite wall.

In the hatch to his left, Raithe could see a laspistol barrel nudging out of the doorway, pointed at Rakkan's head.

'We can do this easy, like,' said the interrogator. 'You go. Get off-world. I take Rakkan in. You're probably just some mercenary anyway, eh?'

'No.'

A pause. 'Who are you, then?'

It was a difficult question. Raithe was not an introspective man, and what self-knowledge he had he kept to himself. Even if he'd wanted to describe who he was, he would likely not be able to find the words.

But, in his own way, he told the interrogator who he was.

By sending a round through two bulkheads, directly into his head.

TWENTY-FIVE

'We pledged you loyalty unto death, not unto damnation.'

– Baroness Thulia Vossa,
in response to traitor forge world Ataxes' call to arms

'That thing,' said Koln. 'It's taken care of.'

'The sergeant is a reliable man – for simple tasks.' Sycorax sipped her vin, gesturing with the glass at the combat before them. 'I believe we're approaching an end here, as well.'

The duellists were huffing, blowing. Tired and making mistakes. Arms fatigued from the deceptive weight of the thin blades. Both dripped with perspiration, their undershirts clinging, pink where the sweat diluted blood.

'Come on,' said Kawe. He was so intent on the fight, Sycorax doubted he'd overheard them at all. 'Close on her. Close on her.'

Sir Galvan's superior reach and strength was beginning to tell. Vossa had cut him twice, but both were superficial. Only one had drawn blood – a good strike to the lungs he'd been forced to parry with his left hand, leaving him with a slash across his forearm.

He was pressing Vossa now, driving her back, controlling the bridge.

'Pity,' said Koln. 'I don't think Baron Kraine will be in a good mood for our initial contact.'

'Mother doesn't look so pleased either,' said Sycorax. 'I doubt she wants to test the High Monarch's favour right now. Too bad. Unless Vossa is drawing him in. If she's that clever.'

'You could stop it.'

Sycorax looked at her. 'What?'

'You're the guest of honour,' she said, as though this was no great matter. 'You could call a hold if you wanted. Bring peace to both sides. Didn't you read your briefing packet?'

Sycorax shook Rakkan's head, stepped out of the sonic dampener field with a release of pressure, like surfacing from water. Read the crowd to find the best avenue of approach.

Whatever resolve Galvan had lacked, it no longer held sway. Before, the two had been testing each other, almost friendly, but now he was sweeping and striking, battering Vossa's blade around. Forcing her to back to the last step and weave a prison of steel around herself. Blocking high, then to the side, the bigger combatant hammering at her like a blacksmith at the forge. One hit smashed her handguard, the metal coming loose and falling to the bridge. Another slashed down on her left shoulder, but it was too unfocused a blow and merely stung her with the flat of the blade.

And then, a lunge.

Sycorax saw the attempted parry come. Knew that the angles were all wrong.

Galvan's blade slashed through the curled wire of Vossa's ornate handguard and pierced the back of her hand. With a powerful outward sweep, her rapier came free, tumbling through the air on a comet tail of blood.

A severed finger tumbled in the basket hilt, like a panicked bird battering itself against its cage.

Galvan slashed back inward, blade tip cutting for Vossa's throat. The swelling roar of House Stryder rose to a crescendo as the blade swung towards the meat of a Rau neck.

'Hold!' Sycorax yelled.

The blade stopped, Galvan's arm bouncing backwards mid-swing as if he'd contacted a refractor field. Sycorax recognised the motion from her training days at the Callidus Temple – a lifetime of tilting field drills and tournament matches had stayed his killing blow.

The rising cries died as she walked up the steps and onto the bridge.

Galvan looked over his shoulder, annoyed, but inclined his head in greeting.

'An excellent display of bladesmanship, Sir Galvan,' said Sycorax, raising a goblet. 'Dazzling performance. And you also, Dame Vossa, well fought. But as the honoured guest I'm afraid peace must be brokered.'

'I did not need your help, sir,' growled Vossa.

'To die?' Sycorax responded. 'No, you had that part quite in hand, cousin.'

'You,' growled Galvan. Sycorax could see his chest heaving under the shirt, his knightly composure barely equal to suppressing the killing urge. 'You picked the moment of my victory to call a hold?'

'Indeed I did, sir,' Sycorax said. 'So that there could be no doubt who won the contest. You are my cousin, Sir Galvan, and I would not steal that from you. But surely you don't want to taint this homecoming with death? This way, you get the honour of the win without splashing her vitae.'

There was a pause, as both combatants breathed, tense. Sycorax let the moment stretch, hoping that the rest would be long enough to crash their adrenaline and let fatigue take hold.

'After all,' she added, 'blood is devilish hard to get off a boot. And those are good ones. Made by the old man in Salvar Street, I assume?'

'They are.' Sweat dripped from Galvan's face, his right arm trembling with the effort of holding his blade at guard in case this was a trick. His eyes darted from Sycorax to Vossa. 'You're in league with Rau, then?'

'I'm in league with court and king,' she said, raising her voice. 'Did you not see the ceremony? I don't blame you, there were a lot of Knight suits there. And Armiger pilots like ourselves can't always see over the shoulders of an Errant.'

Laughter rippled through the crowd at the self-effacing comment. Noble as they were, both Galvan and Vossa were Armiger pilots. On the low end of the aristocracy's ladder. Indeed, that's why their feud had been allowed to come to blows at all – factional conflicts, Sycorax had found, were always spurred by the minds of the old, but fought with the blades and blood of the young.

Old men did so like seeing their grandchildren die to uphold the family honour. But among the crowd were no doubt those, like Kraine, who found the entire thing stupid. A moment at the centre of a jest would be a way to punish them without the need for death.

'We,' sneered Vossa, 'are noble pilots of ancient machines. Our–'

'So it's *we* and *our* now, is it, cousin?' Sycorax turned on her. 'Rakkan the Peacemaker has brought the quarrelsome couple together.'

Vossa clenched her jaw at the laughter that followed. Eyes practically bulging in fury.

Got you, thought Sycorax. From the second she'd seen them sniping, she'd known there was something between them. The electric crackle of mutual attraction, suppressed and curdled by the twisted politics. Vossa, after all, seemed so fixated on him.

Sycorax stepped close. 'Take the loss, cousin. Living with defeat is better than dying with it.'

'You've ruined everything,' Vossa hissed.

'Maybe,' Sycorax said to her, then stepped away and raised her voice. 'All retire in honour from this fight. Galvan has shown the willingness to kill for his house, Vossa the willingness to die for hers. They are equal in valour. And if Dame Vossa wishes to avenge this loss, well, she can challenge Sir Galvan at the tournament tomorrow through the normal procedures.'

'It was to the death, Sir Rakkan!' called a voice in the audience. Sycorax saw a man in red-blue, with a falcon tattooed across his forehead. Lord Lambek-Firscal. 'Words cannot end a duel, only blood. Vossa called for a death-duel – this cannot be undone.'

'Correct, lord,' Sycorax said. 'That is the ancestral tradition. But I believe it is also tradition that if a duellist's weapon sheds innocent blood, the bout is cancelled, yes? And though I am not halfway innocent, I am in no way party to this duel.' In a flash, Sycorax reached out with her free hand, grabbed Galvan's blade, and slid her hand along it like a sheath.

'There,' she said, raising her hand to show the free-flowing blood. 'Is everyone satisfied?'

'Vossa will not thank you,' said Baron Tiberius Kraine. 'But I do.' He raised a goblet and Sycorax clinked it, remembering to nod slightly, and colour Rakkan's cheeks at the compliment.

'I'd like to get to know my cousins before they kill each other,' she said. 'Just for posterity's sake.'

Kraine put a wide forearm over her shoulders, and steered her towards the wall. 'I saw you talking to your mother. No doubt she talked about me?'

'Nothing that bears repeating. You know I don't like these questions, uncle. I'm no one's spy.'

'Of course not, of course not. My pardon. Old habits die hard.

You were still young when you left. But you're no aspirant being shuttled between houses any more – you're your own man, I respect that.'

Sycorax wondered if that was the case, or if Baron Kraine was an even savvier manipulator than Hawthorn. The best antidote for an overbearing mother, after all, was a slightly distant father figure doling out respect.

The kind of person a young man could build masculine rapport with and confide his family problems to. Problems that might provide actionable intelligence for House Rau.

Sycorax said nothing.

'Tell me about the war, then,' Kraine said, crossing his arms and leaning back on a table stacked high with liver-stuffed songbirds. 'Given the house quite a name, it seems.'

Sycorax took a pull of vin and shrugged. 'The hereteks came, and we killed them. Mostly infantry and armour. No Knight-on-Knight victories. And the hated arch-heretek, of course. Not much to say – they were vermin and I killed them as such.'

'And how goes the crusade, at the political level, I mean?' Kraine stuffed a songbird in his mouth and bit it through the breast. Sycorax could hear the bones crunching between his teeth.

'Can't really say. I was at the tip of the lance, mostly. Didn't meet anyone in command until the end.'

'Strange, usually crusade leadership shows a Knight of the realm a little more respect. Includes them in strategic briefings, at the very least. That's how it was when your father and I went on crusade.' Kraine popped the rest of the bird into his mouth and bit down.

'The Freeblade's path is quite different than a full complement,' said Sycorax. 'Especially a mere Armiger. I had a formal reception then was mostly left to my own devices to take my chainblade where I liked. Preferred it that way, in all honesty. No Militarum officer was going to issue me an order.'

'Quite right, Sir Rakkan, quite right.' Kraine nodded and chewed, then extracted a particularly tough leg, looked at the curled, blackened claws, and threw it on the floor. 'Still, it sits badly with me. This house used to command more respect.'

'Rau, you mean, or Stryder?'

'Both. You know that two years ago we got an order to muster and follow you?'

'And why haven't you?'

'Because it was an *order*, not a request,' Kraine sneered. 'It's that damned Guilliman. Thinks he owns the galaxy. Like we're all his vassals. In the old days, the Imperium remembered that we were allies. Treaty partners. We are far older than they are. Hells, the lowest foundations of Gathering Palace were laid before the Palace on Terra. They used to woo us, send diplomats. Now, we simply get an astropathic communique saying we should rally our lances for war? Not calling on our oaths or honour, but *commanding* us. Hah!'

'Perhaps it was an oversight. There is need for urgency, uncle. The Transmuted–'

'That,' said the baron, stabbing Sycorax's chest with a strong finger, 'is exactly what I fear. An oversight. My boy, you have fought in a crusade and think you know the Imperium, but you don't. Because let me tell you, planets die because of oversight. A slip-up in the paperwork and a water table never gets restocked. A system gets too quiet, minds its own business, and suddenly a tactical vassal on Terra decides it's not worth defending from the greenskin savages. If we let this *oversight* stand, if we turn the other cheek without defending our honour, it will be the death of us. Our rights will never be respected again – and if you ask me, that's exactly what Guilliman wants. To erode our autonomy. Bring us all in line, numbers on a ledger, easily counted. They'll want us adopting Imperial law next, I expect.'

'Surely not.'

'They did with Castelaide.'

'What?'

'Sent them a notice that their native land grant system and census didn't comply with the Lex. Forced them to accept a monastery of the Sisters of the Ebon Chalice too, and insisted Navy and Militarum servicemen be immune to local prosecution.'

'They didn't accept?'

'They did. The Knights of Castelaide have always been too...' He mulled the choice of words, then spat one out with venom. '*Flexible*. They felt they had no choice. Their options were to let the Imperials rewrite the treaty, or fight.'

'Mother said she'd fight.'

Kraine shot him a twinkling glance, as if he'd prised the information loose. 'No doubt she would, and it'd be just as ruinous as letting the erosion happen. Too soft and you lose your independence slowly, too hard it goes all at once. But if we put up a brave diplomatic front, insist on the mutual respect both we and the Imperium deserve, we can thread the needle. They want our Knights in the field, and they can't have that if they crush us. Guilliman is ruthless, but he's not stupid.'

'What–' Sycorax started.

'Father,' said a deep voice behind Sycorax's right shoulder. 'You know I loathe it when you speak like that.'

Sycorax turned, raising her goblet to address the stranger, saw a man in his natural forties – free of juvenat treatments. His left ear was augmetic, a disc inlaid in his skull and punctured by a warren of sensor holes to collect sound. Curly hair – only partially combed – gave him a younger appearance. His grey eyes peered from below heavy, straight eyebrows.

'My son,' Baron Kraine nodded. 'Lord Bazile Daggar-Kraine.'

'Lord Daggar-Kraine,' Sycorax bowed. 'You were an inspiration to me as a boy. All of us here, politicking, as you represented our houses in the Tyrannic War.'

'Only the furthest outer edge,' said Daggar-Kraine, matching the bow. Unlike the dark-haired baron, Daggar-Kraine's hair was honey-coloured and parted in the centre, falling to his jawline. His short beard had gone white on the chin. 'I daresay you saw as much combat,. with less armour between you and the foe. But if you'll excuse me' – he turned to Baron Kraine' – I have some words for my father.'

'Say your words,' said Kraine. 'We're all family. And he'll learn of our… disagreement soon enough. I'd rather he heard it first-hand rather than through the poison filter of the baroness.'

'Very well.' He took a goblet from a servant and sipped before starting. 'Lord Commander Guilliman is our ally. An ally in a difficult position, leading a fractious coalition, with the galaxy torn in half. It is more than understandable that he wishes to simplify some arrangements. Besides, his representative said nothing to me about changing the arrangements when I went to renew our oaths.'

'Treaty,' growled Kraine. 'You went to renew our treaty. We do not give oaths to Guilliman.'

'What is a treaty, father, but an oath on paper? An oath we intend to honour the terms agreed?' Lord Daggar-Kraine shrugged. 'It is semantics. Lord Commander Guilliman will not break his agreement provided we honour ours. And ours insists that we come to the common defence when called.'

'Come when called,' said Baron Kraine. 'Those are not Rau words.'

'Our house broke its oath once, father,' said Daggar-Kraine.

'How dare you compare this situation to that dishonour.' Kraine spoke low, nearly whispering, stepping close to his son.

It might have been subaudible were Sycorax's ears not so sharp. 'What would you have had the ancestors do? Make us traitors to fulfil an oath? March at the side of Horus?'

'Of course not. Morvayne and his brood were deeply misguided in putting their oaths to forge world Ataxes above sense. When Ataxes went with Horus, Morvayne went too. Foolishly, it turned out. I don't know why you even let Stryder needle you over it – we showed loyalty to our Imperial allies. But if we fail our oaths – our treaties, if you must – once again we will develop a reputation as mercurial.'

'You are young, son. You don't realise what the Imperium is capable of.'

'And you, father,' Daggar-Kraine responded, sipping, 'are old. And because you are old, you no longer think beyond orbit. Dominion is not its own fiefdom. We are but one Knight in a greater lance. If the lance charges together, we will survive. But if we all break off on our own, we will be destroyed. We can't all of us be Freeblade – no offence meant, dear cousin.'

'None taken,' said Sycorax. She covered Rakkan's flush of embarrassment by taking a songbird's beak between her fingers and twisting off the head, taking pains to mimic how a Knight standing behind the baron had used the sharp beak as a handle to place the skull between her teeth. The savoury brain was not bad – the crisped feathers, though, she could've done without. 'I feel positively spoiled by this homecoming. Particularly the vin, good Dominion vintage. Banish it with a tap.'

They clicked goblets.

Daggar-Kraine turned back to his father. 'You say I don't know what the Imperium is capable of, but I do. And unlike you, who hasn't left this world in decades, I've seen it myself. Under Guilliman, it's capable of change. Of shaking off the stagnation of ten thousand years. And we must be capable of change as well.'

'You see the kind of insurrection I have to live with?' said Baron Kraine, flashing a tight smile at Sycorax. 'Never have children, my boy, they're worse than those rebellious vassals out in the hinterland. I should recall Fontaine and his suppression force, let him take *Axefall* to you.'

Daggar-Kraine *tsked*. 'If he's up to it, he can try. How long does it take our august executioner to crush a rebellion? He's been out there three months.'

'Perhaps he needs some help,' said Sycorax. 'I have yet to pledge to a member of court.'

'You won't pledge to Rallan Fontaine, surely?' growled Baron Kraine. 'Man's a bore. And more importantly, a Stryder. Here's some advice – while the Master of Judgement seems like an exciting position, it's all dry legalism.'

'And everyone hates you,' said Daggar-Kraine, draining his goblet and tossing it on the floor to be retrieved. 'If I were you, I'd pick something closer to power. Less polarising.'

He beckoned and a vassal ran to him with another goblet, kneeling to the floor before proffering it upward with both hands and a bowed head.

'I'll tell you what you want,' said the baron. 'A good Rau master. Yuma's needed a squire for years.'

'Refuses to take one,' said Daggar-Kraine. 'Says all the young ones these days are soft.'

'But you,' said the baron. 'You're a crusade veteran. He might just make an exception…'

'*…if I put in a good word,*' the baron finished, his voice blurred by the playback on the groundcar's spool-slug player.

'Excellent pivot,' said Koln, arcing them around a tight turn on the dirt road and downshifting into the straight. The high-beam headlumens of the groundcar painted the moors that rose up around the dirt track. 'As Kingsward, Yuma has good proximity to the High Monarch, and it looks like you've gotten us in the door.'

'What do you think of him?'

'Yuma? Dangerous. Loyal. Stoic. But that's just my impression through documents and interviews.'

'No, I meant Lord Daggar-Kraine. He strikes me as interesting. With an interest in the big picture that's lacking in his elders.'

'That's true,' said Koln, tilting her head.

She slowed slightly and pulled to the centre to avoid a roadside bonfire. Serfs celebrating the eve of winter tournament. Sycorax saw their wan faces raise as the low groundcar slapped past – a vehicle entirely foreign to this place and its auto-carriages. Silver as a smoked blade, with a curved aerodynamic body.

'He's a tempting prospect,' Koln continued.

'For king?' Sycorax clarified.

'We'd have to work for it,' warned Koln. 'He's fifth in the Lists.'

'So we kill the other four.'

'Subtle,' Koln snorted. 'Might be worth it. Baron Kraine's dislike for the lord commander and Baroness Hawthorn's resentments are not isolated examples. From the vox-captures I made at the feast, this place is bubbling over with sedition.'

'Servants as well?'

'No, the ichthus is rotting from the head it seems. It's mostly the privileged that are souring on the Imperium, which is a problem since they control everything – and after all, it's the Knights we need for the crusade, not the serfs.'

'Think it stems from the High Monarch? He doesn't seem to speak much apart from through his herald.'

'He will at the tournament tomorrow. It's tradition. And tradition matters here.'

A blip in their micro-beads.

'Looks like we're in transmission range,' said Koln. 'Raithe, what are you up to?'

'Solving a problem,' said Absolom Raithe, as he reached inside the open door of the auto-carriage and disengaged the hill brake. He had to reach over the body of the driver, slumped on the wheel, his lifeless foot next to the velocity pedal.

Raithe popped the engine from idle to active, and dropped the corpse's boot on the pedal. He slammed the door as the vehicle rolled forward, picking up speed as the downhill momentum took hold. Five miles an hour. Ten. Fifteen. Twenty.

It was doing thirty when it hit the cliff edge and disappeared, somersaulting down through the air as it passed the grey slate of the rock face.

The carriage struck on its roof, hitting the sea's surface with a slap and bobbing for a moment, bubbles boiling the water around it in bursts of escaping air as the incoming surf tilted it back and forth – slowly sinking until the tyres vanished.

'Executed an ocean dump. The continental shelf drops deep here, they won't find the vehicle.'

'*Tell me you left one alive,*' said Koln in his ear.

'He was forthcoming,' said Raithe, emotionless. 'Hardly had to push. They're Symphonia Dask's men, off-worlders mostly, brought in so they have no previous ties to the houses. Led by Sir Hortius Sabban, nasty character. Dask's unofficial squire and dirty-work man. Which presents a difficulty.'

'*What?*'

'She's expecting him to report back in forty minutes. Which is hard, considering he's in a chilled drawer in the *Stiletto*, and in no condition to talk.'

TWENTY-SIX

> *'Think on your oaths before you swear them. Consider Lady Sakkaran, who in high spirits swore to never remove the mail coat Queen Favla-Astair gifted to her at Midwinter Feast. She kept her word, and now her bones lie at the bottom of Lake Vadlar. We celebrate her for choosing eternal honour over temporary life, but had she chosen her oaths more carefully, she might have had both.'*
>
> – Lucien Yavarius-Khau, High Monarch of Dominion, from his *Meditations on the Code Chivalric*

'So,' said Sycorax. 'What are we going to do now?'

The enemy operative lay in the morgue drawer, his head ending just above the lower jaw. The orphaned lower palate and tongue left enough for roughly a quarter of a dental impression.

'We have a name,' said Koln. 'We have audio and vid-clips. And we have twenty-two minutes. Sycorax, could you pull off a mimic in time to meet Dask? We could learn a lot from the debrief.'

'Difficult without a full face to study and reconstruct.' Sycorax flipped through still images on a data-slate. 'I could create an approximation, get through a few checkpoints, but it won't be convincing in a conversation, especially if Dask knows him well. The look will be off. It'll be missing the mannerisms, gait, hairstyle, little tics. We won't have time to launder the blood off his clothes. She's a trained counter-intelligence officer, she'll get suspicious. And even if I could extrapolate from footage, doing that and arriving in time is impossible. Did you *have* to take a headshot?'

She shot a look at Raithe, who was leaning against the bulkhead, arms crossed.

'Yes,' said Raithe. 'He had a gun on Rakkan. A chest shot risked him discharging a round via muscle spasm or shock. And we'd agreed that Rakkan is useful to us alive for now.'

'*For now*. Thanks for that,' said Rakkan, holding a chemical ice pack to his lap. 'Really, thanks. Good to know where I–'

'But we also agreed,' said Raithe, 'that if Rakkan was discovered we would kill him. Sycorax, do you want to do the honours?'

Sycorax, stepping in front of the pilot, shielded him with her body. 'Raithe, this is harder than any of us thought. If Rakkan had not been advising me, my cover would've been blown already. By his mother. By the dogs. The situation is too complex and evolving to kill him now.'

'Agreed,' said Koln. 'And it would likely mean Gwynne would expose us.'

'We had a plan,' Raithe growled. He drew his Exitus pistol. 'A plan we agreed to follow.'

'And here's my plan,' said Sycorax. 'If you kill him, I'm done. I'll sit on this deck and refuse to take my cover as Rakkan again. You're being ridiculous. Just because you said you would do something, doesn't mean you have to follow through if it doesn't make sense any more.'

Raithe looked at her, straight in the eyes. She could see him deciding whether to kill her, and how. 'Fix this, minimise the exposure risk, and he can live. But do it fast.'

'Sir Sabban will miss his appointment,' said Koln, cutting in. 'And when he does, Dask will send a team to find out what happened. If he was supposed to check in by vox, reinforcements might already be on their way. Rakkan, you said Sabban never used the vox after finding you. Never made any report or update?'

'No,' said Rakkan. 'He just took out his pipe coal and...'

'Nothing picked up by the transmission-thieves,' said Raithe. 'I checked their vox-unit while clearing the scene.'

'Did you keep it?' Sycorax asked.

'Of course,' he said. 'For analysis. Why?'

Sycorax tapped the slate.

'Then it's witchcraft. You know we burn witches here, sir.'

She rewound it, the words reversing in a high squeal. Stared into the plasteel wall, lips moving.

'–itchcraft. You know we burn witches here, sir.'

'You know we burn witches here, *sir*,' she mimicked. 'So we have a vox, we have a voice.'

Sycorax turned to Rakkan. 'Meaning you have ten minutes to tell me everything you remember about Sir Sabban.'

'We'll need vox-codes,' said Koln, pulling on a pair of rubberine gloves. 'I'll have a discussion with the prisoner.'

'Cast lots, cast lots,' Sycorax said into the plastek brick of the hand-vox. She heard the signal buzz then die, and swore at the ancient tech. Moorland wind, sharp as a knife-edge, tossed her replicated hair as she knelt and re-wound the crank on the power unit. Clicked the transmit button experimentally.

Had to be careful with that. Everyone transmitting had their own fist, their own style of clicking the transmitter. Heavy or light. Long or short. A good vox-operator could tell the difference before you even spoke.

'Cast lots, cast lots. This is Outrider. Accept my hail.'

'We have received you, Outrider. Code word accepted. Hold fast.'

Sycorax let out a breath, seeing the mist of her exhalation

twist away in the night wind. She'd ridden hard on a dirtcycle, without lights, to find this isolated moortop. Just in case they tried to triangulate her signal and found it coming from the ship.

'What did you discover?' said the voice. It was cool and hard-edged, like a dagger blade in the winter chill. Accustomed to obeisance.

Baroness Dask? Sycorax could only assume and hope. To confirm it by calling Dask by name, even over a secure vox-channel, would be a major protocol breach. The lady would get spooked and cut the line.

'We followed your orders, ma'am. Full search. But were spotted. The sergeant from the entourage returned. He saw us, opened fire and we retreated.'

'Did you kill him?'

She paused before clicking the transmit button, as if worried about the answer. 'No. We worried that if we had, there would be an enquiry. This way he assumes we're with the hinterland rebels. Bad judgement, landing so far out on the moor. Better for Sir Rakkan to stay in the palace as he was offered.'

'We shall say that if they ask questions. Can this vassal, the sergeant, identify any of your men?'

'Aye, I believe so.'

'That is a difficulty. You know I don't appreciate difficulties.'

'I've taken care of it. You won't be seeing them around. In the drink off the Valsof Cliffs. Off-worlders, no way to tie them to us.'

'Good. When can you report to me?'

This was the dangerous part. The *very* dangerous part. Rakkan's memories of Dask were years old, and likely coloured by the fact that he'd formed them as a younger man. But he had recalled a deep antipathy between Dask and Fontaine. It supposedly reached back to their childhoods. While public allies as the Stryder representatives to court, family gossip was that neither liked nor trusted the other.

'Apologies. The sergeant saw my face. Going to disappear for a while. Make myself useful. I was thinking go out to the hinterlands and check in on Fontaine. Feels like he's dragging his feet on the suppression. Might be something there to know.'

A pause. Longer than Sycorax would've liked.

'*Are you afraid to come back to me, Sabban?*'

'No, no, lady, I… This is the best way to solve our problem. Get some benefit from it. I saved one man, an off-worlder. He can report to you tomorrow at the tournament, blending with the crowd. I'll give him my Saint Judat medal, the one with my initials to prove I sent him. But I have to ring off, I see search-lumens. Do I have your blessing?'

A long pause. Sweat dripped down Sycorax's spine.

'*Yes, send him. And when you get to Fontaine's camp, keep aware of any of those exotic vox-sets. Maybe that girl was with Fontaine, maybe with the rebels, but I doubt it, the kit was too specialised.*'

'I will.'

'*We wouldn't be in this position if you'd taken her alive, you know.*'

'I know.'

'*I'm losing my patience with these missteps.*'

'The lights are close, I have to–'

But the line wasn't answering.

Sound reverberated from the walls of the Sepulchre of Holy Maintenance, bouncing off hard stone, echoing in the side chapels and dissolving ethereally in the shadowed vaults overhead.

Even as the final note buzzed in her sensors, a single tear of lubrication fluid fell from Gwynne's left ocular bionic. This, this was where she belonged. Among her fellow servants of the machine lords. Under the benevolent, bifurcated face of the Omnissiah that was itself a marriage of bone and steel – much like the Knights.

And this ceremony, unworthy as she was of the honour, was to welcome her back.

'All rise, brethren,' said the Arch-Maintenancer from her position on the pulpit. She stretched out her arms as she said it, beckoning them to their feet. Four mechadendrites mirrored the gesture. 'Praise be to the Omnissiah, the creator and sustainer, for seeing His servant Gwynne home to us. And praise Him for bestowing the wisdom and talent upon her to keep noble Knight *Jester* from falling to the hands of the enemy.'

'Praise,' intoned the congregants.

'This ends our services for the evening,' she said. 'Tomorrow is tournament day, please congregate two hours before dawn to say the Invocation of Optimisation. May the Omnissiah be glimpsed through your works.'

'And through your works,' the brethren answered.

Gwynne answered with them – looking at the crowd out of the corner of her right visual quadrant, pleased to once again be among friends.

'Sacristan Gwynne?' said a voice that broke her reverie.

Her breath caught when she saw who called her.

The Arch-Maintenancer herself, halfway through the door in the rood screen behind the altar, beckoning for her to follow.

Gwynne's circuits felt alive when she stepped through the opening, reverberating like the final notes within the sepulchre.

She had never been behind the screen before – nor had she been so close to Arch-Maintenancer Dorthiya Tessell.

Tessell, or at least what organic parts remained of her, was an old woman. She appeared almost shrimplike, given her bent back and the number of mechanical limbs that sprouted from her crimson robe to support her, so that her bare feet hung suspended six inches above the floor.

She looked at Gwynne, and while a vox-hailer in the shape of a smiling mouth had replaced her lips and lower jaw, her eyes, both natural, were a stunning crystal blue.

'Arch-Maintenancer.' Gwynne prostrated herself, and ceremonially opened her data-ports to show she hid nothing. 'I'm unworthy of this attention.'

'Unworthy,' Tessell cackled. 'If you wish to progress, young sacristan, you will abandon the idea of worthiness. We care for the immortal children of the Machine God, His nobility and fury made manifest aeons ago. No one is worthy of that role, and yet someone must do it, so we do.'

'Yes, Arch-Maintenancer.'

'Look at these death masks,' she said, raising her data-cane, so Gwynne could sight along the shaft. 'There is *Shieldmaiden*, who held Lord Macharius' flank against traitor Titans. Below it, *Thunderhead*, so well remembered in *Ballad of the Reactor War*. Across from them, *Splitter of Stars*, who to this day has slain more heretek war engines than any other Knight of Dominion. These are the finest of our fallen, here as an honour for them, but a warning for us. A reminder of our failure.'

'Our failure?' asked Gwynne.

'To keep them operable,' said Tessell, lowering her data-cane. 'These machine demigods might still be with us today if our skills had not been found lacking. These are the ones we could not save, child, and it should haunt us.'

Gwynne saw the pinching around the Arch-Maintenancer's eyes, the regret and burden carried there, and her all-too-organic heart broke for the woman.

'They are war machines, mistress, and war is cruel,' Gwynne said. 'But you have also saved so many. You attended to the

Crown of Dominion after its battle with the heretek Knight *Dawn of Slaughter*, is that not so?'

Gwynne knew it was, but she hoped the reminder of the Arch-Maintenancer's greatest achievement – saving the *Crown* – might salvage the great woman from her melancholy. The damage, from what Gwynne had heard whispered, had been extensive.

'I did, I did. Praise the Omnissiah for sending one of the Emperor's Angels to serve as my right hand.'

'A great deed, mistress, the greatest of a generation.'

'It seems such a lifetime ago that it's like another person did those deeds.' She shook her head. 'How operates your liege lord, *Jester*?'

'It goes well. *Jester* is an excellent warrior with a strong spirit. The right-leg Achilles piston is occasionally obstinate for the first three hundred and twenty-eight seconds of operation.'

'Nothing unusual for a machine of its age.'

'No, mistress, its operational health is exemplary. Its spirit choir is stubborn, as you know, but in a physical sense it is a sound machine, and campaign damage has not changed that.'

'And how have you found… the crusade? Taking to the field amongst our enemies?'

'War is extremely damaging to the machine lords. I hadn't imagined there would be anything bigger than them. And the Transmuted, they are dangerous. Twisted, and under the slavery of a daemonic meme-virus that causes them to torture their bodies into new forms. I had to ensure strict protocols to avoid *Jester* becoming contaminated.'

'I was referring to our other enemies, in the Mechanicus.'

Gwynne paused, wrinkled her brow. 'I found the enginseers helpful when I needed to call upon them. They extended me a great deal of professional courtesy when–'

Tessell whirled around, fast as a feline, her steel spinal column rising as she twisted oddly. 'You did not let them assist with *Jester*? Let them gaze upon the lord's internals?'

'Of course not,' Gwynne said, trembling a little at the Arch-Maintenancer's hard gaze. 'But at times we needed materials and tools. Furnaces to melt the raw adamant and patch armour plating. Equipment for milling replacement parts.'

The Arch-Maintenancer's arched back relaxed.

'Forgive my alarm, Gwynne,' she said, sketching the sign of transgression forgiveness in the air with two gold-inlaid fingers. Gwynne could not tell if the one being forgiven was her or the Arch-Maintenancer. 'I misunderstood.'

'Do we have enemies in the Mechanicus?'

'One enemy, at least,' said Tessell. 'Did you meet any agents or representatives of the heretek Belisarius Cawl?'

'Cawl?' Gwynne asked. 'No, Arch-Maintenancer. The arch-magos dominus is sectors away. At least from what I heard. His name was barely mentioned.'

'Huh. That is exactly what he would like us to think. Did you see any of his Primaris Marines, or his levitating abominations?'

'I have seen Primaris Space Marines, from a distance at least. And when we were formally received by high command. Are these warriors heresies?'

'Of course they're heresies.' The Arch-Maintenancer threw up her four arms. 'Cawl is no longer replicating or improving, not following a template of any kind – he's creating. And what is it, young sacristan, that creates?'

Gwynne swallowed. 'A god.'

'Indeed. A god. And that's what the heretek Cawl thinks he is. He worships *change*, just as much as these Transmuted hereteks your lord so ably fought. There are even rumours that he plans to create new Knight suits, believing he can improve upon the mechanical lords.'

'No,' said Gwynne.

'Oh, yes,' said Tessell, raising her eyebrows. 'He has fashioned a new plasma decimator. Even named it after himself – *Cawl's Wrath*. Imagine such arrogance. Imagine thinking one could improve upon *this*.'

The Arch-Maintenancer spread her arms to indicate the death masks of hero machines that surrounded them, each empty stare judging their custodianship of Dominion's legacy.

'It is impossible,' Gwynne shook her head. 'He could not manage it, he will fail.'

'Yet he has done many impossible things,' said Tessell. 'So let me ask you again, when you were in the circles of politics, did you notice anything unusual? Any hint of the heretek's influence?'

'I did not,' said Gwynne, turning away in shame. 'Though I was not looking for it. Perhaps if I was, if someone had told me…'

'Be not troubled.' The Arch-Maintenancer laid a clammy, comforting hand on her shoulder. 'You left in the night, both you and the human component wounded. Indeed, I am glad to see you functioning so well, given the damage the las-bolt did to your engrammatic banks.'

'I lost only personal memories,' said Gwynne. 'Nothing affecting functionality.'

'That is a comfort.' She paused. 'Dear Gwynne, I know that if I asked, you would do anything for our order.'

'But of course, mistress.'

'What I am about to tell you is in the strictest confidence. It is a fraught time for Dominion, the human component of the *Crown* is showing wear, nearing breakdown. And you know what that might mean for the houses.'

'War.'

'Yes. And if there is war, the lords will be damaged or destroyed.

If there is a conclave to appoint a new king, I will need you to keep your auditories on high alert and tell me of anything you hear.'

'Yes, mistress, but…'

'But?'

'Is not our order apolitical?'

The Arch-Maintenancer chuckled. 'There is no such thing as apolitical, child. In fact, declaring ourselves apolitical is the deftest political move our order ever made. The appearance of neutrality magnifies our influence – influence we use to keep the houses from descending into war. Our single vote has made many a monarch, and prevented many a conflict by swinging the selection towards a compromise candidate. This is known, but what is not known is that our appearance of being above the fray is what gives us that power.'

'Then in this time, your vote must count for a great deal. If something happens, the members of the court will no doubt vote for their own candidates.'

'We shall see,' said Tessell, her mouth turning up on either side of the vox-hailer. 'Baron Yuma is a fair man devoted to the safety and security of the High Monarch and his office above all things. He is a Rau, of course, but his loyalty is to the *Crown*. He could be swayed… You might even steer your human component towards service with him. We could influence his vote. And if your pilot swears fealty to Yuma, I will need you to bring *Jester* to me for reconsecration of its neural uplink, to ensure a strong bond with the hallowed *Throneshield*.'

'I will keep you apprised, and do it well. I know you will be watching.'

'Don't worry about me,' said Tessell, gesturing to the masks, whose empty eye slits seemed to flicker in the shifting light of the votive candles. 'Worry about them. I certainly do.'

TWENTY-SEVEN

'According to legend, we sacristans invented tournaments. Our hope was that the pilots could enjoy the pleasure of violent dominance without actually destroying the machine lords. You know, have a little civil war of their own and feel glorious without actually murdering each other. It works out, mostly.'

— Sacristan Gwynne, pre-operational Interview 11.2, Mission Day: 19

Ninety thousand voices roared when the portcullis went up. Musicians, positioned in raised boxes amid the stands, blew trumpets so long they had to be supported on legs that reminded Raithe of the bipod on his rifle. Servitors wired into armatured exoskeletons twelve feet high, their hands capped with rubberine mallets, beat two bass drums the size of landing pads.

The sound crashed down on Raithe, like the waves that had almost drowned him, rumbling his innards as if it were an explosion. A tremendously heavy sound, both brassy and feral. Louder than some battles he'd experienced.

And then, the Knights entered. First came Sir Renauldus Tarn-Kegga, victor in the summer tournament, with second and third place finishers trailing behind. Mounted in the Knight Warden *Horned Hunter*, Kegga waved at the crowd with his massive thunderstrike gauntlet, white ribbons fluttering in the stiff onshore wind that had blown up the night before.

'Kegga! Kegga!' chanted the crowd, shearing off the name of the mother he so hated.

It must have been bittersweet for Kegga, Raithe reflected. As the reigning champion – and a candidate in the Lists – he would have automatically had an extra vote if Yavarius-Khau died and the court went to conclave. Successions had been decided over less, unless Rau intentionally scuttled him for another candidate.

But now he would need to battle it out again, and risk losing the adamantine mail cape that cascaded down his left pauldron, marking him as the victor, and the Banner of Triumph hanging between his Knight's legs.

Next came the Questoris Knights of the Lists in their quartered blood-red, sky-blue armour, marching in two lines, weapons peace tied. Each wore the trophies of previous wins, banners fluttering from between legs and on poles fastened to their rounded backs. Their tilting shields – ceremonial ones, unmarked by battle and chased with gold – sparkled in the winter dawn. Their massive reactor vents hazed the air above, and their heat-wash melted the coating of frost on the grass of the field.

Then came Rau and Stryder, each in tandem, led by Baroness Hawthorn in *Greyhound* and Baron Kraine in *Firedrake*. Each line of Knights stared straight ahead, refusing to look at their rivals.

And then all stopped, the train stretching from one side of the long tournament oval to the other. Like a Militarum drill team, the two lines of war engines put one foot behind and pivoted smartly to face the other. They presented their right-hand weapons in a salute.

A tunnel of weaponry.

Silence. Wind, and nothing more.

Then from the shadow of the portcullis came a noise like a

great cetacean calling. A howling, singing note that was more predatory and animal than machine. It spiked Raithe's vitals.

Crown of Dominion stalked through the portcullis, its crowned head nearly scraping the spikes of the gate. Its body shone, scrubbed fresh for the occasion, and victory banners hung from each of its massive arms. Even from up in the stands, it looked far more massive than it had in the shadowy basilica.

The two falcon-servitors flew before it, dropping rose petals in its path. Cannons blasted streamers and incense smoke into the air so they fizzled on its ion shield.

Neither beweaponed arm had a peace tie, Raithe noticed. A security protocol. Every battle cannon, thermal spear, and chain-blade on the field was empty of ammunition and fuel save that of the High Monarch. Only his shield sizzled the air.

And he almost missed his cue as the entire population of the grandstands, enough to fill a small city, fell to their knees and bowed.

As Raithe knelt with them, he raised his head enough to look at the massive helm, nearly as large as he was tall.

And thought of the honour he would gain in killing such an impossible target.

'Is everyone in position?' Koln said into the high-gain micro-bead. She could operate it just by moving her throat, without noise, but didn't bother while embedded in the roaring crowd. The device itself was surgically implanted deep in her ear canal, invisible to detection unless someone cut her open.

'*Check*,' said Raithe. '*Moving to meet.*'

'*Check*,' said Sycorax. Hers came in a little strangled, under-water. She was in company and couldn't speak openly.

'Check,' sneered Rakkan beside her, raising a flask in salute, his eyes never leaving the Knights on the field. He took a pull.

'Just like we discussed,' said Koln, her eyes sweeping the sheer number of bodies in the stands. 'Because if anyone gets in trouble, I don't like our options for extraction.'

Sycorax didn't, either. In fact, she couldn't think about much else when she left Gwynne to ready *Jester* for the tournament ground and made her way up from the Armiger depot.

Lowly Armigers didn't march in the royal procession. That was for Questoris-class Knights only. The pilots might rank equally with those in the larger machines – but when mounted the larger machines took precedence.

That was no surprise, she supposed. On an ordinary feudal world, a Knight with an army would wield more power than a lord with a retinue – and each Questoris Knight was as good as an army.

But while tradition barred the Armigers from taking part in the procession, it did leave them time to prepare for the first matches of the day. Around the depot, pilots checked their mounts and sacristans buzzed and tittered – removing peace ties and making final adjustments with their mechadendrites.

There would be a few Armiger competitions, perhaps even a challenge or two, before the bigger Knights took the field.

Sycorax raised Rakkan's hand in greeting at Sir Sangraine, a young Stryder whose Armiger Helverin, *Fencer,* had been prepped in the maintenance bay alongside *Jester,* and who'd chatted with Sycorax about possibly forming a double for a two-on-two match that afternoon.

She'd politely said that she was keeping the first day's schedule open until she'd met with Baron Yuma. No sense being coy or secretive about that, it was universally known that as the Knights jockeyed for position on the field, their pilots were doing the same in the box.

But then Sangraine said, 'Shame about Galvan.'

'What?' she asked, executing the subtle blink Rakkan did when surprised.

'Galvan and Vossa,' said Sangraine, amazed. 'You didn't hear? Galvan and Vossa resumed their duel after the reception. Galvan's dead.'

'Holy Throne.'

'You really should be staying in the palace, Rakkan. You miss a lot sleeping out on the moor. I tried to rush to your mother as soon as I heard, swear as her new squire, but that little snipe Andricus got there before me. Sworn and bonded this morning.'

'Tragic.'

Now as she reached the stair, Sycorax passed Lidya Vossa, already sitting in the cockpit of *Stormrider*. The young woman caught sight of her and stood up in the seat, her fist pointed in Sycorax's direction, a fresh bandage swathing her reattached finger.

A challenge.

'Tomorrow, Vossa, tomorrow,' waved Sycorax, with such a note of patient annoyance that several nearby Knights laughed. 'Haven't you taken enough for one day?'

Vossa dropped down in her cockpit and sulked.

Sycorax noted, in her peripheral vision, that the young woman was tracking her with the pintle-mounted heavy stubber as she climbed the stairs.

Clearly Vossa hadn't taken well to Rakkan saving her life – but that simmering resentment was the least of her worries.

The biggest one, of course, was that Raithe was about to do her job. And despite all his optics, ballistic cogitators and armoured suits, she wasn't sure he was equipped.

It had been Koln's idea. Perfectly logical – though Koln had a voice that made anything seem logical.

Dask expected Sabban to check in after searching the *Stiletto*. Sabban could not do that because he was dead. Sycorax could not impersonate Sabban convincingly enough.

So they had to send someone *else*, made easier by the fact that Sabban, quite cleverly, used off-worlders as his vassal operatives. Men and women who had no ties to either of the houses, and were unlikely to be recognised through family or feudal ties.

Meaning, Symphonia Dask may not have met them personally – indeed, due to the difference in rank almost certainly *wouldn't* have. That's what she kept Sabban around for, to do the unpleasant work that might sully her impeccable honour. While nobility, Sabban's bloodline was low, diluted by an outside marriage to a rogue trader house only one generation back.

Sycorax made it to the top of the stairs, taking a moment to adjust Rakkan's leg augmetics, as she'd seen him do when transitioning from climbing to walking. She looked around the court viewing box to ensure no one from Sabban's family line was there.

None. It was all Armiger pilots. The Questoris Knights were stowing their Knight suits in the underground stable after the royal procession. She caught a snatch of conversation.

'–they have a real arachno-ursid. Do you believe it?'

'Who's facing it?'

'Not me, thank honour.'

It was Sabban's rogue trader family who had sent the exotic wildlife for the games. Sycorax had seen them penned up and braying with terror in the warren of tunnels beneath the tournament field, ready for the beast hunt events. According to the schedule, that would be the third major event after they cleared the field of debris from the team melee and before the first personal challenges.

A few ambulls and arachno-ursids for the Armigers to fight, just to give the crowd something to watch while the tournament master got the challenge matchups in proper order and the nobles refreshed drinks and made bets.

Sycorax hoped Sabban had not been a part of procuring those poor animals. Hoped Dask would not ask Sabban's man for an inside tip.

Because while they were all doing things they weren't trained to do here, Raithe was far out of his depth. They'd considered sending Sycorax to meet Dask, letting Rakkan – the *spare* Rakkan, as she'd joked – compete in the tournament and meet with Baron Yuma.

Sycorax walked past the box's guards, two of Yuma's men, who wanded her with metal detectors. Their devices let out horrid squeals when they passed over her legs, but when she undid Rakkan's belt and showed them the leg braces, their demeanour changed entirely.

'Apologies, my lord,' said one, his face going crimson. 'I had forgotten. We have to take precautions with the High Monarch this close.'

And he *was* close. Or at least appeared to be. At the other end of the court box lay another cordon of men, and beyond that, the shoulder pauldron of the *Crown of Dominion*. The lip of it stuck out so far that the more prominent court figures could nearly stand under it like a sunshade.

In retrospect, her joke about Rakkan had been ill-advised. They'd tried putting Rakkan in the cockpit only to find he could no longer interact with the machine. Even though *Jester* thought Sycorax was Rakkan, it had reformatted enough in the re-dedication that he was no longer compatible with the helm.

So they'd disguised Raithe and Rakkan with facial prosthetics, skin-lighteners and, in Raithe's case, a temporary facial tattoo. Not a total change, but enough to alter their prominent distinguishing marks.

When Sycorax saw him walk up to the guard checkpoint on the other side of the box, she hoped it had been enough.

He wore a spare black jerkin stripped from a corpse, cleaned and pressed. And she was satisfied to see him limping a little like she'd suggested, changing his gait and upright posture. She'd folded his nose over and secured it with an armature in his nostrils so it appeared to have been broken and healed badly. It gave his voice a nasal quality.

He was early. His only symptom of nervousness.

Well, that, and the fact that he'd asked Sycorax to smuggle in his Exitus pistol in case things went south. It rested in a sculpted depression in her waist, tucked under the leg armatures in order to get through the security checkpoint.

'For Baroness Dask,' he told the guards, dangling the medal. 'At her request. Give her this.'

'The baroness isn't here.'

'But she's arriving soon?'

'I can't tell you that.'

'Can I wait?' He gestured to a bench outside the cordon.

'No waiting, come back later.'

For a moment, Sycorax worried the Vindicare might push it, but instead he disappeared down the staircase.

Fire and move, good boy.

Just as she thought it, a noise pummelled her eardrums.

'*Subjects of Dominion–*'

'*–your High Monarch addresses you.*'

Koln swung her attention from the vassals repairing turf on the field to the court boxes at the far end of the tournament field. They straddled either side of a massive alcove in the raised stands, a dais, where the *Crown of Dominion* stood.

'Where is she standing?' she asked Rakkan.

'Left royal box,' said Rakkan. He'd been sullen, but at least compliant, since his failure to pair with *Jester*. 'Right box is for court officials, left box is for the four judges. Dear mother and Uncle Kraine, and one of each house selected from the lower nobility. And Achara, of course.'

Koln enhanced the image in her augmetic corneas, zooming in on the left-hand court box to see Baroness Achara standing before a vox-mic pickup. Waiting for silence. 'She's the announcer, I suppose?'

'Mistress of Ceremonies,' said Rakkan. 'And she'll read the monarch's address. Loud enough that all those noble Knights and dames can hear her even within their armour.'

'Always Achara. How interesting. With Yavarius-Khau silent, she controls every pronouncement, doesn't she? Could even control the kingdom.'

'Unlikely,' Rakkan sneered. 'Two Stryder sit at the High Monarch's table, two Rau. They serve as a check on each other. If one tried to control the monarch, the others would step in.'

'Still, that's power. Perhaps if Sycorax fails to squire to Yuma, we'll get her near Achara.'

'*Your High Monarch wishes to deliver the Midwinter Message and Notices of Official Award and Elevation,*' continued Achara, the crowd having gone from a roar to a murmur. '*He announces news of a great victory against the agri-rebels in the hinterlands. Baron Rallan Fontaine, may he live in the monarch's grace, has raided two manufactorum complexes in Stryder territory and killed or taken three thousand rebels, including their leader, Colline Bek.*'

She stopped, to allow the chorus of boos and jeering.

'*Master of Justice Fontaine executed Bek on the field, and her*

treasonous uprising is near broken. Even now he returns to Gathering
Palace with his forces in triumph. But subjects must remain vigilant.
No harbouring of the king's enemies will be tolerated, even if they be
father or mother, sister or brother. Remember that Yavarius-Khau is
our spiritual father, divinely appointed by the God-Emperor, and your
bond with him is stronger even than flesh and blood. For it is he who
protects his subject-children from the uncaring galaxy, guards against
the horrors of the Archenemy, and received six wounds battling the
heretek House Morvayne to protect this world of Dominion. In addi-
tion, the High Monarch commends the agri-vassals of the southern
continent for a bumper crop that–'

'BEWARE THE TRAITOR, BEWARE THE REGICIDE.'

The crowd, which had been burbling with murmurs and whispers, fell totally silent. Ninety thousand heads turned towards the
Crown of Dominion. The woman next to Koln, a peasant like all
in this section, began to weep and pray in an impenetrable local
sub-dialect of Low Gothic. Three rows down, she saw a man faint.

'What the hells was that?' breathed Rakkan.

For the first time in fifteen years, Yavarius-Khau had spoken
in public.

With her enhanced vision, Koln could see Achara stepping
back from the mic, speaking hurriedly to Kraine and Hawthorn.

'This wasn't planned,' she said.

'The High Monarch,' stumbled Achara, 'commands you to uncover
the recidivists and rebels. For they are tools of the Dark Powers that–'

'THEY ARE AMONG YOU. PLOTTERS. ASSASSINS. ENEMIES
OF THE CROWN. THEY WISH FOR MY BLOOD. TO KILL
YOUR MONARCH AND OVERTHROW OUR ANCIENT WORLD
OF DOMINION. TO DESTROY ITS PROUD TRADITIONS
AND MAKE US PUPPETS. THEIR ALLIES AND AGENTS ARE
ALREADY HERE. STOOGES AND TOOLS OF THE SO-CALLED
LORD COMMANDER, THIS USURPER-REGENT GUILLIMAN

WHO CLAIMS TO SPEAK FOR THE GOD-EMPEROR AND HAS
BROKEN HIS OATHS TO US.'

Koln could feel Rakkan gripping her arm.

The voice rumbled the organs in Sycorax's abdomen. She saw
Sir Mauvec Kawe arriving and slid up next to him.

'Do you know what this is?' she whispered.

Kawe shook his head, pressed a finger to his lips. Absently
passed her a coin purse. 'For Vossa.'

On her right, she saw the Arch-Maintenancer rush up from the
stairway, scuttling like a centipede across the royal box and up
onto the armature to pop open a panel on the *Crown of Domin-*
ion's underside, making rapid adjustments to cabling.

Below, at the foot of the stairs, Raithe put a hand on a steel
support beam as thick as a tree trunk, and felt the voice rever-
berate through it. Next to him, another servant waiting for an
appointment in the royal box – sweating as he tried to work
up his nerve for the meeting – stopped mumbling prayers and
looked skywards.

'FIND THE TRAITORS, BE THEY HIGH OR LOW. PURGE
THEM. THROW THEM OUT OF THEIR HOVELS AND PALACES.
BUTCHER THEM. CARRY THEIR HEADS THROUGH THE
STREET. THUS DO YOU SHOW LOYALTY TO YOUR ANCES–'

The reverberation stopped.

Koln's mind wheeled. Calculated. Tried to extrapolate the possible repercussions.

But she didn't have to; in the next section of the stand, she
saw the crowd roiling. Shouting.

A man stumbled out of the mass and into the stairway
between the benches, blood flowing from his head. A woman

followed him and ripped something from his neck, holding it high. Peasants leaped down after him, beating and kicking him until he tumbled down the stone stairs and lay still on the lower landing.

Koln refocused her eyes on the object the woman held high, and saw it was a silver aquila pendant. Not the baroque local variety with its curved wings and extended tongues that was more falcon than eagle, but the standardised Imperial symbol.

They reached the man, and began to stomp on him before two men dragged him to his feet and threw him over the edge of the stands, into the tournament ground.

'Th-thank you, High Monarch,' said Achara. 'Your, uh, your alle-gorical wisdom is needed to guide us in these trying times. As you say in your parable, we will defend our world from all, even our staunch-est ally the Imperium should we need to. Thankfully, due to your wise leadership, we need not go that far. We shall all look amongst us for hinterland rebel activity. All subjects must report rebel activity to sheriffs and reeves, who will dispense justice under the authority of Baron Fontaine, Master of Judgment. We will remain vigilant, and mob action will not be tolerated.'

The Crown of Dominion stood silent.

'Let the tournament begin!'

Auto-horns blared, and two portcullis gates cranked open. A translucent bubble shield crackled into existence between stands and field.

Hundreds of men and women in rags stampeded out of the spiked gates, fleeing barefoot onto the green grass. Winter sun-light shone on their greasy skins and matted hair.

They were followed by six Armigers stalking to their starting positions, weapons down, ensuring they got no unfair advan-tage from pre-targeting the masses. Autocannon drums clacked as they chambered rounds the size of vin bottles. Thermal spears worked up to idle, crisping the grass beneath them. Chain-cleavers revved in anticipation. A servo-skull hovered above each hunched ogre of a machine, ready to cogitate its kill count.

A horn blared three times, and the captives died.

A Rau Armiger on Koln's left found a tight target grouping and swung up both autocannons. Enormous explosive-tipped rounds blasted the unarmoured targets apart, limbs flying. Another Armiger sprinted into a line of fleeing humans, fast as a leonine, carving into them with its chain-cleaver and firing its thermal spear in a fan into the fleeing mass. Flesh and bone melted.

In the towers, musicians played repetitive fight music. Horns and whining pipes. Drums. Glorious battle-hymns to accompany the slaughter.

'Who are they?' asked Koln.

'Prisoners,' said Rakkan. He swallowed. 'Traitors. Rebels from the hinterland probably.'

'Is this event new? It seems to bother you.'

He shook his head. 'Not new. Older than the Imperium. I grew up with it.'

'So you knew what to expect.'

Koln looked at Rakkan. His face was ashen.

'Yes,' he said. 'But sometimes you have to go away for a while to see your home for what it really is.'

TWENTY-EIGHT

'Baron Yuma, my lord,' Sycorax bowed.

She'd found the Kingsward talking to Achara, in the sequestered judge's box. To get his attention, she'd had to go around the back of the *Crown of Dominion*, along the small maintenance scaffolding connecting the two boxes, its plasteel railings warm to the touch from the proximity of the Castellan's reactor vents.

'*Pistol,*' she heard in her micro-bead.

Raithe.

'*Why?*' she subvocalised, working her throat.

'*I have a feeling.*'

She waved at the baron.

Yuma strode over, domed head and determined face set in a frown. The geometric tattoo on the right side of his head looked more faded up close than it had at the welcome feast.

'Baron, my uncle said I should speak to you at the tournament.'

'You picked a hell of a time to go politicking, son. I've much to do.'

'Then perhaps it's a good time to take on help?'

Yuma snorted, and Sycorax realised belatedly that it was his laugh. 'Son, you have no idea what I have to deal with right now. Trust me, you want no part of it.'

'I am formally submitting myself for a position as squire.'

'Denied.' He ducked the rope, and walked behind the *Crown*, looking up at its structure as if trying to spy cracks in the armour. 'Don't need one. Don't want one. Got along so far without one.'

'In normal times,' said Sycorax, giving Rakkan's wry grin. 'As the High Monarch said, these are not normal times.'

'Didn't you listen? That was allegory. Baroness Achara said so. There are always plots. Nothing different now.'

They came into the court box and Yuma swiped a shot of distilled amasec from a servant, put it away in one drink. 'If I want a squire, I'll come to you. Your eagerness doesn't recommend you much. Means you're in it for the power and influence.'

'I'm in it for Dominion.'

'You're in it for your mother.'

'Uncle is the one who pushed me to come to you,' Sycorax said.

'Same thing,' said the baron, putting down his shot glass and taking up another. 'Stryder, Rau, it's all groxshite. I don't care if you came from your mother, or my brother, or the God-Emperor fashioned you from clay and His divine spit, you're not squiring for me unless I ask.'

'Why?'

'Because Kingsward is a sacred duty, son. It's not an office, or a stepping stone, it's total dedication. You have to lay down your life for the monarch, follow them right or wrong, without judgement. Total singularity of purpose. A determination you didn't exactly show by running off to join the crusade as a *flee* blade.'

'What?'

'A *flee* blade. You ran, Rakkan. A little palace intrigue, a few bullets flying and you were gone. Ditched out on your duty. Blamed the monarch on the way out. Who do you think had to deal with that while you were gallivanting in a warzone, raking up glory and girls, eh?'

'I was not in my right mind, and it was my mother who packed me off. I was two weeks from a battlefront when I gained control of my senses again.'

'Aye, maybe so. But when you combine that with the fact that you're the most recent contact with Imperial forces, well, you heard the High Monarch.' Yuma jerked his head at the *Crown*. 'Not exactly good timing on your part.'

'But that was allegorical,' she reminded him.

'Yes, of course it was.'

'What if I told you that I found myself on the battlefield. Found my sense of duty and dedication. I'll let you in on a secret, lord, but I was never at command headquarters. I'm not even sure the banner the warmaster gave me is real. Maybe she makes them in a factorum, gives them to everyone who distinguishes themselves. To be honest, I barely met her. I was a dog soldier, in the trenches, alongside infantry and armour. They treated me no differently than a Militarum captain. Worse at times. A lone Armiger doesn't exactly rate official attention in a warzone with Baneblades and Dreadnoughts. But I did my duty – and I can do yours.'

Yuma snorted. Tried to look disapproving, but he had little artifice. 'So why me?'

'Because you'll tell me where you stand, always. I'm done being political.'

Yuma laughed at that. 'You pledged to the court, Rakkan. It's a political role. And you served as unofficial representative in the Indomitus Crusade. Political again. But I appreciate the sentiment, at least.'

Yuma glanced out on the field. The tower musicians were playing at a tremendous tempo now, the song having sped up to tell the competitors they were near the time limit.

'Tell you what, son. By law I have to fight one bout at this accursed security nightmare. I always pick the melee, since it's over fastest. Usually I go unaccompanied, but if you can suit up in three minutes, you can join me. Consider it a trial.'

He stuck out his hand, and Sycorax gripped the forearm. 'I won't disappoint you.'

He let go, not noticing the transmitter she'd planted behind his elbow. Within two minutes, it would bore into his flesh, appearing to be nothing more than an insect bite.

'Listen to my commands and you'll do fine. See you on the field.'

Sycorax rushed to the downward stairwell, slamming full tilt into Raithe, who had just finished being patted down by the footmen at the head of the stairs.

'Watch where you're going, peasant,' Sycorax hissed.

'Apologies, Sir Rakkan,' Raithe said, bowing as he slipped the Exitus pistol beneath his robes.

Baroness Symphonia Dask was looking out on the tournament ground, fingering the silver medal, when the footman brought him to her presence.

Below, vassals with push-rakes were clearing bodies from the field. Herding them towards disposal hatches concealed beneath the green grass. On the exterior of the field, duos of Questoris Knights and Armiger support squires were lining up on their marks, ready for the melee.

'So you're Sabban's man,' she said.

'Second feather of the falcon, baroness,' he responded.

'You know the code words, at least,' she said, turning her eyes on him. 'So you're either genuine, or have a singular talent for torture. Sabban would not have broken easily.'

She had violet eyes and a cool demeanour. And where most noblewomen of Dominion favoured double-breasted jackets or genderless tabards, she wore a banded corset and bell skirt, the dress' neckline going halfway up her throat. All of it Stryder blue, and woven with las-reflective flak panels and carapace banding.

Professionalism and competence radiated from her.

And Raithe felt a rare emotion – he was impressed.

He bowed as Sycorax had taught him. 'Rikard Staus, baroness.'

'I don't care. I ask the questions, you answer them,' she said. 'What did you find on the ship?'

'It was a cursory search, baroness, returning nothing but a few pornographic slates and indecent letters in Rakkan's hand.' He held out a few of the scrawled pages they'd mocked up. 'They are here if you wish.'

Dask flicked a disinterested finger and an aide took them.

'You were seen?'

'I was not, I was the lookout. Sir Sabban was good enough to retain me.'

'And no trace of specialised vox-sets, like the girl from the palace?'

Raithe paused, as if considering his answer. It was why they had kept the meeting, rather than simply letting Sabban disappear. To confirm for certain that it was Dask and Sabban who had killed the asset Tessenna Starne. 'No, madam, though I am not familiar with vox-sets enough to know, and I was not there when the woman died. Perhaps you could show me a pict?'

The aide stepped forward with a grimy black-and-white snapshot. Raithe studied it, trying to make something out of the poor quality pict. 'No, I don't think–'

He reached for it and the aide pulled it away.

He heard a starting horn and the crowd roared, drowning him out for a moment.

'No, nothing like that.' He shook his head. 'But I am not familiar with ships.'

Dask's eyes narrowed. 'Come with me. Have you watched the first event, Mister Staus?'

Raithe walked just behind her, letting her lead. She took them around the back of the *Crown* and into the more secluded area there. 'No.'

'Shame. We came out narrowly on top. Stryder took the event, four hundred and thirty-one rebel kills to four hundred and twelve.'

'Congratulations.'

'Would've gone to Rau, but Dame Vossa's mount, *Stormrider*, unintentionally struck two Stryder Knights with four autocannon rounds.'

'An unfortunate accident,' he said, putting enough of a twist on the phrase to communicate his meaning.

'You don't sound like you believe it was an accident,' she said, turning. 'Neither do I. In fact, I don't believe in accidents. Like I don't believe Sabban sent you. Did you intercept Sabban's man? Replace him? Or was it you on the vox the entire time?'

Raithe heard the words, but he was more concerned with the laspistol pressing into his back.

'Who are you really with?'

At the horns, Sycorax broke left and ran as fast as she could push the Armiger.

As a Callidus, she was trained to operate new bodies. To move and adapt to physiologies not her own. Rakkan and Gwynne had even praised her quick progress – but a talented amateur was no match for a ten-year veteran like Rakkan. She felt clumsy, her movements a little too loose, whereas the opposing Armigers dashed and presented arms like they were operating their own bodies. Each movement having a snap that she lacked.

'*You've grown sloppy killing heretek footmen,*' she heard, in the artificial cortex synced with the Helm Mechanicum.

Yuma's voice, via the mind-link shared by Knights and their Armiger squires.

It made her feel dirty, the same way she'd felt soiled when she'd infiltrated the polar research station of the heretek Programmator Quivarian. Then, the artificial cortex had existed to evade mind searches by Quivarian, and prevent her mind from being polluted by the fallen tech-priest's virus, but for some reason this felt just as bad. A push of dominance that came with a physical as well as a psychological pressure.

She *felt* his disappointment.

And tightened up just in time.

Incoming fire alerts painted the left side of her vision, and she slung her ion shield towards the incoming fire and threw herself to the right.

The battle cannon round whistled past her facemask in a pencil-line of movement, punching into the turf where she'd been about to step. The world itself seemed to crack open, and Sycorax saw the grey sky, then the upside-down stands, then the green turf coming up fast.

Impact ground her against the restraint harness so hard, her consciousness disengaged from the helm, and she briefly flashed back to her own body like a dreamer rising, gasping, from a nightmare.

Then, she plunged back into the enveloping world of *Jester*'s senses.

'*Get up. GET UP.*'

Yuma. His imperative splitting through the ringing tone of shell shock.

Not ringing tone, lock tone.

She rolled to the right, a manoeuvre that would've put her on her feet if she were in her own flexible, highly trained body. But in this angular prison of adamant she merely flopped end over end.

But it was enough to dodge the incoming pod rockets that shook the ground where she'd lain, a few corkscrewing munitions blooming into fire against her purpling ion shield.

Whispers in her mind. Not Yuma this time. The helm speaking to her.

Descendant Rakkan is not doing well. He dishonours us. Get up, Rakkan.

A crackle, her micro-bead. Rakkan's voice. 'Get up, Sycorax.'

'GET UP!'

A crackling, blistering sound like circuits frying filled her cockpit and the turf retreated from her face. Sycorax turned *Jester*'s head and saw the admonishing mask of Yuma. His massive Knight Warden, *Throneshield*, had used its thunderstrike gauntlet to grab *Jester* by the carapace armour just behind the construct's head, and lift it like a stray canid pup.

'*Keep your feet, you useless vermin-turd!*' Yuma roared in her mind.

She could see the ion shield on his left side bubbling with hits. His great cage-faced helm turned towards them and tore loose a bright fan of fire with his avenger gatling cannon.

The sound rattled Sycorax's teeth. Shell casings large as bread loaves tumbled from the ejector.

Her steel found purchase on the ground, and she bolted out right.

'*No, stay close.*' Rakkan growled in her micro-bead. '*Tournament fighting isn't war. There's no cover. Advance behind Yuma. Watch his flanks.*'

She retreated, loping backwards like Rakkan had taught her rather than turning her back on the enemy – an act both dishonourable and tactically unwise.

Jester slid into *Throneshield*'s long shadow as a fusillade of gatling cannon rounds peppered the bigger Knight's shield.

'That's mother gunning for you, she wants to embarrass you in front of Yuma and sink your chances of pledging to him. Her mount Greyhound is a Crusader. She'll shoot from long range. Keep your shield up to avoid the gatling cannon, and if a battle cannon round comes in, throw it towards where the ballistic cogitator says it will land. It's the blast you want to avoid. Your shield won't survive a direct hit anyway.'

Yuma was moving, punching cruciform holes in the turf with every step, his upper structure rotated so he approached the challenger's gatling cannon first, one shoulder pauldron thrown forward to take any hits that penetrated his shield.

Sycorax fell in two steps behind him, her eyes level with the knuckles of his gauntlet, the image of it rippling as the translucent power field idled.

She tried to think back to her practice with Rakkan. The mechanical gait, the strange hip rotations. Cursing herself for making the classic mistake of a Callidus – coming under fire and reverting to her natural body movements. That was always the hardest thing: *fighting* like someone else. Keeping the clumsy persona of a Guardsman with a bayonet when your body screamed to execute its enemies with an acrobatic kick or surgical slice.

She thought back to an old assignment, a time she'd needed to meld into a ceremonial Mordian drill team. The precise movements. Every step and rifle spin snappy and intentional.

The mechanical body responded. And just in time.

'Flanker! Sinister quadrant,' she called to Yuma.

An Armiger Warglaive had broken out there, running in

to turn the flank while its master had poured fire at Yuma's fore-quadrant.

Sycorax recognised the sky-blue of Stryder heraldry, the four-winged angel on its banner holding a lightning bolt. *Soaring Blade*.

Andricus. Clever, clever Andricus.

Soaring Blade burned off a shot with its thermal spear, its punctured muzzle blackening as superheated air particles rushed towards *Throneshield*.

Yuma's ion shield roiled like ink spilled in water. Its hue dipped from a light violet to the colour of a bad bruise.

Sycorax pushed Jester out of cover to get a sight line beyond the tint of the damaged ion shield and lit off with her own thermal spear. Thrumming heat blossomed up her metal arm, a pleasant warmth of destructive power that tingled even the now distant ghost of her flesh arm.

Her initial shot went wide, streaking past *Soaring Blade* to blacken the plasteel arena barrier behind him before she swept it over him, painting a violet slash across his shield.

She was about to tear off another shot but Yuma pivoted in front of her and pounded hard towards the Armiger, breaking her line of sight. She sprinted after him, watching their right flank.

In mid-field she saw an Errant-pattern raise its thermal cannon towards Yuma and she leapt to his right side, swinging her ion shield out to intercept the fire on her fresh shield rather than his depleted one.

Heat flash filled *Jester*'s vision and she heard the door-slamming *bang* of *Throneshield*'s ion shield failing. The world went deep purple, and Sycorax realised the enormous melta weapon was now washing over her own shield.

And it was holding.

Her vision cleared and she saw the Errant – Lady Lycan-Bast's *Blood Oath* – turn to meet a threat from her flank.

'*Well done*,' said Yuma.

And Sycorax turned to see a slaughter in progress.

Andricus had tried to scramble away, but his clever flanking movement had pinned him against the wall of the arena and he'd needed to run backwards while turning to escape the hulking Knight.

Not enough room to manoeuvre quickly. Especially stumbling over the partially cleared bodies of the rebels from the last event.

Throneshield's gauntlet crawled with lightning as Yuma brought it down – not in a blow but an enormous open-handed slap that caught the Armiger sidelong, popping its shield, crumpling its thermal spear, and sinking the pointed fingers into the smaller Knight's carapace.

Soaring Blade struggled, lashing and kicking as Yuma lifted it off the ground. Andricus clumsily swept his chain-cleaver down, its whirling teeth showering sparks from the armoured adamantine panels of the gauntlet that held him fast.

Sycorax kept her shield trained to the right, looking for threats, but couldn't help looking with horrified fascination as Yuma raised his gatling cannon and pressed it to the squirming machine.

Muzzle flash stabbed point-blank into *Soaring Blade*, a clean three-round burst directly into its superstructure, before Yuma smashed the limp Knight suit into the steel barrier and flung it backhand.

The mangled *Soaring Blade* landed twenty feet away and rolled. Facemask burned black. Smoke leaking from beneath its holed carapace.

Tournament bouts were conducted on half power. Semi-charged weapon batteries. Specially packed ammunition that ensured any damage would be reparable. What would it be like, she thought, to see these things at war?

And then she threw her shield right, because Vossa was coming for her.

'You're making a mistake,' said Raithe.

'Hands up,' said Dask. She had to shout over the rising cheers of the crowd. They couldn't see it past the *Crown of Dominion*, but clearly something exciting was happening out on the field.

Raithe didn't comply. Raised his voice only enough to be heard. 'There's a lot of loud noises here, baroness. Shots, explosions, crowd howling. That laspistol is a Kastallar model seven, fine piece but light on the trigger. I don't want to be shot because a Knight scored a good hit.'

As if to punctuate the point, the crowd gave a collective noise like they'd been punched in the stomach, then broke into raucous screams and applause.

'*Baron Yuma scores first blood with* Throneshield,' came Achara's voice over the laud-hailers. '*Sir Andricus is honourably eliminated.*'

'What did you do with Sabban?'

'As I said, we searched the ship, found dirty slates and letters. A few war medals in the sergeant's room. Accounts of trade from the combine, we picted them if you–'

'What did you do with Sabban's body? Because the tracker chip I had drilled underneath his skull-port pings every three hours. We can't get a fix on it. Found and destroyed, most likely. I expect you burned him? Dropped the bones down an old well?'

Raithe said nothing. Dask was nearly right. The *Stiletto* had a micro-melta crematorium drawer.

Another cheer went up from the crowd.

'*Baron Tiberius Kraine in* Firedrake *has honourably eliminated Sir*

Mauvec Kawe in Typhoon's Teeth,' intoned Achara, with rising excitement.

'Who are you with?' demanded Dask. 'House Rau? The Crusade's intelligence echelon? Guilliman? The Inquisition?'

'What are you hiding,' asked Raithe, 'that you'd fear the Inquisition?'

Dask's mouth turned down in – what? A frown of frustration? Shame? Fear?

Sycorax would've known, thought Raithe. It should be her here, not him. He was not this kind of specialist. He ended conversations, he didn't draw them out.

'Whoever your masters are,' said Dask, 'I'd like you to deliver them a message.'

'What is it?'

'Don't worry,' she said, raising the laspistol, 'you won't have to remember it.'

And Absolom Raithe's world exploded.

TWENTY-NINE

Autocannon rounds deflected off Sycorax's failing ion shield as she charged Dame Vossa, drinking in the energy of the crowd as ninety thousand voices rose in an anticipatory whoop at the prospect of her revving chain-cleaver striking home.

Vossa's dual lance-like autocannons fired at close range, barrel flare stitching flaming X-patterns in the air.

Jester's shield collapsed with a bang. An auto-round scored its pauldron and two kicked its chestplate, sending a shock through Sycorax's body like she was being socked with an augmetic fist. But with a springing leap she was in range, swinging her cleaver down.

An explosion tore the air, followed by the screaming.

Vossa's Armiger, *Stormrider*, cocked its head around, tripping as it fouled its evading back-pedal and fell. Sycorax pulled the blow, knowing the kill would not be honourable – then noticed the silence, and looked in the same direction as everyone else.

And saw the orange blossom of flame rising up from the royal box.

* * *

'Oh, Throne,' breathed Rakkan. 'Throne. Throne. Throne.'

Koln already had his arm. 'Let's go. Now.'

'What happened?'

'We need to move. After that speech, and whatever *this* is, the crowd is going to get ugly. Head towards the box to see if we can be of assistance but otherwise, we're extracting.'

'It was right in the royal box. The court side. Was that us?'

'No,' said Koln, looking at how the royal box – a hundred feet above the turf – listed to one side as if it might fall at any moment. 'That was a bomb.'

The blast threw both Raithe and Dask to the deck, their position behind the *Crown of Dominion* saving them from the lethal fantail of shrapnel that scythed into the nobles watching the melee on the field. The High Monarch's ion shield boiled with the hit, tinting a neon orange from the kinetic absorption. On Raithe's left, the royal box heeled over like a sinking ship, one of its support pillars bent by the explosion.

A man in Rau livery screamed in indignation as he lay, both legs severed at the knee. Another noble, thrown by the explosion, slid down the suddenly diagonal floor of the box as it listed away from the *Crown*. She made a feeble, wounded grab for a handhold on the deck before disappearing into space. Footmen from the judge's booth hustled by, their autoguns raised, boots slipping on the gory mess that had been Dask's aide.

Standing behind her mistress as was proper – just out of cover.

Raithe heard the shots and stayed down, crawling forward enough to get a line of sight to what was going on.

From the blast pattern, he knew it had been a body-bomb. A particularly nasty implant by the looks of it. Probably detonated at the security checkpoint.

He thought of the servant downstairs, sweating, working his nerve up.

Men and women in peasant clothing stormed up the blast-twisted stairway, firing stubbers into the advancing footmen who opened up with their autoguns.

A body-bomb followed by a storming party. Insurgency tactics. He'd seen it with genestealer cults before.

'While you were questioning me,' he growled at Dask, 'you let the Throne-damn hinterlanders in.'

That irked him. It was unprofessional. Still, he picked up Dask's laspistol and slid it to her. She grabbed it and rose, unsteady, winging a shot towards a rebel that had broken through the footmen.

'I'll get a weapon and cover you,' said Raithe, and bolted towards the judge's box.

He drew his Exitus pistol on the run, dodging to the right side of the *Crown of Dominion* and into the empty judge's box. Stripped off the outer robe as he went.

Baroness Achara was disappearing down the staircase, with two footmen covering her retreat.

Their autoguns snapped towards him, an armed, running man in a black bodyglove.

'Hal-' said one.

Raithe's shot burst his head open.

The other fired, his rifle spitting rounds in the air as Raithe grabbed the barrel and wrenched it skyward. He punched the man's right eye with the barrel of the Exitus pistol, loosening the footman's grip on the autogun. Then he took control of the weapon, using the footman as a body shield as he emptied the auto's magazine down the stairway at the reinforcements coming up.

Bullets buzzed by Raithe as the men in the stairwell returned fire, the body of the captive footman seizing and twitching as rounds punched through his carapace chestplate. Raithe pushed the body down the stairs to serve as an entangling obstacle and darted towards the *Crown of Dominion*. Because no matter how good these hinterlanders were, they weren't going to kill Yavarius-Khau. There was no way. Too disorganised, too lightly armed. They had the necessary zeal, but not the right equipment. Their bomb hadn't penetrated the ion shield.

But Raithe could.

He worked the shot selector on his Exitus pistol to feed from the left side of the dual magazine. Fired two at the *Crown*.

BANG.

The ion shield went down. Two shield-breaker rounds. Usually meant for cracking personal force fields, nothing this big, but the ion shield was already depleted by the bomb blast, and he'd fired two double loads. An unusual requisition he'd ordered specifically for this purpose. The ion shield would probably reset in seconds.

But he only needed it down for a moment.

He holstered his pistol at a run and hopped onto the box's railing, then he leaped – flying through space before smashing against the upper carapace and sliding down the slick enamelled armour. Raithe grabbed a handhold on an ornate rail of golden-edged plate and hauled himself onto the upper armour, sliding himself sideways on his toes as if he were navigating a building's exterior ledge. His shoulder screamed in agony and he triggered pain-suppressors. He hoped the muscle wouldn't tear right off the bone.

Hard rounds spanged off the pauldron to his left and he pulled the pistol from the small of his back and snap-fired a turbo-penetrator round that blew a footman apart, causing his terrified companions to duck back into cover on the stairwell.

Raithe edged around the front of the *Crown*, planted a toe on the top of the meltagun housing and leaped upward, sliding his belly along the smooth red panel and grabbing one of the two mounting rails on its arched back.

Another squall of autogun rounds came from the staircase, and the air tinted yellow.

The ion shield was back on.

But the crowd was wise now. With every eye trained on the chaos at the royal box, it was impossible not to see the man in the black bodyglove scaling the High Monarch's mount, defiling it with his presence.

Raithe hauled himself to a crouch on top of the armoured carapace, keeping low. He pulled his hood up from behind his neck and took the spy mask from its concealed pouch on his pistol holder, unfolding it and clapping it over his eyes and mouth.

He felt the mask contact and activate the electro-magnets embedded in his skull, fastening it in place. Felt the ballistic cogitator interface with his cranial augmetics.

Felt like himself.

'*Raithe,*' said a voice in his mask's internal vox. Koln. '*What's hap–*'

'Commencing kill. Target of opportunity.'

'*That wasn't the plan,*' she said. '*We're not positioned to manage the fallout. We–*'

He clicked off the transmitter.

Then he stood, pistol in hand, and walked towards the top hatch he'd studied every night since receiving this mission. The sealed, armoured hatch with its blast-proof crystal porthole.

Beneath his feet, the *Crown of Dominion* was heartblood-red on the left side, sky-bue on the right. He walked the line where the two colours met, feeling the weight of the moment.

Kill number fifty. Sicarius Primus. First Assassin.

He knelt over the porthole and looked inside.

It was eighteen inches thick and convex, blurring the image of the man inside. Raithe could see pale skin and open eyes, looking at him. Fluid sloshing in the cockpit.

The *Crown of Dominion* hadn't moved. Perhaps hadn't registered him as a threat. Good.

He checked the shot selector, ensuring he was firing the half of the magazine stacked with turbo-penetrator rounds. He was careful. Deliberate. Took it slow, even as the ion shield roiled around him, going from amasec amber to the colour of a sunset at sea. He aligned the barrel with the dome of the porthole, making sure to leave a space of one inch so as not to damage the Exitus with a backfire.

And fired.

The slug lay embedded an inch into the crystal, its penetration smashing the top layer so it flaked and shelved.

He fired again.

This time there was a crack. A surface crack, but one that went down several inches like a break in a glacier. He realigned his pistol on the fissure.

And fired again.

'*The ion shield!*' Yuma roared. The noise slammed both her mind and her eardrums. The Kingsward was broadcasting it loud through his Knight's laud-hailers. '*Fire at the* Crown*'s feet, hit the ion shield but point away from the structure.*'

The melee had taken them down the field, and now every Knight was racing back, eating up ground to get to...

Raithe. She saw Raithe atop the *Crown of Dominion*, kneeling. The flash of a weapon blinking steady as the aviation warning light on a hab-tower's spire.

The mad bastard was going for it.

* * *

Raithe brushed away glass, dug his finger into the tunnel in the crystal to clear the debris. There were spiderweb cracks in every direction now, running deep. Deep purple light, nearly grey, reflected off the shards lying around the porthole. The shield was going down under the heavy ordnance.

Only moments left.

And one bullet remaining.

He prayed, really prayed for the first time in years, that the next shot would strike home. Assassins were worldly, increasingly so as they gained in operational experience. Privy to much that might make another an unbeliever. Raithe, for example, didn't believe in invoking deities to assist his work. If he'd planned and executed properly, he'd get his kill.

But please, God-Emperor, let him not have foolishly wasted a turbo-penetrator round on that footman. Let him not have got this far and end up one round short of his fiftieth kill.

Then, he saw the spot. A place where three deep fissures met.

And he knew that another round would break it.

He lined up and took his shot.

'Seize the off-worlders! The monarch warned us!' screamed the peasant, as he grabbed Koln's shoulder. 'Killers! Traitors! Assass-aaagh!'

Koln broke his wrist and crushed his windpipe.

The crowd closed in on them, a riot of reaching hands and epithets. She swept a spin-kick around them to gain space, smashing a jawbone. Drove her palm up into a nose, blinding an assailant with tears.

Thrust one fist up into the air.

'Close your eyes,' she said to Rakkan, then triggered the photon flash unit in her left thumb.

* * *

The crystal gave way, tumbling into the cockpit and splashing in the liquid below.

Inside, the cockpit was dark, lit only with the eerie glow of control displays diffusing through syrupy liquid.

Raithe could see Lucien Yavarius-Khau, hero of a hundred battles, High Monarch of Dominion, sitting beneath the surface. Eyes boggling up at the man who would be his killer.

The bullet hadn't hit him. So Raithe reached down through the shoulder-width oval porthole with both hands and seized him around the throat. Drew him up to the surface, strangling the king with his gloved hands.

And whatever he did, whether he died here, lived another century, or the rest of the mission descended into a bloody mess, he would have reached fifty kills.

Sicarius Primus.

'The outcome,' he said, whispering the maxim of the Vindicare Temple, 'justifies the deed.'

But the deed wasn't necessary. Raithe could tell from the jellied flesh under his hands, the staring eyes bulging from the sockets, the ice-cold skin and black tongue swelling out of the mouth.

Yavarius-Khau was dead.

And had been for some time.

THIRTY

'Stop! Stop!' screamed Baron Yuma. 'Hold fire!'

But the amount of weapons discharge made him nearly impossible to hear over external laud-hailer – Sycorax stood right next to him, and could barely hear him even with a vox-connection.

So when the *Crown*'s ion shield ruptured, a few stray shots hit the lower superstructure, blackening its legs, melting an adamantine shin plate.

And severing the guy-wires that secured the Knight Castellan to the arena without power.

At first, it seemed nothing would result apart from a few armour replacements.

Then the great machine's head dipped, its carapace shell rolling forward on loose shoulder servos. Unhealthy blue smoke, like the fumes of a bloated corpse, outgassed from the upright reactor vents.

'Holy Terra,' she whispered in her own voice, so stunned she forgot to use Rakkan's.

The antique Knight Castellan, shared by every High Monarch of Dominion since the world declared unity before Horus' betrayal, fell first to its armour-plated knees, and then onto its crowned face.

It hit the hatch to the field's lower gallery, the plating bowing with the Knight's fall. Dirt leapt into the air as if from a battle cannon impact, mixing with the haze of weapons discharge and corpse-smoke venting from the *Crown*'s reactor.

And through her enhanced vision she saw Raithe, clinging to a mounting rail, slide nimbly to the tournament field.

Ninety thousand people, panicking and stunned, began to roar.

For a moment, she did not know what they were saying – but then she made it out.

'Dead! The king is dead!'

Absolom Raithe rolled in the dust plume of the fallen Knight, trying to get his bearings.

His mask cogitators had identified and marked fourteen Knights. Seven Questoris-class, seven Armiger-class. The threat level of their weaponry was unbelievable.

And at first nothing happened.

Then his mask flashed *Incoming fire*.

It took *Jester*'s targeting augurs a moment to cut through the haze of death-smoke and dust, and reacquire Raithe. Enough time for him to get a head start.

Sycorax's thermal spear was at extreme range, too far for accuracy and probably wouldn't hit with killing power. Which is exactly why she fired it before anyone else.

She fired low, scorching the earth where Raithe had just been standing, watching as the heat-wash bubbled the blue-red paint on the *Crown*'s topside. Yuma's gatling cannon smashed her thermal spear down to the ground.

'*Do not hit the king, pursue the traitor. Melee weapons and heavy stubbers only around the monarch.*'

It wasn't mere instruction, it was imperative will, and she was running before she gave *Jester* the signal to do so.

Raithe had leapt onto the *Crown of Dominion*, taking cover in its fallen armour plates, hoping to dissuade their fire by sheltering among the sacred Knight.

Streams of tracer fire zipped downrange from Sycorax's sinister quadrant, and she saw Vossa sprint up alongside her, peppering the *Crown* with suppressing fire.

On her dexter quadrant, another Armiger Warglaive – the friendly Sir Sangraine in *Fencer* – closed in, hunting for a kill.

There was nowhere for Raithe to go. Nothing but open ground and sheer arena walls for hundreds of feet. Sycorax had learned the danger of the open tournament field only minutes ago, and she'd been in a fully armoured and shielded Knight suit.

Her only chance – hells, Raithe's only chance – was if she could get to him before the other Armigers.

And motivating herself to do it was not hard, because she had Yuma's order burning in her mind, spurring her on like a horse feeling the spurs in its flanks, urging her to close with Raithe…

Then rip him apart. But she would deal with that last part when she got there. Right now, she had to use it. She bolted between Vossa and Sangraine, urging her suit to get a nose ahead. Zigging slightly in front of Vossa to interrupt her line of fire.

Then she was at the kill site, armoured feet scuttling on adamant plating. Climbing the dead hunk of metal that once contained the beating heart of Dominion's government. She saw Raithe, sliding into the crook of the Castellan's arm, next to the cold coils of the plasma decimator.

He was doing something there, grabbing and pulling components, trying to get inside the system.

To overload it. Create a backfire detonation of the ammunition – a miniature plasma bomb to get the Armigers off his
back when they came to look for him. Maybe take one or two
with him.

Idiot.

Sycorax revved her chain-cleaver and plunged it down into
the space between plasma weapon and carapace, chewing dirt
and grass, throwing teeth as she accidentally contacted steel. To
anyone watching, it would seem she was digging for the traitor.

Raithe thought so too, because he'd made himself small,
curling up in the elbow joint where the clumsy chain-cleaver
couldn't reach even when the kill imperative in Sycorax's mind
jumped the cleaver in his direction.

Then Sycorax withdrew the weapon and keyed her internal
vox. Clicked her throat twice for *Go.*

And just as Vossa got around her and angled her stubber
down, he made a dashing slide below *Crown of Dominion's* fallen
arm – stubber rounds drumming the panel behind him.

'What are we doing?' asked Rakkan. He was bleeding from a
head wound. The crowd had started ripping up wood from the
stands to build barricades and use as weapons. Gangs of peasants were now creating unofficial checkpoints, beating or killing
anyone they suspected of being part of the murder. Many in the
crowd had crude magnoculars, and had seen Yavarius-Khau's
body lying on the grass.

They'd bludgeoned anyone wearing an aquila. Anyone with
an accent. Rakkan had seen a woman beaten because she
didn't have calluses on her hands, and could therefore not
be a real peasant. Her wails that she worked in a scriptorium
went unheeded.

The mob was jumping barriers, pouring onto the field to

converge on the fallen *Crown of Dominion*, heedless of the Knights running towards it.

Koln had to break them through to the service area, clearing a path of cracked skulls and fractured limbs. One fanatic had hit her directly in the head with a plank of wood. The plank broke, then the man wielding it.

She'd got them past a caged gate and welded it shut with a micro-melta in her index finger. Stolen them a few grey robes matching those the arena servants wore.

'If Raithe has succeeded–'

'Was that the plan? Were you keeping that fro–'

'No,' she snapped. 'It wasn't. He and I are going to have words over it. But if he has succeeded,' she stood aside to let a few panicked servants run past, 'then he needs a distraction if he hopes to get out alive. Something to draw forces towards us and away from him.' She sidled up to a doorway and glanced inside. 'This is it, the mass-refectarium hall.'

Koln ducked inside, scanning the room for threats. It was empty; everyone had panicked and run. She knelt down before a bubbling pot in an alcove oven, and reached beneath it.

'So I helped you find the kitchen – are you going to distract them with food?'

'No, fire,' said Koln, drawing out a burning log and considering it, tilting it so the flame spread. 'Kitchens are where you find the fire.'

Raithe dashed sideways, keeping the superstructure of the *Crown of Dominion* between him and the advancing Knights. They were reluctant to fire at him near the wreck, and he would take advantage of that for as long as possible.

A heavy stubber tore the ground behind him, spanged off the rear armature of a leg he ran behind.

And then, he saw the crowd. Surging. Charging. Coming for him.

'The king!' a woman yelled. 'He's killed the king!'

Hands on him, grasping, pulling.

He lashed out with his pistol, feeling a skull give way as he struck it with the butt. Ducked low and kicked the legs out from another assailant, tripping the two peasants behind.

Weapons activation, right quadrant.

Raithe threw himself backward, scrambling beneath the ankle of the fallen Knight as a Helverin autocannon drilled indiscriminately into the crowd. Blasting chests open, sending limbs flying.

The mob screamed and retreated – but only on that side.

Raithe crawled away – out from under the *Crown*'s foot – to see a fresh charge meeting him.

'Kill *him, kill him. Do not let him escape.*'

Sycorax did not obey, she desired, willed, *acted.*

Yuma had pushed hard, made his imperative *her* imperative. That was how orders worked, when an Armiger pilot bonded to a larger Knight. It hijacked the impulse centre of her brain with an almost undeniable compulsion to kill the traitor who'd murdered her king.

She clawed over the fallen monarch, ready to spring onto Raithe.

To her right, Vossa let off another tearing fusillade at the crowd, her targeting array confused by the number of man-sized targets. She growled in fury, waded into them, trying to find the assassin.

Kill him, howled the ghost choir. *Kill the regicide!*

In the edge of her tunnel-focused vision, she could see Sir Sangraine wading into the crowd with his own cleaver, frantic, the eyes of his Armiger burning red.

Then she sighted Raithe, scrambling under the *Crown*'s leg, and beheld the traitor through a haze of red.

Raithe knew he was done. Surrounded by the mob. Hunted by the Armigers.

The crowd, emboldened and furious, was running into the fallen Knight Castellan now, swarming into the crevices where he'd managed to take shelter.

And his spy mask, his spy mask made him instantly recognisable.

He zigged and zagged to the opposite leg of the *Crown*, batting away hands as they reached for him. Leaping through the loops of cabling that hung in between the Castellan's legs.

A man swung a piece of bench at him.

Raithe took his head off with a pistol shot before ducking under his arm.

Incoming fire.

He juked right, avoiding a meltagun blast from an Armiger that melted four civilians in his path, then took advantage of the hole in the crowd that it had created, splashing ankle-deep through the remains.

Then, a man tackled him. Brought him to the ground.

He was big, the man. Nearly Raithe's size. Raithe hit the ground hard, bracing so his breath would not be knocked out of him. Locked the man with one arm and rolled deeper into the crook of the *Crown*'s leg.

'Kill the traitor!' yelled Yuma.

Kill him, ordered the ancestors.

Kill, kill, kill, urged the ambient thought-network emanating from the two other frenzied Armigers. *Do your duty. Honour the ancestors. Embrace the power of the ancestors. Destroy the regicide.*

There were so many voices. Too many personalities overlaid

one on top of the other. She was Sycorax, in the constructed persona of Rakkan, being simultaneously advised by a choir of ancestors with her will slaved to Baron Yuma. Even her artifice was cracking under the strain, psyche torn between the multiple roles she had to simultaneously inhabit.

Sycorax wanted to save Raithe, Rakkan wanted to kill him to improve his standing, Yuma wanted revenge, the ancestors glory. She could hear the thoughts of Vossa and Sangraine, even those Questoris Knights converging on them, looking for a connection to see or control what the Armiger squires were doing. A bonfire of rage, merging into one. A stir of voices urging Sycorax-Rakkan to kill the traitor.

No, she willed.

Traitor! screamed the ancestral choir. *He is resisting us! Trying to save the assassin. Not Rakkan. Not Rakkan!*

Then she saw him. His mask. Among the crowd. Twenty hands on him, already tearing him apart. His jerkin ripped to shreds, showing pale flesh beneath.

Jester locked a firing solution, and her thermal spear came up nearly of its own accord. Raithe's head and shoulders poked above the over-under barrels of the weapon.

'Nnnnnnggggggggaaaaaah,' she said. Her teeth clenched so hard they nearly cracked as she activated the weapon.

Absolom Raithe was liquefied along with thirteen members of the mob. Their flesh ran like candles on a fire, bones cracking and cooking black, shot through with the orange glow of burning marrow. Leaving no trace, apart from the distorted lump of his spy mask.

And three clicks in her internal micro-bead. They bore Raithe's unique bead signature. *Extraction successful.*

The calculating son of a bitch had put the mask on someone else.

PART THREE

KINGMAKERS

THIRTY-ONE

>>Surveillance Transcript [Device Designation: 22-Beta]
>>Operation: Kingmaker
>>File No. 5782-Gamma-KMKR
>>Mission Day: 23
>>Subject Bugged: Baron Titus Yuma
>>DO NOT TRANSMIT<<

YUMA: How did this happen? How did Dask allow this to happen?

ACHARA: Now, Titus, I don't think assigning blame is–

HAWTHORN: You're sure he's dead?

YUMA: Of course he's dead. He was already in poor shape. Living in the throne too long. One step away from the Dreadnoughts of the Adeptus Astartes.

KRAINE: Why were the houses not told of his condition? Why was I not told? Ancestors' sake, Yuma, I'm your damned brother. You always went on about how great a man he was.

YUMA: He *was* a great man, Tiberius. Great men still get old.

And if his state was fully known, Stryder and Rau would have been tearing at each others' throats.

ACHARA: That's privileged information, Titus.

YUMA: It hardly matters now, does it? After that display at the tournament his incapacity was all too clear.

[AUDIO: Door opening, sealing.]

HAWTHORN: Glad you could join us, Gatekeeper Dask. After all, this is only the greatest crisis in four decades and we have no idea what's going on, so why would we need a spymaster?

DASK: I am afraid that the High Monarch, though of strong body, was slain by the–

[Hawthorn laughs]

YUMA: They know, Symphonia. I told them.

DASK: That could have terrible conse–

YUMA: What did you know, Symphonia?

DASK: Give me a moment, Titus. It's chaos out there. Mobs in the streets, attacking anyone they perceive as enemies of our late monarch. Four of my footmen are out in the basilica square, hanging from lamp posts. Another group seems to have set fire to a wing of the arena. The mobs are furious we shot them up as they tried to catch the killer. And that speech…

YUMA: The plot.

DASK: A hinterland rebel operation. Who knows how they got so far into Gathering Palace. Infiltrated amid the streams of peasants from the near countryside, I expect. They bombed the box checkpoint and sent in a strike force, but apparently that was only a feint to allow an off-worlder, some kind of mercenary based on the partial mask we recovered, to slay our lamented king.

YUMA: An off-worlder you were seen speaking to, I understand.

DASK: What are you suggesting?

YUMA: Always talking about your whispers and rumours,

your agents everywhere – what good did it do, eh? He's dead. Our king is dead on *your* watch and you didn't breathe a hint of a plot.

DASK: Don't shout at me, Kingsward. You're the one who was gallivanting around on the field and leaving the monarch unguarded. The High Monarch's person is your remit. If I failed, so did you.

YUMA: Tell us. Right now. Tell us what you knew.

ACHARA: Yuma, put away that mace.

[AUDIO: Sounds of a scuffle.]

KRAINE: Brother! Brother! Hear her out.

DASK: Months ago my agents discovered a traitor working in Gathering Palace. A court messenger. She was highly trained and broke away from us when she was discovered. We pursued her to a broadcast station. Sir Sabban slew her but she appeared to have broadcast a message off-world.

HAWTHORN: That smacks of the Imperium.

YUMA: And you didn't think this was relevant to the monarch's security?

DASK: It was too inflammatory to get out. You had no compunction keeping the king's health a secret, Yuma.

YUMA: That's different.

DASK: The secessionist faction could have used it as pretext to push the movement forward. And while secession might be popular with the houses, it isn't the policy of this government. You manage the families, we manage the policy, that is how it's always been.

KRAINE: It sounds like it was the policy of its monarch, if you'd let him speak, Achara.

ACHARA: A government is more than its head. The monarch cannot control the court on a whimsy, just as you cannot control all of House Rau. Leadership by monarchic decree is not government, it's tyranny. Particularly when the monarch is a madman.

YUMA: Careful...

ACHARA: He's not monarch any more, Yuma. And has been less so every day. He wasn't a king by the end, just a man in a chair. You know how much that hurts me to say, but it's the truth.

YUMA: She still hasn't told us who the killer was.

DASK: I don't know. He claimed to be one of Sabban's off-worlders, sent to give a report Sabban promised last night. Now I suspect the hinterland rebels intercepted that message, killed Sabban, and replaced his man. I spoke to Sabban not ten hours ago, but his tracking implant has gone silent. The assassin was killed by Sir Rakkan via a thermal spear. Unfortunately the number of bodies and the free use of melta weapons in that brawl mean his body is unrecoverable.

HAWTHORN: Who was Sabban investigating?

DASK: Rakkan. I have sent a summons insisting he come to the palace. I want him watched.

HAWTHORN: You think Rakkan killed the High Monarch? Rakkan? My son?

DASK: He's just returned, and with a retinue of outsiders. I am unsure how he connects to the sophisticated vox-system. But he could be a tool of greater powers. The Inquisition. Perhaps even the Officio Assassinorum–

ACHARA: Don't be silly, Symphonia, everyone knows that doesn't exist.

HAWTHORN: Servants tied Rakkan's shoes until he was ten. His liver looks like an artillery range. Don't mistake me, I love the boy, but he's not overthrowing any governments. Hells, he's an *Armiger pilot*.

YUMA: Let's move away from Rakkan. Because I want to

know – you had suspicions about Sabban's man... you let him in? Some gatekeeper.

HAWTHORN: I admit the snare backfired. I accept–

KRAINE: Where are you going, Hawthorn?

HAWTHORN: Oh, nowhere. Merely to tell House Stryder that the court has been part of a coup against our beloved monarch, that they imprisoned him and tied his hands as an uprising ravaged the hinterland and Imperial spies infested the planet. I think it would convince the fence-sitters to take a greater interest in the Imperial question, don't you?

[Pause: 2 seconds]

[AUDIO: Door opening, sealing.]

TESSELL: You can't do that.

HAWTHORN: My, what sharp ears you have, Arch-Maintenancer. And why exactly can't I? Because it would start a civil war? We would win the war.

TESSELL: No, because by law none of you can leave this room.

ACHARA: She's right. We are in conclave.

KRAINE: You expect us to stay in here, arguing, while the houses spoil for war outside?

TESSELL: Yes, I do. Because it is your duty and a part of who we are. On the death of a High Monarch the court and heads of the houses gather in conclave, and vote for a new monarch. The security forces can handle the streets. Indeed, I have enacted the Conclave Protocol as is my right, and if any of you leave this room the sacristan monks guarding it will use force to prevent you.

[Pause: 1 second]

TESSELL: Non-lethal force, at first. But if you're persistent there are other remedies. My sacristans have put all Knight suits under guard, the ban on mounting the noble machines during conclave is now in force. No one will be going to war, at least not in our ancestral war-gods, until after the coronation.

YUMA: She allowed my monarch to be killed, Arch-Maintenancer. An eternal stain on the honour of both me and my noble machine, a–

TESSELL: A stain that can be wiped away only by good service to a new monarch, Yuma. Let the past be past. All of us have failed. We have here a Kingsward who cannot ward the king, a Gatekeeper who cannot keep the gate, a herald who keeps her monarch silent, and two heads of houses that can't keep their heads straight or houses in line. I myself am a maintenancer who could not keep my monarch well and healthy despite living inside our greatest vessel. Soon, we'll be joined by a Master of Justice who takes months to decapitate a few rebels.

ACHARA: Fontaine is on his way?

TESSELL: Yes, I signalled him. He approaches at the head of the army.

ACHARA: He can't march an army into the streets of Gathering Palace, not with things as they are. The populace will turn on them as traitors and conspirators, they'll tear the palace-city apart.

KRAINE: And I'm not letting any Stryder, even a member of the court, bring an army into Gathering Palace while we're in conclave.

HAWTHORN: We need him.

KRAINE: You need his vote, you mean.

TESSELL: I have sent negotiation broadcasts to Baron Fontaine. He has agreed to abide by law and leave the fyrd at Pikeridge Pass, beyond the mountains, and come alone at all haste. The army's proximity, three days' march from Gathering Palace, can act as a threat against disorder in the streets. Though I'm sure we can expect a few house murders during conclave, as there always are. I'm sure this is satisfactory?

[Pause: 3 seconds]

TESSELL: Good. Now that you have all remembered yourselves and your solemn duties, I think we should call for food and vin. If memory serves, it will take time to choose a monarch.

'After all that. All that castigating about following the plan, following orders, not improvising, being careful about exposure. Insisting on killing Rakkan as too much of a risk. He just… walks up and shoots the monarch.'

Sycorax decapitated the training dummy and sank her phase sword in its belly, spilling the simulated viscera.

She was in her natural form, or at least, the form she'd chosen as a default. Sheathed in her synskin bodysuit with the hood down.

Getting comfortable, Koln supposed. Using her rage to re-familiarise herself with the body she'd no doubt need shortly. In a way, Koln was doing the same – channelling frustration into the chart of hard-copy picts and notes she'd affixed to the inside wall of a command centre disguised as a shipping container. One wall opened like a drawbridge at the touch of a button, and the outside contained enough hazardous materials markings to dissuade even the most enthusiastic search party.

'I'm not thrilled either,' she answered, without looking up from her chart.

Sycorax rebuilt the training dummy and dismembered it again. 'He said he wanted our expertise. That we would use all our skills. He lied. Just wanted to get close enough to take the shot himself. Claim the kill.'

'He's the commander. He can do what he likes…' Koln trailed off. 'Lycan-Bast is a first cousin, or second cousin?'

'Second,' said Sycorax, uppercutting a second dummy's groin so the blade would impale the target's genitals, intestines, stomach, and sever the connection with both lungs. 'So you'll just accept it?'

'Can't change it, I suppose,' said Koln. 'Better to keep an even head, see how we can turn this to our advantage.'

'So he gets to be Sicarius Primus, and we get to figure out how to play speed-regicide with killers encased in Knight armour. Yuma got inside my head, you know. Ordered me. Made his will my own. Felt more than him, too. All those compulsions echoing from the Armigers. It gave me flashbacks to having that heretek Quivarian in my brain.' She stopped, her blade pausing as she quartered a dummy like a game fowl. 'How are you so Throne-damned calm?'

'Active meditation protocols and focus-chants,' Koln breathed through pursed lips, as if she were exhaling lho-stick smoke. 'Aided by a few chemicals.'

'Think I'll join you,' said Absolom Raithe.

He came out of the forward crew compartment, each footstep so quiet no one asked how he'd gotten inside without alerting them. His hair was wet, and combed back. Right arm shoved into a pocket of an exercise bodyglove. In his left hand, he'd managed to weave his fingers around the neck of an amasec bottle and thread three fingers into glasses.

'You,' said Sycorax. 'Nice of you to show up. I see you took the time to shower.'

'Took me a while getting back,' he said, setting the bottle and glasses on an oil barrel and sitting back in a foldable camp chair. Koln thought she detected one eye twitch in a wince when he leaned back, but it was hard to tell with the Vindicare. 'After I clapped the mask on a civilian and you smoked him – thanks for that, by the way – I got lost in the stampede. Found a hatch into the under-pens where they keep the ferocious animals, found a small effluent channel. Started as a ditch, became a pipe. Good thing I brought a throwaway rebreather in addition to the mask. Dumped me out in one of the poorer out-districts of Gathering Palace.'

'We're blown,' said Sycorax, stepping close. Her blade, Koln noticed, was still out. 'You spoke, face to face, with their counter-intelligence chief and then killed Yavarius-Khau in front of every high worthy on Dominion. Started a damned counter-revolution in the streets.'

'I had to fight my way out with Rakkan,' said Koln. 'Started a fire to cover you. Killed a few peasants, I think. It was a bit over-whelming for our guest, he's sleeping. But at least the court, for now, is ascribing it all to hinterland rebels. They think you're an outside mercenary recruited by them, and that the attacks were coordinated. Rakkan is still suspected. He's been summoned back to the palace where he can be watched.'

'We owe a lot to those hinterlanders,' said Raithe. He picked up the bottle in his left hand and poured three drinks, tall ones. 'The operation was almost blown. Dask sniffed me out. Knew I wasn't one of Sabban's crew. Either way I'd have had to go loud to exfiltrate, but under the cover of an attack they'll stop asking who I was with. Better for them to think the High Monarch was killed by rebels than by outside forces. And the mobs provided useful cover. I ran into a few fanatic barricades, but given that I was caked with filth, they let me go as a mute beggar.'

'You just might be, when I get through with you,' snarled Sycorax.

'Have a drink, I always like one after hitting a target.' He raised the glass in a toast. 'To Yavarius-Khau, who still manages to surprise us.'

Sycorax backhanded the glass out of his hand. The crystal shattered on the deck.

'You listen here, you sanctimonious arsehole.' She brought the phase blade around beneath his chin. 'What you did put all our lives in danger. Put the operation in danger. I had to fight that machine to keep it from killing you, and now it's rejected me. The Rakkan identity is blown. *Jester* won't even let me hook into it.'

'I saw an opportunity and I took it. With your improvisational style, I thought you'd appreciate that.'

'Groxshit. You saw an opportunity to get kill number fifty. Become Sicarius Primus. To hell with the rest of the operation, who cares if you died on exfiltration? We'd clean up your mess. As long as you got yours. That's what you Vindicare do. One pull of the trigger, another mark on your rifle stock, and you're gone. You never have to see the aftermath. That's for others, you just get your kill.'

'It wasn't a kill,' Raithe said, picking up another of the glasses. 'You mind if I drink this?'

Sycorax blinked. 'What?'

Koln turned away from her chart, no longer watching peripherally. 'What do you mean, not a kill?'

'I breached the hatch porthole. Took six penetrator rounds to do it. Was out of rounds so I reached in to do him with my hands. He was already dead. No kill.'

'From shock?' Koln asked. 'Cardiac arrest during your attack? My bug recordings say he was in bad health.'

'At first I thought so,' Raithe said. Koln could see him looking Sycorax directly in the eyes. 'Thought it was just a bad shoot. That he'd gone cardiac, or a piece of shattered window crystal embedded in his brain. But he was stone cold. Way past rigor mortis. Bloated, decaying. He'd been dead days, maybe weeks. Terminal before we even arrived here.'

Sycorax withdrew the blade, took a step back, and laughed. It was a cold, rueful sound.

'I've been listening to broadcasts out of the conclave,' said Koln. 'Via the bug Sycorax planted on Yuma. They admitted to the house heads that Yavarius-Khau was mad, that they'd been isolating him and speaking for him to prevent a house war. They didn't say he was *dead*, though. Maybe they were holding that back until the right time.'

'Then who was speaking for him at the tournament?' asked Sycorax. 'That outburst. If he was dead...'

'Someone in the court?' Koln guessed. 'Achara seemed surprised, but she's clearly capable of deception.'

'The Arch-Maintenancer cut it off,' Sycorax said. 'Maybe she triggered it in the first place. Or Dask, who's clearly capable of something that ruthless.'

'Does it matter?' asked Raithe. 'Given that they're in conclave, any stratagem that involves Yavarius-Khau being alive is moot. And if a faction tries to wield the power of the mob during the conclave, we'll know who is responsible. Right now, we have to move fast and hard to put our man or woman on the throne.'

'We have no plan,' said Sycorax.

'Koln has a plan,' said Raithe. He took a sip of his amasec. 'At least she's making one.'

'Things are in flux, but I have ideas. Lord Bazile Daggar-Kraine is by far our best candidate. The most pro-Imperial and with the right bloodline. But being the son of Baron Kraine will mean Stryder will have several other preferred candidates. They won't like putting a direct child of a Rau House head in the pilot throne. We can't just kill one or two to clear the way for him. He likely won't be elected in the first few rounds of voting. This is going to be fluid, and it'll take more than one sanction.'

'Sycorax,' said Raithe. 'You wanted me to trust you two. And we're going to have to work on the fly. Hitting multiple targets, hours apart, and adapting to a fluid situation. Avaaris monitors the conclave and designates the targets, you and I serve as hitters.' Raithe pulled his right hand out of his pocket and rotated the arm in an overhead swim-stroke. Koln saw his jaw tense, teeth pressing together. 'Think we're up to it? I do.'

Sycorax smiled, tapped her teeth with a fingernail, mulling.

'Are you all right?' Koln asked, jutting a chin at Raithe's shoulder.

'Perfectly,' he said. 'Just stretching it. What do you say, Callidus? Ready for a little improvisation?'

'The king is dead,' said Sycorax, smiling her mocking, lopsided smile and raising her glass in a toast. 'Long live the king.'

THIRTY-TWO

HAWTHORN: We have been arguing for nine hours. We should bring it to a vote.

KRAINE: No.

HAWTHORN: Why not? Because you know he'll lose?

KRAINE: Tarn-Kegga is a brilliant candidate.

YUMA: He is impressive on the field. Current Summer Champion.

HAWTHORN: It is midwinter. Past midwinter. His term as champion has lapsed.

ACHARA: Well... that may not be accurate. The Summer Champion passes the Banner of Victory to the Midwinter Champion at the end of the tournament. That is when he ceases to be the champion.

KRAINE: And gives up his extra electoral vote. Therefore he still has it.

HAWTHORN: That is absurd. No one would stand for the fate of this planet being decided on such ceremonial trivialities.

ACHARA: It's not trivial, it's tradition. A sacred institution.

HAWTHORN: You wouldn't consider it so sacred if Kegga

favoured Stryder. And even so you don't have the votes. Do you, Baron Kraine?

FONTAINE: He does not.

DASK: No. Kegga is a good warrior, but doesn't have the constitution for rule. Even calling him Tarn-Kegga sends him into a fury.

TESSELL: Agreed. He is a brute.

KRAINE: And if I offered the Duchy of Waveshatter?

HAWTHORN: Waveshatter? That barren rock? Waveshatter has no reason to exist but to keep shellfish on my plate. If I'm selling the crown, I want more.

KRAINE: What about Raderfall Cairn?

[Pause: 2 seconds]

HAWTHORN: More.

'Renauldus Tarn-Kegga,' said Koln, pegging a pict-capture up with a dagger. He was a lantern-jawed man with thinning hair and a mocking augmetic eye. 'Not unexpected, given he's the Summer Champion.'

'Is he well liked?' asked Sycorax.

'No, strangely enough,' Koln responded. 'He's fairly open in his preference for Rau. At least that's what Rakkan told me in our briefings.'

All had agreed that, with Yavarius-Khau's death, Rakkan's role was largely over, and any further impersonation only risked exposure. They'd packed him and Gwynne off to their quarters in Gathering Palace to fulfil the summons, ensuring that when the escort came, both Koln and Raithe were seen alive and well. All were happy to distance Rakkan from this part of the operation. After all, killing the High Monarch was a sin Rakkan could probably live with given their history, but Koln argued he might not be so sanguine about eliminating, say, Lady Lycan-Bast or Mauvec Kawe.

'Kraine is holding a snap vote,' said Raithe. 'Hoping that civic instability and time pressure might buy him a vote from Arch-Maintenancer Tessell and he can bribe Hawthorn with territory. Will it work?'

'It might,' said Koln. 'The vox-snatchers I planted in the palace are paying dividends. Kegga has separatist feelings, which Hawthorn shares, and she may put that above Stryder interests if Kraine signs over enough domains so she can walk away smiling. Kegga isn't young, after all, and in the meantime, Stryder increases in power. Do you want my estimation?'

'I'd like to hear it,' Raithe nodded.

'Kraine knows this is his best shot, and that to put it through it needs to happen quickly. Hawthorn knows that too. Conclave has broken for the night, but I've detected messengers running back and forth between Kraine and Hawthorn's cells, and one messenger from Hawthorn to Dask.'

'Hawthorn's thinking about it,' said Sycorax. 'She's planning to squeeze Kraine for all he's worth, then throw her and Dask's votes to Kegga.'

'Precisely,' said Koln.

'So tell us about Kegga,' said Raithe.

'He's a beast-fighter, a hunter. Famous for it. His win in the summer tournament was due to tearing apart a carnosaur with his gauntlet.'

'Where is he?' said Sycorax.

'He keeps an exotic game preserve,' said Koln. 'Fifty miles south of here, out past the fens. Predation Manor. Gets most of his stock through the Sabban line, I understand.'

'I've got this one,' said Sycorax, then turned to Raithe. 'You take the next.'

* * *

PREDATION MANOR
22:06 DOMINION STANDARD

Like the fiercest animals, Renauldus Tarn-Kegga was most active at night.

That's when he preferred to stalk, to mount the noble Knight *Horned Hunter* and sprint out on the moorland, gunning down the flocks of razorkin he specifically bred so that he always had dangerous things to kill.

But special animals – the particularly dangerous or illegal specimens – were kept down here in the dungeon menagerie. A place of reinforced cages, chains rigged on pulleys, and the sweet stench of butchered meat.

Kegga knelt in front of the cell, ensuring that he kept six feet away from the bars. He held his chin in his right hand, as he often did while thinking, his index finger massaging his bottom lip.

He was watching how the beast moved.

'I know they are your vassals, lord,' said Vorcius Arun, the old reeve looking uncomfortable. 'And you are free to treat them as you will. But…'

'Come to the point,' Kegga growled. 'Bad enough that *Horned Hunter* is locked up in the stable, and *they* have to follow me everywhere.'

Kegga jerked his head towards the half-dozen footmen in his personal livery who stood in the centre of the room. Against one wall stood a combat servitor, its cable-wired arms replaced with a clamp and a shock prod.

'Now you bring me peasant grumblings.'

'Perhaps it would be better to discontinue the dead tithe while you are under consideration for the throne, lord.'

'Why?'

'For… political reasons. Your reputation, lord.'

'Baron Kraine is arranging it. What peasants think of me means nothing. Besides, it's not so much to ask.'

'It is their bodies, lord.'

'Only once they're dead,' Kegga snarled defensively. 'What are they going to do with them, put them in the ground? Waste of good feed-meat. Besides, how else am I supposed to satisfy this creature?' He threw a hand out towards the cage, then drew it back when he saw an unlidded purple eye shine in the dark.

'Grox, lord?'

'It does not like grox. It likes people. Alive, generally, but I'm no monster.' He nodded at a basket of freshly quartered body parts. 'Pass me an arm.'

Arun reached into the basket, grabbing an arm that seemed to be the least likely to stain his robes, and passed it to Kegga. In the depths of the cage, ink-black scales raced and bunched.

Kegga held the arm out towards the cage, and with a sound of scraping parchment, it was gone. Arun had a brief impression of movement, iridescent scales, and a triangular head long as a lasrifle with hooked teeth meant for snagging flesh.

'This will be the last one I kill in *Horned Hunter*,' Kegga said, almost wistful. Arun could see the lord's eyes shine with tears. 'Before the coronation, I'll let it loose in the chalk tunnels and track it down. By then, the hunger and shock-prodding will have made it aggressive enough to keep things interesting. I will miss *Hunter*, Arun. The *Crown* is all ranged weapons, nothing so primal as a thunderstrike gauntlet. But think of what I could kill in that massive hulk of machine. And what wild freaks of nature I could acquire if I became High Monarch.'

'Yes, but that's such a slippery word,' said Arun, stepping back.

'What word?'

'If,' said Arun, as he placed a foot between Kegga's shoulder blades.

And shoved.

Kegga sprawled forward, tumbling, arms out to catch himself. Eyes wide and mouth open in panic. He slapped onto the rockcrete, frantically pushing away from the bars on the palms of his hands.

Too late. The enormous serpent seized him by his right arm, dragging him bodily towards the enclosure.

Sycorax's enhanced senses let her note every detail. She read the fear in Kegga's eyes, the way the fingernails of his free hand shredded as he tried to find purchase on the flagstone. How he kicked out at the armoured purple eyes of the greater malkavan constrictor.

The *clang* of his body as it hit the bars. And the dry parchment sound as a tail as big around as a barrelhead snaked around his midsection, pinning him there.

She was already running when the footmen responded. Las-bolts flashed past her, into the darkness of the cage grille. In her peripheral vision, Sycorax saw a footman run to the stricken Kegga and try to haul the coil off his chest as the lord's face went purple.

Another grabbed her by the robes.

She didn't care, she was changing as she ran. Her slim, wiry form was loose in the reeve's robe so that she shed it like the malkavan constrictor shed its skin, so that the footman's hands were still entangled in the empty robe when she whirled and took his head off with the phase blade.

Sycorax pulled up her hood and sprinted left, hearing the *crack-crack* of laspistol fire whipping past. One las-bolt clipped the falling body of the decapitated footman and sent it tumbling.

Sycorax zigzagged towards the two firing at her, then dropped and slid between them, scything one down at the knees before leaping in a corkscrew rise that buried the flickering xenos blade into the other's back.

She went low, minimising her profile while getting her bearings in the fight. Realised how much chaos she'd caused. One footman had Kegga by the arms, trying to drag him away from the serpent's grip. Another aimed a laspistol point-blank at the reptile's head, recoiling and sheltering his eyes as his shots ricocheted off the reflective scales.

The other remaining footman was behind the combat servitor, trying to find its activation stud.

Then the tactical calculus changed all at once.

Kegga broke, his spine and ribs splintering with a wet crunch and chest folding in half as the strangler pulled his body through the bars.

And the combat servitor's glass eyes flared red.

The servitor hurtled towards her, the hiss of its pneumatic stimm-injectors firing and its shock-goad sparking. The weapon lit its pallid, mortified flesh in snaps of electric blue.

Sycorax drew the neural shredder from the small of her back, felt the hum of it as the gas activated, and let loose a billowing cone of empyric energy that washed over the servitor and its handler.

The footman collapsed against the wall, his nervous system ravaged and voluntary movement impossible. But the servitor, more augmetic than flesh, came on.

It snapped at her with the vice-claw, and she weaved low and under, slashing through its guts. The phase blade flickered in and out of reality, past armoured augmentations and scything flesh.

Exactly what she *didn't* need.

The vice came down on her back like a hammer, staggering her with the blow. A red dagger flashed in front of her face, temporarily blinding her in a blue haze as it overwhelmed her eyes with its light.

They were shooting at her. The footmen, caring nothing for

the servitor, were blazing into the combat. She threw up her phase blade in a guard, turned to dash around the servitor's side so its bulk could screen her from–

Bang. Electrical discharge. Charred synskin and flesh. Cold stone on her back.

Heartbeat palpitating in her temples, like she'd taken too big a hit of polymorphine.

Shock-prod. In her ribs by the feel of it. Threw her clear across the room and into a wall, knocking her skull across the stonework.

She lay still. Willed herself to stop breathing.

Servos whined as the servitor slowed its charge, depressants flooding its body as it sensed its task complete. It still continued towards her, one step at a time.

Thunk. Thunk. Thunk.

'Is it dead?' asked a voice.

Thunk.

'Throne, it moved fast. You see how it moved, Nek?'

Thunk. Thunk.

'I saw. It looks like a woman.' By his voice, Nek was rattled. Not thinking straight. 'But it was the reeve. *In* the reeve. Is it a daemon? It killed Lord–'

Thunk. Thunk.

'Keep your head. We'll put a few rounds in it to make sure.'

One advantage of the Callidus bodysuit was that its hood-lenses screened your eyes. Made it so the enemy never knew where you were looking. Right now Sycorax was looking at the servitor's approaching feet, judging the moment when she could move, plotting her route.

And it came. The servitor got close, fouling the aim of the footmen, and she took off at a slithering crawl, using the poly-morphine in her system to wriggle into shadows and deform herself through the bars of empty cages.

'Hells!' Nek shouted and fired two las-bolts that scorched the wall, and another that thumped into the servitor's back.

Sycorax gathered herself up in the shadows, climbed a cage to get above them as the pair wheeled around, firing at anything that moved.

And in a room full of captured game, *everything* moved.

'Come out!' the senior one ordered. 'There's no escaping. We have a hundred footmen in the manor.'

'Your men don't concern me,' Sycorax said.

They spun and fired up to where she'd been standing. Their fusillade stained the upper galleries red.

Sycorax was already behind them, legs wrapped around one of the hanging chains, descending head first so smoothly the links didn't even rattle.

'You've created a bloody mess,' said Nek. 'Evidence. The Master of Judgment will find you.'

'No,' she said, sounding rather bored. 'The grox-strangler will take care of the bodies.'

They spun towards her.

Just after she hit the activation rune that dropped the gate.

The enormous serpent came for them low and fast, their las-shots bouncing from its scales.

They were still screaming when Sycorax leapt off the top of the chain, and clambered through the grated skylight.

Six minutes later, she lay flat near the moor road, watching the windows of Predation Manor blink with gunfire.

When the sleek groundcar pulled up with its top down, she hopped into the passenger seat rather than opening the door.

'Good kill?' asked Raithe, his hands sheathed in soft driving gloves.

'Good kill,' Sycorax answered. 'No pursuit.'

Raithe offered her a lho-stick, and when she took it, she

noticed it had already been clipped in half. 'Why, Absolom. You don't have an...'

Raithe clicked an igniter. 'Koln said that's your usual.'

'You know,' she said, leaning forward to get a light, cupping the flame in one hand so it wouldn't be seen from a distance. 'As character flaws go, overpreparation has its attractions.'

Raithe hit the velocity pedal, causing the groundcar to leap into a sprint, barrelling down the back road with its forward lights doused. The illumination of the instrument panel was an island of light in the black moorland.

Sycorax leaned back, blowing smoke into the night and feeling the rush of acceleration in her hair.

'Okay,' she said, giving her tilted half-smile. 'So who's up next?'

KRAINE: And you had *nothing* to do with it?

HAWTHORN: He was a vicious boy who kept vicious creatures and died viciously. It's no mystery.

DASK: My men have found no indication of slaying, but the evidence was heavily digested.

YUMA: My lords, may I suggest urgency? This uncertainty is not good for stability. A mob has tried the palace gate three times today. Every hour we bicker, elements of the populace become more convinced Yavarius-Khau was killed in a coup.

HAWTHORN: I'm confused. Are we talking about the coup this court perpetrated for years, or a different coup?

DASK: No jests, Hawthorn, people are dying. Sir Lowwek and Dame Sedana are out in the square, hanging by their throats from a guildhall window. Lord Batalla is with the chirurgeons. Someone dropped a flagstone from a window and caved in his skull.

FONTAINE: Under siege by our own peasants.

TESSELL: I have a candidate suggestion. Lord Bazile Daggar-Kraine, pilot of *Holdfast*. He is moderate, has the right blood–

HAWTHORN: No.

TESSELL: He is relatively free of house politics. His combat exper–

HAWTHORN: No.

YUMA: You're fighting a losing battle, Dorthiya.

HAWTHORN: We will not be making Baron Kraine's son the High Monarch. Should I throw Rakkan's name in? He is moderate and has combat experience. Maybe we should plug *him* into the *Crown of Dominion*?

KRAINE: Don't be absurd. Name a serious candidate.

HAWTHORN: Fine. Sakas-Varn.

ACHARA: That fire-eating secessionist?

[Pause: 1 second]

FONTAINE: She's worth considering.

'Lady Vagara Sakas-Varn,' said Koln, sliding the pict across the camp table. Despite the image grain, Raithe made out the woman's knife-thin face and the gathered pile of her hair. A tube ran up one nostril.

He committed the face to memory. 'I can do it. Where is she?'

'Part of the contingent that made it out to their estates after the tournament,' said Koln. 'But I think we can arrange for her to return, catch her on the road.'

'Are you right for this one, Raithe?' Sycorax raised an eyebrow. 'It might look suspicious if her head explodes during transit.'

'My operational capabilities go far beyond–'

'Relax, I'm baiting you.'

'Actually,' said Koln, 'I thought we might all collaborate on this one.'

* * *

Lady Vagara Sakas-Varn's head hit the cushioned ceiling of the auto-carriage, and she cursed the driver.

She thumped the ceiling with a fist. 'What the hells are you doing up there?'

'Sorry, lady,' he said through the armoured screen. 'The roads.'

'The roads, the roads,' she mimicked. 'If he gives me another jolt like that I'll tie him to the back of the carriage and let him see the roads up close.'

Her squire, Sir Padgraine, laughed and wrote the quip on his slate.

That was his job – to laugh and write. Recording the triumphs, observances, cutting retorts, and every blow she struck on the tournament field. Since they'd been seventeen, he'd been building a record of Sakas-Varn's deeds. A complete history of the woman who he believed, even when the possibility seemed remote, would one day be High Monarch.

And if that had meant a little assistance from him here or there – a bit of addler venom slipped into an opponent's cup before a tournament match, a vicious scandal planted and discovered, or made up from nothing – well, that was just the business of court.

That old crone Achara thought the duty of a herald was to serve as a mouthpiece. A communication channel. A conduit – Throne help us – between the ruler and the ruled.

Padgraine cared little for such old-fashioned notions. As Sakas-Varn's unofficial herald, he'd helped create her. They'd served as partners in her elevation, an active participant in his lady's rise.

And now, she would rise higher than ever – taking Padgraine with her.

'What are you smiling about?' asked Sakas-Varn. She said it with snap, but not without warmth.

'Thinking about myself on that dais, at your right hand, and Achara down in front of us. You think she'll cry when you take her off the court?'

'I hope so. I think we'll see a few tears on coronation day, don't you?' She stretched like a feline. 'Read it again, will you, Roddie?'

Padgraine opened the message on his data-slate. This would be the seventh or eighth time he'd recited it, and it was starting to get a little old without spicing it up with a tease.

'From Symphonia Dask,' he started, then paused with an impish grin.

'Don't start that game again. The rest! The rest!'

'Hail, Lady Varaga Sakas-Varn. Conclave seriously discussing your candidacy. You will likely have the votes by afternoon. Come at once, as presence in capital is vital given security situation. Due to unrest, please use the trunk road through Latarin Moor. May I give you my...'

'Oh, don't start that again.'

'It's gone.'

'What?'

'It... it was here on the slate, but now it's gone. Strange.'

Sakas-Varn leaned over to his side of the auto-carriage, her brow wrinkling. 'What did you touch?'

He was about to say something when they heard shouting.

Range to target: .82 miles

Air temperature: +5.3 degrees from Freeze Point

Wind speed: 15 miles per hour, north-northeast

Humidity and temperature above acceptable equipment tolerances

Raithe watched the auto-carriage through his mask optics, the read-outs painting the sides of his vision. The bulky auto-carriage bounced and swayed on the bad dirt road, driver exposed to the elements.

It was his reserve mask. A little older. Its efficiency was about five per cent below the one destroyed at the tournament, but when plugged via cable into the rifle scope, it performed nearly as well.

It was a big carriage, opulent, built on a cargo-hauler base. Six inflated rubberine tyres, neck-high on a standing man, kept the passenger compartment and driver's cab off the ground.

From his shooting hide, atop a seven-hundred-foot tor and shielded by an ancient stone cairn, he could see all the little details – gilded edging along the carriage's lines, golden statues of Questoris-pattern Knight suits decorating each corner of the roof. Each statue held a lightning bolt in its outstretched hand and had a hooded falcon on its armoured shoulder. They glinted in the winter afternoon.

Raithe sent a mind-impulse to his mask. It tinted the eye-lenses to ensure a stray reflection of sunlight didn't dazzle him when he scoped onto the target.

'Approaching interception point,' he said.

One click in his micro-bead. Sycorax acknowledging.

Movement on the moor. He watched peripherally, keeping his eyes on the auto-carriage. Dark shapes crawled forward at the crest of the hills surrounding the road.

Koln hadn't found it hard to provoke the attack. Indeed, she'd done it in hours. Sycorax had only needed to drop into a few taverns, start a few rumours. Nail a few crude handbills to the doors of guildhalls and chapels. Lady Sakas-Varn was a traitor. Sakas-Varn had helped kill the king. Sakas-Varn was coming to take her corrupt prize – the crown of their slain monarch – that afternoon, by the Latarin Moor Road.

Sakas-Varn, who was ever so good at wiping out peasant-criminals in the arena.

Koln had done her work well. Sycorax had mixed into the peasant ambush below, but she hadn't needed to lead or incite.

Yavarius-Khau had broken the dam, Koln only had to direct the flow.

The auto-carriage passed out of sight behind a low hill, and Raithe settled in behind his scope, training it on his pre-calibrated sector of fire where the dirt road passed between the hills. The scope's auditory sensors registered a rising yell and the crack of stubber fire a moment before the gunshots echoed across the moorland and washed over his near-proximity mask sensors. It also picked up engine acceleration.

He rolled his shoulder forward, then back. Whatever he'd done to it climbing the *Crown* had not been good, and his rope ascent up the tor had aggravated it. Just building a shooting hide from the cairn's rocks and lifting his rifle into position had triggered a deep burn in the ligaments along with a disquieting weakness.

The recoil, he knew, would hurt.

Hopefully not enough to spoil his second shot.

Range to target: .82 miles

Air temperature: +5.4 degrees from Freeze Point

Wind speed: 14 miles per hour, north-northeast. ATTN: Beware localised wind tunnel at target location

Then the auto-carriage was in his scope, rising up on the road. Stubber fire hammered it from above, chipping the gilded statues of Questoris Knights and cracking the reinforced windows. A mob of peasants sprinted into the roadway to block the carriage's path, and the driver accelerated to run them down.

Raithe slid his sights one point left to align them, found the target and squeezed the trigger.

The Exitus hammered his injured shoulder like a pile-driver and he felt tendons grate and slide. He sucked cold, heather-scented air through his teeth, covering the sound of the rifle's cough and the bullet zipping downrange.

The unbalanced auto-carriage pitched forward on its burst

tyre and slewed to one side so hard it went up on two wheels for a moment. The crowd recoiled, fearing they'd be crushed.

Raithe had the second tyre in his scope, right where the tread met the road.

He fired, and shouted in pain.

'Lady,' Padgraine shook Sakas-Varn. 'Awaken, lady! Varaga, wake, we have to go!'

Lady Varaga Sakas-Varn opened her eyes to find one seeing red. Bloodshot, she realised. 'What...?'

'Hinterlanders,' said Padgraine. 'Or peasants. We overturned.'

She sat up, pressing a hand to her head, seeing how it came away bloody. 'We'll go into the cab,' she said. 'Get the vox. Call assistance from Gathering Palace. I am to be queen, and these dirt-eating peasants aren't capable of killing a queen.'

But then a workingman's crowbar slammed into the gap between the warped door and its armoured frame, and a handheld melta-torch, the kind used in the Gathering Palace armouries, whispered its hushed song of melting steel.

And when the door opened, she found out exactly what peasants were capable of.

'*Good kill,*' voxed Sycorax. Raithe heard it in his internal micro-bead, as he zipped up his guncase left-handed.

'Good kill,' he responded, as he slung the case and anchored the mono-filament cable from his descent kit, paying out a line from the sensor-controlled spool on the small of his back. 'Meet you at the bottom.'

Then he leapt into space, arms outstretched, controlling the descent spool with his left hand – because he couldn't feel his fingers on the right.

* * *

DASK: I told them to stay where they were. I told *all* of them.

YUMA: One candidate dead on the eve of a vote might be coincidence, but twice smacks of a plot.

ACHARA: Except...

FONTAINE: What?

ACHARA: It's a complicated environment out there. Uprising. Blood feuds between houses. More than one candidate has been slain in the last few days, it always happens. Sir Kazar-Sthall was shot at through his window. Two candidates are with the palace medicae, and he suspects poison. It will not stop until we decide.

HAWTHORN: Lady Katline-Denshain?

TESSELL: I'd rather Lord Tavona-Akava. He has a more serious demeanour and his family has long ties with the Cult Mechanicus.

KRAINE: I'm for Tavona-Akava.

HAWTHORN: Of course you are, he's a secret Rau. In which case I think I'll back Katline-Denshain.

TESSELL: In that case might I suggest that, for the sake of speed and stability, instead of voting on each individually we adjourn to reflect and cast votes on one against the other?

YUMA: I think that is best, given the rising body count. But understand that no one is to leak that we are considering these candidates – it could be dangerous for them.

'Lady Baldonna Katline-Denshain.' Koln tapped the pict on her board, and followed a red string to another pict. '*And* Lord Sammel Tavona-Akava. We have our first double bill.'

'You'll need both of us, then,' said Sycorax. She was casting an eye at Raithe, Koln noticed, as if appraising him.

Raithe sat with his hand in his pocket again, looking on edge. 'Will you need a long shot?'

'Actually, I thought I'd take care of these myself.'

'Don't you have to man the vox?' asked Sycorax.

Koln drifted over to a cogitator, looked at a line of data-chains, and clicked a few keys. 'I've already knocked out one candidate without leaving the ship. They don't always have to be killed. Just made... unpalatable.'

'If you think you can handle it,' said Raithe, standing and stretching. 'You have my confidence.'

He turned towards his quarters.

'Sycorax,' said Koln. 'I wonder if you'd do a small errand for me?'

Flames below in the city made the thick panes of the leaded window glow with an unearthly light. Below, Dask's footmen had spent three days besieging a district armoury seized by the mob. The rebels insisted that the conclave name a new High Monarch and execute all found responsible for Yavarius-Khau's death. The footmen, tiring of the stand-off, had set the building alight – arresting anyone who emerged.

In the archive, the scriptorium thralls still passed between the high bookcases, robes whispering across the floor. None looked up from their work as Rakkan passed.

He was being watched, he knew that. The guards at the door of his childhood chambers were there as much to record his comings and goings as to protect him.

Most of the palace was secured, locked down – but the archive and librarium were not. Dask hoped, apparently, that the nobles could be kept docile if given access to enough reading material.

And Rakkan wanted to oblige.

>*What is the duty of a wounded Knight?*

For a day, he'd been able to do little and see no one. Quarantine, all over again. Yet with even more alcohol supplied.

Yet when he'd uncorked the first bottle of amasec, with dinner, he hadn't tasted it. Even the smell made him ill, bringing back the odour of the pipe coal searing his flesh. He ordered raenka, but it was the same. He had a glass of red vin with his dinner of cold mutton, but he didn't finish it.

Instead, he stared at his father's helmet. Put it on. Ignored the tang of blood.

>*What is the duty of a wounded Knight?*

He'd been in the archive twice now, over the past two days, consulting table-sized folios of Fang family history.

His father's line was old. That he knew. And strange.

One child. Each generation had one child – unless one died, in which case they had another child. And while that was standard in the modern age, this stretched back three millennia, as far as records went.

And those children. Always piloting *Jester*. Never rising above their station. Other families branched, created sub-families. Rose and fell in fortune. But the Fang were just... *there*. Every large battle, they rode, but never distinguished themselves. A footnote in every history. The only battle they had missed was the defence of Dominion itself, during the heresy. Sir Blastin Fang was too ill to rise from his bed, missing the action.

When Rakkan got too far back in time, and the chronicles ceased, he tried the old settlement songs. They were spotty and unreliable. Stories about *Stormbringer*, the mythical Rau Knight Valiant that duelled *Crown of Dominion* over the honour of seating the monarch – and destroyed itself in sorrow at its defeat. Most stories were fanciful, verging on embarrassing. Knights had children with fae folk, battled giants and hobgobs, and acted without pilots.

There was only one Fang reference – a story about a noble, Dame Sakaava Fang, befriending the shaggy Green Man who stalked the woods and wilds, gobbling up any who looked upon him. A common peasant superstition. When Rakkan was a small child, hinterlanders still reported seeing the creature.

It seemed merely amusing, until his eye got to the bottom of the page.

You are wounded, said the Green Man. Near death. If you ride against these invaders, you will die. What is the duty of a wounded Knight?

Rakkan turned the page – and found the next one torn out.

'We have him,' said Sir Jarak Theofan. 'He's in the archive. Let the lady know. Run, *quietly.*'

The messenger nodded, and jogged.

'Come on,' Theofan said, cocking his head. Two men, Rau footmen, followed him.

An archivist glanced towards them and they swept left into a canyon of leather-bound volumes. Into the vital records section. Two cases down, they found him.

Theofan could hear the archivist following. Slow on his aged joints.

'Goodmasters? Goodmasters?' A voice, wavering and dry as scraped vellum. 'This is a closed area.'

One of the footmen grabbed the old archivist by the throat and whispered in his ear. He left them alone, face white, kissing a silver charm on his neck and muttering that he'd seen nothing.

Theofan came up on Rakkan as he pushed a slim document in between the accordion files, the trailing ribbon of its seal dangling below the shelf.

'Sir Rakkan,' grumbled Theofan.

His footmen flanked him, trapping Rakkan in the narrow ravine of bookcases.

Rakkan turned, and Theofan saw the fear and confusion in the pilot's eyes. Rakkan was not small, but he was nowhere near Theofan's mass – nearly seven feet tall, wide and solid, with muscles specially trained by weighted armour. His shadow spilled across the smaller man.

Rakkan opened his mouth to speak, and Theofan slapped him, hard.

'Not a sound,' he said. 'You're coming with us. Without trouble. We're your fellow squires, hey-ho? All of us on the same side.'

'Where–'

Theofan slapped him again, backhand. Then flexed his fist, knuckles stinging from the blow. 'Ask me again, I'll pull your joints apart like a chicken. Maybe hook you up behind *Red Sky*, and drag you through the courtyard for a few hours.'

Footsteps behind him. His messenger returning.

'Sir–'

'What?' He half-turned, annoyed at the interruption.

'The lady… the lady says you must be mistaken. Rakkan is in his quarters reading. She can see him and his sacristan through the window.'

Theofan's eyes locked with the messenger, trying to divine if this was a jest.

The messenger was looking over Theofan's shoulder, trembling.

Theofan pursed his lips, turned slowly back towards Rakkan.

Rakkan was smiling a wry, tilted smile that didn't match his face.

'Oh, boys, boys, boys,' Rakkan said, in a light chiding voice. 'You picked the wrong Rakkan.'

A green blade sprang from Rakkan's sleeve.

They were dead before they even thought to scream.

When the Gatekeeper's guard arrived, they could not make head nor tail of it.

Four men, dead. Killed in what appeared to be a spontaneous affray, without making a sound.

Their only clue was the document half-pulled out of the bookcase, with its purity seal dangling a ribbon that made it impossible not to notice.

As soon as they read it, all became clear. They showed it to the old archivist, who hustled away on his old joints to show the baptism certificate to his chief.

For it proved that Lady Baldonna Katline-Denshain – a candidate in the Lists – had given birth seven years ago at her country estate.

The assassins came for Lord Sammel Tavona-Akava as he slept. His personal footman died when the first assassin approached him with an outstretched hand, and when he reached out and locked forearms in greeting, the second drew a laspistol and put two bolts through his heart.

But while the shots roused him, it was the splintering of his door frame which got him on his feet and set the servant girl under his sheets to screaming.

The light spilling in his open door blinded him, and though he raised his hands to defend himself, the assassin's blow struck directly between his open palms, breaking his nose. Tavona-Akava felt his back hit the wall, knocking the breath from him, and he only didn't fall because of the hands holding him up by the shirt.

'You traitor,' the assassin growled. 'You murdering bastard.'

'L-Lisille?' he stammered. His eyes adjusted to the sudden lantern-light, and the scarred face of Lycan-Bast nearly pressed to his own. 'W-what is this–'

'Two of my cousins are with the medicae, getting their stomachs pumped and systems flushed.' She hauled him forward and slammed his back against the wall. 'Qualla poisoning. One might die. Xanthius, I understand, he's in the Lists, but Tollin is only fourteen.'

'I didn't,' he said. 'I never–'

'There's an apothecary phial,' said the second one. In the half-light, Tavona-Akava saw it was Lycan-Bast's personal footman. The one she was rumoured to tangle with. He was sniffing an uncorked tube. 'It's qualla.'

'Lisille. Lisille, I don't know where that came from,' Tavona-Akava wavered. The look on her face made his bladder let go. 'It's a plant. I'm being–'

'Don't kill me,' said the servant girl. The footman had her by the wrist, pulling her out of bed. 'Please. I bought it for him. In the city. A day ago. I didn't know why he wanted it.'

Lycan-Bast gave her a withering stare. 'Will you testify to that?'

'Yes.'

'Then you can live,' she said. 'And you, my lord, I will be ejecting from the palace.'

'Th-thank yo–'

He only realised what she meant when she whirled him around and let him go. When his spine hit the window with bone-crushing force and bowed it outward – and with a sound of cracking wood and splintering glass, he felt the cold night air on his skin.

And saw Lycan-Bast, framed in the glowing window, getting smaller as he fell into darkness.

Raithe ran his cleaning rod through the barrel, scouring it, readying it for the next kill.

He wished his body could be so easily cleaned and prepared. The wear and fouling of its use so cleanly scraped, oiled, and broken down. Pain radiated from neck to fingertip. A constant dull ache gave way to bolts of electricity racing down his bicep every time he worked the bristled rod through the barrel. There was nothing to be done. No rest. No sleep. He couldn't stop.

So he sat at his desk, ensuring that his rifle, at least, was in good shape to fire.

Turning the wheel lock to enter his cabin suite had been agony. For the first time in years, he'd recited the Litany of Transcending Pain.

He stopped cleaning the rifle and stretched, rotating the shoulder in a slow backstroke, one hand on the muscle, sucking air over his teeth as he felt it grind and pop.

'You're injured,' said Sycorax.

He glanced over his shoulder, saw her in his peripheral vision. Not on the bed this time, at least. Instead she leaned against the door frame, arms crossed.

'I thought we agreed you had to be invited,' he said. 'And no, they're just pre-operational stretches. Working out some bruising from the recoil.'

'That was a good shot back there, clean. I can see why you've got such a reputation.'

'Thank you.'

'But you're still an idiot.'

Raithe put down the barrel, the meditation of the cleaning broken, and turned in his chair.

His neck would not turn without dizzying pain, so he rotated at the shoulders instead, turning his whole body in the chair. 'Why?'

'Because you're hurt, and you've been hiding it.' He tried to speak but she cut him off. 'Don't deny it, look at you. You're locked up, torn muscle probably. Nerve, maybe. I might've noticed before but I was too busy hating you.'

'Leaders... need to inspire confidence. If I had told you–'

'You don't know much about leadership, do you?'

'No,' he admitted. 'They taught me to be a marksman. Conditioned me as a killer. But no one trained me to do this. To be honest, I'm feeling as misused as you are.'

'Team members need to know each other's limits. So they can step in if needed.'

'And I suppose you're going to step in and take the reins. Declare me incapable. And you wonder why I didn't bring it up?'

'No, grox-brain, so I can step in and help you.' She stepped close and knelt, her brown-green mosaic eyes – he noted, casually, that they had been coin-silver yesterday – fixed on his shoulder. 'Let's see it.'

Raithe gathered the bottom of his exercise tunic and pulled it over his head. He got it halfway up his arms before he stopped, and let out a cry of pain.

'Big yelp for a man with so many scars.'

Raithe caught a glance at himself in the mirror. It had been a long time since he'd looked at his body. Really looked. Image didn't concern him; function was his sole concern. How the muscles moved under the skin, the mechanical push and pull of tension and release. The network of scars he largely dismissed as aesthetic.

'This one' – he gestured to a puckered white line across his stomach, using his left hand – 'was a drukhari wych. Synskin weave saved me there. This one, on my side–'

'Looks messy, lot of tearing.'

'On Govii, fifth mission. Jackal Alphus caught me in an ambush. Took a hard spill on a dirtcycle.'

'Bet it paid for it.' She laid a hand on his shoulder. 'Rotate it – *slowly.*'

He did, feeling it crackle like a kid crushing a handful of plastek packing material.

'Golden Throne, Raithe. You're dumber than I thought. I'm amazed you can turn a doorknob. How long has it been like this?'

'During my last operation, so… a few months.'

'You should've had surgery. Maybe an augmetic.'

'Risky. If it doesn't go perfectly it can throw the rifle off. That'd mean decades of training and experience out the airlock. And you know what happens if they pull you off operational, you never know if you'll get back on. I'd rehabbed it to ninety per cent before this mission, but I've been hard on it since...'

'Now do it backwards.'

'Gaaaggghhh!'

Sycorax shook her head. 'You're lucky you didn't tear it completely off the bone. No patch-up job in the galaxy could help then.' She pulled out a needled phial.

Raithe shrank away.

'Don't tell me a man with that much scar tissue is afraid of needles?'

'What's in it? No painkillers. It can impact visual perception and reaction times.'

'It's polymorphine. A micro-dose. Helps the muscles find their proper place. Reknit and heal.'

'I...' He thought. 'It can do that?'

'Temporarily.' She stuck him with the needle. Activated the syrette. 'Good old polymorphine. If you were trained, the healing might be more permanent. But that would take years of focused meditation, higher doses and body-conditioning. Now rotate.'

He pulled the shoulder around, blinking. There was pain, but less pain. Like a bad bruise rather than a bayonet wound.

'Keep working it, don't stop. Just do rotations for twenty minutes or so. It'll hurt worse before it gets better. But it will get better. Effects should last a few hours, more if you treat it nicely. Not a permanent fix, but enough to give you a break. Unless I've got the dosage wrong, in which case the fix will be permanent, in that your shoulder will have liquefied.'

'Thanks,' he said, rotating the arm. 'No chance I could get a few of those phials for the next shoot, is there? Just in case.'

'The Callidus Temple guards it jealously,' she said, standing. 'Especially from our rival temples.'

He nodded, mouth turning down.

'But I won't tell them,' she said, setting a phial on the desk, 'if you don't.'

TESSELL: So we're all agreed?

DASK: Before we vote, I wish to note that all candidates are under guard. We will not be having any more surprises.

HAWTHORN: A little late for that.

TESSELL: You've had the night. Now on the question of the *Crown of Dominion*, who casts their electoral vote for Lord Bazile Daggar-Kraine. I vote aye.

YUMA: Aye.

FONTAINE: Nay.

ACHARA: Aye.

DASK: Nay.

KRAINE: Aye.

TESSELL: Baroness Hawthorn?

HAWTHORN: He's a Rau. The son of a Rau. You will not convince me otherwise. And he's a coward on the Imperial matter.

TESSELL: This is not a time for speeches, baroness. Say either aye or nay.

HAWTHORN: But… Tiberius has agreed to give me half of the uplands so… long live High Monarch Daggar-Kraine, I suppose.

KRAINE: Is that an aye?

HAWTHORN: Aye.

THIRTY-THREE

*'On the spirits of my ancestors, on the glories of my house, I
swear to defend Dominion from all evils within and without.
To lead these noble houses in a manner consistent with the
honours of the past and the achievements of the future. To
remain pure in thought and noble in action, to defend any
kinsman and battle any foe. By this I abandon all oaths
to house or family, and pledge my remaining life to serve
Dominion as High Monarch.'*

– Coronation Oath of the *Crown of Dominion*

'I never thought I would see this,' said Rakkan. 'A coronation,
I mean.'

'Did you not, lord?' responded Koln, in her engine-master
disguise. 'Yavarius-Khau was an old man.'

'Yes,' said Gwynne. 'The lamented monarch – may his soul
echo forever in the *Crown* – had suffered much loss of function
due to the extended wear on his biological parts.'

They were walking through the fortifications in front of the
basilica, earthen ramps and sandbag positions thrown up during
the riots and guarded by Stryder-Rau footmen. Most of them
were from Daggar-Kraine's personal house, Rakkan noticed, a
gift to the new monarch-elect from his father, Baron Kraine.
Given that the basilica faced the marshalling fields, they had a
flat kill-zone leading all the way to the snow-laden mountains.

An officer, seeing Rakkan's personal arms and the corresponding patches sewn on Gwynne, Koln and Raithe, waved them through the basilica's great double doors.

'I know he was old,' Rakkan said, waving a hand at the officer in dismissive thanks, 'but he seemed so solid. Eternal. I never thought–'

'Rakkan.'

They turned, the retinue hastily bowing when they saw who had approached.

To Rakkan's left, Dame Vossa strode out of the baptistry chapel. She was in her formal court attire, the gorget seal-lock of her pilot suit engraved in gold, the red tabard lying atop it carrying Baron Kraine's device of a storm drake spewing lightning from its mouth.

'We're missing an Armiger pilot for the honour guard,' she said, beckoning. 'Too many dead in the crisis. And by tradition we need one crusade veteran among the Armigers. You're the only one we have.'

'But *Jester*'s in the stable…'

'You'll pilot *Red Sky* manually,' she snapped. 'Make haste! We don't want to miss the procession to Gathering Palace.'

She turned towards the door, and he followed, shrugging at his retinue.

He saw Koln and Raithe exchange a glance, before they slipped into the basilica.

The trumpets sounded.

Within minutes, a new monarch would be crowned – and Dominion's new era would begin.

Rakkan heard the trumpets when they were halfway down the cloister. The sound echoed hollow among the columns of the covered walkway. Behind, the muffled sound of the sacristan choir seemed to emanate from the basilica's stones.

It prickled Rakkan's skin, the transition between the packed, hot interior of the cathedral and this deserted cloister. The knowledge that the worthies of Dominion had all gathered, yet he was headed the other way, across a deserted courtyard.

'This is my fortune, exactly,' he said. 'The only coronation in my lifetime, and I'll miss it.'

'Your mother wanted you in the honour guard,' Vossa said, growling. 'Baron Kraine too. He's nobody's squire, but everyone is so sweet on Rakkan.'

'Still, I...'

'Would you rather watch history, or be a part of it?'

'When you put it that way...'

So many nobles stood in the basilica that from where Gwynne stood, Lord Bazile Daggar-Kraine looked the size of a doll as he mounted the golden staircase leading to the open hatch of the *Crown of Dominion*.

Daggar-Kraine, every part of his armour streaming with ribbons and purity seals, took each of the fifty steps with the Arch-Maintenancer by his side, reciting the oaths of investiture. He'd spent last night in the company of the sacristans, preparing himself to merge his soul with the venerable machine, descending deep into the crypts below the Cathedral of Maintenance to endure a second harrowing. A second Becoming ritual.

It was said his screams could be heard for hours.

From her place in the rear of the crowd, Gwynne could not see whether Daggar-Kraine bore any ill effects from the ritual. The most important nobles – court members, generals returned from the field, and the two house heads – stood in the front of the crowd, beneath the shadow of the great throne-machine. Then came the most important of the house nobles, separated by the centre aisle and arranged in order of rank.

Only then came the Armiger pilots, and the nobles of the Lists – at least what remained of them after the bloodshed of the last few days. It would, after all, have been gauche to have the first image a new High Monarch saw through the *Crown's* oculars be their possible replacements.

Only then, at the very back of the basilica, came the retinues.

<We helped put him there,> Gwynne transmitted to Koln, in binharic. <And here we are at the back.>

She was standing with Koln and Raithe, in the thin crowd of vassals at the rear. Wind blew in behind them, lifting robes and chilling her steel augments and data-inputs so they ached against her natural skin. They were lucky to be there at all – many full nobles had not rated an invitation, and were on a ballroom balcony at Gathering Palace, waiting to cheer the *Crown of Dominion* as it emerged. Others were still in the countryside, managing estates.

<That's the way, for us,> Koln responded. Given the noise of the choir there was no chance of being overheard, but she used the machine language just in case. <We change each place we come to, never acknowledged for it. But we prevented a war.>

<Dominion stands and many will live because of us,> said Gwynne, then added, <and we can't tell anyone.>

<No,> transmitted Koln. <You can't.>

Gwynne knew a threat when she heard one, and ended the connection.

The coronation was starting.

'Sycorax,' Raithe murmured subaudibly. 'What–'

'–*do you see up there?*'

Up in the shadow of the vaults, Sycorax crouched on a falcon-headed gargoyle. Around her clustered eagles, skeletons wielding swords, roaring manticores and twisting dragons.

A crowd of fierce beasts. Fitting company for her, she thought.

'Moment,' she whispered.

She leapt to get a better line of sight, gripping a crossbar and swinging upward under it like a gymnast, passing between two banners and landing on another bar.

It was harder than usual, loaded down as she was. Raithe had asked her to carry his gear, just in case things went sideways. The weight of the zip-case on her back had given her an idea of why he'd torn that shoulder.

There was little organisation up here. Banners hung haphazardly on chains or were mounted in rows on rods that stretched across the whole of the basilica. No one but the servitors had been up here for centuries, and she chose her landing spots carefully, avoiding those that might prove too fragile and give way. Even her careful passage triggered micro-draughts of air, stirring loose threads and gold flakes from the disintegrating battle honours. They drifted down like snow, caught in the high air circulation of the massive vault, and dispersed.

Had anyone noticed, they would've seen that the shower of dust motes was moving towards the front.

'I have eyes on Daggar-Kraine,' she said, nestling down where a bar met a support pillar. A perfect vantage point, looking down through the threadbare gauze of a banner that screened the view of her from below. They couldn't get this far and mess it up now. That was why she was up here, to watch for unpleasant last-minute surprises.

Forty feet below, she could see Lord Daggar-Kraine settling into the command throne of the *Crown of Dominion*. In Sycorax's enhanced senses, she could make the words out as he swore to defend any kinsman and battle any foe, his face set in a frown of dutiful concentration.

'*He's in the throne?*' asked Koln.

'Affirmative,' Sycorax responded. 'I hope they cleaned it first.'

It was strange, she reflected, to see the *Crown of Dominion* without its face mask.

Yavarius-Khau's death mask lay between the Castellan's feet, nestled in a bouquet of yellow and white flowers – the colour of mourning, Koln had said. Apparently the old king's ashes were sealed in a compartment behind the eyes.

Soon he would be hung above the great altar with the other monarchs, and the *Crown* would take on the new mask, which lay beneath a velvet drape, watched over by the servitor-falcons.

'No threats?' asked Raithe. *'Everyone in their place?'*

'I don't see Baron Fontaine,' Sycorax shot back.

'With the army, beyond the mountains,' Koln said. *'Ensuring there's no mutiny during the coronation.'*

'A few squires missing,' whispered Sycorax. 'Vossa, Hawthorn's new one... Andricus, was he? A few from Stryder and Rau nobles.'

'The honour guard,' said Koln. *'They guard the procession out. Vossa took Rakkan for it. Apparently–'*

'He's taking the oath,' said Sycorax. 'Not long now. Thirty minutes?'

'We did it,' said Koln. *'Throne save us, we did it.'*

'But I don't understand,' said Rakkan. 'Why do I need to do this in *Red Sky*?'

Twenty Knight Armigers stood ready in the basilica stable, ranked up alongside twenty Questoris Knights. An honour guard for the ages. Stryder. Rau. Court colours. Like nothing Rakkan had ever seen.

Though he had never seen a coronation.

'Theofan died in the crisis,' said Andricus. He was a minor cousin of Rakkan's, still a teenager, and seemed almost too small for the squire's tabard his mother had bestowed him with after Vossa slew Galvan. 'We need you to take his place.'

Rakkan had paused on the lower rung of the mounting stairs, the ring of squires bracketing him in. Vossa seemed to be the leader, but there was also Sir Brovan Mortau, a Rau Knight squired to Lord Palladius. Dame Dasteva Calthanis, squire to Lady Gersanna of Stryder. There were more, perhaps twenty, arrayed like teeth of mismatching colour.

Only squires, the Knights were in the basilica.

'But... I should process in *Jester*, surely? This Knight will not like being mounted so soon after losing its pilot.'

Rakkan was not sure he could command *Jester*, any more. Manually, of course, but he would need to reformat and reconsecrate the Knight before pairing with it again. He should be grateful his ruse had not been discovered.

But this felt...

'There's no time,' said Vossa. 'The coronation has started. We need to be in position. There's no time to dally. Go!'

Rakkan took one step up, another. Vossa followed him, herding him up the stairs. 'Now get in.'

Rakkan looked down at the squires as they stared up, expectant. And he saw what bothered him.

They were Rau and Stryder. Standing next to each other. No jostling, no sniping jibes. Squires who had crossed swords in back alleys stood quietly among each other as natural as tools in a drawer. And... hadn't Vossa killed Galvan, so why was she with his replacement? Behind them, a semicircle of sacristans buzzed and hummed, bobbing in little bowing movements.

'What is–'

Vossa grabbed him, snarling, pushing his head towards the cockpit. 'Help me, you fools! Get the neural jack.'

They came up the ladder as swift as hounds and grasped him in their hands. Clawed at him, lifting him, dragging him onto the upper carapace of the Armiger and towards the open hatch.

He kicked out with his augmetic braces, sending one squire tumbling off the Knight. He caught another in the jaw with a weak punch. Then Vossa was jamming his father's helmet over his head, locking the seal, shoving him down into the hatch and the unfamiliar, warm darkness of the Armiger. He felt a neural jack scraping at his skull-port as he fought, head hitting the spongy leather padding of the cockpit walls.

'Embrace them, Rakkan!' growled Vossa. 'Embrace your ancestors.'

'Embrace the Power of Eight,' echoed the squires.

'He's almost done,' said Sycorax. 'Looks like we've wrapped this up. Prepare to be non-operational.'

Daggar-Kraine finished the oath, and the Arch-Maintenancer picked up the crown that lay on a pillow supported by one of her mechadendrites.

She held it up.

'The honourable crown of Dominion!' Dorthiya Tessell intoned. Internal hailers boomed her voice far beyond its natural range. 'Given freely via the laws of this domain, with all fairness and nobility. By the electors and heads of houses, by the court and sacristan order, to King Daggar-Kraine.'

The crown was old, and not much to look at – a simple circlet of gold inset with jewels, with three finials at the front to represent the houses and sacristan order. In the rear was a skull input on a hinge, and when the Arch-Maintenancer lowered the crown onto Daggar-Kraine's head, she gingerly reached back and rotated the data-spike into the new king's implant.

Then she kissed the data-cable in the Throne Mechanicum, and connected it to the crown.

'Dominion!' she declared, standing back. 'Hail your High Monarch!'

Daggar-Kraine went stiff, his eyes rolling back as the *Crown* merged with his mind. He jerked once, twice, in seizure. Foam dribbled from his mouth. Sycorax could hear reactor hum, smell an odour like circuits cooking.

'*I sense ozone,*' Koln warned.

'He's taking it hard,' she whispered. 'But so did I.'

The upper hatch closed to preserve the king's modesty, and Tessell raised her arms in wonder and bowed as servitors dragged the rolling mounting stairs aside.

'Your monarch!' said Tessell. 'Your monarch addresses you!'

The *Crown*'s head stirred, lifted. From the mouth-mounted hailer, exposed and insectile with the mask removed, came a booming voice.

'*SUBJECTS OF DOMINION. WE FACE A CRISIS UNLIKE ANY WE HAVE FACED BEFORE. AS THE CONCLAVE DEBATED, NO DOUBT THIS WAS PARAMOUNT IN THEIR MINDS – WE HAVE BEEN CALLED TO WAR.*'

'Here we go,' said Sycorax.

Rakkan slammed his leg armatures straight, rocketing his helmet upward into Vossa's unprotected face. He felt a cracking scrape on the helmet's dome, and something small tumbled down, clicking as it hit the control console.

The data-jack dropped limp behind him, and he grabbed for purchase, trying to find anything that could give him enough leverage to pull himself upright. But all Knights were unique, and when he blindly reached for where *Jester*'s interior hand-rail should be, the rail moved.

He heard a howl of pain above him, and the slapping, scratching hands retracted, plunging the cockpit into darkness.

Only when he looked up did he realise what had happened. He had yanked the emergency hatch lever and slammed the top door right onto them. In one corner, he could see worms wriggling in the rubberine hatch seal, disappearing as they drew themselves out.

Fingers. Fingers slammed in the hatch.

And in the oval porthole above him, he could see the snarling, animal face of Dame Vossa, blood leaking from her mouth.

Rakkan grabbed the manual controls, awakening the Knight suit. He pivoted the machine at the waist, shaking humans off the upper carapace, sending bodies sliding and tumbling.

Then he slammed the sticks forward and set *Red Sky* into a clumsy run, nearly stumbling as his first leap crushed a fallen squire.

They were scrambling for their machines, hoping to pursue. He swept *Red Sky*'s Helverin autocannons back and forth, catching a sacristan in the back and sending them flying. He punched the firing studs, but the guns did not respond.

Unloaded? Deactivated?

There was no way he could escape. If he went to the open marshalling field, they would run him down. If he fought, he'd die in seconds – no manually piloted Knight could defeat an opponent joined with his machine.

But the basilica stables had only one other exit large enough to accommodate an Armiger: the catacombs.

So he turned, and dashed down into the darkness.

'WHEN THE HOUSES OF STRYDER AND RAU HAVE BEEN CALLED TO FIGHT, WE HAVE ALWAYS RESPONDED. AND THROUGH ANCIENT TRADITION, ALL HOUSE WARS AND VENDETTAS MUST CEASE WHEN WE MARSHAL FOR CONFLICT.'

Lubricant tears slipped down from Gwynne's oculars, tasting of machine oil when they beaded on her lips. She had never seen a coronation, even from the back – she thought of her parents, who fixed auto-carriages, and prayed their spirits were with her to see this.

Their daughter, hearing the words of a king.

She could feel them, she thought, close. Pressing on her mind, like a finger pushing on the vox-pickup unit behind her right ear.

'IN THAT SPIRIT, THE FOLLOWING MEMBERS OF THE HOUSES WILL PRESENT THEMSELVES.'

'Power of Eight,' she heard, and frowned. It triggered a memory. A sense. Wasn't that what the Archenemy had chanted on the line? When she and *Jester* had fought them?

'BARONESS HAWTHORN ASTAIR-RAKKAN, OF STRYDER.'

How strange. She tried to isolate the sound, to lock it down. A memory? A trauma?

'Embrace the Power of Eight.'

'BARON TIBERIUS KRAINE, OF RAU.'

A broadcast. A data-packet streaming into her auditory system. She reached up and switched off her binharic transponder.

'Your transponder,' Gwynne gripped Koln's arm. 'Turn it off.'

'What?'

'You have cranial augmetics with receivers,' said Gwynne. 'It's the conqueror_wyrm, someone's broadcasting it. Turn external receivers off, now!'

She shouted loud enough that it echoed off the pillars around them.

Deeper, deeper into the catacombs. Past the weak glow-globes that snapped on at his passage. Past the arms of houses living and dead.

Each line had their vault. While the masks of kings, heroes and court figures hung in the basilica, the others lay entombed here.

Rakkan passed them with *Red Sky*'s lunging, mechanical stride, pitching back and forth like an auto-carriage with bad suspension.

An object clicked and rattled on the control console, and Rakkan suddenly realised it was a tooth. A canine. And there on his lap, a shovel-like incisor. He barked a laugh, remembering Vossa's bloody mouth as she stared in through the porthole.

'See you smile at me now, cousin.'

As he picked the teeth off his lap, he noticed a gleam of leather nestled beside the pilot seat – a holdout laspistol, with a hot-shot cell. The kind pilots placed inside their suits in case they had to bail out.

It might come in useful. Vossa was pursuing. Rakkan was sure it was her. He could hear echoes down the tunnel. And the automatic glow-globes were a telltale sign of his path.

He would have to get out soon. Proceed on foot. Get into the smaller side-chambers where a Knight couldn't...

Rakkan felt the neural cable slither along his back a moment before it coiled around his throat, cutting his airway like a strangling serpent, throttling him against the seat he'd never bothered to buckle himself into.

His gloved fingers wrestled at the thick bundle of cords about his neck as he felt the tapping, probing neural jack scraping against his skull-port.

Power of Eight, sighed *Red Sky*, as its console glowed a lurid purple.

'SIR PALLADIUS OF RAU. LADY GERSANNA OF STRYDER.'

The list went on, booming so loud Sycorax couldn't make out the thin buzzing in her implanted micro-bead. There was weird interference, perhaps because she was so close to the *Crown*'s hailer.

'Can –ou see –ch –te–cer?'

Sycorax clicked her throat three times to convey the message *Did Not Receive*. 'Try again once he's done speaking,' she said, in case her own message went through. 'Should be soon, stage is almost full.'

Below her, the dais swarmed with nobles, divided between Stryder and Rau.

'NOW ALL OF YOU, TAKE THE HANDS OF YOUR RIVAL AND SWEAR TO DO NO VIOLENCE TO ONE ANOTHER, TO SET ASIDE ALL EVILS AND BE KINSMEN. MAKE A NEW OATH OF LOYALTY, TO BE SHRIVEN NO MORE AND JOIN IN THE FACE OF THE GREAT THREAT.'

Below her, Sycorax saw Hawthorn clasp Kraine's arm. Rau and Stryder from across the upper ranks of the houses, swearing brother- and sisterhood to one another, along with their squires.

Many looked confused, but smiled with the sudden bridging of the divide.

The court figures, on the other hand, stood in the front alarmed and whispering.

'THIS IS OUR WAY. HOUSES JOINED IN CONFLICT TO FACE A GREAT ENEMY. OUR OLDEST FOE. TO ROOT OUT THE TRAITORS AND SCHEMERS IN OUR MIDST AND HEAL OLD WOUNDS. LORD-COMMANDER GUILLIMAN CALLS US TO WAR.'

Rakkan reached behind him, grabbing the data-jack, wrestling it as if it were a dagger a foeman was trying to plunge into his neck. With his right hand, he grasped the hotshot laspistol.

Not much air now, not much time. The cockpit was grey. Even the sickening purple light of the console was gauzy and colourless.

Power of Eight, growled the Armiger. A deep, canine sound. A braying.

No, not an Armiger – a War Dog.

Rakkan laid the laspistol across his shoulder and fired. Muzzle flash strobed the interior of the cockpit white with shot after shot as he emptied the hotshot magazine directly into the systems of the Helm Mechanicum. Then his vision went dark, and the constriction around his throat ended.

If it were not for the cool, painful breaths, he would've thought he had died.

But it was not him that was dead – it was *Red Sky*. Systems dark. The serpent of its neural cable lay across his shoulder, twitching with death spasms.

Rakkan threw the cable off him and reached up for the emergency hatch lever. Threw it.

Thanked the Emperor when he saw the thin light of the tunnel glow-globes above.

Then he clambered out, into a city of the dead.

Raithe didn't like this. It felt off. The bloody division coming together too quickly.

And the broadcast. Where was that broadcast coming from?

Then he heard the thunder. So easily covered by the sound of trumpets and pipe organ. Drowned out by the sacristan choir.

Gwynne and Koln had pushed forward in the crowd, trying to get to the Arch-Maintenancer and warn her to switch off her receivers. Order the other sacristans to do so.

Raithe detached from the crowd and headed for the open basilica doors. Clear winter light spilled in, snow flurries drifting inside to dissolve among the heat of burning candles and pressed bodies.

'WE WILL ONCE AGAIN BE ONE HOUSE, UNDIVIDED, ON CRUSADE AS IN THE PAST.'

'Raithe,' transmitted Sycorax. 'I don't like this, something isn't right.'

'AND WE WILL HEAR LORD-COMMANDER GUILLIMAN'S

CALL AND MARSHAL TO THE FIELD OF COMBAT. WE WILL DECLARE WAR AGAINST THE ARCHENEMY, AS HE HAS REQUESTED.'

'I know,' said Raithe, slipping past the doors of the basilica and into the shadow of an arch. He saw footmen outside, scurrying into position behind stone monuments and the headstones of dead vassals.

Then he raised his eyes to the horizon, and felt his stomach go cold.

'WE WILL RIDE AGAINST OPPRESSION AND TYRANNY – BY DECLARING WAR AGAINST GUILLIMAN AND HIS SO-CALLED IMPERIUM OF MAN.'

'I think I found Baron Fontaine,' said Raithe, eyes fixed on the mountains.

The first thing he saw were the las-beams and tracer fire cutting across the sky. Dominion's air defences on the southern continent were engaged in a full-scale repulse. A battle was going on behind the mountain range.

And coming out of the mountain pass onto Gathering Plain marched a party of Knights. At the head was the noble Knight *Axefall*, mount of Baron Fontaine. Behind him, a lance of Questoris-pattern suits.

And flanking him on either side, two Knights in the magenta armour Raithe knew from the briefing books.

'...AND WE WILL DO SO,' boomed the High-Monarch, *'REUNITED WITH OUR SIBLINGS IN HOUSE MORVAYNE.'*

THIRTY-FOUR

Six yards of the forward firestep at Heaven Defence West blew inward, evaporating three heavy stubber teams and the mortar battery behind it.

Captain Staalheim saw sky and earth, earth and sky, plasteel ditch spikes spinning around him in the air before he crashed down again. Rapid-fire battle cannon hit, he thought, dragging himself up to what was left of the firestep.

It had come from a Knight of Morvayne, a corrupted Crusader-pattern – the first traitor Knight to land on Dominion since the Heresy. Since the days when *Leviathan* – the Knight without a pilot – had sacrificed itself to kill the traitor Baron Morvayne.

But that was not what terrified Staalheim. What terrified him were that there were familiar shapes loping among the towering Morvayne Knights and harrying the defences.

The Knight Helverin *Drumbeat*, piloted by Sir Brovan Mortau. *Killing Talon*, Dame Sarissa's machine. Blue-and-red shapes dodging and firing.

The footmen of Heaven Defence West were fighting their own

lords. He'd trained for it. At times, when the bastards displaced a village or raised grain tithes, even wished for it. But from the fire stitching across the sky, he knew the fire-control centre in the middle of this star fort was fighting a battle. Contesting a planetary landing by the traitor Knights.

In the defensive battery behind Staalheim, a volcano lance powered up. Its red-orange shot tore through the air above him, making his next breath taste of the forges he'd grown up downwind of. Halfway across the plain, he saw the lance beam burst an ion shield and batter into a Morvayne Knight's shoulder joint, staggering it and causing its gatling cannon to shelve away. The massive weapon crushed a dozen tainted Mechanicus thralls that scuttled around its feet.

Celebratory cheers rang from the lance battery, barely audible over the weapon's down-cycling.

'*Traitorbane! Traitorbane!*'

That was the Knight they'd stripped the lance from, ten thousand years ago, the last time Dread House Morvayne had set their traitor feet on Dominion. Three dozen Stryder-Rau Knights died that day, along with half a million footmen. At that time, Dominion had no air defences – not like it had now.

Now, it had Heaven Defence West and Heaven Defence East. And while they stood, almost anything Morvayne had could be stopped in orbit. Rapid-fire battle cannon *Tilting Field* slammed out a shot from another corner of the star fort, its shell bursting on a Morvayne ion shield.

Both houses, and three Morvayne Knights, were coming for them.

But Captain Staalheim thought of those half-million footmen dead. Thought of the thing Dask had told them from their first day tithed into her Gatekeeper's Guard.

No matter who it was, no one must be allowed to take the

fire-control. It didn't matter if it was the house heads, the *Crown of Dominion*, the God-Emperor arisen or their dear old grand-mums. All must be denied with force.

The corrupted Crusader pivoted on its hip joint and stitched fire up the star fort's glacis with its gatling cannon, each round kicking up man-sized clods of earth as the spiral of tracers walked fire up into *Traitorbane*.

The venerable lance exploded, its battery rupturing with an eardrum-cracking sound of las-discharge and flying acid. Staal-heim looked behind to see the barrel fall forward and roll down the inner ring of the star fort and into the moat between defensive layers.

'Lascannon crews!' he roared. 'Make ready! Prepare to repulse at close range!'

Denied with force, he thought, but for how long?

Silence reigned in the basilica. Sycorax looked down on the kneeling crowd, trying to read their faces. Even from high up, she saw the shock written there.

Those on the dais, already pledged, moved back to make room.

The servitor-falcons leapt into the air and took flight, dragging the mask from beneath the velvet drape.

It hung on the chain between them, halved diagonally. One half red, one half blue – merging in a slash of Morvayne purple.

'IF ANYONE WISHES TO JOIN OUR ENDEAVOR, STEP FORWARD AND SWEAR OATHS NOW.'

No one moved, then came a scuffle at the front of the kneeling crowd.

Yuma stood, or tried to. Achara gripped his arm, trying to pull him back. On the other side, Dask whispered harshly into his ear.

'Let go,' he shouted. 'Let *go*.'

He threw them off and turned to the crowd.

'You're cowards,' he told the kneeling crowd. 'All of you.'

'No, Yuma,' Sycorax breathed. 'No.'

'You knelt to this man. Accepted him as your king. Gave your votes to him, some of you.' Yuma glared at Dask and Achara. 'Well, you may not remember what that means, but I do. He is our king.'

Yuma stepped up to join the Knights on the dais. His brother, Baron Kraine, greeted him with an arm grip.

'WHO ELSE WILL RISE AND FOLLOW? WHO DARES DEFY?'

A few Knights trickled to the front, heads bent as if to keep their identities hidden.

'THIS WORLD OF DOMINION,' said High Monarch Daggar-Kraine, *'HAS NO MERCY FOR TRAITORS.'*

She saw movement in the crowd – Koln and Gwynne, pushing forward, yelling something at Dorthiya Tessell as she stood atop the mounting stairs.

She opened her mouth to warn them, yelled, 'Koln!'

Just as the *Crown of Dominion*'s plasma decimator began to keen, and its coils heated to an incandescent blue.

Rakkan slid beside a funerary pillar, unsealed his helmet for a moment, and listened for pursuers. Catalogued what he could hear.

Dripping water. The muffled silence of the underground. And…

There. Movement. Large feet splashing through the brackish water that seeped in through the stone. This part of the catacombs, the Rau section, was close to the sea.

Faster splashes, the scrape of metal on a wall. Adamant scraping adamant.

Vossa had found the dead *Red Sky*.

The smell was still on him, the acrid stink of burned electronics, undercut with sizzling flesh. Not everything inside, wrecked by the hotshot fusillade, had been machine.

He relocked the helmet, slipping deeper into the catacomb tunnel, using the two stablights built into his helmet to guide him.

By chance, fate, or long-buried memory, he knew where he was headed.

A tunnel of searing blue energy carved through the crowd, blasting twelve Knights and their retinues into ash and blinding six more who simply looked at the discharge.

Koln grabbed Gwynne and pulled her behind a pillar, shielding her from the backwash of scorching air. White motes washed over them, and for a moment Koln thought the shot had punctured the roof field and let in a blizzard of snowflakes. Then she gagged on it and realised it was the cremated remains of the dead nobility.

To her right, reaching towards the safety of the pillar, were the clawing skeletons of a group that had not made it to cover.

'STAND YOU WITH THE FALSE PRIMARCH GUILLIMAN? AGAINST YOUR KING?'

Dusted in human ash, her Stryder-Rau livery white, Koln activated the lasweapon in her right hand and dragged Gwynne closer to the dais.

The red spear of the volcano lance flashed beneath Sycorax as she danced through the vaults. Burning bright, it sliced diagonally through a pillar and flashed up into the ceiling, its heat-wash igniting the frail banners clustered around her.

Ancient tapestries curled at the edges, embers drifted and

caught. Splashes of superheated liquefied masonry spattered upward and melted banner poles.

Then the plasma decimator fired again, lighting the vaults blue just before the rising heat of the barrage reached flashover point and the entire shrouded ceiling burst into flame.

'Koln!' she shouted, leaping through the inferno. 'Koln!'

'*I need you,*' Raithe voxed back. She could hear gunshots. '*At the main doors, right now.*'

'Copy,' said Sycorax, leaping for a chain that held a line of burning flags aloft. She landed, wrapped one arm around the chain, sprang her phase blade, and slashed through the links.

Sycorax dropped from the incendiary hell of Stryder-Rau's ruined legacy – and swung down into a massacre.

The nobility of Dominion fled wholesale from their king, an outrushing tide of screaming faces. Unmounted pilots fell, to die crushed under the boots of squires who funnelled towards side chapels and the main door.

Sycorax made her body rubbery and slim, slipping through the press of bodies. She could see the grey rectangle of winter light above the heads of the milling crowd.

But then heavy stubber rounds tore through the door and thumped into the massed flesh of fleeing nobles.

Clack-clack. Clack-clack.

Four footmen went down, tight grouping. Close range. One fell away from the tripod-mounted heavy stubber that had just sprayed a burst through the basilica's double doors. They were rushing the open doors of the basilica, pinning the fleeing nobles inside.

Raithe thanked the Emperor for gifting him with such acute paranoia. Otherwise he might not have bothered to sneak in the Klavell compact. With Sycorax holding his gear, it hadn't seemed necessary.

But it was necessary. It completed him.

And despite the cataclysm, he was glad his role had suddenly become simple.

Put bullets in bodies.

Raithe saw a footman draw an autogun up to his shoulder. He swung the iron sights onto the man's head and drilled a neat hole in his skull.

'We're not getting out this way,' Raithe said. 'They have support weapons.'

'Better out there than in here,' shouted Lisille Lycan-Bast. She and most of the Lists – what remained of them – sheltered in a baptistry. No one had any weapons. Weapons apart from swords were, generally, not allowed at a coronation for fear someone would kill the monarch.

Too bad it's the other way around this time, Raithe thought.

'Sycorax,' he sub-vocalised. 'While you make your way here, see if you can herd some nobles to the baptistry. At the end of this, we want some pilots left.'

He gave them about ten minutes before they were overrun. And that was if the *Crown* didn't finish them first.

Rakkan expected the gate to squeal as it opened, given the dampness of the tunnel and salt encrustation on the walls.

But no. It swung inward on hinges as well oiled as those on a Knight's joint. As he pushed it, Rakkan realised that while the door itself was ironwork, its hinges were corrosion-resistant adamantine.

The iron lattice formed curling, spiralling wave patterns that overlapped one another. In the centre a sword emerged from the waves. And above it, an arching scroll device read FANG.

Rakkan had been so small when he'd last been here. The place had appeared so much bigger then, when they'd laid his father's lead-lined casket inside. A chamber twelve-feet high, stone niches piling the dead four deep.

Now, he saw how cluttered and claustrophobic it was. A far cry from the marble vaults of his mother's Astair line. The Fang had always been of little prestige. A servant line, one step above vassalage. Even Baron Kraine had not bothered much – it was out of the way, and over the centuries the stone niches had all been taken. Rather than expand the space, caskets had simply been stacked along the walls like crates in a storage depot.

As far as Dominion was concerned, the soul lived in the Knight. The body was just rotting matter.

Rakkan found the casket easily. It was the first inside the gate, on the right, pressed sideways against the weeping masonry of the stone wall.

'Hail, father.'

He unlocked a glove and laid a hand on the lead box, feeling the embossed letters.

Sir Selkar Fang
Knight-Pilot of Jester
Saviour of High Monarch Yavarius-Khau
Slain in Victory

Rakkan's hand curled into a fist, and he thumped it on the metal.

'I tried, father. I truly did. Spent my life trying to better myself. Escape this poor man's bloodline. Be more than you were, than your mother was, to stop the cycle. Be the first Fang to pilot a Questoris Knight. To be no man's squire… and look where it's led me.'

The sob crept up, hidden behind the anger. He sucked air, eyes misting. And he all at once felt like he was drowning, looking at a smoke-twisted sky and choking on his own fluids. Text repeated in the corner of his helm's vision. Scrolling. Looping. Idiotic.

>*What is the duty of a wounded Knight?*

>*What is the duty of a wounded Knight?*

'I don't know!' he shouted. 'I don't know. You weren't here to teach me. All the tenderness you showed, and all I can remember of you is dying, burdening me with your charge. What the hell were you thinking, knowing I would inherit *Jester*? That I would have to see you like that, feel you like that. Leaving me a message devoid of love or care, just, *Tell my son to rise from his blood.*'

>*ENTRY: TO RISE FROM HIS BLOOD*

>*Entry Accepted*

>*Fang Line Established*

>*Declare Yourself, Knight*

Rakkan stopped at the sound of movement.

Large movement.

In the rear of the vault, the coffin-laden wall pivoted on its axis, revealing a glowing light beyond.

>*Declare Yourself, Knight*

'Linoleus Rakkan.'

>*Hail, Linoleus Rakkan, scion of the Fang Line, son of Selkar Fang, pilot of noble Knight Armiger Jester.*

>*THREAT NOTICE: Planetary alarms triggered. Ship detected in upper atmosphere. Hostiles in sector seven-two. Heaven Defence West besieged. Detestable House Morvayne has landed.*

>*Defence Activation Authorised*

>*Will you ride to the defence of the realm?*

Tentatively, drawn by the light, Rakkan stepped through the swinging wall. Took off his helmet so he could better see.

So awestruck was he, he didn't even notice when the door closed behind him.

'*I have been waiting,*' said a voice like thunder over the red sea.

* * *

'The baptistry!' Sycorax shouted, trying to herd the crowd. 'There, there's shelter.'

Smoke filled the basilica, and it was impossible to see. Terrified nobles with drawn faces and terrible slick burns kept storming out of the haze. She pushed them towards safety. Many failed to listen, having never seen her before.

There had been a lot of survivors at first, now not so many.

'Koln? Gwynne?' she voxed, not bothering to hide her voice.

A blue glow lit the smoke, and she threw herself flat, a streak of solar radiation splashing a pillar thirty feet in front of her, heating it until the stone ran and dripped like wax.

'Raithe? How's the door?'

'*Holding, for now.*' She could hear the pop-pop of gunfire behind his voice. '*I need my gear.*'

'Coming.'

A form, ash-covered, staggered from the smoke. At first she mistook its shape for a robed sacristan, but then she saw it was a woman.

It wasn't until she coughed and turned her face towards her that Sycorax realised who it was. She had a scalp wound and part of her hair had caught fire and burned. Her bell skirt was in shreds.

'Baroness Dask?'

'Who…?'

'Get to the baptistry, baroness, there's shelter there.'

Dask nodded and staggered backwards, holding a palm to her head wound.

Then Sycorax heard the whine of a las-cell bank and turned to see the volcano lance, the red glow in its throat visible as she looked right down the barrel.

'Keep going, keep going,' said Koln.

They sprinted along the side of the basilica vault, dodging in and out of chapels, vaulting fallen shrines and ranks of devotional candles.

But then, they met the choir.

A sacristan staggered out of the steps to the choir loft, mechadendrites waving. Its ocular augmetics were a deep purple with a light that matched the sickly glow from the *Crown*'s own lenses.

The corrupted thing twisted its head around unnaturally far to look at them, hissed and clicked like an aggressive insect.

'Eiggggggghhhttt…' it said.

Koln shot it through the head. Put a second las-bolt in its brainpan as they passed. Her digital weapon was ancient, with a clear beam – low noise, no visual giveaway.

'They're Transmuted,' Gwynne said, trying to hold back a digestive system purge.

'We'd be too if you hadn't cued me,' said Koln. 'I just hope the Arch-Maintenancer managed to kick hers off as well.'

'And if she didn't?' Gwynne asked.

Koln dropped to one knee and stitched three shots into an incoming sacristan, who scuttled at them on all fours like a lizard.

Behind them there was a spectacular rumble and crash as part of the upper vault arches fell, shorting out the ceiling field. Winter sunlight ghosted through the smoke.

'Then we deactivate her,' said Koln. 'Permanently.'

'Here,' Sycorax threw the bag to Raithe, who caught it with his left hand, and drew his Exitus pistol from the outside holster pocket. 'We have maybe one minute before the *Crown* gets here.'

'Have you seen Rakkan?' said Raithe.

Heavy bolter rounds crashed into the basilica door above his head. He spun into the open and put two shots into the weapon's ammo hopper, detonating it.

'If they took him with the honour guard, either he's joined, or he's dead.'

'That lot in the baptistry keep asking for him. They think he's a war hero, that he'll know what to do.'

Sycorax swore and reached for the injector embedded in her thigh.

'I'll take care of it.'

Lisille Lycan-Bast was holding a prayer, a last prayer for deliverance, when Rakkan walked into the baptistry.

No one asked why he was wearing an armoured black bodyglove, sprayed in the quartered colours of Stryder-Rau, a detail Sycorax was grateful she'd seen to, thinking that in a pinch she'd better blend into a crowd.

Kawe was the first to see him.

'Rakkan!' he said, jogging over and gripping his cousin's arm. 'Glad to see you here.'

The others looked up from praying. They were spooked, defeated. Weaponless and unmounted. Betrayed.

There were Lycan-Bast and Lambek-Firscal. Sir Sangraine, the amiable pilot of the Armiger *Fencer*. Mauvec Kawe. Lady Catalea of the Rau Warden *Aegis of Hope*. A few other Questoris and Armiger pilots.

And Symphonia Dask, shell-shocked.

'We could use a veteran campaigner,' said Lycan-Bast. 'Save Baroness Dask, none of us have been in a war.'

'Well, good news,' said Rakkan, flashing a grin. '*This* is a war. And you've survived so far. Which means we're all veterans now.'

The floor shook, and rockcrete powder spilled down from the ceiling above.

'Now, we haven't got much time, so who knows this basilica best?'

* * *

It was the silhouette that gave Tessell away. So many arms, so many mechadendrites. No one else had a shape like that.

Too bad they only saw her through the armoured window of the communication tunnel next to the dais. Too bad it was double-locked with a data-port and internal pin.

The *Crown of Dominion* was behind them, still sweeping towards the gates, venting its wrath on any survivors it found. Everyone else was gone.

Traitor Knights, Transmuted sacristans.

All that were left were the bodies.

'Where does this lead?' Koln asked.

'The Cathedral of Maintenance Altar,' Gwynne said. 'Our shrine.'

'And what's there?'

Gwynne shrugged. 'Ritual objects. Masks of the dead heroes. Our records and monasteries.'

'Any military assets?'

'No, just...' Gwynne's eyes widened. 'Oh, Omnissiah. Our store of Knights. The unformatted ones, ready for their human component.'

'You reroute the door control, I'll handle the lock.'

Gwynne plugged into the access port, brow furrowing as she cycled combinations. Koln activated the melta-torch in her finger and found the locking pin. Within moments, she'd sliced through it.

'How are you–' she began.

The hatch slid open.

'Access granted,' said Gwynne, then stopped when she saw the body inside. 'Is that...?'

'Holy Throne,' said Koln. 'I think it is.'

It was hard to tell, given all the blood – but Baroness Achara, herald of Dominion, lay dying at their feet.

* * *

'Waiting?' asked Rakkan. 'Waiting for what?'

'*For thee, Sir Rakkan,*' the voice answered. It filled the chamber with a rolling echo.

'What is this place?' asked Rakkan. He shaded his eyes so he could see it better. He could ken no point to it. An underground dome-cavern, thirty feet wide, with a plasteel grating floor. Below the floor was green seawater underlit by spotlights. The rippling liquid cast an ethereal spirit-light on the ceiling and walls, and he realised this sea-cavern must be deep enough to be below the algae layer.

In the centre of the room, a circular hole in the decking gave access to a curved thing coming up from the water. Rakkan first thought it was some kind of animal, until the hatch opened and he saw the lights of control consoles dancing inside.

'*This is your legacy,*' said the voice. '*The legacy your father left for you. That his mother left for him. And her father left for her. All the way back to the unremembered days. The secret he would have told you, had he not died so young and unexpectedly – but he left you the key. I had not thought it would take so long for you to discover it. But I have been patient.*'

'You knew my father.'

'*All too briefly. But a good man. He would have done much if called. What will you do, now that Morvayne has defiled the sacred soil of our kingdom? Will you mount up, and rise from the bloody sea?*'

'You are a Knight? I... I am not bonded to you. I've never piloted anything but a humble Warglaive. And how can you speak–'

'*You will find it natural. My controls resemble a Warglaive. You've already piloted the squire, now it is time to pilot the Knight.*'

'The squire?' he asked.

'*Noble Knight* Jester. *It is my pair. We are bonded. Have been so since before the rockets left Terra. The pilot of one is the pilot of the other.'*

Rakkan found himself drawn to the upper shell of the machine. From its time underwater, green kelp had grown on the hatch, lying shaggy on the otherwise thick adamantine. Rakkan lowered himself inside, if only to see what the controls were like. Old leather creaked as he lay in the seat.

'You want me to ride for glory, I presume,' he said, glancing at the control panel.

'*No,*' rumbled the Knight.

Rakkan could feel it vibrate under him, a Throne Mechanicum so powerful it was nearly alive. 'But...'

'*This machine is a defender. Bound to Dominion. There is no honour in this charge, no cheers of victory on the tournament field, no campaign badges or banners. It only does its duty.*'

'And what duty is that?'

'*To rise from the bloody sea, take the enemies of this world, and hurl them screaming back into the darkness. To bring song to the hearts of friends, and terror to the hearts of foes. Is that what you want?*'

Rakkan smiled. 'Yes, that would be splendid.'

'*Then don your father's helmet, Sir Rakkan.*'

He slipped it on, attaching the cable of the Throne Mechanicum.

Hail, Sir Linoleus Rakkan, the helmet said. *Will you pledge to ride to the defence of the realm?*

'Yes,' said Rakkan, teeth clenched, ready for what must come next.

The data-spike snapped down into his skull, and in an instant, he saw battlefields and tournaments. Burning stars and stomach-dropping voids. Places he had no memory of and monsters unnumbered. A kaleidoscope view of a thousand lives, smashing and separating. Mosaics of memory.

And his father. He felt his father.

Tell my son to rise from his blood.

And when he opened his eyes, he was another being entirely.

Seventy yards. That's how far it was to the crypt entrance. Seventy yards of nearly open ground in front of a rampaging Knight Castellan.

But they couldn't go out the doors. They couldn't go back into the basilica. And they couldn't stay here – the damn structure was coming down around them.

Which left the run.

And maybe one trick.

Raithe hefted the rifle, feeling its adjusted weight with the ploin-sized rifle grenade slotted into the stock rather than a barrel. He glanced around the side of the door, letting his mask get range. A hundred yards, maybe. The *Crown* picking its way around an enormous hole it had burned in the floor.

'Remember,' said Rakkan/Sycorax. 'Just to the first pillar.'

Raithe took a breath, rehearsed the move in his mind, then spun around the wall and took the shot.

Tonk.

The grenade arced a shallow parabola up and into the vaults, then down right into the Knight's face.

'Go!'

They ran.

A blue cloud, flecked with silver tinsel and shot through with lightning, bloomed in front of the Castellan. The ion shield flared amber, and the *Crown* bellowed, striking out with its meltaguns.

Blind.

Raithe slammed his back against the first pillar, sliding his head to the side to get a look at the armoured monster.

It stalked to the right, shaking its great head.

'Load,' he said.

Rakkan loaded and twist-locked the second haywire grenade into the rifle stock. Raithe had brought them in case they'd needed to get past an Armiger or two in order to kill Yavarius-Khau.

An Armiger *or two*, though. This was their last grenade. Even given the high priority of Assassinorum requisitions, the logistical strain of the Indomitus Crusade had meant the Mechanicus could only deliver two.

He felt a pat on his shoulder, saw Rakkan give an unusually lopsided smile. 'Ready.'

He spun and fired, and they ran.

A siegebreaker shell burst against the basilica wall, shattering a mosaic and sending multicoloured tiles the size of autogun rounds zinging through the air. One tile embedded itself in the skull of an Armiger pilot Raithe didn't know. Chunks of stone buttress the size of groundcars fell across their scattered knot of running figures, crushing Sir Kestegal of Rau. Along with the masonry came a huge downrush of particlised grey stone, reducing visibility to a few feet.

Raithe vaulted the debris and slid across the smooth top just as footmen stormed through the basilica's double door, the hailstorm bursts of their lascarbines darting red and ultra-visible above him in the dust-laden air.

He heard the screams as *Crown of Dominion*, still blind, opened up on them with the plasma destructor. His next breath stung, full of atomised stone and the heat-wash of plasma ordnance.

Without his mask, Raithe's visual acuity was little better than the Castellan's. For a moment he thought he'd lost his bearings, until Rakkan – no, Sycorax – reached out of the grey shroud and dragged him into the shelter of the crypt stairwell.

'Headcount?' he asked, coughing to clear his lungs.

'All but three of them made it,' Sycorax said, leaning close. 'Considering the circumstances, I think that's pretty good.'

THIRTY-FIVE

'Is she dead?' asked Gwynne.

'If she isn't,' said Koln, 'she will be soon.'

Even so, she took the time to pick the laspistol out of Achara's limp fingers. No sense inviting surprises.

'Hold this.' Koln handed the pistol to Gwynne. 'Point it down the corridor. If anyone comes at us, shoot. Don't bother aiming, I'll take it from there.'

'R-R... kan,' Achara stuttered. Heat-wash from a plasma hit had seared her robes to her skin, and flash-burned the rolls of parchment that hung from her pilot suit. She'd been shot in the chest, an abdominal hit likely flooding a lung. When she spoke, pink foam leaked from one side of her mouth.

'Baroness, I have water.' Koln uncapped a small canteen and tipped it to the herald's lips. Most spilled down her front, but she swallowed enough to clear her throat.

'Rakkan,' said Achara. 'You're Rakkan's people.'

'What happened, baroness? How did you get here?'

'Got hit in the initial blast. Thought I was dead.' She swallowed.

Koln didn't know exactly what she meant, whether Achara had thought she'd died, or the traitors thought she was dead. Probably both. She didn't interrupt to ask.

'Had... had pistol. Was in my boot, so it was sheltered. Cell didn't cook off.' She coughed, a choking sound that brought more pink foam.

'What were you trying to do?'

'Kill her.'

'The Arch-Maintenancer?'

'She got me instead.' Achara's head dipped towards the gunshot. 'Useless. I'm so useless.'

'No. Tell us what we need to know and we can finish the job. You're the herald, speak.'

'Symphonia... she thought you were Inquisition, you know. Paranoia, I said. But maybe. Maybe...'

'She was right,' said Koln.

One of the core tenents of the Vanus Temple: never correct a mistake in your favour.

'Huh,' said Achara. 'Funny. Always knew you'd find us out. Always knew we couldn't... hide it... forever...'

Achara's eyes drooped, then shut. Her chin sank down on her chest. Pink spittle drooled from her open lips.

'No, you don't,' said Koln. She pulled the tip off her left middle finger, exposing a syringe, and punched it through Achara's chest wall and into her heart. Triggered the injection with a muscle twitch.

Achara's head arched back, mouth opening in a gasp like a drowning victim coming back to air. Her blue lips coloured to grey.

Resuscitation shot. Adrenaline and revivicant cocktail direct to the bloodstream, paired with an integral micro-shock to restart the heart.

Koln tipped another drink of water into her mouth.

'What were you hiding from us? What did you think we'd find?'

'Tha– chhh.' Achara spat out the water. Blood was in it. Not just enough to pink it this time. There were chunks of coagulated red with comet tails that spiralled around them.

'Tell me, and I might be able to catch her.'

'He was a good man.'

'Who?'

'Yavarius-Khau. Good man... the best man really. We failed him. At the Battle of Blazing Heaven. He was wounded. So badly. *Dawn of Slaughter* nearly killed him. Would have, if Selkar Fang hadn't sacrificed himself. That's when we betrayed him. We thought,' she coughed. 'We thought we were saving him.'

'He was corrupted,' finished Koln.

'Tessell suspected, I think. So did all of us, if I'm honest. It speared him with so many strange projectiles from its harpoon batteries. I thought... thought...'

'Thought what?'

'They looked like data-spikes,' said Achara. Her head was drooping. 'We ignored it. Were lost. Lost without him. Without his leadersh...'

Koln reached forward and raised Achara's head, lightly slapping the herald's cheek. 'And then?'

'Tessell saved him. A miracle. He was diminished, of course. The Throne Mechanicum and his support systems kept him alive. We fed him through tubes. Our own little Emperor on his throne.'

'But he was mad,' said Gwynne.

'Not at first.' Achara gave a weak shake. 'For months, years he was lucid and normal. His old self, mentally. A great man. The greatest monarch in generations. Our only unifying figure – and when he was not himself, we protected him. From the intrigue, from plots, from himself. If we had done what he'd said, there would've been revolt. Whatever the *Dawn of Slaughter* had put in him was taking control. So we closed the circle, started speaking for him. It was selfish too, of course. No guarantee we would have kept our places if we got a new monarch. But it was also for him. Poor king, my poor king.'

Tears were rolling down Achara's cheeks, mixing with the blood on her chin.

'Now tell me the rest,' said Koln. 'Tell me the rest and I'll let you go.'

'He was the best man,' she said. 'The greatest. He fought it. But the episodes stretched. By the end he wasn't himself. Too erratic. And then Dask found your woman, the Inquisition agent. There would be an investigation, they'd find our monarch was tainted, assume all of us were too. Purge us, destroy our beautiful machines. And... and... we decided to remove the tubes. He wasn't there any more. Just a raving, broken man whose mind was unable to fight the darkness any more. It wasn't murder, we just... let him go.'

'When?'

'A month ago now. But it took longer than we anticipated. He was still speaking for days, he was tough, you see. The Arch-Maintenancer remotely piloted the *Crown* from the data-ports at the back. Our puppet king, waiting until things were calm enough to invest a new monarch.'

'Impossible,' said Gwynne. 'Logically insufficient. Yavarius-Khau spoke at the tournament. He could not have been dead. Tessell could not have done that.'

'Maybe his spirit, his madness, was still echoing through the machine. That's what I told myself when things like that happened. That he'd joined the ancestors inside the Throne

Mechanicum. All we had to do was install a new monarch, one without the taint, and all would be well.'

'Why did that not work?' asked Koln. 'Was Daggar-Kraine subverted or infected before taking the throne?'

Achara shook her head, sputtering. 'She... she knows. Your sacristan. See it in her eyes. Ask her creed.'

'The machine does not serve the man,' repeated Gwynne. 'The man serves the machine.'

'Oh, God-Emperor...' Koln's head sank between her crouched knees. A deep sickness churned her stomach. 'It wasn't Yavarius-Khau that was infected, it was the *Crown of Dominion.*'

Gwynne groaned.

'The king...' Achara coughed, the pink foam returning. 'He was stopping the taint, controlling it. Keeping it in check so it didn't take over the *Crown*. For ten years he succeeded, even when it drove him mad. Then, we killed him. And there was no one to fight it. He was the strongest man I knew. And we snuffed him out and let Morvayne in. I'm sorry... so... so...'

Achara's head lolled. Koln spiked her with the adrenal shot again.

'How did the others get tainted? What's the infection vector?'

Nothing happened. It was like stabbing a side of meat.

'She has no more data to surrender,' said Gwynne. 'Dorthiya Tessell will tell us the rest.'

'The Arch-Maintenancer has much to answer for,' said Koln, standing.

'She's no Arch-Maintenancer,' sneered Gwynne, hefting the laspistol. 'She gave up that title when she embraced Morvayne.'

PART FOUR

CRUSADERS

'It laid in among them, the great machine. Older than settlement it was, the only Knight to slay without a pilot. And that day it became the horror of its enemies. The foul Knight Eye of Blades it disembowelled. Scarhelm it burned to ash. And at the height of the combat, the Pride of Rau, the Knight that walks alone, duelled the dread engine Loyal Unto Death and its hateful pilot Catallius Morvayne.

It tore the traitor screaming from its cockpit. Crushed the patriarch of Morvayne beneath its tread. Then – its quest complete – the wounded machine collapsed into the sea.

Thus died the Leviathan.

And the Knights of Dread House Morvayne have never since returned to Dominion.'

— Sagas of Dominion, Tale Twenty: 'Morvayne's Rebellion'

THIRTY-SIX

Deny them. Deny them to the last shot. Those were their orders.

So he drew his sidearm.

Staalheim fired his laspistol at the behemoth looming above him, calling retreat as the beast's coaxial stubber butchered his footmen. One stubborn woman, Chelsa, ducked behind the gunshield to take a last desperate burst even as the beast's laser desecrator powered up with the keen of a tortured animal.

She disappeared totally, along with her artillery piece and sixteen feet of wall. Staalheim stumbled as the earthen firestep began to collapse beneath him and slide towards the breach.

'TERMINUS REX!' the beast bellowed, chains of skulls swinging from its superstructure. Coming on them like a hate from the old stories, a carnivorous giant screaming for meat and bone. One clawed gauntlet, twice as tall as a man, crackled with warp energy that vaporised six soldiers as it grabbed a handhold and hauled itself onto the battlements. 'TERMINUS REX!'

Staalheim assumed that was the giant's name.

'Go!' he yelled at his footmen. 'Up! Up to the next firestep! Fire everything, throw mortars if you have to!'

Their great guns were all gone. *Tilting Field*, *Traitorbane*, *Foehammer*, even *Faithful Servant*. With their shield down, fixed artillery positions were no match for the mobile firepower of the Knights. The lascannon batteries had taken down the ion shield around *Terminus Rex*, but did little more.

'Retreat!' he screamed, crossing the earth bridge, and clawing his way up the narrow stair that brought him to the dubious safety of the inner fortress.

His micro-bead burbled. It was hard to make out amid the din.

'Anyone catch that?' he yelled at his command retinue. 'Are they ordering us to flee?'

'The sea,' corrected his vox-artisan. 'He said the sea is boiling.'

More monsters. Surrounded by beasts.

Behind him, he heard the ogre's talons bite earth as he climbed the higher inner glacis of the star fort.

Each blow, *boom-boom-boom*, shook bricks loose from the stairway beneath Staalheim's feet.

He gained the top and turned, only to see the horrible visage rising above the parapet, sending the men inside fleeing. Four crackling talons grabbed the barrel of the dead lance *Foehammer* and it pulled itself halfway above the parapet, its golden skull-maw howling a curse that washed Staalheim with its foul inorganic breath, bursting one eardrum when he turned his head away from the corrupted gust.

The power of the noise shook him so badly his legs went out, and he fell, held upright only by one hand thrown backward.

Deny them. That was the order.

Not to deny them until the position became untenable. Not deny them until casualties became too great. Not to deny them so long as you can stand.

Deny them.

'Hold fast!' Staalheim yelled, raising his laspistol.

His hand shook so much the barrel made figure-eights in the air. And despite the beast's size he actually worried he might miss. Staalheim fired and hit the thing's left pauldron. Then its arming cap. The third struck the palm of the thunderstrike gauntlet as it reached for him.

The missile passed directly over his head, popped the weakened ion field with a painful discharge of air, and hit the Morvayne beast with the sound of a crashing mag-train. Armour plates fractured and crumpled. The monster reared back for a moment before jolting forward again, its adamantine helm clanging against the burned husk of the volcano lance.

An enormous harpoon had impaled it in the space between the head and the carapace, warping the traitor Knight's upper armour with its passage.

The claws of its gauntlet sank into the firestep six feet from Staalheim's boots.

Staalheim felt liquid dripping and looked up to see a great anchor chain, thick as his waist, groaning with tension. His eye followed it over his shoulder, where he saw a nightmare come to life.

His pistol fell from nerveless fingers.

At first, he thought he was seeing the Green Man, the shaggy giant who lived in the deep woods, and whose mouth ran with the blood of foresters who had cut more lumber than needed. But that foolishness only lasted until it took a step forward, and he scrambled to the side to get out of its path.

The behemoth strode across the top of the fortress, the forests of kelp clinging to its frame waving and dripping with each step. Harpoon chain retracting, it dragged the wounded *Terminus Rex* onto the parapet like a landed fish.

The traitor raised its decimator and lightning bounded down the harpoon chain, splitting the air and triggering systems deep inside the fallen machine to rupture and burn. One of its eye-lenses burst outward with a cough of green, and flames licked from its armoured ribcage like an overfed boiler.

One enormous four-toed foot swung over Staalheim as he scrambled out of the way, briefly showering him with water before planting itself on the traitor's rising head. The wounded Knight Desecrator feebly clawed at the armoured leg, scraping away kelp to reveal a panel red as heartblood.

With a motion like an industrial steel press, the giant ripped its harpoon free and crumpled the traitor's head. Then it looked down the edge of the fort at the enemy Knights below it, smashed its conflagration cannon twice upon its tilting shield, gave a foghorn bellow, and threw its arms wide in a gesture of challenge.

No sound returned but its own voice, echoing back from the distant mountains.

It was then that Staalheim realised what he was looking at. The Knight Without a Pilot. The Saviour of Dominion. Slayer of Old Man Morvayne. Terror of Traitors.

And he found his voice.

'It's the *Leviathan*!' he shouted, the words ripping out of his throat with a joy born of desperation. '*Leviathan*! *Leviathan*!'

The footmen took up the chant, raising their swords, screaming the Knight's name. Beating weapons to their armoured breastplates as they rallied to their positions.

'*Leviathan*! *Leviathan*! *Leviathan*!'

Even encased in so much adamantine, Rakkan could hear the voices lifting up around him.

Not the refined cheers and howls of the king's box on the

tournament field, but the wild, joyous swelling of the grand-stand. It was a clamour of hope, but a bloodthirsty hope. Hope not just for salvation, but to see one's enemies torn asunder. To see them punished.

For the abominations of Morvayne to quail in fear of Dominion's own monster.

Below, two Questoris Knights of Morvayne looked up at him from the foot of the glacis. A few War Dogs – tainted Armigers in Stryder-Rau colours – weaved about at their feet.

He lowered the harpoon to point at the Morvayne Knights below, each individually in challenge.

'Know me, traitors,' he said, and felt his seat rumble as the laud-hailers amplified his words. 'I am *Leviathan* – and you are mine.'

Then he leapt off the parapet and came down on them like an avalanche.

Chabon Fawl wore a purple armband to show his allegiance, his Rau livery defaced with handprints of the purple ink they'd found when they looted the palace scriptorium.

Well, that was not strictly accurate. They had not found purple ink. Purple was the colour of Morvayne, and had been banned on Dominion since the dread lord and his Knights had honoured their oath to the Mechanicus and left to join Horus.

But the scriptorium had plenty of Rau red and Stryder blue – and when they mixed it?

Morvayne purple. Almost as if it were planned that way, that the galaxy had come into order, the walls separating oceans breaking down.

He turned the autogun down the corridor, and kept his patrol. There were still rebel holdouts, those who had refused to join King Daggar-Kraine, in the palace. Death squads like his were sweeping to find the rebels and eliminate them. Just as he'd done with the hinterland rebels in the provinces.

'Advance,' he whispered to the two men at his back. 'Slowly into the corridor now. Watch the flanks.'

An explosion rattled through the palace, dropping palm-sized pieces of plaster from the ceiling. There was a hell of a siege going on at Heaven Defence West, it seemed. Dask's personal units were contesting it.

Fawl had served Baron Kraine for twelve years, and was good at it. Good enough that he'd not questioned things overmuch when Kraine began talking about their enemies in the Imperium. After all, there were enemies in House Stryder, and the court, and even as Yavarius-Khau had predicted, in the very populace amongst them. And those were his fellow Dominionites.

Given that there were enemies within, it would make sense that there were enemies without. And what had Morvayne's great sin been? Fighting the Imperium that was now their enemy.

So he barely glanced at the wall, with its delta-shaped splashes of blood and bullet holes. At the bodies of the palace staff lying in heaps at its foot.

Fawl crouched in the doorway, taking cover. 'Kalbrait, Verren, move up.'

He heard nothing. Not the whisper of fabric, nor creak of floorboard.

He didn't look away from the corridor; that was a good way to get killed.

'Kalbrait, Verren,' he whispered, urgent. And finally he felt a body at his shoulder.

Absolom Raithe wound the garrotte around the footman's neck twice to choke off the scream, then shook him until the spine broke.

'Clear,' he whispered into his micro-bead, covering the corridor with his Exitus pistol.

'Good God-Emperor,' whispered Lycan-Bast, looking at the dead patrol. She was at the head of the column, moving at a crouch in a line to stay below the windows. She picked up an autogun and passed it down the line, taking a stub pistol for herself. 'Where did Rakkan find a specimen like you?'

'Militarum,' said Sycorax, from behind. 'They have loads to spare.'

'Really?' said Dask, appraising a body with a professional eye. 'If we survive this, sergeant, I might have work for you in the future.'

He motioned for Dask and the others to stay, and crept into the corridor, peering up above a window ledge.

'It is impressive,' said Sycorax, into her micro-bead. She was keeping the rearguard position in case any footmen or tainted sacristans came up behind them. 'I always thought of you as more a long-range man.'

Raithe saw the fixed positions on the Hall of Fields – turncoat footmen in Stryder livery behind hasty barricades of grain sacks and palace furniture. Military-looking, probably Fontaine's household. A few Transmuted sacristans, the purple burn of their augmetic eye-lenses visible even from his vantage point.

Sycorax slid her head up below the window, peered out with one eye to keep her profile minimal. 'What's your read?'

Raithe's mask tagged targets, calculated firing solutions. Measured climatic conditions.

Air temperature: +5 degrees from Freeze Point

Wind speed: 11 miles per hour, west-northwest

Humidity and temperature above acceptable equipment tolerances

'We have traitors in prepared positions on the Hall of Fields. Crew weapons, hard cover. Going to be hell getting past them. Especially without heavy weapons.'

'We have the rifle.'

'I can't follow you across if I use it. I'd need to set up in a position, give the go order, and you run the gauntlet as I clear a path. Then after the fire support I'll have to move before they find me.'

'Once we're in the Knight suits, you'd be left behind anyway. And it would be good to have a spotter when we take on Morvayne.'

Raithe nodded. The plan had developed organically as they made their way up through the crypt tunnels, Sycorax, Dask and Lycan-Bast taking the lead.

Marshal the Knights, ride to battle, strike the traitor Stryder-Rau Knights and their Morvayne allies as they draw up forces for an attack on Gathering Palace.

'There's another aspect,' he said. 'In addition to Morvayne Knights gathering on the plain, Heaven Defence West is under heavy assault. Can't see much from the window, but the weapons discharges suggest Knight-level ordnance.'

'They're trying to land,' she said. 'Take out the fire-control centres.'

'I'm guessing a few Morvayne Knights teleported or dropped into the hinterlands to join Fontaine.' Raithe dropped his rifle bag and unzipped it, assembled his rifle as he spoke. 'They probably don't have the capability to teleport a whole complement. Not with Knights.'

'If I'm going to get across this bridge,' said Sycorax, 'I need to do it as myself. Which means shaking the nobles.'

'Handle that however you think best,' he said, taking one last look. 'I know a good shooting position.'

Sycorax tapped his shoulder as he began to slide away. Pressed something into his palm. 'Good luck, Absolom. Take care of yourself.'

It was a micro-dose syrette of polymorphine.

'Thanks,' he said, as he slipped into the shadows. 'I'll be watching out for you.'

'Dask!' Sycorax hissed, and beckoned.

The Gatekeeper came, struggling to keep low on old joints.

'There were other pilots, were there not? Waiting to see the procession from the viewing platform. That's close, isn't it?'

'Not far, no,' said Dask. 'Three rooms that way.'

'The more pilots, the better chance we have once we're mounted,' said Sycorax. She ran her hand through her hair, like Rakkan did when under stress. 'Take the rest of the group. Liberate as many as you can. Bring them back here in fifteen minutes.'

'What are you going to do?'

'I'm going to take the Hall of Fields.'

Four hundred tons of adamantine, steel and righteous fury crashed down on the two Knights of House Morvayne. Rakkan wielded the long thundercoil harpoon like a mace, stoking its generator so the serrated head crackled with electricity as he leapt from the top parapet over the moat, then vaulted into the thick of the traitor Knights.

'Stryder-Rau!' he shouted, activating his broad-spectrum vox. 'Heaven Defence West is besieged. *Leviathan* returns. Rise. Fight for Dominion.'

The first traitor was a twisted Errant-pattern, its thermal cannon already amputated and trailing wires from the stump. Rakkan brought his harpoon down on that defenceless side as he landed, the blow splintering its pauldron and driving the Knight to one knee before Rakkan slashed the harpoon sideways to parry a slice from the whirling chainsword of its companion.

Their weapons locked, the electrical feedback of a completed circuit making the steel weapons stick, and the fell thing speared out at Rakkan with a meltagun shot while he responded in kind.

The exchange of fire overcooked both their ion shields, throwing them apart with a bone-shattering *bang* as the two energy bubbles overloaded and broke the electrical circuit.

Rakkan took a step backwards and refocused on the wounded Knight, who was rising chainblade-first in a thrust towards the larger machine's hip assembly.

The blow might have landed, but a decade of combat in a Warglaive had – he was surprised to find – adequately prepared him for the close-confines fighting of the Valiant. A pilot used to the Questoris-pattern with their long-ranged cannons and elegant reaper chainswords would've struggled with the short striking range of the harpoon and conflagration cannon. But Rakkan was used to the butchery of the chain-cleaver, and had years of experience with infantry attacking him from below.

'Don't think so,' he breathed.

He sidestepped into the blow, so the chewing teeth of the chainblade hit his kneeplate and skipped upward, where he trapped it vertically between his harpoon arm and hip superstructure.

Its teeth whirred harmlessly – there was only one cutting edge to a reaper chainsword, and now it was chewing nothing but air.

He bashed downward with his conflagration cannon, crushing the blade's motor before he turned the tri-barrel flamer on the Knight and washed it with fire until the domed armour crinkled in on itself.

A War Dog – one of the tainted squires – forced its way around the burning Knight and opened up with twin autocannons, dimpling Rakkan's ion shield.

He kicked it with a massive foot, caving in its side and sending the panicking machine scurrying away on its gun barrels, dragging its crushed legs behind it.

'*Leviathan*!' came the chants from the smoking star fort. '*Leviathan*! *Leviathan*!'

'*Go*,' came the word in Sycorax's micro-bead. And she went.

She came out onto the Hall of Fields strolling, wearing a purple armband and overlarge jerkin looted from a dead footman.

'Hail,' said Sycorax. She raised a hand in greeting, and a captain came out from behind a grain-sack heavy stubber nest.

'Halt there!' he shouted. 'Make yourself known!'

She was still ten yards away, too much in open ground for this to work. Sycorax slowed as if to comply, but kept walking.

'Sorry?' she yelled, holding a hand to her ear. 'Lots of shooting inside. Head's ringing bad. And…'

She gestured towards Heaven Defence West.

The scene there nearly stopped her. At the foot of the glacis, three Knights brawled, smashing each other like boxers. Firing weapons at close range. Two purple Knights, and one that appeared a patchwork of red and green. A stray battle cannon shell arced well over the Hall of Fields, whistling in its passage and prompting the gun crews of footmen to duck.

'I said *halt!*'

Sycorax centred her focus.

'*Waiting for code word*,' said Raithe.

'Yuma sent me,' she shouted, slowing her pace but still moving forward. 'To fetch my Knight *Jester* and ride with our cousins in Morvayne.'

The stubber-gunner chambered a belt feed.

Sycorax stopped, hands up. Judged the distance.

The captain drew his autopistol. It'd be a hard shot to dodge, standing still at this range. She could see his eyes searching her. 'Show me a written order, *sir*. Or we open fire.'

Hesitancy there. No one knew who, exactly, was who. He

didn't believe her, that was clear, but centuries of his peasant ancestors being killed for merely disrespecting the higher orders created just enough doubt.

'No trouble, cousin, no trouble,' she said, reaching into her jacket. 'I have an order from Baron Kraine, the kingmaker.'

The stubber operator's head exploded, blinding the loader with chips of ejected skull.

Sycorax whipped the throwing dagger through the air so fast it buried hilt-deep in the captain's eye before he even had a chance to look and see why the loader was screaming.

She dashed past, mercury-smooth, using his falling body as cover from a footman in the grain-sack redoubt who levelled an autorifle at her.

Sycorax went into a slide, snatched up the captain's fallen auto-pistol, and fired a three-round burst that pitched the footman backward, blood puffing into the air from two chest penetrations.

'*One's pushing up on your eleven o'clock,*' voxed Raithe.

Sycorax backed up against the outside of the sack strongpoint, dragged the autorifle off the parapet where the dead footman had left it, and blind-fired it over the parapet at the eleven position. Hot casings rattled the stone between her feet.

'*Down,*' said Raithe.

Sycorax, feeling the polymorphine dose she'd taken blaze inside her, threw off the big jerkin that hid her equipment, and changed into who she really was.

Air temperature: +5 degrees from Freeze Point

Wind speed: seven miles per hour, west-northwest. Cross-eddies due to distortion of force field proximity

Gravitic distortion of fields: .22 degrees concave

Targets remaining: 21

Raithe let out a long breath and squeezed the trigger. Winced at the hard kick of the Exitus on his shoulder. But it was a *good* pain. The pain of doing what he was meant to.

In his scope, a fast-moving sacristan with data-flails for arms tore in half.

Hellfire round. Spinal.

Targets remaining: 20

Sycorax was in the bottom of his scope, stripping off a looted jacket that concealed her phase blade, neural shredder and the back-mounted power unit. Taking fire now that the initial shock of her assault had worn off.

He'd known this window would be the perfect vantage point since he had seen it on their first day at Gathering Palace. High up above the gateway to the Hall of Fields, yet still within the arcing tunnel of sheltering energy. Wind coming through the shattered window, blowing in his face. Winter wind, sharp as a blade.

Sharp as he felt.

In fact, traitor footmen had posted their own marksman team here, though they wouldn't be complaining about Raithe usurping their spot – now that they were stacked in a corner.

They'd been messy, anyway. Rifle poking out of the section they'd broken through the mosaic window, ration trash scattered about. Piss-stink in one corner.

Raithe lay with his barrel a foot back from the removed window section. He was impossible to spot from below.

Sycorax was moving now, fast and smooth, low to the ground like a lizard. Wriggling, moving in a way so utterly inhuman Raithe stopped to watch for a moment. She found a hole in a sandbag emplacement, barely larger than her head. Behind it, a footman swept for her. Sycorax flowed through the hole, shoulders flattening, body serpentine. She came up under the footman and gutted him with her phase blade. He fell in two pieces.

Red tracers darted past Sycorax and he navigated his crosshairs up to the crew-served multi-laser. A Faber-pattern. Old make. Discontinued on most forge worlds due to the unstable battery load. He worked the shot selector for a turbo-penetrator round and followed the cable with the crosshairs to where it ended behind the thick pew the crew were using as a barricade.

The spy mask stripped away layers, read power outputs. The battery burned yellow, pulsing. Depleting fast as the crew poured on the las-fire.

Squeeze. Kick.

Yellow sparks leapt skyward like fireworks. A fizzing spray of unleashed las-energy boiled and billowed outward like a bad spirit unleashed.

Pretty.

Targets remaining: 17

He let go of the rifle and let it rest on its bipod. He rotated his shoulder to loosen it. The used polymorphine syrette lay beside his gear bag.

In the distance to his right, at Heaven Defence West, a mottled green-red Knight duelled a Morvayne Knight Rampager. Ion shields flashed and bruised. Armigers scampered around, peppering the bigger Knight's ion shield with fire. A few stray autocannon rounds from the fight arced high and splashed against the right-hand energy field on the bridge, blooming it amber.

On the horizon, he could see two Stryder-Rau Questoris Knights heading into the fray.

Incoming fire.

A warning across his vision arrived a microsecond before las-bolts splashed through the upper panels of the mosaic window, showering him with multicoloured glass.

Ballistic cogitators estimated the line of fire from its angle of attack, marking four squares of his vision-grid in red. He found the offending marksman on the far end of the bridge, and settled his crosshairs a hair above and to the left of her head, to compensate for her shooting position nestled up against the right-hand field.

He smiled.

Squeeze.

Kick.

Enemy reinforcements had come. Reinforcements he was too busy to look at.

Rakkan bashed the Knight Rampager with his shoulder, pushing it back and gaining himself room.

A battle cannon round whistled past Rakkan and fountained dirt from the fort's glacis. A thermal cannon blast howled through his ion shield and cooked the siegebreaker cannon on *Leviathan*'s left shoulder, vaporising it so fast that liquid adamantine spalled off and spattered across his upper carapace.

At least it evaporated the ammo rather than cooking it off, Rakkan thought.

The Knight Rampager on his right squealed, lowered its head and came at him, foot talons pawing the ground as it charged, chainsword scything the air, gauntlet reaching.

A mistake.

Rakkan launched the harpoon through its abdomen and reeled it in, slamming the frantic Knight in close, enveloping its form with his beweaponed arms so he held it to him cranium-to-cranium like a lover as the two twin meltaguns on his chest mounts bored into its armour and cooked the pilot alive.

He turned, holding it like a shield between him and the reinforcements.

And it was only then that he saw who the Knights were.

Close was *Firedrake*, raising its thermal cannon for another shot.

Behind, in the distance, *Greyhound*.

His uncle. His mother.

Rakkan threw the fused, stiff traitor on top of its companion and levelled his harpoon at Baron Kraine.

The chanting let them know they were getting close.

Close to Dorthiya Tessell, close to the truth.

The reserve sanctuary was massive, an underground chamber seven storeys high, its ceiling criss-crossed with boxy crane assemblies and hanging chain-harnesses. Incense smoke pooled around everything as if it were an obscura addict's den.

Despite the fact that Koln had not seen a living soul other than the two of them in the past forty-three minutes, the room felt crowded – a forest of Knight suits stood shoulder to shoulder, an army of stone giants without the spark of life. Here and there they lay under sheets, but most stood with their chins to chests, weapons crossed in front of them. Unpainted, bare metal bodies making them appear like funerary statues.

Koln and Gwynne moved slowly, carefully.

'Point that las down,' advised Koln. 'You're not trained to use it, which makes you as dangerous to me as you are to her.'

Gwynne nodded, swallowed. Koln expected the young sacristan had never been to the reserve sanctuary – the facility that held the future of Stryder-Rau, its insurance of continued existence, was too hallowed for a mere Armiger sacristan.

Koln motioned her towards an inert Armiger, and pulled her close.

'There will be a vox-set. Something powerful to communicate with the surface.' Koln opened a data-channel and shunted her a packet. 'Find it, transmit what we've discovered to Raithe and

Sycorax. Tell them they cannot by any means allow the *Crown* to survive. They have to destroy the Throne Mechanicum along with Daggar-Kraine. A kill is not enough.'

'Acknowledged.'

'Come on,' she motioned towards a long, clean room tented by plastek tarps. 'We can move under cover better through here.'

They slipped through, Koln lifting the slit plastek curtain of the door so it didn't crinkle, and began to creep through the laboratory.

'Armigers,' said Gwynne. 'The sacred blueprints of the Armigers.'

'What?'

Gwynne gestured towards yellowed parchments strip-taped to the clapboard walls. 'These are Armiger schematics. Look, there's Vossa's *Stormrider*. And *Raptor's Claw*, Andricus' noble machine. This' – she pointed to a slateboard of numerals – 'is behavioural code. We're not supposed to learn that, but you see it from time to time on the more exotic damage read-outs. And we had to learn to look for signs of...'

'Oh, Throne,' said Koln. 'The squires. The squires were all missing at the coronation. That's how she did it. The infection vector.'

Then her dataveil tagged a draped sheet in the corner, stained with red. Koln drew it back, her augmetic pupils rotating at the revelation.

'What is it?' asked Gwynne.

'An astropath,' said Koln, dipping two fingers into the excavated, vivisected cranium. 'Throne help us, it's an astropath.'

'What does that mean?' asked Gwynne.

'It means,' she said, 'we've been exposed utterly. It means someone either knows who we are already, or will very soon.'

Sycorax spun away from the stream of autogun fire, landing backwards on her hands and scuttling like a crab behind a barrel.

She was at five kills and counting, but they were everywhere. Frontal assault was not her preferred combat environment, and were it not for Raithe providing covering fire, she'd be lying a hundred yards back in a pool of blood.

Might still happen, she thought, as a footman came up above a plasteel barrier, his arm cocked back and a grenade in his hand.

Sycorax swung her neural shredder on him but suddenly the footman's arm was gone. He stood stunned for a moment, before throwing himself down to frantically search for the grenade at his feet and dive on it.

The frag detonated, throwing the wounded soldier's body into the left-hand field where it stuck and juddered. His plasteel door barrier fell forward, exposing two other footmen who'd been saved by his sacrifice.

Sycorax put them down with an empyric blast from the neural shredder, the wave of green energy severing the pathways in their brains so they dropped and lay still – not even a twitch.

'Moving,' she said into her micro-bead.

'*Confirm*,' said Raithe. '*Watch your one, incoming Transmuted.*'

Sycorax somersaulted over a burned barricade and activated her phase blade.

The Transmuted came on armed with maintenance tools. Sacristans of the stable, lower initiates of the maintenancer temple. They were hunched and insectile, clicking and keening, moving sideways and in diagonals as they advanced.

The first swung a double-sided hammer and she danced backwards, slicing the head of it off so it clunked hard on the bridgeway. Then she spun downward and cut through his knee before going for the second. This one had an adamantine clamping claw sutured to one arm, and as he opened it, she saw whirling circular saws deep in its throat. A tool for extracting pilots from armour too crushed to operate hatches, she realised. Specialist equipment. Higher class than a simple forgeshrine menial.

The taint ran deep.

She ducked the swipe, feeling the jaws of the clamp snap just above her head as she dived and rolled past. A backhand chop to the spine put the sacristan on the floor, and Raithe exploded whatever remained of its brainpan.

Sycorax sprinted, flashing left and right to confuse the five-man fire-team who stood in front of the door to the Knight stables. Two las-bolts creased her thigh. A hard round clipped against the xenos metal of her blade, falling in two pieces.

She ripped it across a footman's neck as she ran past, not waiting to see the head fall, and broke her run into a wide arc to come at the others from the side and behind.

'*I have to withdraw,*' said Raithe. '*Search team on the stairs.*'

'Copy,' said Sycorax, blasting past the fire-team and throwing so much momentum behind her run that she sprinted an arc up the wall of the stable. Her neural shredder caught three as they turned around, trying to follow the blur attacking them. Before they hit the rockcrete, she sprang off the wall and landed on the last man, pinning him to the stone with her phase sword.

'Bridge clear.'

'*See you on the field,*' Raithe said. '*I'm repositioning. Going up the citadel of Gathering Palace. Best unobstructed view. Better change back to Rakkan, I see Dask and her crew on this end of the bridge.*'

'We never get any credit,' mumbled Sycorax subaudibly as she changed her face while dragging the big doors of the stable open. 'Have you ever noticed that?'

THIRTY-SEVEN

Rakkan charged *Firedrake* straight-on, his remaining shoulder-mounted battle cannon hammering a dual shot that burst Kraine's ion shield. Targeting augurs floated in his vision.

Target lock: *Greyhound*.

He loosed the shieldbreaker missiles, hoping the harassing fire would keep her at bay temporarily as he dealt with his uncle.

'Traitor!' he roared.

Haze from Kraine's thermal cannon boiled over *Leviathan*'s ion shield, purpling his vision just before the baron's stormspear rocket pod let loose. Rakkan jerked forward in his restraints and *Leviathan* staggered, punched twice in the chestplate. A third twisted high, sizzling past the upper carapace.

Leviathan hungered. It wanted Kraine. Almost alone its harpoon arm came up and hammered out its projectile chain.

Kraine turned, leaning *Firedrake* back to deflect the blow.

Instead, when the great harpoon glanced off his chestplate and pauldron, it slammed him backwards and he unbalanced.

Firedrake fell, arms flailing, crashing into the dirt of the world it had betrayed.

The great Knight crawled backwards as *Leviathan* approached, Rakkan retracting the harpoon with deliberate slowness. Locking the weapon home before raising it to point at *Firedrake*, scrambling to right itself.

'A challenge,' Rakkan bellowed. 'I want you, Kraine.'

Kraine must have heard the challenge, because when he got *Firedrake* to its feet, Kraine ran.

Towards the tournament ground.

The citadel had one staircase. A spiral.

The footmen came down at him one after the other. A seemingly endless supply.

A spiral staircase, Raithe knew, gave tactical advantage to the defenders above. An attacking force could only climb single file, tiring with every step, unable to watch both their footing and the defenders raining blows on them from above. And of course, its chief advantage was that on a spiral stair, the size of an attacking force did not matter – since enemies could only fight each other one-on-one.

That tactical calculus changed, however, when one of those two opponents was a Vindicare operative, one of the deadliest killers in the Imperium of Man.

Raithe blasted out a kneecap with his pistol and let the man tumble past. Punched a second in the throat with the barrel of the gun then gripped his unhelmeted head and rammed it into the pillar of the winding staircase. The next man stabbed out with a bayonet and Raithe felt a searing pain in his abdomen, but didn't stop to examine it before he put his utility knife through the footman's throat.

Abdominal wound, he thought, looking at the blood on his hands. Painful. Not fatal. He could feel the synskin suit tighten and cinch off the blood flow as he grabbed a pistol that was blind-firing around the next bend, tore it out of the footman's grip, and smashed the gunframe into his face.

Then he came up the landing using the man's body as a shield, and ventilated two incoming sacristans with turbo-penetrator rounds. The third leapt on him, scouring his face with its mechadendrite mouth feelers. He rolled onto his back with the blow, keeping the human shield between them, then planted a boot into the unconscious hostage's midriff and threw both over his head. Straight through a stained-glass window.

He ejected his pistol magazine, slid home another and pulled the slide, ignoring how blood was creeping past his mask seal. Outside the shattered window, he could see the green Knight charging a red Rau machine. The Rau unleashed a trio of missiles – one flew high.

Tracking… tracking…

It struck a lower floor of the citadel, rocking the tower.

Raithe hoped that would help him.

But there was still half the staircase to go before he reached the ideal vantage point, and there would be more footmen coming up behind. Probably marshalling in force, waiting to develop a large storming party. Maybe the rocket had wiped some out.

But Raithe never counted on luck.

He threw down his bag, ripped out a black butterfly kit of pressure plates and tripwire, and began to make life hard for any pursuers.

A footman came down the stairs wielding a battle axe, howling fury for his house and his gods. Raithe shot him without looking up from his work.

'Arch-Maintenancer Dorthiya Tessell,' said Koln, walking out into the maintenance bay of the forgeshrine.

Tessell paused in her incantation, her arms quivering with… what?

Fear? Rage?

'Engine-Master Dak,' said Tessell, turning away from the cogitator she'd been operating, the fat cables snaking out the back and into the cockpit of a Knight Armiger. 'Though I think we can dispense with the formal titles, particularly those we did not earn, yes?'

'Are you trying to figure it out?' asked Koln. 'Now that he's gone?'

Tessell's face did not move, the matronly eyes impassive. But the hand of her third right arm clicked its thumb and middle finger, a nervous tic like a crow tapping on a window. 'Whoever do you mean?'

'Your miracle worker, the Techmarine.'

Her head inclined, Tessell's features were shadowed and dark. 'Who told you? Gwynne? Remembered, did she?'

Koln walked a circle, not wanting Tessell to be able to fix her easily with a weapon if she tried to attack. 'Tell me if I have solved the equation, would you? The Battle of the Blazing Heaven. Your High Monarch has fallen. Not only is he dying, but the *Crown*'s Throne Mechanicum is dying. Data-spikes, embedded deep. You think he's been poisoned, maybe even know he's poisoned by Chaos, but they can't give him up. He's too special, too strong. They want a miracle you can't provide – then behold, a miracle appears.'

'It did.'

'The Iron Hands Techmarine. Or so he told you. He did what you could not. He healed Yavarius-Khau and the *Crown of Dominion*. Counteracted the corruption. Stabilised the king. In fact, now the ancestors speak to the king in a louder voice than ever. Am I accurate so far?'

Tessell straightened, raising her chin.

'Except he didn't cleanse the infection. He nurtured it. Used his data-jack to upload the heart_wyrm virus – it could only be imported manually then, as opposed to the broadcast version now – which fully corrupted the *Crown* and gradually, Yavarius-Khau himself. Probably he was an Iron Warrior, not an Iron Hand. How would you know? You'd never met an Astartes on this backwater.'

'Careful.'

'But everyone calls you a miracle worker. Your position of Arch-Maintenancer is guaranteed for life. Which is good, because the houses are spoiling for war as the king becomes more and more incapacitated. Threatening your precious machines. All these petulant children who share your sacred things. You fear a civil war. And then you find a solution – use the same program that healed Yavarius-Khau to make the ancestors speak louder and give the machine power to control the man. This new technology–'

'New technology is heresy, this is a spiritual practice. I would not expect you to understand.'

'Spiritual practice, then. But it's hard to spread. Knight systems are highly locked down, impossible to corrupt via broadcast like idiot tech-priests and data-thralls. Especially idiot sacristans who jack directly into a Throne Mechanicum in an effort to fix it – which is how it corrupted you.'

Tessell dashed for her, legs scuttling on the plated decking, and Koln dodged between a pair of Armigers, activating a data-cloak and weaving into the forest, losing herself.

'But whether fool or corrupt,' she said, using the auditory dampener to bounce her voice, 'you found a solution. You couldn't infect the Questoris Knights – too suspicious. Too many questions. Pilots are so close to them, always in the centre of attention.'

Koln watched Tessell scuttle in the wrong direction, her centipede body wriggling between Knight legs.

'But Armigers,' Koln said. 'No one pays attention to lowly Armigers. Low bloodlines, the inglorious sacristans. And once you infected them, whenever they were squired to a Knight, the mind-link passed the infection to the Questoris-pattern. The Armigers got the will of the Knight, the Knights got the infection of the Armiger. That's how you got Kraine and Fontaine. Hawthorn Astair-Rakkan eluded you, but you got tainted Vossa to kill her squire in a duel and lined up one of your circle. In fact, it wouldn't surprise me if the "victors" in all these Stryder-Rau duels just happened to clear the way for an infected squire.'

Koln slipped between the legs of a Knight Castellan.

'But you missed Yuma and Achara, who didn't want squires, and Dask, who's had the same one since Blazing Heaven. Really very clever.' Koln paused, scanning the darkness for her. 'Is that why you tried to kill Gwynne?'

Tessell came at her from the side, moving faster than Koln thought possible. Insectile arms struck out at her one after the other and she turned the blows with her augmetic hands, batting and twisting, using all her speed to block the incoming claws, steel ringing on steel like a knightly battle of old as her cogitation implant analysed the pattern and broke it.

She thrust forward with the palm of one hand, letting loose a kinetic blast that threw Tessell back into the incense shroud.

Koln heard scuttling in the dark. Legs on decking, on adamantine armour. Knew Tessell was climbing the Knights.

'Gwynne found you out,' Koln taunted. 'A low-born little daughter of engine-thralls who worked on dirtcycles and autocarriages discovered your secret. Maybe you tried to bring her in, or that irrepressible curiosity of hers just wouldn't be constrained. But you had to kill her.'

'That little bitch said she was working for me. I'm the Arch-

Maintenancer, no one should be out of my control. She was hiding things from me. Concealing.'

Koln saw a shadow in the smoke and let loose a las-blast that illuminated the incense red, but hit nothing.

'Easy problem to solve, Gwynne. Just a corruptible footman and a stub pistol, a cheap murder. But he was an amateur. He was messy. He tried the hit when Rakkan was there, and Gwynne dived on him. Backfire. Everyone thought mad old Yavarius-Khau tried to kill his great-nephew. Gwynne was a hero. Hawthorn shipped them off as Freeblades to protect them. Ruthless as she is, she's still a mother. But you had one stroke of luck – the shot blew Gwynne's engram-banks. She remembered nothing about the plot.'

'You don't understand.' The voice was pleading, shaken. 'Everything I did, I did for these machines.'

'I do understand,' said Koln, stalking through the Knights, right hand configured to shoot. 'The virus didn't work like he promised, did it? No one stopped fighting. The fighting got worse. And the secession talk. Fontaine, dragging out the hinterland uprising to give him time to build an army made for a coup. And worst of all, your own growing paranoia. Doubting whether your thoughts were your own. All those intrusive ideas about breaking away, visions of past glories, irrational hatred for the Mechanicus, questions about whether Morvayne was truly that bad.'

She found Tessell by the sound of her weeping. The Arch-Maintenancer was doubled over, her flesh-hands covering her face.

'But you knew they were that bad, you knew because you'd seen what was inside *Dawn of Slaughter*. How twisted and perverse the traitor Knights became. You understood that you had brought that fate upon both your houses. And now, you're trying to reverse it.'

'But I can't,' she wailed. 'It's not my fault, it's not my fault.'

Click-click. Gwynne's signal for *message sent*.

'In my experience,' said Koln, raising her digi-weapon, 'hereteks never think it is.'

Tessell struck out at her, her kind eyes now burning mauve.

'Ride, ride!' Sycorax slammed the hatch on *Typhoon's Teeth* and knocked the crystal twice, giving Mauvec Kawe a thumbs-up as his dual reactors cycled up and lifted the Knight out of its mounting crouch.

'Are you hearing this, Linoleus?' he said through the laud-hailers. *'On the vox. They're saying the* Leviathan *has come. That it's single-handedly turning an assault on Heaven Defence West.'*

'Leviathan,' Sycorax said into her helmet's vox-system, saying it with awe, but unsure what it meant. She hit the toggle on the mounting stairs and wheeled them away as the Knight Gallant took a first step, shaking the chamber. 'A good omen.'

'The best,' said Kawe, stomping towards the gateway. *'I lay good odds on us this day!'*

Apart from Sycorax, the entire loyalist force was mounted and moving. With the sacristans corrupted – she'd had to kill a few who were trying to disassemble the loyalist Knights – there was no one to help the Questoris pilots into their cockpits.

So she'd taken the duty herself – and all that remained was for her to mount up herself.

A buzz in her internal micro-bead. 'Raithe?'

'Negative,' voxed Raithe. *'Not me.'*

It was an insect drone, far away. She dialled it in, cleaned up the transmission.

'Hailing Rakkan. Hailing Rakkan. Acknowledge.'

'Gwynne?' she said, so shocked she did it aloud. 'We thought you were dead. Is your escort with you?'

'Yes. Please digest the data-packet.'

Sycorax climbed into *Jester*'s cockpit and closed the hatch, connecting the neural cable to the helmet's link. 'Gwynne, I'm busy and don't have background data-processing, can you summarise?'

'It's not Daggar-Kraine who's tainted, it's the Crown of Dominion. *You must destroy the Throne Mechanicum, kill the Thro–'*

The signal cut.

'Raithe, are you hearing this?'

'Yes, reading it.'

'Any good news? Any useful angle we can play other than–'

'Charging directly at the most dangerous machine on this world and trying to murder it? No.'

'Excellent,' she said. 'For a moment there, I thought we might win.'

Then she dropped the helmet on her head and entered a chorus of screams.

Not Rakkan! Traitor! Imposter! Killer of kings! Who are you? WHO ARE YOU?

The spirits howled in her mind, gnawed at her ears, battered her psyche. The data-spike ground and twisted, like a knife when a killer wants his enemy to suffer.

'I'm an assassin! And you are mad fools – what do you say to that?'

Quiet. The data-spike stopped twisting.

How dare you sp–

'No, how dare *you*. You ridiculous dead, insisting your children bow and worship you. You've ruined this kingdom, you know that? With your pride and arrogance. Your insistence that your descendants live up to your deeds. You know what they've done in pursuit of that? They've sullied their noble machines and declared for House Morvayne.'

That… A lone voice now. *That is not possib–*

'Yavarius-Khau was mad and corrupted, the *Crown of Dominion* is a temple to Chaos. Your venerated machine-monarch has gone sentient and withdrawn from the Imperial treaty, and Morvayne marches on Gathering Palace. Read this if you don't believe me.'

She opened her full mind to them then, not just the false cortex, and streamed the data-packet into the machine.

Fallen!

Fallen!

Our houses are fallen!

'So now you know who I am, and you have two choices,' Sycorax said, through gritted teeth. She was being hailed by the other Knights. No time for this. 'You've been fighting me this whole time. Now will you partner with an outsider and an assassin, or will you sit inert in the stable as Dominion falls – that is unless I give you what you deserve and drop an incendiary grenade in here?'

Jester's chain-cleaver revved to full spin, and its right leg stepped forward.

'Nice riding with you,' she said.

Avaaris Koln knew anatomy.

The pain in her mid-abdomen was a ruptured kidney, the cable-shears of Tessell's third right arm having smashed through her chest wall and broken two steel-reinforced ribs. One femoral artery was open, her synskin suit cinching tight to try and keep her from bleeding out and staining Tessell's robe an even darker red. The second left arm was in her lower abdomen; she could feel the acid spilling inside her.

But Koln's augmetic hands were locked around the Arch-Maintenancer's throat. Tessell's face was turning blue, the vox-unit that replaced her mouth crumpling under the adamantine fingers.

'Sanction delivered,' Koln said, and triggered her digi-weapons.

The Arch-Maintenancer's face burst into an inferno, the melta weapon melting away skin and flesh. The laspistol drilled through the back of the neck and severed the spine. A kinetic field emitter in the palm blew the Arch-Maintenancer out of Koln's grip and into a primer-grey Knight Errant.

But Tessell was no longer a mortal tech-priest. She was Transmuted, a creature of warp-data, daemonic chants encoded into her logic chains. Her steel skull gleamed as she gripped the front of the Knight suit, scuttling down to the floor even as her robes cooked away. And her form was more awful than Koln could have imagined. A true centipede, plated with bone and rearing up ten feet high.

'Dorthiya Tessell,' a voice said.

The heretek looked, head wrenching nearly all the way around.

'As an adept of the Order of the Maintenance Altar and a true follower of the Omnissiah, I declare you a heretek and a traitor,' Gwynne said.

Through Koln's fading vision, she saw Gwynne had no weapon but a cable.

A cable linked to her wrist-cogitator – and trailing to an Armiger Helverin, its autocannons pointed at the twisted sacristan.

Gwynne stopped firing when the drum magazines clicked empty. By that time, Koln had stopped moving.

THIRTY-EIGHT

Together they rode. Loyalists, competitors in the Lists, Stryder and Rau, friends and rivals. High and low.

They rode for the Gathering Plain.

'Gwynne says we have to kill the *Crown*,' said Sycorax. She'd sent on the data-packet, not that anyone had time to read it. Clever Koln had stripped any language mentioning the Assassinorum, leaving nothing but damning facts. 'Not just kill Daggar-Kraine, but the Throne Mechanicum itself.'

'*An engine-kill if we can manage it,*' cut in Dask. The poor baroness, the ranking member of the group, was nominal leader. But the other loyalists were nearly all young, either from the succession Lists or the lower ranks rescued from the viewing platform. Their combat experience came only from the arena, and they were not accustomed to following military rank structures. '*The formation is coming in from the mountains,*' Dask continued. '*Hoping to reinforce the initial lance besieging Heaven Defence West. We ride to intercept them, and lift the siege to keep the air defence grid firing. We're a team now, no one try to be a hero.*'

A weak speech, the ghosts in the helm whispered. *Practical, without inspiration. The young Knights are quaking in their seats, yet she offers no bravery.*

Sycorax looked to her right, past Dask. She opened her vox.

'Loyal Knights,' she said. 'We are now players in a fable. Our monarch turned traitor. Dread Morvayne come. *Leviathan* is risen. We here are fortunate to breathe the air of legend. Look to your dexter side, see how the traitors flee from *Leviathan*!'

Cheers over the vox, over the sounds of running pistons. Despite the bouncing of full sprint, all could see Kraine's *Firedrake* scrambling away from the legendary giant. The Knight Valiant's stature was only more imposing due to the fires that licked from his kelp-draped armour.

'By riding today,' she continued, 'our names will not be forgotten. If we are slaughtered to a man, our enemies will weave chants about how dear we sold our blood. And if victory shines upon us, our masks will hang high in the basilica. Children will point and say, "There is *Typhoon*! And noble *Sprinter*! And the *Aegis of Hope*, who fought against two foes as if they were one. These are the heroes who rode with *Leviathan*." Is that not right, baroness?'

Louder cheers, almost raucous, drunk on adrenaline and the singing ancestral choirs. Even as *Leviathan* disappeared from sight behind the tournament ground.

'It is,' said Dask. 'Stay together, support each other. The goal is to get close to the *Crown*. Wedge formation. Drive into them. Put my thermal cannon in range and let *Typhoon*'s Teeth deliver the killing blow.'

That was Dask's plan, to soften the *Crown* up with the thermal cannon on her own machine *Basilisk's Gaze* and let Kawe carve him up with the *Typhoon*'s reaper chainsword and thunderstrike gauntlet.

It was a good plan. A sensible plan. And when Sycorax looked down their line of Knights, built for war and armoured against all comers, their banners fluttering in the winter wind, sprinting twice as fast as a man, she almost believed her own words.

To see Sir Mauvec Kawe in *Typhoon's Teeth*, head down and running, his reaper chainsword long as a battle tank, and Dask in *Basilisk's Gaze*, her honour pennants flying. Her badge of the stone eye stared from her pauldron, as it had stared unblinking upon traitor Knights and xenos devils. She was the only one of them who had battled the Dread House.

Sir Sangraine was in *Fencer*, loping with long strides alongside *Jester*. Autocannon barrels shone in the winter light. Every step demonstrated his pride to be among such heroes.

And so many others. Lord Lambek-Firscal in the Crusader *Galeforce*; his younger half-brother – who had stood with him among the Lists candidates at the coronation, despite the fact that it was not allowed – in the Warglaive *Sprinter*. Lady Catalea in *Aegis of Hope*, her avenger gatling cannon already cycling in preparation for her first shot, the lights on her rocket pod toggling to green to show they were live. Some, Sycorax didn't know – straggler survivors from Stryder or Rau, minor nobles that had not rated a photo or card on Koln's chart, but were now riding to die for their world.

Only now you see, whispered *Jester's* spirit choir. *This is what we are. The grandeur and glory.*

And Sycorax did see, and thought of the ones not there. The murdered and the missing. Achara in *Voice of Authority*. Lord Daggar-Kraine, now good as dead, in *Holdfast*. Even Sabban in *Mauler*.

All the ones she herself had killed – how useful would their shields have been now.

Because as they rounded the edge of the knoll and saw the

enemy, she remembered what they were up against – an enemy lance larger than they'd imagined, strung out in loose column formation, using the tournament stadium as cover to approach Heaven Defence West.

Rallan Fontaine in *Axefall*, his reaper chainsword replaced with an enormous bearded poweraxe. At least ten Questoris Knights of Stryder and Rau. Two in the magenta colours of Morvayne. A pack of Armiger squires weaving beneath their legs.

And at the heart of the enemy host, the *Crown of Dominion*, guarded by Yuma's *Throneshield*.

The charging formation faltered on the hill, coming to a standstill as they regarded the enemy.

'What is our cry?' asked Lambek-Firscal.

It was traditional, in war, to call the name of one's king – but they had no king. A house, but they were without one. They could not scream the name of a famous victory, a crusade or an honoured ancestor.

'We cry Leviathan,' said Mauvec Kawe. 'And we cry for what we've lost.'

He stepped forward and clanged his tilting shield twice, and shouted, Leviathan!'

'Tavell!' howled Sir Sangraine. Calling for his pledged lady, burned to ash in the basilica. 'Tavell and Stryder! Tavell and Stryder!'

And then all howled together, in pain and pride. Of houses they had always favoured, but refused to admit due to their candidacy. Of noble machines sitting empty. Or the name of *Leviathan*. The Firscal brothers called for their father, fallen at the Blazing Heaven. Dask yelled for Achara, who though a Rau, had always been her closest companion. And in the cover of the din, Sycorax could not help but howl for the slain Rakkan.

But then Lycan-Bast called for vengeance, and like a spirit choir the many voices became one.

They charged: for *Leviathan* and vengeance.

Absolom Raithe lay in the bell tower of Gathering Palace, watching the maddest scene he'd seen in decades of operational work.

The Stryder-Rau Knight lance was in a full-tilt charge towards the opposing force. Percussive steps threw up clods of earth the size of groundcars, tearing across Gathering Plain where the house armies traditionally assembled for war. Weaving and firing, their ion shields flashing with hits. Stormspear rockets zipped off their carapace mounts to detonate among the defending foe, who only now were turning their low-slung heads to the assault.

And the first solid hits came. Lambek-Firscal in *Galeforce* – flanking west in a fire support position – set a Morvayne knight aflame before the *Crown* holed it through the body with a volcano lance. The Crusader exploded, tearing apart in a dazzling white flash of reactor overload that sent burning parts spinning away like comets. An engine kill so violent that Raithe's view of it rattled as the shockwave passed.

Twice their number. The enemy was nearly twice their number. In fact, as he watched the charge he could see a unit of traitor Knights peel off and run west. A horde of War Dogs, loping and snapping at one another.

Flanking manoeuvre? Possible. But that was a lot of firepower and it made no sense for the fast skirmishers to entirely turn their backs on the charge.

He raised his head, zeroed his mask optics for optimum range, and swung the sight around at the diminishing figures.

'Sycorax, we've got a reposition. It's most of the old Stryder-Rau squires. They're heading west... towards the *Leviathan*.'

'*Can he take them?*'

Raithe shook his head and panned his scope over, calculating intercept lines. Past the arena.

'Throne,' he said. 'Disengage. Disengage. The big ones are going to tie you up while *Leviathan*'s overwhelmed and cut to pieces, then the War Dogs will go for defensive works.'

Too late. The charge was committed.

Even from two miles away, he heard the sky-splitting crack of adamantine meeting adamantine.

Sycorax sidestepped from behind Dask and fountained melta fire at *Axefall*. His ion shield failed and adamantine bubbled along his upper thigh and hip, cables twisting and curling with the heat.

She'd hoped to slow him. It wasn't working.

Incoming fire alerts blared in her mind's eye and she dived into a roll, dodging out of the fire cone of the answering volley from his rocket pod. Beside her, *Sprinter* was not so lucky. Its ion shield depleted in the charge, the rockets blasted the Armiger open like a ration tin hit by a las-bolt.

Fontaine turned towards *Jester*, raised his great axe and lunged for her.

But as he took the long leap forward, *Aegis of Hope* slammed into his blind side, the fist of its thunderstrike gauntlet striking his head with such shield-splitting discharge that his mask spun away and landed in the turf. Sycorax took her cue, and ran.

Jester felt good. Very, *very* good.

She had never realised how much the machine was fighting her. She weaved among the larger machines like a serpent, striking and disappearing; darted like a hound through their cumbersome legs, using her smaller stature to score damaging hits to crucial pistons and weaken armour plating the bigger Knights could exploit.

Jester was agile, nimble, and more than anything, *fast*.

She did not need to move like it – she could make it move like her.

'*Sycorax*,' Raithe voxed. '*Stay on Dask, she's in trouble.*'

Ahead, she could see *Basilisk's Gaze* pushing towards Yuma, ion shield thrust forward on one shoulder as she drove into a storm of gatling cannon fire. The ion barrier broke and the spirals of tracer drilled her Knight's sinister-side armour, stripping her pauldron with its stone eye to bare metal and detonating her chest-mounted heavy stubber.

And stepping up behind came the *Crown of Dominion*, levelling its plasma decimator for the kill.

Sycorax revved her chain-cleaver and dashed into an intercept path. *Basilisk's Gaze* threw up an arm in defence and took the plasma beam directly on its thermal cannon. Armour plating glowed and metal warped under the bombardment, and still she came on.

Then the gas canisters in the weapon's stock cooked off, and the melta weapon's sudden decompression tore the *Basilisk's* arm apart. Sycorax sheared away, shrapnel pelting her shield and thumping off her upper carapace as *Basilisk's Gaze* went down on one knee before *Throneshield*, which raised its thunderstrike gauntlet in a fist and smashed the Knight Errant to the ground.

The blow let off a shockwave that rattled Sycorax in her cockpit.

'*Three seconds!*' Raithe yelled.

'What?'

'*Fire on* Throneshield *in three seconds!*'

'Fire on *Throneshield* in three seconds,' she voxed the lance. 'One!'

'*Two!*'

* * *

Absolom Raithe heard another trip-mine go off below. Another round of screams and falling masonry. They were getting closer. Soon they'd be on him.

No matter.

'Three,' he said.

And sent the shield-breaker round downrange.

Throneshield saw Lycan-Bast incoming, saw her lower her paladin's rapid-fire battle cannon and brace for the recoil, chainsword swung out behind her for a balanced shot.

Yuma's ion shield shimmered up just in time to take the hit, gatling cannon rotating in its eagerness to return fire. But then his ion shield collapsed like a lanced boil and the battle cannon round struck him dead centre.

Throneshield staggered backward, its gatling fire spraying the dirt as its shell-shocked pilot triggered it accidentally. Sycorax saw her moment, and darted in to cook its mask, blinding the big Knight.

Blood Oath was on him, Lycan-Bast slashing and carving with her chainsword, driving *Throneshield* into the smouldering wreckage of *Basilisk's Gaze* so he entangled his feet, and couldn't get distance to put his gauntlet in play.

'*Mauvec!*' Lycan-Bast shouted. '*Go! Go!*'

Typhoon's Teeth, the fiercest Knight on the tournament field when it came to close fighting, charged the *Crown of Dominion*. The *Crown* had no melee weapons, while the *Typhoon* was dedicated to them. Kawe's weapons flew out wide, the gesture of taking all comers, as his ion shield rippled under the assault of the *Crown*'s volcano lance.

Typhoon's chainsword bit deep into the upper carapace, thunder-strike gauntlet gripping the coil of the plasma decimator and crushing it, and for a glorious moment a backfire of plasma lit both machines in silhouette, shadow-puppets locked in battle.

And then the *Crown* angled its two twin meltaguns directly into the *Typhoon's* chest and liquefied it, fusing its arm joints into inoperability.

Sycorax could hear Kawe scream over the vox. He screamed that his controls were not answering, that he could not breathe. That the cockpit was on fire.

Then the vox cut and the *Typhoon* fell, sliding down the bigger machine.

'Raithe!' Sycorax called.

'*Everyone's engaged*,' he answered. '*And I doubt your weapons are enough*.'

'But there's no one else,' she said. 'Take out those meltaguns, and have a penetrator round ready.'

'Circle around and re-engage,' Raithe said.

Another mine detonation. Two floors below this time. They were cutting it close.

Raithe stuck the last polymorphine phial in his shoulder, and rotated it. It hurt, God-Emperor did it hurt, and he worried for his accuracy at this range.

The last shield-breaker had come in high, almost too high – but he'd keep shooting.

Another explosion below him, this one a directional trip-mine. That distinctive cough of steel balls blowing out from the casing and rattling on walls.

Raithe popped his magazine. With dextrous fingers he ejected each round and reordered the stack.

Turbo-penetrator.

Turbo-penetrator.

Shield-breaker.

Turbo-penetrator.

Shield-breaker.

Then he slotted it back into his rifle and chambered the first shield-breaker round. Got behind the scope.

Range: 2.3 miles

Wind speed: 8 knots west-northwest

Gravitic conditions: normal

Visibility: light haze, melee obstructions

Deep breath in, hold. Out through the lips.

Crosshairs on the left meltagun.

Squeeze-kick. Squeeze-kick.

As Sycorax sprinted through duelling Knights, ducking below a stream of gatling fire and throwing her ion shield sideways to catch battle cannon shrapnel, she saw the left melta sponson on *Crown of Dominion* rupture and catch fire.

The big Knight reared back and trumpeted in confusion, head lowering to search for its attacker, when the second sponson exploded and burned.

'You better fire when I need it, Raithe,' Sycorax swore, plunging towards the hulking war engine.

Though she ran directly for it, it still looked over her little machine, searching for the mightier weapon that had damaged it.

She came on sidelong, thermal spear out in front of her in a formal challenge, weaving past the remains of *Basilisk's Gaze*, only ripping off with her thermal shot when she leapt onto the smouldering wreck of *Typhoon's Teeth* and inside the *Crown's* guard.

It was the vision of Rakkan's father that had inspired her, the way the traitor Knight *Dawn of Slaughter* had gotten between the *Crown's* main weapons, so it was unable to fight back with anything but its close-support meltaguns.

The meltaguns *Crown of Dominion* no longer had.

Jester's thermal spear fired into the *Crown's* chestplate like a boring laser, bubbling the paint and burning the plating brown.

The Knight Castellan bayed and tried to step backward, but *Jester* was a fast machine and it wanted this kill even more than Sycorax did. She stayed on the High Monarch, melta-beam wavering hotter and hotter as his tripartite breastplate buckled inward and cracked, as the ceramite-sculpted scroll stamped with the name *Crown of Dominion* ran into illegibility. It seemed to do nothing, its arms paralysed.

My controls aren't responding, Kawe had said. The extreme, focused heat had locked up the system. Just as she was locking up Daggar-Kraine.

Until her thermal spear sputtered dry.

A concussive blow hammered her down, once, twice.

The world went sideways as she staggered, just managing to stay upright.

And saw the volcano lance batter down on her again.

She threw up her thermal spear and caught the blow, wincing at the phantom pains as the weapon housing cracked under the strain.

'This is for Rakkan!' she roared out of her laud-hailer. Stepped inside its guard again. Cycled up the chain-cleaver, and rammed it tip first into the buckled chestplate.

The chain-cleaver was not a cutting weapon; it was a chopping, *digging* weapon, originally meant as a tool for constructing settlements rather than war. Dual chains of teeth running all the way around, making it closer to an excavator than a saw. And that's what she did. She dug into the damaged chest. Quarried it. Tore away the breastplate and bored upward, feeling the tension release of punching through the collapsing plate and digging into the soft cabling beneath.

Up, up into the systems behind the head. Up towards the cockpit.

The *Crown of Dominion* screamed.

Oils and unguents bathed *Jester*'s vision, the cleaver sinking up to its arm mount in the larger Knight. It was revving uselessly now, its teeth stripped by the effort and motor nearly burned out. Still she drove it deeper.

The impaled creature tried to pull away from the gutting blade.

And its backwards movement only made it easier for Sycorax to lever the chainblade forward and crack the massive Knight open – its front superstructure breaking away and taking the head with it, exposing the internal wires and cockpit.

And letting her look Daggar-Kraine directly in the eyes.

Daggar-Kraine was not the man Yavarius-Khau had been. The conqueror_wyrm had taken him fully, purple candle flames licking up from his withered eyes. Ectoplasm spilled from his mouth, and ran down from the crown where it tore his paper-thin skin.

He had aged forty years in the last hour.

No, it was the opposite. The *Crown* had drained him.

'*Rakkan*,' he said, as the tri-pointed crown clamped around his head lifted him out of his throne, the slithering neural cable affixed to it dangling his body like the lure on a deep-sea fish. '*You have done your worst, but damage can be repaired. All things are possible with the Power of Eight, unlocked by my code-father, Quivarian.*'

'Raithe, kill this abomination.'

Raithe settled his crosshairs on the doll-like figure at the edge of his range. The oddly silent struggle of a drama happening miles away.

Laid a finger on the trigger.

The tower rocked, his aim bouncing out of true. Last trip-mine. Voices on the stairs.

In his scope, *Crown of Dominion* ducked low, Daggar-Kraine dipping behind *Jester* – shot obscured.

He snatched out with his left hand and grabbed his pistol,

dropping the first footman on the stairs with a belly shot, then as he doubled over, shooting the Transmuted sacristan coming up behind him. They fell backwards into their companions.

Back to the scope.

'Come on, come on, clear the shot.'

'Who is this wraith, Rakkan? Let us see.'

Sycorax swung her dead chain-cleaver at the pilot and he caught it with his hand, his warp-strengthened fingers crimping the metal.

And she felt him in her head, the intrusive push of the mind-link or the heretek Quivarian.

She pushed back, so hard that she could no longer hold the Rakkan persona and her true face pushed through his disappearing features.

Daggar-Kraine's eyes crinkled in confusion, as if he had reached for a stick and realised it was a snake.

'I know you. My code-father knows you.'

'Because I killed Quivarian,' she said. And rammed the muzzle of her broken thermal spear under his chin, lifting it above her carapace, back into Raithe's line of fire.

'Now hold still.'

Raithe saw the head come up into his sights, the grimace of pain and anger in the mouth. A brief moment when the candle-flame eyes looked directly at him through the scope and realised what was about to happen.

His head, lined up directly with the Throne Mechanicum.

Squeeze. Kick.

There are shots where a marksman knows the bullet will hit. Shots where you can nearly see the bullet flying downrange in the scope, arcing in a perfect moment of terminal physics. This was one of those.

Raithe kept his eye glued to the scope – willing himself not to blink – and saw sunlight glimmer on the round. It bored a hole through the trident crown, shattering it into two pieces, and ploughed a tunnel through Daggar-Kraine's skull, fountaining purple warp energy into the air.

And with a sound that echoed off the mountains and raised panicked wails across the palace, it cleaved the Throne Mechanicum in two. The ejected shell casing clinked on the stonework, like a sound of two glasses clicking together.

For an instant, Raithe thought he imagined stretched faces bleeding out of the destroyed cockpit and diffusing in the air, but when he blinked, they were gone.

Rakkan crashed through the arena's gate with a shoulder charge, taking it off its hinges with a crash.

Empty. Stands and field dark. Long shadows of afternoon stretching in the empty tournament ground.

'*Nephew,*' said Kraine's voice, echoing over the system amplifiers. '*Is that you in there? Of course. It could only be you. It was never supposed to go this way.*'

Rakkan pushed *Leviathan* to midfield, panning his head side to side, keeping an eye on his rear threat grid.

'You knew,' he said.

'*Yes. As the head of the house, I was privy to the secret. I steered that helmet to you. Tried to don it myself, but only you have your father's memories. That's how it stays in the line. Thought you'd join us, once you realised the enormous gift of responsibility I'd given you. Last of the Fang. That's why we were so eager to marry off your father – we needed a child to pilot the weapon. For the day Rau would rise again. Your father was always so parochial about keeping the secret. That it only be used for defence, and never in house war.*'

Rakkan caught a blip on his rear threat grid and pivoted

directly around at the waist, unleashing a gout of flame from his conflagration cannon. He put a wall of promethium burn between himself and the oncoming enemy, catching it in the spread.

A low, hunched form sprinted away, its upper carapace afire.

An Armiger.

No, a War Dog.

'We are not tainted dupes, you know. It was the ancestors who told us to do it. They spoke to us, convinced us over years of conversations. Showed us how we needed to recapture the glories of the past. Of an independent Dominion, when no Imperium had us yoked and collared.'

'Lies,' Rakkan said to himself. 'Lies of a heretek code-virus. They corrupted the ancestors, and the ancestors lied to you.'

Another threat, this time hard on the dexter side. Rakkan rotated his siegebreaker cannon and dead-eyed the Armiger as it rushed out of a field gate and tried to get behind for a shot at his reactors.

The dual shells smashed into the scuttling Chaos mount, bypassing its ion shield and shattering it, smashing the broken form against the arena wall.

'We should have joined Morvayne ten centuries ago, when they rose against Imperial tyranny. They have no restrictions. No lord commander telling them to cease their feuds or discontinue blood sports. Indeed, if we destroyed every Stryder that joined House Morvayne with us, Morvayne would praise us for our strength. The Emperor offers stagnation. Eternal, responsible stalemate. Morvayne offers victory. Morvayne offers a future.'

The War Dogs came at him from every side, then. The squires, five of them, rushing all at once. His ion shield lit up with autocannon hits and thermal strikes. He sprayed fire in an arc before him, warded off a chain-cleaver with a shattering crack of electricity from the harpoon, felt a thermal spear burn into his hip joint from the rear, locking the ball mount.

Rakkan leapt backwards and kicked out, sending a War Dog flying through the air and crashing into another.

And then he saw Kraine strolling out from a gate, his thermal cannon fixed on Rakkan.

'I'm sorry,' said Kraine, through his laud-hailer. 'You cannot see that future.'

The battle cannon round blew the ground out from under Kraine, causing *Firedrake* to stumble and go over on its back, arms flailing to push itself up again.

It never got the chance.

Greyhound was true to its name. Quick, agile. Baroness Hawthorn came out of the shadows, crouching low, pinning the fallen baron to the ground of the tournament field. Her gatling cannon tore into him at point-blank range, battering through his chestplate like a rock hammer until blood spattered and cooked on the rotating barrel.

Then she gave a low whistle.

The War Dogs withdrew, scampering away to her side.

They nuzzled their faces against her armoured legs, blurting inhuman sounds.

Rakkan saw Vossa and Andricus among them, no longer moving quite like a Knight did as they loped and snapped at one another.

'The presence of Morvayne was too much for them,' she said through Rakkan's vox. Not shouting through her laud-hailers. Speaking to him. 'They've lived with the taint long enough that it's accelerated once the touch of a true traitor Knight came close enough. Morvayne does not have squires, it has mind-slaves. I suppose… we have mind slaves. In that house, the machine rules the flesh.'

'Traitor.' Rakkan lowered his harpoon at her in challenge.

'No,' she said. 'No, I don't think so. You wouldn't kill your mother,

Linoleus, and I would never hurt you – or let that bastard Kraine do it. You must understand that I did this for you, for us. Even after my mind-link with Andricus – when I saw the truth of our folly and what must be done – I made sure you were not in the basilica. So you could choose. My boy, with Morvayne you could rise so high. They appreciate a man who claws his way to the top, who refuses to accept vassalage. Come with us, bring over Leviathan *and you can become the mightiest of them. Stryder-Rau is broken, you cannot rebuild a schism like this. The Inquisition will kill you all for the mere possibility of taint.'*

Rakkan took a step forward, harpoon raised.

Vossa growled.

'Well… you always were headstrong. And you've done well considering, haven't you?' Her head cocked, as if listening to something. *'I…'*

Greyhound turned, hearing animal bellows and trumpet calls on the horizon.

'The monarch…' she said. And he was not sure if it was the vox or her voice that was breaking. *'The monarch is dead. The true monarch. Not just its meat-puppet, but the* Crown of Dominion. *I felt it when it went. I would like to know how you managed that.'*

Rakkan beat his harpoon on his tilting shield, once, twice.

'No, son. Not this day. Perhaps on the field.'

With a pop of discharge, a crown of flame ignited above her upper carapace. A ring of wych-fire, expanding, circling, flames feeding on nothing. Inside, reality split like a shattered mirror, bleeding from each crack the awful incandescent light of another realm. The War Dogs bellowed and nuzzled her in fear.

Behind them he could see a cavernous interior – a ship, perhaps – and the hulking shadows of corrupted Knights.

He rushed them, aiming to grab her, force her out of the growing circle of the hex.

'Mother!' he yelled.

'*Goodbye, son. Your traitor mother is proud of you.*'

And with a thunderclap of air rushing to fill a vacuum, she and the War Dogs were gone.

CODA: MISSION DEBRIEFS
AFTER-ACTION REPORT
>>Operation: Kingmaker
>>File No. 5782-Gamma-KMKR
>>Mission Day: 41
>>Drafted By: Absolom Raithe
>>Cleared for Reading: Sycorax, Vindicare Temple [Pacificus], Callidus Temple [Pacificus], Vanus Temple [Pacificus], Master of Operations
>>Clearance Level: Vermilion Special Privileged
>>DO NOT TRANSMIT<<
>>DO NOT DUPLICATE<<
>>PURGE DATA AFTER READING<<

Please find enclosed a brief summary of residual matters involving Operation KINGMAKER.

As directed, operatives RAITHE [Commander], SYCORAX and KOLN deployed to Dominion with directives to eliminate High Monarch YAVARIUS-KHAU and manage aftermath to prevent a succession crisis that would deprive the Imperium of an ally's crucial military assets.

As you are aware from our previous reports, local conditions proved more complicated than expected. An infiltration/infection of the Stryder-Rau Knights by the meme-virus 'conqueror_wyrm' triggered a large-scale defection and brief civil conflict, leading to the loss or elimination of a dozen Knight suits [see attached list].

While this would at first appear to breach mission parameters, I believe our presence was crucial to preventing a total loss of Dominion and all its assets. Given that the losses are minimal and that we did, in fact, kill the High Monarch of Dominion – that being High Monarch DAGGAR-KRAINE – I consider this assignment to be successfully concluded on all points.

However, I understand and respect that some opinions already differ on this point.

As for personnel matters, I wish to commend both SYCO-RAX and KOLN for their professionalism and ability in extreme circumstances. The mission would not have been a success without either one of them. [See attached documents for citation requests.] I regret to inform the Vanus Temple that KOLN's honours must be given posthumously.

Following the Morvayne-sponsored uprising, our team guided a new monarch to the throne, and quietly advised a reorganisation of Dominion's governmental structure.

Crusade leadership will be pleased to note that Dominion no longer elects its monarch as part of a partisan process. A slate of reforms helped by the fact that many of the survivors were themselves candidates in the Lists.

After the weeks-long Diet of Gathering, a dual-monarchy system emerged. Dominion henceforth has *two* High Monarchs – bonded by marriage. One represents Rau, and the other Stryder. While not without flaw, the system has several advantages. Each monarch can serve as a check on the other, and both houses have representation in leadership. The Lists were abolished, with candidates sorting themselves into whichever house they wished.

The greatest advantage, however, is that there will always be a monarch on Dominion. One monarch will go to war, while the other stays to safeguard the kingdom against the now reinforced hosts of House Morvayne.

During negotiations over who should take the role of monarchs, a dark-horse candidate emerged in Linoleus Rakkan. Given his leadership during the crisis, and the fact that he challenged and defeated the previous monarch in single combat, he seemed the logical choice. The problem of his low bloodline was remedied when a page torn out of his ancestral book was rediscovered in the archives, proving that Rakkan's grandfather was not an Imperial admiral, but Baron Lovau of House Stryder. This paternity was concealed, the document says, due to Baron Lovau's ambition to take the crown and the ban on candidates having children. [Note: Before her file is formally closed, and she is declared killed in action, I wish to place a commendation in Operative Koln's service record, praising her abilities in document forgery. The page was accepted without question, and streamlined the aftermath.]

This, along with his marriage to Lady Lisille Lycan-Bast and her ascension as co-monarch, quieted the more traditionalist elements as to his low birth status.

As for Stryder-Rau's participation in the Crusade, the first contingent of Knights should arrive at the battlefront in eight days' time under Baron Mauvec Kawe, Master of Judgment.

The rest of the Knights of Stryder-Rau, along with High Monarch Rakkan, will follow once the coronation ceremonies conclude, Rakkan is formally rechristened with the name Lovau-Rakkan, and installed in the new seat of power, the

Knight Castellan *Throne of Dominion*. That will take some time as the reserve Knight suit slated to become the *Throne*, along with a complement of replacement sacristans, are currently being imported as diplomatic gifts from House Castelaide.

Since the target of this mission, YAVARIUS-KHAU, was dead before our arrival, no operative will be able to list the elimination in his or her service record. As for who gains formal credit for the elimination of DAGGAR-KRAINE, High Monarch of Dominion: given the nature of the operation I ask that it be split three ways – between KOLN, SYCORAX and myself – as a gesture of good faith and cooperation among the temples.

The outcome justifies the deed.

ABSOLOM RAITHE, DOMINION STATION

Sycorax dropped the communique on the table. 'You're dividing credit.'

'Yes,' said Raithe, pushing a glass of amasec towards her. The surface of it vibrated slightly with the purr of the *Stiletto*'s engines. A third glass stood untouched on the table. 'It seemed like the right thing to do.'

'Why?'

He sat back, sipped at the drink. 'The nobles of Dominion were so focused on who they thought they were – their house, their family, their vision of the future – they didn't see what they were becoming. Or could become.'

'True.'

'Whenever they got what they wanted, it ruined them. Because they never thought about the cost of it. If Stryder had destroyed Rau, or Rau did Stryder, what was their next move?' He shrugged. 'Achara saved her king and damned him, killed him and let something worse loose.'

'I don't see how this relates to you becoming Sicarius Primus.

You know I don't care about kill counts, especially not a third of a kill. Koln wouldn't mind if you took her third, either.'

'But,' said Raithe, 'I've been thinking that what Koln told you was right. They sent me on this mission to kill me. No one really *wants* a Sicarius Primus. Best case, I'm poached by Operations and spend the rest of my life planning other operatives' missions. Dealing with Terran politics.'

'But if you don't claim the kill,' said Sycorax, her mouth twitching up in a smile, 'you stay operational.'

'Not only that, one-third credit? No one will accept it. Temples will argue until no one gets the kill – but as mission commander I can always revise it and credit the kill to myself. Meaning that with a single file submission I reach fifty kills and Primus status.'

'Leverage,' said Sycorax.

'They used us,' he smiled. 'So let's turn the tables. Use them for a change.'

'No wonder you're so relaxed. You know it's not healthy, sleeping as much as you have been – you should put more hours in at training or you'll atrophy.' She took a sip. 'So what are you going to do with all that leverage?'

'Stop being someone else's tool. Stay in the field, pick my assignments,' he said, with a shine in his brown eyes. 'And my teams.'

'Not eager to get back to being a solo operator, then?'

'I'm beginning to think interesting people make for interesting missions,' he said, and raised his glass. 'To new beginnings.'

'Creating messy endings,' she said, meeting the toast.

The glasses clinked with the sound of a shell casing bouncing on stone.

'I admit it,' said Queen Lycan-Bast. 'I'm jealous.'

'Sorry,' Rakkan replied. 'It's the way it has to be. The court wouldn't have it any other way. You know how Dask is. Even more paranoid now.'

'High Monarch Rakkan, off fighting the crusade for our allies,' she said, running her fingers over the wet masonry, not even trying to disguise the bitterness. 'And his wife, Queen Lycan-Bast, sitting at home.'

'Defending the realm. Rebuilding. Training our new group of Knights – we lost most of our pilots. You will create the heroes of our future. And you are also a High Monarch, no mere queen.'

'It sounds dull, and inglorious.' She rolled her eyes. 'You've become very stentorian and duty-bound since the coronation, Linoleus. Makes me wonder what you saw through the *Throne of Dominion*'s eyes.'

He paused. 'Not much different than what I see now. It's quiet in there. Very quiet. A fresh Throne Mechanicum. Arch Maintenancer Gwynne says I'll get used to it, that the ghosts imported from *Jester* will start to make themselves known.'

'I know we're co-monarchs,' she said, 'but it doesn't feel like it with you enthroned in a Knight Castellan and me still riding a paladin.'

'We could only wrangle one suit out of House Castelaide. Besides, you like *Blood Oath*. And you are needed here. Morvayne is gathering their strength. They will return.'

'And here I'll be, with *Blood Oath* and our least experienced Knights.' When he failed to answer, she said, 'Why are we here, anyway? Is this some ritual, you need to inaugurate me into the Fang line?'

'Something like that,' he said, opening the ironwork door.

'Very mysterious and sinister, husband.' She raised her eyebrows, twisting the last word with playful irony. Then, remembering where she was, she softened. 'Is this about your father?'

They were not a couple, not really. And never expected to be. More partners than lovers. She still had her footman, and that was fine with him. Neither was used to it yet, but there was friendliness and mutual respect, and that was a good start. The rest would come later, if it ever did. But the most important thing was to keep the peace.

Rakkan laughed. 'We're here to give you your wedding present.'

He held out the battered helmet.

'This is your wedding present?'

'Put it on.'

Lycan-Bast looked at her new husband expectantly, as if he would say more.

Then she sighed and slipped the helmet over her eyes.

>*Retinal scan: successful*

>*Fang line confirmed [by marriage]*

>*Hail, Lisille Lycan-Bast, Monarch of Dominion*

Behind the words, she saw the rear wall swing on its axis, green light spilling from the portal. And when she walked through, she saw a giant, a thing from fae stories, arising on lifts from the grated floor.

The Green Man. The Terror of Morvayne. Saviour of Dominion and Slayer of Traitors. The Knight Without a Pilot.

Leviathan.

'He's been in the shadows twelve thousand years,' said Rakkan. 'Back then, they worried he would become a prop for the house war. That having two active Dominus-class suits would prove unbalancing when there was only one throne. But... well, there are two thrones, now.'

'But Linoleus,' she whispered, 'he has no pilot.'

'He does now.'

>*Lisille Lycan-Bast, will you ride to the defence of the realm?*

'Yes,' she whispered.

And in the red mask, two emerald eyes awoke.

It was raining in the city of Yanzagore. Heavy rain, drops the size of thumbnails that drummed off the tin roofs of the clapboard houses and streamed into the gutters slum residents had dug into the hard clay. Whole neighbourhoods were known to collapse if the monsoon storms got too heavy.

At least it provided a break from the unbearable humidity of the last five days – a visible haze of suspended water. It caused clothes to stick. Sweat to run. It got into her hands, past the heat cracks that had burst open when she'd immolated the thing that was Dorthiya Tessell.

Koln flexed her right augmetic, noting how the ring finger followed a step behind the others. She would have to adjust them again.

Her augmetic eyes pierced the rain, scanning for the roving bands of ganger jacks that patrolled the outhab shanties clustering around Shautin's astropathic relay citadel.

Upper classes didn't live here. Proximity to the relay's psychic emanations were correlated with birth defects, aggressive cancers and occasionally even mutation. Anyone who could stay away, did.

Yet the last signal origin had come from here.

When Koln had seen the astropath lying vivisected on Tessell's table, she knew the implications immediately. It was Drusus Mak, the astropath the Assassinorum had planted on Dominion. And the coin-shaped subliminal astropathic vox-implant in his brain was missing.

Even then, Koln knew she could not return from Dominion alive. The knowledge would be taken out of her hands. Buried, for fear that the Inquisition would start digging into Assassinorum affairs. She'd be told to forget about it, then sent on mission after mission until her convenient death removed all memory of the missing implant, and all it meant.

So she had worked with Gwynne to give her masters the death they wanted – and proceeded alone.

Because the implant had not stopped transmitting. Whoever took it had cracked the Vanus encryption, and was sending messages. Official Assassinorum messages in a cypher she was not able to decrypt by brute force.

Except for one word:

Vendetta.

So Avaaris Koln, rogue operative, put up her hood and disappeared into the rain.

Towards the spire of the Shautin relay. And a revelation that might kill her, easy as a bullet.

ABOUT THE AUTHOR

Robert Rath is a freelance writer from Honolulu who is currently based in Hong Kong. He is the author of the Warhammer 40,000 novel *The Infinite and the Divine*, and the Warhammer Crime novella *Bleedout*. His short stories include 'War in the Museum', 'Glory Flight', and the Assassinorum tales 'Divine Sanction', 'Live Wire' and 'Iron Sight'.

YOUR NEXT READ

VOLPONE GLORY
– by Nick Kyme

As war rages across the Sabbat Worlds, the Volpone Bluebloods are sent to Gnostes to liberate the Agria island chain from the entrenched Blood Pact. Can they emerge victorious from their bloodiest campaign yet?

An extract from
Volpone Glory
by Nick Kyme

If he wanted to live, Darian knew he should take the pistol. The dead man had no use for it, but the lowborn were not permitted to bear arms. They would likely hang him for taking it. Or whip him to death. He'd seen a man take five hundred lashes before finally expiring. Darian didn't want to die like that. He didn't want to die at all.

But death was coming all the same. And it wore a devil's face.

Maybe he could hide it, wedge it beneath the belt. He might need it. In a last-ditch moment of desperation, a pistol would be useful. The east flank had collapsed. That was the word rushing down the line like a sea of hellfire. Panic rode its waves.

The earth shook again, spilling clods of dirt into the trench as the barrage pounded the Ankish line and the air grew thicker with aerosolised blood and soil. It was like pitching through fog, only adhesive, and it caked the body like a second skin. A heavy cannonade answered the barrage, drumming in staccato. Our guns, their bombers. An impasse about to be overcome.

Our forces would prevail, they had said, those men in the finely tailored uniforms with metal clinging to their chests like it was any sort of guarantee.

The blood cults were coming, this much Darian knew. Just like he knew he should take that Throne-damned pistol and put it to use. The enemy had broken the flank and soon the line would be overrun. He might be very glad of a lasgun then.

Darian regarded the weapon clutched in a dead hand and the blank-eyed officer with half his face missing. The gun remained, but he could not. He hefted the belt of canteens across his shoulder and trudged on.

It had been a decent trek back to town and from there a return to the trench, its long and winding course like an arterial vein poised to be severed. Darian passed the burnt-out shells of tanks in the mustard camo of the Pardus Armoured, slumped like lonely metal bunkers, distant islands in the fog, eerily still and inert. A Ministorum priest murmured solemn words over a row of quiet men lying on their backs, seemingly unconcerned with what was coming. A band of Tunnel-Rats in dirty ochre fatigues and bucket-shaped helmets ran the other way. They were grinning. Darian looked back despairingly as he watched them disappear into the fog. He hastily made the sign of the aquila to the priest to show that he was pious and hurried on.

As he worked his way deeper into the trench network he passed other men: some in the rugged drab of the Diggers, others in plainer uniforms wearing the caducei of medics. A second platoon in ragged forest green came his way, stern-faced and swarthy. Darian didn't recognise the regiment as they trailed past, headed towards the sounds of a distant skirmish. There were so many auxiliaries, reduced to bits and pieces in an ill-fitting puzzle. He saw spotters and riflemen, a few crew-served heavy stubbers and missile tubes, a voxman tinkering with a boxy comms unit but eliciting only static. As the bombardment persisted and the guns answered, most of the troopers with more mediocre weapons hunkered down. And waited.

Few paid Darian any heed. As a mil-serve, he was largely beneath their notice, a servant and a non-combatant. Most didn't understand his purpose but no one reached for his canteens, they all knew not to do that. His cargo wasn't for them; even the burly Diggers, fearsome and headstrong as they were, knew the pecking order. And the Bluebloods sat at the top. The 'bastard' Royal Volpone.

They didn't stir as Darian entered the Volpone part of the trench, not the sentries who had been posted there should the enemy get this far into the trench, nor the ranks who kept their hooded eyes forwards, waiting for something to materialise out of the fog. Standing in line, their finely made laslocks gleaming, their grey uniforms pressed and nigh-pristine, their fine armour and iconography shining – what proud popinjays they were. But rigidly focused. No casual chatter here, or fatalistic camaraderie.

Darian kept his eyes down nonetheless.

The trench opened out, chambers breaking up the labyrinthine monotony, the edges reinforced with additional steel revetments and flakboard. It delineated the entire southern edge of Lodden, the fortified town they had occupied for the last six months. Several firing holes had been cored out, tripod-mounted heavy bolters sitting snugly within. All Praxis-pattern, well made. Three more gunnery nests were in process. Diggers hacked at them with shovels and picks, dark sweat patches under their armpits like old bloodstains. The Volpone watched but did not participate. Menial work was not for the Bluebloods, though a few of the sergeants congratulated the Diggers on the quality of their labour and had stronger drink brought down the line to them.

A phonograph was playing, the sound tinny and the needle

scratching. The rousing strains of 'Volpone, On To Glory' led Darian to the officers' bunker where some of his lords had amassed.

An ornate electro-sconce hung over the room, swaying as motes of dirt spiralled from the ceiling like dying moths. The light flickered, illuminating a map table, three chairs and several charts affixed to the wall. A sweaty-faced adjutant was pulling files from a cabinet and stuffing them hastily into a large pack. Another mil-serve stood nearby, ready to receive it. Lenna. She gave Darian a quick smile and he felt warmer despite the chill air, returning the smile when he thought the officers weren't looking.

The officers stood together. There were three of them surrounding a vox, listening intently to a scratchy broadcast. A cadre of silent adjutants attended them. All had grim faces.

'It's done then,' uttered one as the broadcast concluded, leaning across the map table to switch off the vox. 'We're giving up the town. We've lost the guns.'

Fair-haired like many amongst the Volpone, with a sharp nose and clear grey eyes, he was the youngest of the three and the least scarred. A lieutenant called Armand Culcis. He had a strong bloodline, and a good family history. Fourth generation Blueblood. His family were amongst the middling nobles of the Volpone aristocracy, hence his officer's rank.

Darian knew the history of all of the officers in the 50th. Not an insignificant number, but it was wise for a vassal to know his kings and which of them he should be wary of.

'Shitting hells,' Shiller growled, and started pacing. 'I need a damn drink…'

A slab of a man, Isaac Shiller had the hooded eyes common to the Volpone aristocracy, with shoulders like the bulwarks of a fortress and a red beard that framed a portcullis of a mouth. Shiller was sixth generation, a captain, and from a long line of high-ranking military men. He had lofty aspirations, but bad habits.

As he paced, Shiller looked up and caught sight of Darian. His expression changed from disconsolation to annoyance.

'Ah, you're here at last. Just in time for our disgrace.' Shiller glared, taking in Darian's dishevelled appearance. 'And look at the state of you. A bloody shambles. I should have you reprimanded.'

Darian murmured apologies into his dirt-caked boots as he gave a canteen to the red-haired officer. Shiller took a swig, swallowed and then scowled.

'What's this piss?' he snapped, and tossed the canteen back at Darian, who caught it. This only irritated Shiller all the more. 'Give me spice wine, you useless deg.'

In the background, Lenna looked afraid. She had been on the receiving end of Shiller's temper before. Darian raised his hand surreptitiously to signal it was all right.

A bomb hit close, shivering the walls, and sent a decanter crashing. Glass shattered. Shiller swore. He was still righting himself when Darian offered the wine.

'Fegging deg...' Shiller spat, his gaze like a lance thrust.

Culcis interjected. 'Is that strictly necessary, captain?'

Turning his ire on the lieutenant, Shiller looked about ready to unleash another barrage when the third officer, Major Regara, took an interest. He had been reviewing the map table intently, lost in thought, stoically bracing himself against its sides when the room shook.

'Decorum, Captain Shiller,' he warned, and glanced at the canteen. 'And also a modicum of restraint. If that explosion and the snap-fire I can hear not so far away is any indication, our withdrawal is imminent. I need you sober. I'll have good order when we leave.'

Shiller cooled immediately, his respect for the major ingrained. Some of the colour returned to Lenna's cheeks.

'Of course, sir.'

Where Shiller was thick, Regara was trim and sharp as a knife-edge, with greying hair that made him look distinguished rather than old. He also wore fine armour and carried an artisan sabre. His left leg was a chrome-plated bionic. Darian didn't know how Regara had lost it, possibly the same war that gave him the scar across his face. Vasquez Regara was thirteenth generation and could trace his lineage back to the Macharian Crusade. Upper-tier nobility.

'And give that man a drink, will you,' he snapped, turning his attention back to the map table. 'He looks like he's run ten miles.'

Darian blinked.

'Well, go on then,' urged Shiller when Darian didn't immediately partake. 'Take a pull. Of the water, mind you. Can't have the degs rolling around drunk now, can we.'

The word 'deg' meant 'degraded' and was a slur some of the officer class used to describe the mil-serves. It was frowned upon, but had yet to be stamped out. Darian declined with good grace, though he was parched as a dry desert wadi.

'Suit yourself,' said Shiller with an irked glare and drained the wine, supping it like milk from his mother's teat.

Culcis stepped into Regara's eyeline. 'Sir... what is our course of action here?'

Regara took a calming breath. A vein pulsed in his neck. 'We have no choice. This position has become untenable.'

'We'll reoccupy the town,' said Shiller, the Blueblood in him reluctant to accept defeat.

'They're in the bloody town, captain. All over it. We have to withdraw from Lodden entirely and retreat, as per Voke's order, to marker nine.'

'That's Ankishburg, sir,' Culcis interjected.

'I know where it bloody well is, lieutenant. Marker nine,' he repeated. 'Platoons to fall back along the town outskirts. Keep them in staggered formation and do it by degrees.' He muttered an expletive. 'Stretched across the length of the damn map… And have the Agrians mine the trenches. I want the damned Archonate writhing in blood and earth when they retake it.'

'And the guns, sir?'

'Can they be spiked? Do we have time for that?'

'The magos reports that we can wreck the turning mechanism and limit their function, but that's all.'

Regara swore under his breath again, then said, 'Have the Martian do it. We don't really have authority to destroy them anyway, or the time to seek approval. I want us long gone before the Pact get them facing in our direction. Shiller, you've got Lance and Shield Company, the second and third auxiliaries and the Pavis. Have the tanks maintain a barrage for the rank and file to retreat under. Put some heavy metal on the east flank. It might slow the collapse and give us more time. And get the bloody platoons back together, for Throne's sake.'

Shiller gave an ugly smile. 'I'll have them pounded to the hells and back.'

'See that you do, captain.'

Regara stood up straight from the map table. They were spread out, too far. Voke had tried to match the Archonate line, to engage on every front. It had left them vulnerable and the town at risk.

'The entire Ankish line.' Regara shook his head. 'It won't stand,' he said bitterly. 'It won't bloody stand.'

Then he walked over to Darian, took a canteen of spice wine and drained it.

* * *

The leg ached. Despite the fact it hadn't been there for years, it ached. Old memories returned, of Nacedon and everything Regara had lost there. Some pains didn't go away. Not really.

'Are you all right, sir?' asked Culcis.

The major waved off his lieutenant's concern, though he knew he must look grim. His eyes drifted to the sky and the silhouette of the Arvus lighter slowly disappearing as it spirited away General Voke and his command staff. Regara had declined a seat, preferring to see out the retreat on foot with his regiment. Besides, Major Pallard was dead, and an officer of rank was needed to coordinate the withdrawal of the other Volpone companies and the auxiliaries. It had seemed a noble gesture at the time. Now, with his leg hurting like a bastard, he couldn't see past the folly of it.

They were half a mile from the extraction zone, Lodden well behind them, and trudging through sodden earth and persistent rain. It was sparse terrain, a few farms and outhouses the only structures. Chimera transports trundled past, fighting through the mud and flanked by teams of Agrian 22nd sappers, in case they needed rescuing. Regara watched the armoured carriers with undisguised longing. He had also refused the offer of a ground transport when Culcis had managed to scrounge it up, leaving it solely for the ferrying of the dead and injured. Even then, the armoured carriers weren't enough and trains of stretcher-bearers trailed through the ever-worsening conditions.

The entire regiment was strung out, weary and defeated. They kept good order, even the auxiliaries, though most had been reduced to scraps.

'Damned leg,' he admitted, scowling at the state of his boots as he lumped through the mire. 'Martian forged, chrome plated, but doesn't like the damp. Or maybe I don't.'

Regara cast a glance to the eastern flank. Now they were out of the trench and well on their way, he could fully appreciate the guns. The weapon they had been forced to abandon.

'Throne above, Culcis,' he rasped, 'what have we allowed to happen?'

Godsword, the men called it, because it was said that the effect where its power fell was like the sword of the Emperor Himself. It was well named. Its four long macrocannon barrels stabbed into the sky like huge funnels tilted on their axis, their ends blackened by explosive expulsion. Lesser but still-devastating weapon batteries surrounded it, a defensive measure, but Regara couldn't see these.

It had anchored the line, conjoined with the fortified town, a marvel of Martian engineering that was supposed to have been the key to unlocking the way south into Archenemy territory. The Pact had let them raise it, even fire it, and then they had taken it. Six months and Godsword was theirs.

'Reinforcements are incoming, sir. The guns will be retaken.'

Regara didn't comment. Through a magnocular, he watched as red-plated ants scurried across the macrocannon battery, the Pact feasting over their hard-won prize. He didn't know how long it would take their engineers to fix the rotatory mechanism that enabled the immense machine to turn; he only hoped it would be long enough for the Volpone and their auxiliaries to get out of range.

He lowered the magnocular and the weapon grew far away again, a towering spear thrust into the smoke-choked air above Lodden.

Distant booms revealed that the main enemy forces had met the trench line and the mines left by the Diggers. A score of lesser detonations undercut it as the Pardus kept up their barrage but the tanks were pulling out now to join the rest of the retreat, wary of the massed infantry headed their way.

Setting off again, Regara noticed the mil-serve from earlier floundering with his heavy belt of canteens.

'Culcis,' he said to his lieutenant, indicating the other man. The mil-serve was young, maybe twenty-five Terran standard, though war made men look older than they really were. Dark stubble covered his head like a skullcap from where his hair had been shaved. Despite his lowborn provenance, he had a strong profile and fierce blue eyes.

'Sir?'

'Tell him to leave it. No one falls behind, not even the servants. I'll have every man and woman accounted for, by Throne.'

Culcis nodded, then turned and raised his voice. 'Cut the strap, deg,' he yelled. 'And move your arse. Quickly now!'

The mil-serve nodded, unbuckling the canteen belt and letting it fall. At once, his pace increased.

'And, lieutenant...' Regara added, a hard glance at the mil-serve slogging across the earth.

'Sir?'

'Don't call them that. He is either mil-serve or you learn his name. Bad enough that Shiller is an ignorant swine with no breeding without having to put up with it from you too, lieutenant.'

'Sir,' answered Culcis, suitably contrite.

The mil-serve suddenly stopped and turned. Something had made him look up, and then he started waving frantically at Regara, shouting, 'My lord, my lord!'

The major followed his gaze to a growing speck on the horizon. A low buzzing materialised on the breeze, audible above the general retreat with the conclusion of the tank barrage. Several of those tanks, those with enough elevation on their primary armaments, angled their long cannons skywards.